Extraordinary acclaim for Donato Carrisi's

The Whisperer

"*The Whisperer* is one hell of a ride. This story screams high tension, high stakes, and high velocity. Superb." —Michael Connelly

"Brilliant and very creepy.... A great book." —Ken Follett

"A gripping read. I defy anyone to guess the denouement."
—Laura Wilson, *The Guardian* (UK)

"*The Whisperer* employs the graceful turns of phrase common to literary fiction.... Carrisi's villain is a suitable cohort for Hannibal Lecter, and his detectives are intelligently nuanced, each struggling, sometimes failing, to cope with the depravity into which they immerse themselves in the name of good. A haunting, disconcerting, devastating portrait of evil." —*Kirkus Reviews*

"Profiler Mila Vasquez and criminologist Goran Gavila race headlong against time, following obscure and elaborate clues laid out by a serial killer who seems almost prescient; whichever way the police turn, their quarry seems forever one step ahead, taunting them. Thanks to Carrisi's intricate plotting, the criminal also keeps at least one step ahead of the seasoned mystery reader, ensuring a couple of major surprises as the novel draws to a close. *The Whisperer* has already won several literary awards abroad and has been a bestseller all over Europe. I predict no less for it here." —Bruce Tierney, *BookPage*

"Donato Carrisi has a unique gift for blending fascinating forensic detail, mind-bending plot twists, and empathetic characters into a seamless, powerful narrative. *The Whisperer* intrigues, informs, and haunts simultaneously, a novel that will linger in the mind long after you've finished." —Michael Koryta

"Exquisite. Readers who appreciate manipulation, both of plots and themselves, by the author, and those who appreciate a shock of bloody horror will be absolutely enthralled by this offering."

—*Library Journal* (starred review)

"Brutally awesome.... Thomas Harris by way of Ian Rankin."

—Will Lavender, *New York Times* bestselling author of *Obedience* and *Dominance*

"More than delivers on its ghoulish promise.... You might not want to read this alone in the house."

—*Time Out London*

"Intriguing.... An engagingly gruesome tale."

—*Publishers Weekly*

"Serial killer books are a horror staple. With Donato Carrisi's *The Whisperer,* the genre is not only receiving a breath of fresh air; the book is taking dark literary thrillers to a new level.... A great, creepy, tension-filled thriller that keeps a frenetic pace for more than four hundred pages. Carrisi's prose is sharp and his phrasing has a distinctive literary slant that helps make even the grisly portions of the novel a pleasure to read."

—Gabino Iglesias, *HorrorTalk*

"In this stunning thriller, Donato Carrisi has created a masterful balance of good and evil, deftly shaded by the flawed humanity of those who seek to impose some order on crime and violence.... From that first eerie graveyard to the shocking ending, nothing in this tale is predictable. Shock waves tremble throughout an impressive and deeply satisfying piece of work."

—Luan Gaines, *CurledUp*

"Carrisi's narrative is unforgettable and disturbing, one that will have you waking up at night and making sure that the doors to your home are locked and your children are safe. *The Whisperer* will take you places that you have never been by routes you will never find again. Prepare to be terrified."

—Joe Hartlaub, *BookReporter*

"A murder mystery. A puzzle. A challenge. An intriguing portrait of society, of you and me."

—Emilina Minero, *EDGE Boston*

THE WHISPERER

A novel

Donato Carrisi

Translated by Shaun Whiteside

MULHOLLAND BOOKS

Little, Brown and Company
New York Boston London

Mulholland Books / Little, Brown and Company
Hachette Book Group
237 Park Avenue, New York, NY 10017
mulhollandbooks.com

Originally published in Italy as *Il Suggeritore* by Casa Editrice Longanesi S.p.A, 2009
First English-language edition published in Great Britain by Abacus, June 2010
First published in hardcover in the United States by Mulholland Books / Little, Brown and Company, January 2012
First Mulholland Books paperback edition, January 2013

Mulholland Books is an imprint of Little, Brown and Company, a division of Hachette Book Group, Inc. The Mulholland Books name and logo are trademarks of Hachette Book Group, Inc.

The publisher is not responsible for websites (or their content) that are not owned by the publisher.

The Hachette Speakers Bureau provides a wide range of authors for speaking events. To find out more, go to hachettespeakersbureau.com or call (866) 376-6591.

Library of Congress Cataloging-in-Publication Data
Carrisi, Donato
[Suggeritore. English]
The whisperer / Donato Carrisi ; translation by Shaun Whiteside. —1st ed.
p. cm.
ISBN 978-0-316-19472-3 (hc) / 978-0-316-20722-5 (pb)
1. Serial murder investigation—Fiction. I. Whiteside, Shaun. II. Title.
PQ4903.A666S8413 2012
853'.92—dc23 2011026452

10 9 8 7 6 5 4 3 2 1

RRD-C

Printed in the United States of America

THE WHISPERER

■■■■■■ Prison
Penitential district no. 45

Report of the Director, Alphonse Bérenger
23 Nov

For the attention of the Office of the
District Attorney, J. B. Marin
Subject: CONFIDENTIAL

Dear Mr. Marin

I wish to inform you about the strange case of one of our inmates.

The individual in question is prisoner number RK-357/9. We can only refer to him in this way, since he has consistently refused to supply his personal information.

His arrest occurred on 22 October. The man was wandering at night—alone and naked—along a country road near the town of ■■■■■.

A comparison between the subject's fingerprints with those contained in the archives ruled out his involvement in previous crimes or in cold cases. Nonetheless, his repeated refusal to reveal his own identity, even before a judge, earned him a sentence of four months and eighteen days in prison.

Since the moment he set foot in the penitentiary, inmate RK-357/9 has never shown any sign of indiscipline, and has always respected prison rules. The subject is of a solitary disposition and reluctant to socialize. Perhaps for that reason no one has been aware of one particular trait of his, which has only recently been noticed by one of our warders. Prisoner RK-357/9 wipes and rubs with a piece of felt each object with which he comes into contact; he collects all the hairs that he loses each day; he polishes to perfection the sink, the taps and the toilet each time he uses them.

We are plainly dealing with someone with a mania for hygiene, or, more likely, an individual who wants at all costs to avoid leaving behind "organic material."

We therefore seriously suspect that prisoner RK-357/9 has committed a particularly serious crime and wants to prevent us from taking his DNA to identify him.

So far the subject has been sharing his cell with another recluse, which has certainly helped him in his task of mixing up his own biological traces. Thus our first measure since discovering his habit has been to remove him from this social setting and put him in isolation.

I am informing you of the above to start the appropriate investigation and request, if necessary, an urgent measure to force prisoner RK-357/9 to provide a DNA sample.

The matter is urgent because in precisely 109 days (on 12 March) the subject will have served his sentence.

Respectfully yours,

Director

Dr. Alphonse Bérenger

1.

Somewhere near W.
5 February

The big moth carried him along, moving by memory through the night. It quivered its dusty wings, weaving through the mountains that lay like giants sleeping back to back.

Above them, a velvet sky. Below, the dense forest.

The pilot turned towards the passenger and pointed ahead to a huge white hole in the ground that looked like the glowing throat of a volcano.

The helicopter veered off in that direction.

Seven minutes later they landed on the verge of the highway. The road was closed, and the area was guarded by police. A man in a blue suit walked beneath the blades and welcomed the passenger, holding down his flyaway tie as best he could.

"Dr. Gavila, we've been expecting you," he said loudly to keep his voice from being drowned out by the noise of the rotors.

Goran Gavila didn't reply.

Special Agent Stern went on: "Come with me, I'll explain on the way."

They walked along a makeshift path, leaving behind them the sound of the helicopter, which was gaining altitude again, sucked up into an inky sky.

The fog rolled like a shroud, blurring the outlines of the hills. Around them, the aromas of the forest, mixed and sweetened by the damp of night that rose up inside their clothes, creeping coldly along their skin.

"It hasn't been easy, I assure you: you really have to see it with your own eyes."

Agent Stern walked a few steps ahead of Goran, pushing his way through the bushes with his hands, talking to him without looking round.

"It all kicked off this morning, at about eleven. Two little boys are walking along the path with their dog. They enter the forest, climb the hill and come into the clearing. The dog is a Labrador and, as you know, they're dogs that like to dig...so suddenly the animal goes mad because it's caught a scent. It digs a hole. And out comes the first one."

Goran tried to keep pace as they made their way into increasingly dense vegetation along the slope that was gradually becoming steeper. He noticed that Stern had a little tear in his trousers, at knee height, a sign that he had come this way several times that night.

"Obviously the boys run away immediately, and alert the local police," the officer continued. "They arrive, carry out an examination of the place, the hills, looking for clues. So far, all routine activity. Then someone thinks of digging again to see if there's anything else...and out comes the second one! At this point they called us: we've been here since three now. We still don't know how much stuff there is under there. So, here we are..."

A little clearing opened up in front of them, lit by spotlights—the volcano's shining mouth. Suddenly the scents of the forest vanished, and the men were struck by an unmistakable stench. Goran lifted his head, allowing the smell to fill him. *Phenic acid,* he said to himself.

And then he saw it.

A circle of little graves. And about thirty men in white overalls digging in that Martian halogen light, armed with little spades and brushes to move the earth as delicately as possible. Some of them were combing the grass, others taking photographs and carefully cataloging everything they found. They moved in slow motion. Their gestures were precise, calibrated, hypnotic, wrapped in sacral silence broken only by the occasional little explosions of the flashes.

Goran could see special agents Sarah Rosa and Klaus Boris. And Roche, the chief inspector, who recognized him and immediately came striding over. Before he could open his mouth, Goran cut in with a question.

"How many?"

"Five. Each one is fifty centimeters long, by twenty wide and fifty deep...What do you think you would bury in holes like that?"

One thing in all of them. The same thing.

The criminologist stared at him expectantly.

The reply came: "A left arm."

Goran turned to look at the men in the white overalls working away in that absurd woodland cemetery. The ground yielded only decomposing remains, but the origin of the evil that brought them here must lie somewhere before this unreal and suspended time.

"Is it them?" Goran asked. But this time he already knew the reply.

"According to the PCR analysis they're female. They're also Caucasian and between the ages of seven and thirteen..."

Children.

Roche uttered the phrase without any inflection in his voice. Like spittle that leaves a bitter taste in your mouth if you keep it in.

Debby. Anneke. Sabine. Melissa. Caroline.

It had started twenty-five days before, like a little story in a provincial magazine: the disappearance of a young student from a prestigious boarding school for the children of the rich. Everyone thought she'd run away. The girl in question was twelve and her name was Debby. Her schoolmates remembered seeing her leaving at the end of lessons. They'd only noticed her absence from the girls' dormitory during the evening register. It looked very much like one of those events that make a middle-sized article on the third page, and then fade quietly away into Other News, waiting for a predictable happy ending.

And then Anneke had disappeared.

She was from a little village with wooden houses and a white church. Anneke was ten. At first they had thought she'd got lost in the woods, where she often went on her mountain bike. The whole of the local population had joined the search party. But without success.

Before they could work out what was really going on, it had happened again.

The third was called Sabine; she was the youngest, seven years old. It had happened in town, on Saturday evening. She had gone to the fairground with her parents, like lots of other families with children. There she had climbed onto a horse on the merry-go-round, which was full of children. Her mother had watched her go round once, and waved. And a second time, and waved again. The third time, Sabine wasn't there.

It was only then that someone had started thinking that three children disappearing over three days might amount to an anomaly.

Searches had started on a large scale. There had been television appeals. Suddenly people were talking in terms of one maniac or several, perhaps a whole gang. But there were no clues to help them narrow it down. The police had set up a dedicated hotline to collect information, including anonymous tip-offs. There had been hundreds of leads; it would have taken months to check them all. But of the little girls not a trace. To make matters worse, since the disappearances had happened in different places, the local police forces couldn't agree about which one had final responsibility.

That was when the violent crimes unit, run by Chief Inspector Roche, had been called in. Missing person cases didn't normally come under its jurisdiction, but because of the mounting hysteria these had been treated as an exception.

Roche and his men were already on the case when child number four disappeared.

Melissa was the oldest: thirteen. Like all girls of her age, she had been under a curfew from parents who feared she might become another victim of the maniac who was terrorizing the country. But her enforced seclusion had coincided with her birthday, and Melissa had other ideas for the evening. She and her friends had come up with a little escape plan to go and have a party in a bowling alley. All her friends arrived. Melissa was the only one who didn't show up.

From that point onwards a hunt had begun for the monster, one which was often confused and improvised on the spur of the moment. People had mobilized themselves, ready to take justice into their own hands. The police had set up road blocks all over the place. Checks on people who had been condemned or suspected of crimes against minors had been stepped up. Parents didn't dare send their children outside the house even for school. Many schools had been closed for lack of pupils. People left their homes only when it was strictly necessary. After a certain time of day, towns and villages were deserted.

For a few days there had been no news of fresh disappearances. Some people had started to think that all the measures and precautions applied had had the desired effect of discouraging the maniac. But they were wrong.

The abduction of the fifth little girl was the most sensational.

Her name was Caroline, aged eleven. She had been taken from her bed, as she slept in the room next to her parents, who hadn't noticed a thing.

Five little girls kidnapped in the course of a week. Then seventeen very long days of silence.

Until now.

Until these five buried arms.

Debby. Anneke. Sabine. Melissa. Caroline.

Goran looked around at the circle of little trenches. A macabre game of ring-around-the-rosy. He could almost hear them chanting.

"From now on it's clear that we're no longer dealing with a case of missing persons," Roche said, beckoning everyone around him to deliver a brief speech.

They were used to this. Rosa, Boris and Stern joined him and listened, eyes fixed on the ground and hands clasped behind their backs.

Roche began: "I'm thinking of the person who has brought us here this evening. The person who predicted that all this would happen. We are here because he wanted us to be, because he imagined it. And he has constructed all of this for us. Because the spectacle is for us. He has prepared it all very carefully. Savoring the moment, savoring our reaction. To take us by surprise. To let us know who's big and powerful."

They nodded.

Whoever was responsible for this had gone completely unnoticed.

Roche, who had for some time included Gavila in the squad to all intents and purposes, noticed that the criminologist was distracted, his eyes motionless as he followed a train of thought.

"So, Dr. Gavila, what do you think?"

Goran emerged from the silence that had fallen, and said only, "The birds."

At first no one understood.

He continued, impassively: "I hadn't noticed on the way here, I've only spotted it now. It's strange. Listen..."

The voices of thousands of birds rose from the dark forest.

"They're singing," said Rosa, startled.

Goran turned towards her and gave a nod of agreement.

"It's the floodlights...they think this light is daybreak. And they're singing," Boris observed.

"Do you think it makes sense?" Goran went on, looking at them this time. "And yet it does...Five buried arms. Pieces. Without the bodies. We could say that there's no real cruelty in all this. Without the bodies, no faces. Without the faces, no individuals, not even people. We just have to ask ourselves, 'where are the children?' Because they aren't here, in these trenches. We can't look them in the eye. We can't see that they're like us. Because there's nothing human in any of this. There are only *parts*...No compassion. He didn't grant them any. He left us with nothing but fear. You can't feel pity for these little victims. He wants to let us know *only* that they are dead...Do you think that makes sense? Thousands of birds in the darkness, forced to sing in response to an impossible light. But it's the product of an illusion. And you have to be careful with illusionists: sometimes evil deceives us by assuming the *simplest* form of things."

Silence. Once again the criminologist had caught a small and telling symbolic meaning. What the others often couldn't see or—as in this case—hear. The details, the outlines, the nuances. The shadow surrounding things, the dark halo in which evil hides.

Every murderer has a "plan"—a precise form that brings him satisfaction, even pride. The hardest task is to understand what his vision is. That was why Goran was there. To banish that inexplicable evil with the reassuring notions of his science.

At that moment a technician in a white overall approached them and spoke directly to the chief inspector with a confused expression on his face.

"Mr. Roche, there could be a problem... *there are six arms.*"

2.

The music teacher had spoken.

But that wasn't what had struck her. It wasn't the first time. Lots of lonely people give voice to their own thoughts when they're in the safety of their own domestic walls. Even Mila sometimes talked to herself when she was at home.

No, it was something else that was new. And it was her reward for a whole week of waiting; sitting in the cold of her own car, constantly parked outside the brown house, peering inside with a little pair of binoculars at the movements of that fat, milky-white man in his forties as he moved calmly in his orderly little universe, always repeating the same gestures, weaving a web that only he was aware of.

The music teacher had spoken. But what was new was that this time *he had uttered a name.*

Mila had seen it emerging, letter by letter, on his lips. Pablo. It was the confirmation, the key to enter that mysterious world. Now she knew.

The music teacher had a guest.

Until almost ten days before, Pablo was only an eight-year-old boy with brown hair and bright eyes, who liked speeding around the area on his skateboard. And one thing was certain: if Pablo had to run an errand for his mother or his grandmother, he skated there. He spent hours on that thing, up and down the street. For the neighbors who saw him passing by their windows, little *Pablito,* as they all called him, was like one of those pictures that have become part of the landscape.

Perhaps that was why no one had seen him that February morning in the little residential district where everyone knew everyone else by name and houses and lives all seemed the same. A green Volvo station wagon—the music teacher must have chosen it because it was like so many other family cars parked in the driveways—appeared in the deserted street. The silence of a perfectly normal Saturday morning had been broken only by the slow squeak of the tarmac beneath the tires and the gray scrape of a skateboard progressively gaining speed...It was six long hours before anyone noticed that something was missing from the sound of that Saturday. That scrape. And that little Pablo, on a cold, sunny morning, had been swallowed up by a creeping shadow that wouldn't give him up, parting him from his beloved skateboard.

That four-wheeled plank had ended up lying motionless in the middle of a swarm of policemen who had taken over the area as soon as the report had come in.

Now, ten days later, it could be too late for Pablo. Too late for his frail child's psyche. Too late to wake up untraumatized from his nightmare.

Now the skateboard was in the boot of the policewoman's car, along with other objects: toys, clothes. Clues that Mila had sniffed out as she tried to find a trail to follow, and which had led her to this brown lair. To the music teacher, who taught in an institute of higher education and played the organ in church on Sunday morning. The vice president of the musical association that organized a little Mozart festival every year. The shy, anonymous bachelor with the glasses, the incipient baldness and the soft, sweaty hands.

Mila had observed him very carefully. Because that was her *gift*.

She had joined the police with a precise purpose and, after leaving the academy, had devoted herself to it completely. She wasn't interested in the criminals, let alone the law. That wasn't why she ceaselessly searched every corner where shadows lurked, where life rotted undisturbed.

As she read Pablo's name on the lips of his jailer, Mila became aware of a searing pain in her right leg. Perhaps it was from too many hours spent in the car waiting for that sign. Then again, perhaps it was from the wound in her thigh, which she had stitched herself.

I'll treat it properly later on, she promised herself. *Afterwards, though.* And as she formulated that thought, Mila realized that she was ready to enter the house, to break the spell and bring the nightmare to an end.

"Officer Mila Vasquez to headquarters: have identified suspected kidnapper of Pablo Ramos. The building is a brown house at 27 Viale Alberas. Possibly dangerous situation."

"Fine, Officer Vasquez, we're sending backup, but it'll be at least thirty minutes."

Too long.

Mila didn't have that much time. *Pablo* didn't.

The terror of having to utter the words "it was too late" when giving her account of events impelled her towards the house.

The voice on the radio was a distant echo and—pistol in her fist, arm lowered across her body's center of gravity, eyes alert, quick, short steps—she reached the cream-colored fence that surrounded the rear of the little house.

An enormous plane tree loomed above her. The leaves changed color with the wind, showing their silvery outlines. Mila flattened herself against the fence and pricked up her ears. Every now and again the blast of a rock song reached her, carried on the wind from somewhere nearby. Mila leaned over the wooden gate and saw a well-tended garden, with a shed and a red rubber hose that snaked through the grass to a sprinkler. Plastic furniture and a gas barbecue. All very normal. A mauve door with frosted glass. Mila stretched an arm over the gate and delicately lifted the latch. The hinges squeaked and she opened the gate just wide enough to step into the garden.

She closed it again so that no one inside, looking out, would notice a change. Everything had to stay as it was. Then she walked as she had been taught in training, carefully weighing her steps on the grass—just with her toes, so as not to leave footprints—ready to leap if the need arose. A few moments later she found herself beside the back door, on the side from which she would cast no shadow when she leaned over to look inside the house. The frosted glass meant that she couldn't make out the interior, but from the outline of the furniture it looked like a sitting room. Mila ran her hand towards the handle on the opposite side of the door. She gripped it and pushed it down. The lock clicked.

It was open.

The music teacher must have felt safe in the lair that he had prepared for himself and his prisoner. Soon Mila would find out why.

The linoleum floor creaked beneath her rubber sole with each step she took. She tried to control her footsteps to keep from making too much noise, then she took off her trainers and left them beside a chair. Barefoot, she reached the entrance to the hall, and she heard him talking:

"I would also need a roll of kitchen paper. And that cleaning product you use for polishing porcelain…yes, that one…Then bring me six tins of chicken soup, some sugar, a copy of the TV guide and a few packets of cigarettes, lights, the usual brand…"

The voice came from the sitting room. The music teacher was shopping by phone. Too busy to leave the house? Or perhaps he didn't want to leave—he wanted to stay and keep an eye on his guest's every move?

"Yes, number 27 Viale Alberas, thank you. And bring change for fifty, because that's all I've got in the house."

Mila followed the voice, walking in front of a mirror that reflected a distorted version of her own image. Like the ones you see at funfairs. When she reached the door to the room, she stretched out her arms holding the pistol, took a breath and burst into the doorway. She expected to surprise him, perhaps from behind, with the receiver still in his hand, standing by the window. A perfect living target.

Which wasn't there.

The sitting room was empty, the receiver resting quite normally on the phone.

She realized that no one had made a phone call from that room when she felt the cold lips of a pistol resting like a kiss on the back of her neck.

He was behind her.

Mila cursed to herself, calling herself an idiot. The music teacher had prepared his lair well. The garden gate that *squeaked* and the linoleum floor that *creaked* were the alarms to signal the presence of intruders. Hence the fake phone call, the bait to attract his prey. The distorting mirror so that he could take up a position behind her without being seen. It was all part of the trap.

She felt him stretching his arm out in front of her, to take the gun from her. Mila let him do it.

"Shoot me, but there's no escape for you now. My colleagues will be here soon. You can't get away, you'll have to surrender."

He didn't reply. She could almost see him out of the corner of her eye. Was he smiling?

The music teacher took a step back. The barrel of the gun detached itself from Mila, but she could still feel that extension of magnetic attraction between her head and the bullet in the magazine. Then the man turned towards her and finally entered her field of vision. He stared at her for a long time. But without looking at her. There was something deep in his eyes that looked to Mila like the antechamber of darkness.

The music teacher turned round, fearlessly turning his back on her. Mila saw him walking confidently towards the piano against the wall. Reaching the instrument, the man sat down on the stool and looked at the keyboard. He set both pistols down on the far left.

He raised his hands and, a moment later, let them fall back on the keys.

As Chopin's Nocturne No. 20 in C sharp minor filled the room, Mila breathed hard, the tension spreading along the tendons and muscles of her neck. The music teacher's fingers slipped lightly and gracefully over the keyboard. The sweetness of the notes made Mila feel like a spectator at this performance, hypnotized by it.

She struggled to remain clearheaded and let her bare heels slide backwards, slowly, until she was back in the corridor. She got her breath back, trying to calm her thumping heart. Then she started searching quickly around the rooms, pursued by the melody. She inspected each of them, one by one. A study. A bathroom. A larder.

Until she reached the closed door.

She pushed it with her shoulder. The wound in her thigh hurt, and she concentrated her weight on her deltoid.

The wood yielded.

The faint light from the corridor burst ahead of her into the room, whose windows appeared to have been walled up. Mila followed the glow into the darkness until she met two terrified, liquid eyes that returned her gaze. Pablito was there, on the bed, his legs drawn up against his thin chest. He was wearing only a pair of underpants and a sweater. He was trying to work out if there was anything he should be afraid of, if Mila was part of his nightmare or not. She said what she always said when she found a missing child.

"We've got to go."

He nodded, stretched out his arms and clung to her. Mila kept an ear out for the music, which was still pursuing her. She was worried that the piece wouldn't last long enough, and that there wasn't enough time to get out of the house. A fresh anxiety took hold of her. She had put her own life and the hostage's at risk. And now she was scared. Scared of making another mistake. Scared of stumbling at the last step, the one that would take her out of this horrible lair. Or discovering that the house would never let her go, that it would close in on her like a silken net, holding her prisoner forever.

But the door opened, and they were outside, in the pale but reassuring light of day.

When her heartbeats slowed down, and she was able to forget the gun that she had left in the house, and press Pablo to her, shielding him with her warm body to take all his fear away, the little boy leaned towards her ear and whispered…

"Isn't *she* coming?"

Suddenly heavy, Mila's feet were rooted to the ground. She swayed, but didn't lose her balance.

Fueled by the strength of a terrifying realization, she asked, "Where is she?"

The little boy raised his arm and pointed to the second floor. The house watched them with its windows and laughed, mockingly, with the same gaping door that had let them go a moment before.

It was then that the fear fled entirely. Mila covered the last few meters that separated her from her car. She sat Pablo on the seat and told him, in the solemn tone of a promise, "I'll be right back."

Then she went back to let the house engulf her.

She found herself at the bottom of the stairs. She looked up, without knowing what she would find up there. She started climbing, gripping the banisters. Chopin's notes went on undauntedly, following her exploration. Her feet sank into the steps, her hands stuck to the banisters which seemed to be trying to hold her back.

Suddenly the music stopped.

Mila froze, her senses alert. Then the dry report of a gunshot, a dull thud and the disjointed notes from the piano beneath the weight of the music teacher as he collapsed onto the keyboard. Mila quickened her pace as she continued on her way upstairs. She couldn't be certain that it wasn't another trick. The stairs curved round and the landing stretched into a narrow corridor covered with thick carpet. At the end, a window. In front of it, a human body. Frail, slender, against the light: feet stretched on a chair, neck and arms stretched towards a noose that hung from the ceiling. Mila saw her trying to slip it over her head and gave a cry. The girl saw her and tried to speed up the operation. Because that was what he had told her, it was what she had been taught.

If they come, you must kill yourself.

"They" were the others, the world outside, the ones who couldn't understand, who would never forgive.

Mila hurled herself towards the girl in a desperate attempt to stop her. And the closer she got, the more she seemed to be running back in time.

Many years before, in another life, that girl had been a child.

Mila remembered her photograph perfectly. She had studied it closely, feature by feature, running through her mind every fold, every expressive wrinkle, cataloging and repeating all distinguishing features, even the tiniest imperfection of the skin.

And those eyes. A speckled, lively blue. The eyes of a ten-year-old child, Elisa Gomes. Her father had taken the picture. An image stolen at a party as she was busy opening a present and didn't expect it. Mila had imagined the scene, with the father calling her to make her turn round and take the picture by surprise. And Elisa turning towards him, without time to be surprised. A moment had been immortalized in her expression, something imperceptible to the naked eye. The miraculous beginning of a smile before it opens up and spills onto the lips or brightens the eyes like a rising star.

So Mila had not been surprised when Elisa Gomes's parents had given her that particular photograph when she had asked for a recent picture. It certainly wasn't the most suitable photograph, because Elisa's expression was unnatural and that made it almost unusable for re-creating the ways in which her face might change over the course of time. Her other colleagues who had been put on the investigating team had complained. But Mila hadn't cared, because there was something in that photograph—an energy. And that was what they should have looked for. Not a face among others, one child amongst so many. But *that* girl, with *that* light in her eyes. As long as no one had managed to extinguish it in the meantime…

Mila grabbed her just in time, clinging to her legs before the rope could take her weight. She kicked out, struggled, tried to scream. Until Mila called her by name.

"Elisa," she said with infinite gentleness.

And the girl recognized herself.

She had forgotten who she was. Years of prison had erased her identity, a little piece every day. Until she had become convinced that this man was her family, because the rest of the world had forgotten her. The rest of the world would never save her.

Startled, Elisa looked Mila in the eyes. She calmed down and let herself be rescued.

3.

Six arms. Five names.

With that mystery, the squad had left the clearing in the middle of the forest and joined the task force waiting on the highway. Snacks and fresh coffee seemed to clash with the situation at hand, although they did provide a semblance of control. But no one on that cold February morning touched the buffet.

Stern took a box of mints from his pocket. He shook it and slipped a few into his hand before throwing them straight into his mouth. He said they helped him think. "How is it possible?" he asked, more to himself than anyone else.

"Fuck…" Boris muttered, shaking his head. But it came out so quietly that no one heard him.

Rosa concentrated her attention on a spot inside the camper. Goran noticed. He understood—she had a daughter the same age as those girls. It's the first thing you think about when you find yourself faced with a crime against minors. Your own children. And you ask yourself what would happen if…But you don't get to the end of the sentence, because even the very thought is too painful.

"He's going to make us find them in bits," said Chief Inspector Roche.

"So that's our task? Collecting corpses?" asked Boris with a hint of annoyance. A man of action, he didn't want to see himself relegated to the role of gravedigger. He wanted a perpetrator. And so did the others, who quickly nodded at his words.

Roche reassured them. "The priority is always an arrest. But we can't avoid the heartrending search for remains."

"It was deliberate."

Everyone stared at Goran, pondering his words.

"The Labrador scenting the arm and digging the hole: it was part of the 'plan.' Our man had his eye on the two little boys with the dog. He knew they took it into the forest. That's why he put his little graveyard there. A simple idea. He completed his 'work,' and he put it on display."

"Do you mean we're not going to catch him?" asked Boris, unable to believe his ears, and furious.

"You know better than me how these things go..."

"But he's really going to do it? He'll kill again..." This time it was Rosa who didn't want to give up. "He's got away with it so far, he'll do it again."

She wanted someone to contradict her, but Goran had no reply. And even if he had had an opinion on the matter, he couldn't have translated into humanly acceptable terms the cruelty of having to divide himself between the thought of those terrible deaths and the cynical desire for the murderer to strike again. Because—and they all knew this—the only chance of catching him would be if he didn't stop.

Chief Inspector Roche went on: "If we find the bodies of those little girls, at least we'll be able to give their families a funeral and a grave to weep over."

As usual, Roche had put it in the most diplomatic manner possible. It was a rehearsal for what he would say to the press, to soften the story to the advantage of his own image. First mourning, grief, to take time. Then the investigation and the finding of the culprits.

But Goran knew that the operation wouldn't be successful, and that the journalists would hurl themselves on every scrap, greedily stripping the matter to the bone and spicing it with the most sordid details. And more than anything, from that moment the police would be forgiven nothing. Their every gesture, every word, would acquire the value of a promise, a solemn undertaking. Roche was convinced that he could keep the hacks at bay, feeding them a bit at a time with whatever they wanted to hear. And Goran left the chief inspector with his fragile illusion of control.

"I think we're going to have to give this guy a name...before the press does," said Roche.

Goran agreed, but not for the same reason as the chief inspector. Like all criminologists who present their work to the police, Dr. Gavila had his own methods. First and foremost that of attributing traits to the criminal, to transform a still rarefied and indefinite figure into something human. Because, faced with such fierce and gratuitous evil, we always tend to forget that the one responsible for it, like the victim, is a *person,* often with a normal life, a job and perhaps even a family. In support of his thesis, Dr. Gavila told his university students that almost every time a serial killer was arrested it came as a complete surprise to his neighbors and family.

"We call them *monsters* because we feel they are far away from us, because we want them to be 'different,'" Goran said in his seminars. "And instead they're like us in every respect. But we prefer to remove the idea that someone like us is capable of so much. And we do so in part to absolve our own nature. Anthropologists call it 'depersonalization of the criminal' and it is often the greatest obstacle to the identification of a serial killer. Because a man has weak points and can be caught. Not so a monster."

For that reason, Goran always had on the wall of his lecture theater a black-and-white picture of a child. A chubby, defenseless little man-cub. His students saw it every day and always grew fond of the picture. When—more or less towards the middle of term—a student summoned the courage to ask him who it was, he challenged them to guess. The answers were extremely varied and fantastical. And he was amused by their expressions when he revealed that the child was Adolf Hitler.

After the war, the leader of the Nazi movement had become a monster in the collective imagination, and for years the countries that had emerged victorious from the conflict had been opposed to any other vision. That was why no one knew the photographs from the Führer's childhood. A monster couldn't have been a child, he couldn't have had any feelings other than hatred, or a life like that of his contemporaries who would later become his victims.

"For many, humanizing Hitler meant 'explaining' him in some way," Goran would tell his class. "But society insists that extreme evil cannot be explained, it cannot be understood. Trying to do so means trying to find some kind of justification for it."

In the task force van, Boris suggested that the creator of the arm cemetery should be called "Albert," after an old case. The idea was welcomed with a smile by everyone there. The decision was taken.

From that point onwards, the members of the unit would refer to the murderer by that name. And day after day, Albert would acquire a face. A nose, two eyes, a life of his own. Everyone would imbue him with his own vision, rather than seeing him only as a fleeting shadow.

"Albert, eh?" At the end of the meeting, Roche was still weighing up the name's media value. He moved it around on his lips, he tried to catch its flavor. It could work.

But there was something else that tormented the chief inspector. He mentioned it to Goran.

"To tell you the truth, I agree with Boris. Holy Christ! I can't force my men to pick up corpses while a crazed psychopath is making us look like a bunch of idiots!"

Goran knew that when Roche talked about "his" men he was really referring to himself. He was the one afraid of coming away without a result. And he was always the one who feared that someone would talk about the inefficiency of the federal police if they couldn't arrest the culprit.

And then there was the question of arm number six.

"I thought I wouldn't disseminate the news of the existence of a sixth victim for the time being."

Goran was disconcerted. "But how will we find out who it is?"

"I've thought of everything, don't worry..."

***

In the course of her career Mila Vasquez had solved eighty-nine missing-person cases. She had been awarded three medals and a great deal of adulation. She was considered to be an expert in her field, and was often called in to help, even by other forces.

That morning's operation, in which Pablo and Elisa had been freed at the same time, had been called a sensational success. Mila had said nothing. But it annoyed her. She would have liked to admit all her mistakes. Entering the brown house without waiting for reinforcements. Underestimating the environment and the possible traps it contained. She had put both herself and the hostages at risk by allowing the suspect to disarm her and aim a gun at the back of her neck. Finally, not preventing the music teacher's suicide.

But none of that had been mentioned by her superiors, who had instead stressed her merits as they were immortalized by the press in the ritual photographs.

Mila never appeared in those snaps. The official reason was that she preferred to protect her own anonymity for future investigations. But the truth was that she hated having her photograph taken. She couldn't even bear to see her image reflected in a mirror. Not because she wasn't beautiful, quite the contrary. But at the age of thirty-two, hours and hours of training had stripped her of every trace of femininity. Every curve, every hint of softness. As if being a woman were an evil to be eradicated. Even though she often wore male clothes, she wasn't masculine. There was simply nothing about her that suggested a sexual identity. And that was how she wanted to appear. Her clothes were anonymous. Jeans that weren't too tight, worn trainers, leather jacket. They were clothes, and that was that. Their function was to keep her warm or cover her up. She didn't waste time choosing them, she just bought them. Lots of them were identical. She didn't care. That was how she wanted to be.

Invisible among the invisible.

Perhaps that was also how she was able to share the district changing room with the male officers.

Mila had spent ten minutes staring at her open locker as she ran through all the day's events. There was something she had to do, but her mind was elsewhere at the moment. Then a stabbing pain in her thigh brought her back to herself. The wound had opened up again; she had tried to staunch the blood with a tissue and sticky tape, but it hadn't worked. The flaps of skin around the cut were too short and she hadn't been able to do a good job with needle and thread. Perhaps this time she really would have to consult a doctor, but she didn't want to go to hospital. Too many questions. She decided she would put on a tighter bandage, in the hope that the bleeding would stop, then try again with new stitches. But she would have to take an antibiotic to avoid contracting an infection. She would get a fake prescription from one of her contacts who gave her information every now and again about the new arrivals among the homeless at the railway station.

Stations.

It's strange, thought Mila. While for the rest of the world they're only a place you pass through, for some they're a terminus. They stop there and they don't leave again. Stations are a kind of ante-hell, where lost souls congregate in the hope that someone will come and collect them.

An average of twenty to twenty-five individuals disappear every day. Mila knew the statistic very well. All of a sudden these people vanish without warning, without a suitcase. As if they had dissolved into nothing.

Mila knew that most of them were misfits, people who lived off drugs and dodges, always ready to sully themselves with crime, individuals who were constantly in and out of jail. But there were also some—a strange minority—who at some point in their lives decided to vanish forever. Like the mother who went shopping at the supermarket and didn't come home, or the son or brother who boarded a train never to reach their destination.

Mila's belief was that each one of us has a path. A path that leads to home, to our dear ones, to the things we are most bound to. Usually the path is always the same; we learn it as children, and each of us follows it for the whole of our lives. But sometimes the path breaks.

Sometimes it starts again somewhere else. Or, after following a series of twists and turns, it returns to the point where it broke. Or else it remains hanging there.

Sometimes, however, it is lost in the darkness.

Mila knew that more than half of those who disappear come back and tell a story. Some, though, have nothing to tell, and resume their lives as before. Others are less fortunate; all that remains of them is a mute and silent body. Then there are the ones you never hear about again.

Amongst those there is always a child.

There are parents who would give their lives to know what happened. Where they went wrong. What act of negligence produced this silent drama. What happened to their little one. Who took their child, and why. There are those who question God, asking what sin they are being punished for. Those who torment themselves for the rest of their days in search of answers, or who die pursuing those questions. "Let me know at least if he is dead," they say. Some end up wishing it was so, because they want only to weep. Their sole desire is not to give up, but to be able to stop hoping. Because hope kills more slowly.

But Mila didn't believe the story of "liberating truth." She had learned that by heart, the first time she had found a missing person. She had felt it that afternoon, after bringing Pablo and Elisa home.

For the little boy there were cries of joy in the district, festive car horns and parades of cars.

Not for Elisa; too much time had passed.

After saving her, Mila had brought her to a specialist center where social workers had taken care of her. They had given her food and clean clothes. For some reason they're always one or two sizes too big, Mila thought. Perhaps because the people they were meant for wasted away during those years of oblivion, and had been found just before they vanished away entirely.

Elisa hadn't said a word all that time. She had allowed herself to be looked after, accepting everything they did to her. Even when Mila had told her she would bring her home, she had said nothing.

Staring at her locker, the young officer couldn't help seeing in her mind the faces of Elisa Gomes's parents when she had turned up with Elisa at their door. They were unprepared, and even a little embarrassed. Perhaps they thought she would be bringing them a ten-year-old child, and not that fully grown girl with whom they no longer had anything in common.

Elisa had been an intelligent and very precocious little girl. She had started talking early. The first word she had said had been "May"—the name of her teddy bear. Her mother, however, would also remember her last one: "tomorrow," the end of the phrase "see you tomorrow," uttered in the doorway before she went off for a sleepover at a friend's house. But that tomorrow had taken too long to arrive. And her yesterday was a very long day that showed no sign of coming to an end.

In her parents' minds Elisa had gone on living like a ten-year-old girl, with her bedroom full of dolls and Christmas presents piled up around the fireplace. This was immortalized like a photograph in their memory, imprisoned as if by a magic spell.

And even though Elisa had returned, they would go on waiting for the little girl they had lost. Without ever finding peace.

After a teary hug and a predictable emotional outburst, Mrs. Gomes had brought them in and offered them tea and biscuits. She had treated her daughter as you would treat a guest. Perhaps secretly hoping that she would leave at the end of the visit, letting her and her husband return to the sense of deprivation that they had come to find so comfortable.

Mila had always compared sadness to an old cupboard that you'd like to get rid of but which ends up staying where it is, and after a while emanates a certain smell that fills the room. And over time you get used to it and you end up being a part of the smell yourself.

Elisa had come back, and her parents would have liked to shake off their own mourning, and give back all the compassion bestowed on them during those years. Never again would they have a reason to be sad. How much courage would it take to tell the rest of the world about their new unhappiness at having a stranger walking around the house?

After an hour of civilities, Mila had said good-bye, and she had felt as if she had noticed a plea for help on Elisa's mother's face. "Now what do I do?" the woman cried mutely, terrified about coming to terms with this new reality.

Mila too had a truth to confront: the fact that Elisa Gomes had been found purely by chance. If her abductor had not felt a need to enlarge the "family" by taking Pablito as well, no one would ever have known what had happened. And Elisa would have remained closed away in that world created for her alone, and for the obsession of her jailer. First as a daughter, then as a faithful bride.

Mila closed the locker on those thoughts. *Forgetting, forgetting,* she said to herself. *That's the only medicine.*

The district was emptying, and she felt like going home. She would have a shower, open a bottle of port and roast chestnuts on the hob. Then she would sit and look at the tree outside the sitting room window. And perhaps, with a bit of luck, she would go to sleep early on the sofa.

But as she prepared to reward herself with her usual lonely evening, one of her colleagues appeared in the changing room.

Sergeant Morexu wanted to see her.

A gleaming layer of damp covered the streets that February evening. Goran got out of the taxi. He didn't have a car, he didn't have a driving license; he let someone else bother about taking him where he wanted to go. Not that he hadn't tried driving, and been rather good at it. But it's inadvisable for someone accustomed to losing himself in the depths of his own thoughts to sit behind the wheel. So Goran had given up.

Having paid the driver, the second thing he did after setting his size nines on the pavement was to take from his jacket the third cigarette of the day. He lit it, took two drags and threw it away. It was a habit he'd formed when he had decided to give up smoking. A kind of compromise, to trick himself about his need for nicotine.

As he stood there, he met his image reflected in a shop window. He stopped to contemplate himself for a few moments. The untidy beard that framed his increasingly weary face. His glasses and his tousled hair. He was aware that he didn't take much care of himself. But the person who did had given up the role some time before.

The striking thing about Goran—everyone said—was his long and mysterious silences.

And his eyes, huge and piercing.

It was nearly dinnertime. He slowly climbed the steps. He went into his apartment and listened. A few seconds passed and, when he got used to that new silence, he recognized the familiar, welcoming sound of Tommy, who was playing in his room. He went towards him, but only observed him from the door, without having the courage to interrupt what he was doing.

Tommy was nine. He had brown hair, he liked the color red, basketball and ice cream, even in winter. He had a best friend, Bastian, with whom he organized fantastical "safaris" in the school garden. They were both in the scouts and that summer they were going to go camping together. Lately they hadn't talked about anything else.

Tommy looked incredibly like his mother, but he had one thing of his father's.

A pair of huge, piercing eyes.

When he became aware of Goran's presence, he turned and smiled at him. "It's late," he said.

"I know. Sorry," Goran said defensively. "Did Mrs. Runa leave a long time ago?"

"She left to get her son half an hour ago."

Goran was annoyed: Mrs. Runa had been their nanny for some years now. She should have known he didn't like Tommy being left at home alone. And this was one of those little inconveniences that sometimes made the business of getting on with life seem impossible. Goran was finding it difficult to resolve everything on his own; the only person who possessed that mysterious power had forgotten to leave him the book of magic spells before she left.

He would have to talk to Mrs. Runa and perhaps even be a little harsh with her. He would tell her to stay in the evening until he came home. Tommy became aware of his thoughts, and his face darkened. So Goran suddenly tried to distract him, asking, "Are you hungry?"

"I ate an apple and some crackers and I drank a glass of water."

Goran shook his head, amused. "That's not a proper dinner."

"It was my snack. But now I'd like something else…"

"Spaghetti?"

Tommy clapped his hands at the suggestion. Goran stroked his head.

They cooked the pasta together and set the table; each had his own tasks and carried them out without consulting the other. His son was a quick learner, and Goran was proud of him.

The last few months hadn't been easy for either of them.

Their lives risked unraveling. Goran tried to hold the scraps together and make up for absence with order. Regular meals, precise timetables, established habits. From that point of view, nothing had changed from *before,* and that was reassuring for Tommy.

They had learned together to live with that void, but when one of them wanted to talk about it, they talked about it.

The only thing they never did anymore was say her name. Because that name had left their vocabulary. They used other ways, other expressions. It was strange. The man who was concerned about christening every serial killer he came across no longer knew what to call the one who had for a time been his wife, and had allowed his son to "depersonalize" his mother. She could be a character in one of the fairy tales he read to him every evening.

Tommy was the only anchor that still kept Goran bound to the world. Otherwise it would only have taken a moment to slide into the abyss that he explored every day out there.

After dinner, Goran went and hid in his study. Tommy followed him. It was another ritual. Goran sat in his creaking old chair and his son lay belly down on the mat, resuming his imaginary dialogues.

Goran studied his library. The books of criminology, criminal anthropology and legal medicine were beautifully displayed on the shelves, each one with its damask spine and gold blocking. Others were simpler, more modestly bound. They contained the answers. But the difficult thing—as he was always telling his pupils—was finding the questions. These books were full of disturbing photographs.

Wounded bodies, tortured, martyred, burnt and dismembered; all rigorously sealed in shining pages, annotated with precise captions. Human life reduced to a cold study.

That was why, until a short time before, Goran had not allowed Tommy to touch the books in the library. He worried that his curiosity would get the better of him, and that by opening one of those books he would discover how violent life could be. Once, however, Tommy had transgressed. He had found him lying, as he was now, flicking through one of those volumes. Goran still remembered him lingering over the picture of a young woman fished from a river, in the winter. She was naked, her skin purple, her eyes motionless.

But Tommy didn't seem at all disturbed, and rather than shouting at him, Goran had sat cross-legged beside him.

"Do you know what this is?"

Tommy had considered impassively for a long time. Then he had replied, diligently listing all the things he could see. The tapering hands, the hair in which frost had formed, the eyes lost in who knows what thoughts. In the end he had begun to fantasize about what she did for a living, about her friends and where she lived. Then Goran became aware that Tommy noticed everything in the photograph except one thing. Death.

Children don't see death. *Because their life lasts a day, from when they get up to when they go to sleep.*

That time Goran understood that, however much he tried, he could never protect his son from the evil of the world. Just as, years before, he had not been able to rescue him from what his mother had done to him.

Sergeant Morexu was not like Mila's other superior officers. He cared nothing for glory, or for having his picture in the paper. That was why Mila expected him to haul her over the coals for the way she had conducted the operation at the music teacher's house.

Morexu was brusque in his manners and moods. He couldn't hold an emotion for more than a few seconds. So one moment he would be furious or sullen, and immediately afterwards he would be smiling and incredibly kind. Also, to avoid wasting time, he combined his gestures. For example, if he had to console you, he would put one hand on your shoulder and walk you to the door at the same time. Or he would speak on the phone and scratch his temple with the receiver.

But this time he wasn't in a hurry.

He left Mila standing by his desk, without inviting her to sit down. Then he stared at her, his feet stretched out under the table and his arms folded.

"I don't know if you realize what happened today…"

She anticipated him. "I know. I made a mistake—"

"And yet you saved three people."

The statement froze her for a long moment.

"Three?"

Morexu sat back in his chair and lowered his eyes to a piece of paper in front of him.

"They found a note in the music teacher's house. Apparently he planned to take another one…"

The sergeant handed Mila the photocopy of a page from a diary. Beneath the day and the month, there was a name.

"Priscilla?" she asked.

"Priscilla," repeated Morexu.

"Who is she?"

"A lucky little girl."

And that was all he said. Because it was all he knew. There was no surname, address, photograph. Nothing. Only that name. Priscilla.

"So stop beating yourself up about it," Morexu went on and, before Mila could reply, he added, "I saw you today at the press conference: it looked as if none of it mattered to you."

"It doesn't."

"For God's sake, Vasquez! Do you realize how grateful the people you saved should be to you? Not to mention their families!"

You didn't see the look on Elisa Gomes's mother's face, Mila wanted to say. Instead, she merely nodded. Morexu looked at her, shaking his head.

"Since you've been here I've never heard a single complaint about you."

"And is that good or bad?"

"If you can't work it out for yourself, you've got big problems, my girl... That's why I decided you'd enjoy a few days working with the unit."

Mila didn't agree. "Why? I do my job, and it's the only thing that interests me. I'm used to managing that way. I'd have to adapt my methods to somebody. How can I explain that—"

"Go and pack your bags," Morexu interrupted, dismissing her complaint.

"Why the hurry?"

"You're leaving this evening."

"Is it some kind of punishment?"

"It isn't a punishment, and it isn't a holiday either: they want advice from an expert. And you're very popular."

Mila's face grew serious.

"What's it about?"

"Five abducted children."

Mila had heard it mentioned on the news. "Why me?" she asked.

"Because it looks as if there's a sixth, but they don't know who it is yet..."

She would have liked further details, but Morexu had clearly decided that the conversation was over. He went back to being brusque, merely holding out a file with which he pointed at the door.

"Your train ticket's in here as well."

Mila took the bundle of papers and made for the door. As she left the room she repeated the name in her head. *Priscilla*.

4.

The Piper at the Gates of Dawn, 1967. *A Saucerful of Secrets,* 1968. *Ummagumma* was 1969, as was the sound track of the film *More*. In 1971 there had been *Meddle*. But before that there was another one…in 1970, he was sure of it. He couldn't remember the title. The cover, yes. The one with the cow. Damn, what was it called?

I've got to get some petrol, he thought.

The fuel gauge was on empty, and the warning light had stopped flashing to settle into a peremptory red glare.

But he didn't want to stop.

He had now been driving for a good five hours, and had traveled almost six hundred kilometers. And yet putting that remarkable distance between himself and what had happened tonight didn't make him feel any better. He held his arms stiffly on the wheel. The tense muscles in his neck ached.

He glanced behind him for a moment.

Don't think about it…don't think about it…

He kept his mind busy by running through familiar, reassuring thoughts. Over the past ten minutes he had concentrated on the entire discography of Pink Floyd. But over the previous four hours it had been the titles of his favorite films, the players in the last three seasons of the hockey team he supported, the names of his old schoolmates, and even the teachers. He had got as far as Mrs. Berger. What had become of her? He would have liked to see her again. Just to keep *that thought* at bay. And now his mind had got stuck on that stupid album with the cow on the cover!

And that thought had come back.

He had to chase it away. Send it back to the corner of his mind where he had managed to confine it at various times during the night. Otherwise he would start sweating again, and every now and again he would burst into tears, despairing of the situation, even if it didn't last long. The fear came back and gripped his stomach. But he struggled to stay clear-headed.

Atom Heart Mother!

That was the title of the record. For a moment he felt happy. But it was a fleeting sensation. In his situation there wasn't much to be happy about.

He turned round again to look behind him.

Then, again: *I've got to get some petrol.*

Every now and again a gust of ammonia rose up from the mat at his feet to remind him that he had lost control of himself. The muscles in his legs were starting to ache and his calf had gone to sleep.

The storm that had been beating down on the motorway almost all night was moving away beyond the mountains. He could see its greenish flashes on the horizon, while a voice on the radio delivered yet another weather report. Soon it would be daybreak. An hour before he had come out of a tollbooth and emerged onto the motorway. He hadn't even stopped to pay the toll. His purpose at the moment was to carry on, to get further and further.

Following the instructions he had received to the letter.

For a few minutes he let his mind wander elsewhere. But inevitably it kept coming back to that memory.

He had reached the Hotel Modigliani the previous day, at about eleven in the morning. He had done his work as a salesman in town all afternoon and then in the evening, as planned, he had had dinner with some of his clients at the hotel bistro. Just after ten, he had gone back to his room.

Having closed the door, he had loosened his tie at the mirror and, at that moment, his reflection had shown him, along with his sweat-drenched appearance and his bloodshot eyes, the true face of his obsession. That was what he turned into when the desire took hold of him.

Looking at himself, he had been surprised at how he had been so good at hiding the true nature of his thoughts from his colleagues all evening. He had talked to them, listened to their inane chatter about golf and demanding women, laughed at the irritating jokes about sex. But he was elsewhere. He was savoring the moment when, back in his room, the knot in his tie loosened, he would let the lump of acid that was choking his throat rise up and explode in his face in the form of sweat, labored breathing and a treacherous expression.

The true face beneath the mask.

In the seclusion of his room he had finally been able to give vent to the urge that had been pressing in his chest and in his trousers, making him fear that it too might burst out. And yet it hadn't happened. He had managed to control himself.

Because soon he would be leaving.

As always he had sworn to himself that this would be the last time. As always, that promise was repeated *before* and *after*. And, as always, it would be denied and then renewed the next time.

He had left the hotel at about midnight, at the peak of his excitement. He had started idling: he was early. That afternoon, between tasks, he had made sure that everything was going according to plan, so that there would be no glitches. He'd been preparing this for two months, carefully grooming his "butterfly." Waiting was the down payment required for any kind of pleasure. And he had savored it. He had checked all the details, because any one of them could expose everything. But that wouldn't happen to him. It never happened to him. Now that the graveyard of arms had been found, he had to take additional precautions. There were a lot of police around, and everyone seemed to be on the alert. But he was good at making himself invisible. He had nothing to fear. He just had to relax. Soon he would see the butterfly in the driveway, at the spot they had agreed the day before. He was always afraid that they might change their minds. That something would go wrong. And then he would be sad, that rotten sadness that took days to dispel. And what's worse, you can't hide it. But he went on repeating to himself that this time too everything would be fine.

The butterfly would come.

He would quickly help her into the car, welcoming her with the usual pleasantries. The ones that help things along, make everything nice, take away the doubts produced by fear. He would take her to the place he had chosen for them that afternoon, turning off into a little side road from where you could see the lake.

The butterflies always had a very penetrating scent. Chewing gum, gym shoes. And sweat. He liked that. That smell was now part of his car.

Even now he could smell it, mixed with the smell of urine. He wept again. So many things had happened since that moment. Things had moved quickly from excitement and happiness to fear and disaster.

He looked behind him.

I've got to get some petrol.

But then he forgot and, taking a mouthful of that polluted air, he immersed himself once more in the memory of what had happened next…

He was sitting in the car, waiting for the butterfly. The opaque moon appeared from time to time among the clouds. To dispel his anxiety, he ran through the plan again. At first they would talk. But he would mostly listen. Because he knew that the butterflies always needed to receive what they couldn't get elsewhere: attention. He played his part to perfection. Listening patiently to his little prey which, by opening up its heart to him, made itself weaker. It lowered its guard and let him move undisturbed into deeper territories.

Close to the cleft of the soul.

He always said just the right thing. He did it every time. That was how he became their master. It was nice to teach someone about their own desires. Explain properly what it takes, show them how it's done.

It was important. To become their school, their training ground. Give a lesson in what is pleasant.

But just as he was composing that magical lesson that would throw open all the doors of intimacy, he had glanced distractedly into the rearview mirror.

At that moment he had seen it.

Something less solid than a shadow. Something you might not really have seen, because it comes straight from your imagination. And he had thought of a mirage, an illusion.

Right up to the fist on the window.

The dry click of the door opening. The hand snaking into the gap and grabbing him by the throat, clutching it. No chance of reacting. A gust of cold air had filled the inside of the car and he clearly remembered thinking, *I forgot to lock it! The locks!* Not that they would have been enough to stop him.

The man was remarkably strong and he had managed to drag him out of the car with only one hand. His face was covered with a black balaclava. As the man held him in midair, he had thought of the butterfly: the precious prey he had taken such trouble to attract, which was now lost.

And this time he was the prey.

The man had slackened the grip on his neck and flung him on the ground. Then he had lost interest in him and gone back towards his own car. *He's gone to get the weapon he's going to use to finish me off!* Driven by a desperate survival instinct, he had tried to drag himself along the damp, cold ground, even though the man in the ski mask would have needed to take only a few steps to reach him and finish what he had begun.

People do such pointless things when they're trying to escape death, he thought now, in the stale air of his car. Some people stretch out their hands when they're faced with the barrel of a gun, and all that happens is that the bullet perforates their palm. And to escape a fire some people throw themselves out of the windows of buildings... They're all trying to escape the inevitable, and they make themselves ridiculous.

He hadn't thought he belonged to that group of people. He had always been sure that he could confront death with dignity. But that night, he had found himself wriggling like a worm, naively begging for his own safety. He had just managed to limp a few yards.

Then he had lost his senses.

Two dry blows to the face had brought him to. The man with the balaclava had come back. He loomed above him, staring at him with two dead, dark eyes. He wasn't carrying a weapon. He had nodded to the car and said only, *"Go now and don't stop, Alexander."*

The man with the balaclava knew his name.

At first it had struck him as reasonable. Then, thinking about it again, it was the thing that terrified him most.

Getting away from there. At the time he hadn't believed it. He had got up from the ground and staggered to the car, trying to hurry for fear that the other man might change his mind. He had immediately sat down at the wheel, his eyesight still misty and his hands trembling so much he couldn't start the engine. Then at last his long night on the road had begun. Far from there, as far as possible…

I've got to get petrol, he thought, becoming practical again.

The tank was running on fumes. He looked out for signs for a filling station, wondering whether or not this was part of the task he'd been set the night before.

Don't stop.

Two questions had filled his thoughts. Why had the man with the balaclava let him go? What had happened while he had been unconscious?

He had had the answers at one o'clock in the morning, when, his mind clear for a moment, he had heard *the noise*.

Something rubbing against the bodywork, accompanied by a rhythmic, metallic beating—*tom, tom, tom*—grim and ceaseless. He must have done something to the car; *sooner or later one of the wheels will loosen and detach itself from the axle and I'll lose control and crash into the guardrail!* But nothing of the kind happened. Because the noise wasn't mechanical. But he'd worked that out only later…even if he still wasn't able to admit it to himself.

At that moment a road sign had appeared: the nearest filling station was less than eight kilometers away. He would get there, but he would have to be quick.

At that thought he turned around for the umpteenth time.

But his attention wasn't focused on the motorway that he was leaving, or the cars in his wake.

No, his gaze stopped before he got there, long before.

What was pursuing him was not on the road. It was much closer than that. It was the source of the sound. It was something he couldn't get away from.

It was the thing in his luggage.

That was what he kept staring at insistently. Even though he was trying not to think about what it might contain. But by the time Alexander Bermann turned around to stare straight ahead, it was already too late. The policeman at the edge of the carriageway was gesturing to him to pull over.

5.

Mila got off the train. Her face was bright and her eyes swollen from her sleepless night. She walked under the roof of the station. The building consisted of a magnificent nineteenth-century main hall and a huge shopping center. Everything was clean and orderly. And yet, after a few minutes, Mila knew all its dark corners. The places she would look for missing children. Where life is bought and sold, where it nestles or hides.

But that wasn't why she was there.

Two colleagues were waiting for her in the office of the railway police. A stocky woman of about forty, with an olive complexion and big hips, too big for the jeans she was wearing. And a man of about thirty-eight, very tall and well-built. He made her think of the lads from the village where she had grown up. She'd gone out with a couple of them at middle school. She remembered how clumsy their advances had been.

The man smiled at her, but his colleague merely stared, with one eyebrow raised. Mila stepped over for the introduction ritual. Sarah Rosa mumbled her name and rank. The man, however, held out his hand, saying clearly, "Hello, I'm Special Agent Klaus Boris." Then he offered to carry her canvas bag: "Let me."

"No, thanks, I can do it myself," said Mila.

But he insisted: "It's not a problem."

His tone, and the stubborn way he smiled at her, told Mila that Agent Boris must be a bit of a ladies' man, convinced that he could work his charm on any woman who came within range. She was sure that he'd decided to have a try as soon as he had seen her in the distance.

Boris suggested having a coffee before setting off, but Sarah Rosa glared at him.

"What's up? What did I say?" he pleaded.

"We don't have much time, remember?" the woman shot back dismissively.

"Our colleague has had a long journey and I was just thinking that—"

"There's no need," Mila cut in. "I'm fine, thanks."

Mila had no intention of getting on the wrong side of Sarah Rosa, who didn't seem to appreciate the fact that Mila was there to work with them.

They reached the car in the car park, and Boris sat down in the driver's seat. Rosa sat next to him. Mila got into the back, along with her canvas bag. They pulled out into the traffic and headed down the road that ran along the river.

Sarah Rosa seemed rather annoyed to have to act as escort to a colleague. Boris didn't seem to mind.

"Where are we going?" asked Mila shyly.

Boris looked at her in the rearview mirror. "Headquarters. Chief Inspector Roche needs to talk to you. He's going to be giving you your instructions."

"I've never had anything to do with a serial killer case before," Mila pointed out.

"You won't have to catch anyone," Rosa replied acidly. "We'll take care of that. Your only task is to discover the name of the sixth child. I hope you've been able to study the file...?"

Mila ignored the note of smugness in her colleague's voice as she thought of the sleepless night she had spent on that envelope. The photographs of the buried arms. The sparse medico-legal data about the age of the victims and the chronology of the deaths.

"What happened in that forest?" she asked.

"It's the biggest case for ages!" Boris said, taking his hands off the wheel for a moment, excited as a little boy. "Never seen anything like it. If you ask me, the shit's about to hit the fan at the top level. That's why Roche is bricking it."

Boris's vulgar slang annoyed Sarah Rosa, and Mila too, in fact. She had never met the chief inspector but she already knew that his men didn't hold him in especially high regard. Certainly, Boris was more direct, but if he took these liberties in front of Rosa it meant that she agreed with him, even if she didn't let on. *It's not going well,* Mila thought. She decided to judge Roche and his methods for herself, not be swayed by the comments she might come to hear.

Rosa repeated a question and only then did Mila notice that she was talking to her.

"Is that blood yours?"

Sarah Rosa had turned in her seat and was pointing at a spot at the bottom. Mila looked at her thigh. Her trousers were stained with blood; the scar had opened up. She put a hand on it and hastily came up with an explanation.

"I fell when I was jogging," she lied.

"Well, try and get that wound healed. We don't want your blood contaminating any of our samples."

Mila felt suddenly embarrassed by the rebuke, not least because Boris was staring at her in the mirror. She hoped it would stop there, but Rosa hadn't finished her lesson.

"Once, a rookie who was supposed to be keeping an eye on the scene of a sexual homicide went and pissed in the victim's bathroom. We spent six months chasing a ghost, thinking the murderer had forgotten to flush."

Boris laughed at the memory. Mila, though, tried to change the subject. "Why did you call me? Couldn't you find the girl by just glancing at the list of disappearances for the past month?"

"Don't ask us…" said Rosa spicily.

The dirty work, thought Mila. It was only too obvious that that was why she had been called in. Roche had wanted to give the thing to someone outside the unit, who wasn't too close to him, to let them take the fall if the sixth corpse were left nameless.

Debby. Anneke. Sabine. Melissa. Caroline.

"What about the families of the other five?" asked Mila.

"They're coming over to headquarters too, for the DNA test."

Mila thought of those poor parents, forced to subject themselves to the DNA lottery to be certain that the blood of their blood had been barbarously killed. Soon their lives would change forever.

"And what do we know about the monster?" she asked, trying to distract herself from that thought.

"We don't call him a monster," Boris observed. "That would depersonalize him." As he said it, Boris exchanged a meaningful glance with Rosa. "Dr. Gavila doesn't like that."

"Dr. Gavila?" Mila repeated.

"You'll meet him."

Mila's unease increased. It was plain that her scant knowledge of the case put her at a disadvantage over her colleagues, who would be able to make fun of her over it. But once again she didn't say a word to defend herself.

Rosa, on the other hand, had no intention of leaving her in peace and pressed her indulgently: "You see, my dear, you shouldn't be surprised if you don't understand how things stand. I'm sure you're good at your work, but this is different, because serial killers have different rules. And that applies to the victims, too. They've done nothing to deserve it. Their only crime, most of the time, is that they happened to be in the wrong place at the wrong time. Or they were wearing one particular color rather than another when they left the house. Or, as in our case, their crime was to be little girls, Caucasian, and to be aged between nine and thirteen...Don't take this the wrong way, but you can't know these things. Nothing personal."

Yeah sure, I believe that, thought Mila. Since the very moment when they met, Rosa had made everything personal.

"I learn quickly," Mila replied.

Rosa turned and looked at her, her face hard: "Do you have children?"

Mila was startled for a moment. "No, why? What's that got to do with it?"

"Because when you find the parents of the sixth little girl, you'll have to tell them the 'reason' why their beautiful daughter was treated like that. But you will know nothing about them, about the sacrifices they made to bring her up and educate her, the sleepless nights when she had a temperature, the savings they'd put aside for her studies, to make sure she had a future, the hours spent playing with her, or helping her with her homework." Rosa's tone was getting increasingly angry. "And you will never know why three of those girls wore the same shiny polish on their nails, or that one of them had an old scar on her elbow because maybe she fell off her bike when she was five, or that they were all young and pretty and their dreams and desires of that innocent age have been violated forever! You don't know these things because you've never been a mother."

"'Hollie,'" was Mila's brusque reply.

"What?" Sarah Rosa stared at her without comprehension.

"The brand of nail polish is called Hollie. It's the shiny kind, coral dust. It was a freebie that was given away a month ago with a teenage magazine. That's why all three of them had it: it was really successful. Also, one of the victims was wearing a charm bracelet."

"We haven't found a bracelet," said Boris, who was starting to get interested.

Mila took one of the photographs out of the folder. "It's number two, Anneke. The skin near her wrist is paler. A sign that she was wearing something there. The murderer might have taken it off, perhaps she lost it when she was being kidnapped or during a struggle. They were all right-handed except for one: she had ink stains on the side of her index finger, she was left-handed."

Boris was impressed, Rosa startled. Mila was a river in full spate. "One last thing: number six, the one whose name we don't know, knew the one who vanished first, Debby."

"How the hell do you know that?" asked Rosa.

Mila took the pictures of the arms out of the folder one by one. "There's a little red dot on the tips of both their index fingers. *They're blood sisters*."

The Department of Behavioral Sciences of the Federal Police dealt chiefly with savage crimes. Roche had been head of it for eight years, and he had been able to revolutionize its style and methods. He had been the one, in fact, to open the doors to civilians like Dr. Gavila who, with his writing and research, was unanimously considered the most innovative amongst current criminologists.

In the investigative unit, Agent Stern was the information officer. He was the oldest and the most senior. His job involved collecting data that would then be used to construct profiles and trace parallels with other cases. He was the "memory" of the group.

Sarah Rosa was the logistics officer and computer expert. She spent much of her time studying new technologies, and she had received specific training in the planning of police operations.

Finally there was Boris, the interrogating officer. His responsibility was to question the people involved using the most appropriate method, and to make the possible culprit confess. He was a specialist in all kinds of techniques that would achieve that goal. And usually he reached it.

Roche issued the orders, but he didn't materially direct the unit: it was Dr. Gavila's intuitions that guided investigations. The chief inspector was a politician more than anything else, and his choices were often dictated by his career. He liked to appear in public and take the merit for investigations that were going well. In the ones that were unsuccessful, however, he divided responsibility around the whole group or, as he had called it, "the Roche unit." This method had brought him the dislike and often the contempt of his subordinates.

They were all in the meeting room on the sixth floor of the building that was home to the midtown Department headquarters.

Mila sat down in the back row. In the bathroom she had treated the wound in her leg again, closing it up with two layers of sticking plaster. Then she had changed her jeans for another identical pair.

She looked around, setting her bag on the floor. She immediately recognized a gangling man as Chief Inspector Roche. He was talking animatedly to an unassuming man with a curious aura about him. A gray light. Mila was sure that outside that room, in the real world, the man would have vanished like a ghost. But in here his presence had a meaning. He was plainly the Dr. Gavila that Boris and Rosa had been talking about in the car.

There was something about the man that immediately made you forget his crumpled clothes and untidy hair.

It was his eyes, huge and piercing.

As he went on talking to Roche, he shifted them onto Mila, catching her in flagrante. She looked away, awkwardly, and after a while he did the same, going to sit down not far from her. From that point onwards he ignored her completely, and a few minutes later the meeting officially began.

Roche stepped onto the platform and began to speak with a solemn gesture of his hand, as if talking to an enormous audience rather than an auditorium of five people.

"I have just heard the scientific report: our Albert has left no clues behind. He really knows what he's doing. Not a trace, not a fingerprint in the little graveyard of arms. He just left us with six little girls to find. Six bodies…and a name."

Then the inspector invited Goran to speak, but Goran didn't join him on the platform. Instead he stayed in his place, with his arms crossed and his legs stretched out under the row of chairs in front of him.

"Albert knew from the start how things would go. He predicted them down to the smallest detail. He's the one running the show. And six is a complete number in the formula of serial murder."

"Six-six-six, the number of the beast," Mila interjected impulsively. Everyone turned to look at her with expressions of reproach.

"Let's not resort to that kind of banality," said Goran, and Mila felt herself sinking into the floor. "When we talk about a complete number we are referring to the fact that the subject has already completed one series or more."

Barely noticeably, Mila frowned and Goran guessed that she hadn't understood, so he explained it better: "We call someone a serial killer if they have killed three times using similar methods."

"Two corpses only make a multiple murderer," added Boris.

"That's why six victims are two series."

"So it's a kind of convention?" Mila asked.

"No. It means that if you kill for the third time you don't stop," said Rosa, bringing the discussion to an end.

"The inhibitory brakes are relaxed, the sense of guilt is lessened and now you're killing mechanically," Goran concluded and turned back to the others. "But why don't we know anything about corpse number six?"

Roche broke in. "We do know one thing now. From what I have been told, our distinguished colleague has supplied us with a clue that *I* consider to be important. She has linked the nameless victim to Debby Gordon, our number one." Roche said it as if Mila's idea were in fact his own. "Officer Vasquez, if you would be so kind as to tell us the results of your investigative intuition."

Mila found herself at the center of attention again. She lowered her head to her notes, trying to bring some order to her thoughts before starting to speak. Meanwhile Roche nodded to her to stand up.

Mila got to her feet. "Debby Gordon and child number six knew one another. Of course this is just a supposition on my part, but it would explain the fact that they both have an identical mark on their index fingers…"

"What is it exactly?" Goran asked curiously.

"Well…it's that ritual of pricking your fingertip with a needle and mixing your blood by bringing your fingertips together: an adolescent version of the blood pact. You usually do it to consecrate a friendship."

Mila herself had done it with her friend Graciela; they had used a rusty nail because needles had struck them as too girly. The memory suddenly flooded into her mind. Graciela had been her playmate. Each knew each other's secrets, and once they had even shared a boyfriend, even though he hadn't known anything about it. They had allowed him to believe that he was the clever one who managed to go out with both friends without their noticing. What had happened to Graciela? She hadn't heard from her for years. They had lost contact too soon, never to see one another again. And yet they had promised each other eternal friendship. Why had it been so easy to forget her?

"If that's the case, child number six should be a contemporary of Debby's," she concluded.

"The Barr body test carried out on the sixth limb bears out this thesis: the victim was twelve," said Boris, who couldn't wait to gain points in Mila's eyes.

"Debby Gordon went to an exclusive boarding school. It isn't plausible that her blood sister could have been a schoolmate, because none of the other students are missing."

"So she must have met her outside of the school setting," Boris butted in again.

Mila nodded. "Debby had been at the school for eight months. She must have felt very lonely far from home. I would guess that she had trouble bonding with the other girls. So I suppose she met her blood sister in different circumstances."

Roche said, "I want you to go and take a look at the girl's room at the school: something might come out of that."

"I'd like to talk to Debby's parents too, if possible."

"Sure, do what you see fit."

Before the chief inspector could continue, there was a knock at the door. Three quick taps. Immediately afterwards a short man in a white shirt made his entrance, even though no one had invited him in. He had bristly hair and unusual almond eyes.

"Ah, Chang," said Roche by way of welcome.

The man was the medical examiner dealing with the case. Mila realized almost immediately that he wasn't actually oriental. His name was Leonard Vross, but everyone had always known him as Chang.

The little man came and stood next to Roche. He carried a dossier that he opened straightaway, even though he had no need to read its contents because he knew them by heart. Probably keeping those pages in front of him gave him a sense of security.

"I'd like you to listen carefully to what Dr. Chang has discovered," said the chief inspector. "Even though I know that it might be difficult for some of you to understand certain details."

The reference was to her, Mila was more than sure.

Chang put on a pair of glasses that he kept in his shirt pocket, cleared his throat and began to speak. "The state of preservation of the remains, in spite of their having been buried, was excellent."

This confirmed the idea that not very much time had passed between the making of the arm graveyard and its discovery. So the pathologist expanded on a number of details. But when Chang finally had to illustrate the method by which the six little girls had been killed, he got straight to the point.

"He killed them by cutting off their arms."

Lesions have a language of their own, and they use it to communicate. Mila was well aware of that. When the medical examiner turned the page of the file to the enlargement of the photograph of one of the arms, she immediately noticed the reddish halo around the cut and the break of the bone. The seepage of blood into the tissue is the first indication of whether the lesion is lethal or not. If it has been inflicted on a corpse there is no activity from the cardiac pump, so the blood flows passively from the torn vessels, without settling in the surrounding tissues. If, on the other hand, the blow is delivered when the victim is still alive, the heart is pushing the blood into the injured tissues in a desperate attempt to scar them. In the little girls, the lifesaving mechanism had stopped only when the arm had gone away.

Chang went on: "The lesion occurred halfway down the brachial biceps. The bone isn't shattered, the break is clean. The killer must have used a precision saw: we haven't found any iron filings along the margins of the injury. The uniform section of the blood vessels and the tendons tells us that the amputation was completed with what I would call surgical skill. Death was caused by bleeding." Then he added: "It was a hideous death."

At this phrase, Mila felt an impulse to lower her eyes in a sign of respect. But she immediately noticed that she would have been the only one.

Chang went on: "I would say he killed them straightaway: he had no interest in keeping them alive longer than necessary, and he didn't hesitate. The methods of killing are identical for all the victims. *Except for one...*"

His words hung in the air before raining down on his listeners like a shower of icy water.

"What do you mean?" Goran asked.

Chang pushed his glasses back from the tip of his nose and stared at the criminologist. "Because for one of them it was even worse."

Absolute silence settled on the room.

"The toxicological examinations have revealed traces of a cocktail of pharmaceuticals in the blood and the tissue. In this case: antiarrhythmics like disopyramide, ACE inhibitors and atenolol, which is a beta-blocker..."

"He reduced her heart rate, lowering the pressure at the same time," added Goran Gavila, who had already understood everything.

"Why?" asked Stern, for whom it wasn't clear at all.

A grimace, like a bitter smile, appeared on Chang's lips. "He slowed down the bleeding to make her die more slowly...he wanted to *enjoy the show*."

"Which child was it?" asked Roche, even though they all knew the answer.

"Number six."

This time Mila didn't need to be an expert on serial killers to work out what had happened. The medical examiner had effectively stated that the murderer had altered his modus operandi. Which meant that he had become confident about what he was doing. He was experimenting with a new game. And he liked it.

"He changed because he was happy with the result. He was getting better and better," concluded Goran. "From what we can tell, he was enjoying it."

Mila suddenly felt a strange sensation. It was that tickle at the base of the neck that alerted her every time she was getting close to a solution to one of her missing-person cases. It was hard to explain. When it happened, her mind would reveal an unexpected truth. Usually that perception lasted for longer, but this time it disappeared before she could grasp it. Some words from Chang swept it away.

"One more thing…" The doctor turned to face Mila: even though he didn't know her, she was the only strange face in that room, and he must already have been informed about the reasons for her presence. "The parents of the missing girls are in the next room."

From the window of the traffic police station, hidden away among the mountains, Alexander Bermann was able to enjoy a complete view of the car park. His car was down there, in the fifth row. From that observation point it looked very far away.

The sun, already high in the sky, made the sheet metal gleam. After last night's storm he could never have imagined a day like this. It was like late spring, and it was almost hot. A faint breeze came through the open window, bringing a sense of peace. He was strangely content.

When he had been stopped at the road block at dawn, he hadn't been flustered, he hadn't panicked. He had stayed inside the car, with the annoying sensation of dampness between his legs.

From the driver's seat he had an excellent view of the officers beside the police car. One of them was holding the envelope containing his documents, running through them, dictating to the other the data which the other man then passed on by radio.

Soon they're going to come over and make me open the boot, he thought.

The officer who had pulled him over had been very polite. He had asked him about his fog lamp, and been sympathetic as he told him that he didn't envy him for having been forced to drive all night in that awful weather.

"You're not from around here," he had announced, reading the numberplate.

"No, you're right," Alexander had replied. "I'm from somewhere else."

The conversation had ended there. For a moment he had thought of telling him everything, but he had changed his mind. The moment had not yet come. Then the officer had walked off towards his colleague. Alexander Bermann didn't know what would happen, but for the first time he had relaxed his grip on the wheel. The blood had started circulating in his hands again, and their color had returned.

And he had found himself thinking about his butterflies again.

So frail, so unaware of the spell they cast. While he had stopped time for them, making them aware of the secrets of their fascination, the others merely drained them of their beauty. He took care of it. What could they accuse him of, after all?

When he had seen the policeman coming back towards his window, those thoughts had suddenly fled and the tension, which had relaxed for a moment, had mounted again. They had taken too long, he had thought. As he came over, the officer held one hand at his hip, level with his belt. Bermann knew what that gesture was. It meant that he was about to draw his gun. When he was finally nearby, he heard him say something that he wasn't expecting.

"We'd like you to follow us to headquarters, Mr. Bermann. Your logbook is missing from your documentation."

That's strange, he had thought. *I was sure I put it there*. But then he had understood: the man with the balaclava had taken it out when he had been unconscious…And now here he was, in this little waiting room, enjoying the undeserved warmth of the breeze. They had shut him up in here after confiscating his car. Without knowing that the threat of an administrative sanction was the last of his worries. They were holed up in their offices, completely unaware, making decisions about things that no longer had any importance for him. How do you change the hierarchy of priorities for a man who no longer has anything to lose? His most urgent thought at the moment was that the caress of that breeze shouldn't cease.

Meanwhile he still had his eyes fixed on the car park and the comings and goings of the policemen. His car was still there, in full view. With its secret locked away in the boot. And no one noticed anything.

As he reflected on the uniqueness of his situation, he noticed a squad of policemen coming back from their midmorning coffee break. Three men and two women, all in uniform. One of them seemed to be telling a story, and waved his arms about as he walked. When he finished, the others laughed. Alexander hadn't heard a single word of the story, but the sound of laughter was contagious and he found himself smiling. It didn't last long. The group passed close to his car. One of them, the tallest, suddenly stopped, letting the others continue on their own. He had noticed something.

Alexander immediately spotted the expression that had formed on his face.

The smell, he thought. *He must have caught the smell.*

Without saying anything to his colleagues, the policeman started looking round. He sniffed the air, trying to find the faint trace that had for a moment put his senses on the alert. When he found it again, he turned towards the car next to him. He took a few steps in that direction, then froze by the closed boot.

Alexander Bermann, seeing the scene, sighed with relief. He was *grateful*. Grateful for the coincidence that had brought him here, for the breeze that had been granted him and for the fact that he would not be the one who opened that damned boot.

The caress of the wind subsided. Alexander got up from his seat by the window and took his mobile out of his pocket.

The time had come to make a phone call.

6.

Debby. Anneke. Sabine. Melissa. Caroline.

Mila silently repeated those names as she gazed through a pane of glass at the family members of the five identified victims, who had assembled in the morgue of the Institute of Legal Medicine. It was a gothic building with big windows, surrounded by bare parkland.

There are two missing, was Mila's obsessive thought. *A father and a mother that we haven't yet managed to find.*

They had to give a name to left hand number six. The girl Albert had tormented the most, with that cocktail of drugs to slow down death as painfully as possible.

He wanted to enjoy the show.

She thought again of the music teacher case, when she had freed Pablo and Elisa. *And yet you rescued three,* Sergeant Morexu had said, referring to the note found in the man's diary. That name…

Priscilla.

Her boss was right: the little girl had been lucky. Mila became aware of a cruel link between her and the six victims.

Priscilla had been chosen in advance by her executioner. It was only by chance that she had not become his prey. Where was she now?

What was her life like? And was there a part of her, deep and hidden, that was aware of escaping a kind of horror like that?

From the moment she had set foot in the music teacher's house, Mila had rescued her. And she would never know. She would never be able to appreciate the gift of the second life that had been granted her.

Priscilla, like Debby, Anneke, Sabine, Melissa, Caroline. Predestined, but without their destiny.

Priscilla, like number six. A faceless victim. But she at least had a name.

Chang maintained that it was just a matter of time, that the identity of the sixth little girl would emerge sooner or later. But the idea that she had disappeared forever made it difficult to consider any other option.

But now she *had* to be clear-minded. *My turn,* she thought, as she looked through the glass separating her from the parents of the little girls who already had a name. She studied the human aquarium, the choreography of those silent, grief-stricken creatures. Soon she would have to go in there to talk to Debby Gordon's father and mother. And she would have to give those parents what remained of their grief.

The morgue corridor was long and dark. It was in the basement of the building. It was reached by a flight of stairs or a lift that wasn't usually working. There were narrow windows on either side of the ceiling, which let in a very small amount of light. The white glazed tiles covering the walls didn't manage to reflect it, which had probably been the plan when they were put there. The result was that it was dark there even by day, and the fluorescent lights on the ceiling were always lit, filling the spectral silence of the place with their unceasing hum.

What a horrible place to face the news of the loss of a child, Mila reflected, still studying those suffering parents. There was nothing to comfort them but some anonymous plastic chairs and a table of smiling old magazines.

Debby. Anneke. Sabine. Melissa. Caroline.

"Take a look," said Goran Gavila, standing close behind her. "What d'you see?"

First he had humiliated her in front of everyone. And now he was being familiar.

Mila went on observing for a long while. "I see their suffering."

"Take a better look. There's more."

"I see those dead children. Even though they aren't there. Their faces are the sum of their parents' faces. That's how I can see the victims."

"And I see five nuclear families. Each one with a different social background. With different incomes and different lifestyles. I see couples who have, for various reasons, had only one child. I see women who are long past forty, and for that reason can't biologically hope for another pregnancy...that's what I see." Goran turned to look at her. "*They* are his true victims. He has studied them, he has chosen them. An only daughter. He wanted to strip them of any hope of overcoming their grief, of trying to forget their loss. They will have to remember what he did to them for the rest of their days. He has amplified their grief by taking away their future. He has deprived them of the possibility of passing on a memory of themselves to the years to come, of surviving their own death...and he has fed on that. It is the reward for his sadism, the source of his pleasure."

Mila looked away. The criminologist was right: there was a *symmetry* in the evil that had been done to these people.

"A pattern," Goran stated, correcting her thoughts.

Mila thought again about girl number six. There was no one to mourn her yet. She had a right to those tears, like all the others. Suffering has a task to perform. It rebuilds the bonds between the things of the living and those of the dead. It is a language that stands in for words. That changes the terms of the question. It was what the parents on the other side of the glass were doing. Minutely rebuilding, with their pain, a scrap of the life that no longer existed. Weaving together their frail memories, binding the white threads of the past to the thin ones of the present.

Mila summoned her strength and crossed the threshold. The parents' eyes immediately moved to her and there was silence.

She walked towards the mother of Debby Gordon, sitting beside her husband, who rested his hand on her shoulder. Her footsteps sounded grim as she stepped in front of the others.

"Mr. and Mrs. Gordon, I need to talk to you for a moment..."

Mila pointed the way with a movement of her arm. Then she made them walk ahead of her towards a second little room, with a coffee machine and a snack dispenser, a worn sofa against the wall, a table with blue plastic chairs and a rubbish bin full of plastic cups.

Mila asked the Gordons to sit on the sofa and went to get one of the chairs. She stretched her legs, feeling another little pang in the wound in her thigh. It wasn't all that strong: she was getting better.

Mila screwed up her courage and began by introducing herself. She talked about the investigation, without adding any details to what they knew already. Her intention was to put them at ease before asking them the questions that interested her.

The Gordons hadn't stopped looking at her for a moment, as if she somehow had the power to stop the nightmare. Both husband and wife were attractive and elegant. Both lawyers. The kind that are paid by the hour. Mila imagined them in their perfect home, surrounded by selected friends, with their gilded lives. It made sense that they could send their only daughter to study at a prestigious private school. Both husband and wife must be two sharks in their profession. People who can deal with the most critical situations in their own field, who are used to smashing in the teeth of their opponents, and never being discouraged by adversity. But now they were both completely unprepared for a tragedy like this.

Once she had finished the exposition of the case, she got to the point: "Mr. and Mrs. Gordon, are you by any chance aware of any special friendship that Debby might have made with a girl her age outside of the boarding school?"

The couple looked at one another as if, rather than an answer, they were trying to find a plausible reason for the question. But they couldn't find it.

"Not that we know of," said Debby's father.

Mila, however, wasn't satisfied with that meager reply. "Are you sure that Debby never talked to you on the phone about anyone who wasn't a schoolmate?"

As Mrs. Gordon struggled to remember, Mila found herself studying her outline: that flat stomach, the toned muscles of her legs. She understood immediately that the choice to have only one child had been carefully mulled over. This woman would not have weighed down her physique with a second pregnancy. But it was too late now: her age, close to fifty, would not allow her to have any more children. Goran was right. Albert hadn't chosen them by chance.

"No...but lately she had sounded much more at ease on the phone," said the woman.

"I imagine she must have asked you to bring her home..."

She had hit a sore point, but she couldn't help it if she wanted to get to the truth. His voice cracking with guilt, Debby's father admitted: "It's true: she was out of her element, she said she missed us and Sting..." Mila looked at him, baffled, and the man explained: "Her dog...Debby wanted to come home, to her old school. Well, she never actually said that. Perhaps she was afraid of disappointing us, but...it was apparent from her tone of voice."

Mila knew what was going to happen: these parents would forever reproach themselves for not listening to their daughter's heart when she begged them to let her come home. But the Gordons had put their ambition before her, hoping that it was something that could be genetically transmitted. There was really nothing wrong about their behavior; they had wanted the best for their only daughter. Basically, they were just behaving like parents. And if things had gone differently, perhaps one day Debby would have been grateful to them. But that day, sadly for them, would never come.

"Mr. and Mrs. Gordon, I'm sorry to have to insist, I can imagine how painful this is, but I must ask you to think back to the conversations you had with Debby: the people she saw out of school might turn out to be very important to the solving of the case. Please, think back, and if anything comes to mind..."

The two of them nodded at the same time, promising they would try to remember. Mila glimpsed a figure behind the glass of the door:

Sarah Rosa, trying to attract her attention. Mila apologized to the Gordons and left. When she stood face-to-face with Sarah Rosa in the corridor, the woman said only a few words.

"Get yourself ready, we have to go. They've found the body of a little girl."

Special Agent Stern was still wearing a jacket and tie. He preferred brown or beige or blue suits, and shirts with thin stripes. Mila worked out that his wife was keen on him walking around in well-ironed clothes. He looked well-groomed, his hair combed back with a little brilliantine. He shaved every morning, and the skin on his face was soft rather than smooth; it smelled good. He was a very precise character, Stern. One of those who never change their habits, for whom an orderly appearance is more important than being fashionable.

And he must have been very capable in his work as a collector of information.

During the car journey that brought them to the place where the body had been found, Stern threw a mint into his mouth, then quickly set out the facts as he knew them.

"The arrested man is called Alexander Bermann. He's forty years old and he's a sales representative—machine parts for the textile industry. He's a great salesman, apparently. He's married, and he's always lived a quiet life. He is highly regarded, and well known in the city where he lives. His work brings him in a fair income: he's not rich exactly, but he's doing OK."

"He's clean, then," added Rosa. "Not the kind you'd expect."

When they reached the traffic police station, the officer who had found the body was sitting on an old sofa in one of the offices. He was in shock.

The local authorities had handed the place over to the violent crimes unit. And they got to work with the help of Goran and under the eyes of Mila, whose role consisted simply in checking the presence or otherwise of useful clues that would let her do her job more easily without actively intervening. Roche had stayed in the office, letting his men reconstruct what had happened.

Mila noticed that Sarah Rosa kept her distance from her. She couldn't help being pleased about that—even though the policewoman was keeping an eye on her, waiting to catch her out, she was sure of it.

A young lieutenant offered to walk them to the exact place. Trying to look confident, he was at pains to make it clear that nothing had been moved. But all the members of the unit knew very well that it was probably the first time he had faced a scene of this kind. In a career as a provincial policeman, you don't often come across such a horrible crime.

Along the way, the lieutenant set out the facts with extreme precision. Perhaps he'd rehearsed the speech beforehand, so as not to get it wrong. So it came out like a written statement: "We have ascertained that yesterday morning Alexander Bermann arrived at a hotel in a village very far from here."

"Four hundred miles away," Stern specified.

"It would appear that he drove all night. The petrol tank was almost empty," the lieutenant added.

"Did he meet anyone at the hotel?" asked Boris.

"Apparently he dined with clients. Then he retired to his room...that's what the people who were with him say. But we're still checking their versions."

Rosa jotted this down in a notebook, and Mila glimpsed the note from over her shoulder: *Collect hotel guest version re timetables*.

Goran broke in: "Bermann hasn't said anything yet, I suppose."

"Suspect Alexander Bermann refuses to speak without a lawyer present."

They reached the car park. Goran noted that white screens had been arranged around Bermann's car to conceal the spectacle of death. But it was only one hypocritical precaution among many. Agitation is often a mask used to respond to terrible crimes. That was something that Goran Gavila had learned early on. Death, especially violent death, exerts a strange fascination on the living. Corpses always arouse our curiosity. Death is highly seductive.

Before reaching the scene of the crime, they put on plastic shoe covers and caps to hold their hair in, and the inevitable sterile gloves. Then they passed around a small container of camphor paste. Each of them took a little to rub under their nostrils to keep any kind of smell away.

It was a tried and tested ritual, which needed no words. But also a way of finding the right level of concentration. When she received the tub from Boris, Mila felt like a participant in that strange act of communion.

The traffic police lieutenant, having been invited to walk ahead of them, suddenly lost all his confidence and hesitated. Then he left.

Before crossing the boundaries of this new world, Mila caught Goran looking at her with concern. She nodded, and he seemed reassured.

The first step was always the hardest. Mila wouldn't easily forget her own.

In those few square yards, where even the sunlight was altered by the cold and artificial glare of the halogen lamps, there was another universe, with physical rules and laws entirely unlike those of the known world. The three dimensions of height, width and depth were joined by a fourth: the void. Every criminologist knows that it is in the "voids" of a crime scene that you find the answers. By filling those spaces with the presence of the victim and the executioner you reconstruct the crime, you give a meaning to the violence, you cast light on the unknown. The first impression at a crime scene is always the most important.

Mila's first impression was the smell.

In spite of the camphor, the smell was penetrating. The scent of death is both nauseating and sweet. It's a contradiction in terms. First it hits you like a blow to the stomach, then you discover that there is something deep within it that you can't help liking.

The team members quickly arranged themselves in a circle around Bermann's car. Each of them occupied an observation point, their eyes creating a grid that covered every square inch.

Mila followed Goran to the rear of the car.

The boot was open, as it had been left by the officer who had found the body. Goran leaned into it and Mila did the same.

Inside the boot there was nothing but a big black plastic bag within which the outline of a body was just visible.

The bag had clung perfectly to its form, molding itself to the features of the face and assuming its shape. The mouth was wide in a mute cry. As if the air had been sucked out by the dark abyss.

Like a shroud of flesh.

Anneke, Debby, Sabine, Melissa, Caroline…Or was it number six?

The eye sockets could be seen, and the head, thrown backwards. The body had not given up its life without a struggle; on the contrary, the posture of the limbs was stiff, as if it had been struck by lightning midleap. In that statue of flesh, something was plainly absent. An arm was missing. The left one.

"Fine, let's start the analysis," said Goran.

The criminologist's method consisted in asking questions, some of them simple and apparently insignificant; questions to which they would all try to find an answer. Even in this context, every opinion was accepted.

"First of all the *orientation,*" he began. "So, tell me: why are we here?"

"I'll begin," suggested Boris, who was standing on the driver's side. "We're here because of a missing logbook."

"What do you think? Is that enough of an explanation?" Goran asked, looking around the group.

"The roadblock," said Sarah Rosa. "Since the little girls went missing there have been dozens of them, scattered all over the place. It was a possibility, and it happened…it was luck."

Goran shook his head: he didn't believe in luck. "Why should he take the risk of driving around with this compromising cargo?"

"Perhaps he just wanted to get rid of it," Stern suggested. "Or perhaps he was afraid that we were onto him, and he was trying to shift the clues as far as possible from himself."

"I agree that it might be an attempt to throw us off the trail," said Boris. "But it went wrong."

Mila worked out that they had already made their minds up: Alexander Bermann was Albert. Only Goran seemed still to be slightly perplexed.

"We've still got to work out what his plan was. That's why we've got a corpse in a boot. But the first question was a different one, and we still don't have an answer to it: why are we here? What has brought us together around this car, looking at this body? Since the outset, we've taken it for granted that our man was clever. Perhaps even more intelligent than we are. He's tricked us several times, managing to kidnap the little girls even when everyone was on full alert...Can you really imagine, then, that it was the lack of a stupid logbook that gave him away?"

Everyone considered this in silence.

The criminologist turned back to the traffic police lieutenant, who had stood apart in the meantime, silent and as pale as the shirt he wore under his uniform.

"Lieutenant, a short time ago you told us that Bermann requested the presence of a lawyer, is that right?"

"Exactly."

"Maybe a duty lawyer would do, because for now I'd like to have a talk with the suspect, to let him refute the results of our analyses when we've finished here."

"Do you want me to give instructions now?"

The man was waiting for Gavila to dismiss him. And Goran was about to do as he wished.

"Bermann has probably found a way to get a version of the facts ready. Better to take him by surprise and try to catch him out in a contradiction before he learns it off by heart," Boris added.

"I hope he's had time to examine his conscience while he's been locked up in there."

As the lieutenant spoke, the team members looked at one another in disbelief.

"You mean you've left him alone?" asked Goran.

The lieutenant was uncomfortable. "We put him in solitary, in line with police practice. Why, what—"

He didn't have time to finish his sentence. Boris was the first to move—with a leap he found himself outside the enclosure, and he was followed in turn by Stern and Sarah Rosa who, as they left, quickly took off their shoe covers to keep from slipping when they ran.

Mila, like the young traffic lieutenant, appeared not to understand what was going on. Goran dashed after the others, shouting back, "He's an at-risk subject: you should have kept an eye on him!"

At that moment both Mila and the lieutenant understood the risk the criminologist was talking about.

A few moments later they met up by the door of the cell where the man had been locked up. There was a surveillance officer who hurried to open up the spy hole when Boris showed him his card. Through that little chink, though, there was no sign of Alexander Bermann.

He's chosen the blind corner of the cell, Mila thought.

As the guard opened the heavy locks, the lieutenant went on trying to calm everyone—but himself most of all—by stressing once again that the procedure had been followed to the letter. Bermann's watch, his belt, his tie and even his shoelaces had been taken away. He had nothing that he could hurt himself with.

But the policeman was proved wrong as soon as the iron door was flung open.

The man was lying in a corner of the cell. The blind corner.

Back against the wall, his arms were abandoned in his lap and his legs spread wide. His mouth was drenched in blood. A black pool surrounded the body.

He had used the least traditional of ways to kill himself.

Alexander Bermann had torn away the flesh of his wrists with his teeth, and waited to bleed to death.

7.

They would take her home.

With that unvoiced promise, they had taken delivery of the little girl's body.

They would do her justice.

After Bermann's suicide it was hard to keep that commitment, but they would try anyway.

That was why the corpse was here, at the Institute of Legal Medicine.

Dr. Chang arranged the microphone hanging from the ceiling so that it was perpendicular to the steel morgue table. Then he turned on the tape recorder.

First of all he took a scalpel and rapidly slid it along the plastic bag, tracing a very precise straight line. He set down the surgical instrument and, with his fingers, delicately picked up the two flaps that he had made.

The only light in the room was the glare from the lamp above the operating table. All around, the chasm of darkness. And balanced on the edge of that abyss were Goran and Mila. None of the other members of the team had felt they had to take part in the ceremony.

The medical examiner and the two guests had put on sterile gowns, gloves and face masks so as not to contaminate the evidence.

With the help of a saline solution, Chang slowly began to spread out the edges of the bag, detaching the plastic from the body beneath, to which it had perfectly adhered. A little at a time, with great patience.

It gradually began to appear... Mila immediately saw the green corduroy skirt. The white blouse and the woolen waistcoat. Then she began to see the flannel of a blazer.

As Chang carried on, new details came to light. He reached the thoracic section, the arm of which was missing. The jacket wasn't actually bloodstained there. It was simply cut off level with the left shoulder, from which a stump protruded.

"He didn't kill her with these clothes on. He rearranged the corpse afterwards," the pathologist said.

That "afterwards" was lost in the echo of the room, plunging into the chasm of darkness that surrounded them, like a stone bouncing off the walls of a bottomless pit.

Chang slipped the right arm out. On the wrist there was a bracelet with a key-shaped pendant.

Reaching the level of the neck, the doctor stopped for a moment to wipe his brow with a little towel. Only then did Mila notice that the pathologist was sweating. He had reached the most delicate point of the operation. The fear was that when the plastic was detached from the face the epidermis might also come away.

Mila had been present at other autopsies. Usually the medical examiners didn't have such scruples about the way they treated the bodies under examination. They cut them apart and sewed them up quite carelessly. At that moment, however, she worked out that Chang wanted the parents to see their child one last time, in the best possible state. That was why he was so apprehensive. She felt a surge of respect for the man.

Finally, after a few interminable minutes, the doctor succeeded in completely removing the black bag from the little girl's face. Mila recognized her straightaway.

Debby Gordon. Twelve years old. The first to go missing.

Her eyes were wide open. Her mouth was still gaping. As if she was desperately trying to say something.

She was wearing a clasp with a white lily. *He's combed her hair*. How ludicrous, Mila thought suddenly. It had been easier to be compassionate with a corpse than with a living child! But then she deduced that there was another reason why he had taken such care of her.

He made her beautiful for us.

Her hunch made her furious. But she also understood that at that moment those emotions did not belong to her. They were meant for someone else. And soon she would have to go in there, overcome the profound sense of darkness and inform two parents, already destroyed, that their life was truly over.

Dr. Chang exchanged a glance with Goran. The moment had come to establish what kind of murderer they were dealing with. Whether his interest in this child had been generic, or horribly targeted. In other words, whether or not the little girl had been subjected to sexual violence.

Everyone in that room was torn between the desire that she had been spared that final torment, and the hope that she hadn't. Because in the latter case there would be a greater chance of the murderer leaving organic traces that would enable them to identify him.

There was a precise procedure for cases of sexual violence. And Chang, having no reason to diverge from it, started the physical examination.

It usually began with the marking and identification of the clothing on the body. Then came the search for any suspicious stains on the clothes, any threads, hairs, leaves. Only then did the pathologist move on to *subungual scraping,* which consisted in collecting from the victim's nails, with a kind of toothpick, possible residues of the murderer's skin—if the victim had defended herself—or earth or various fibers to identify the location of the killing.

But the result was negative. The condition of the corpse—apart from the amputation of the limb—was perfect, her clothes were clean.

As if someone had taken the trouble of washing her before putting her in the bag.

The third phase was the most invasive and contained the gynecological examination.

After a few minutes, Chang lifted his head towards Goran and Mila, stating coldly, "He didn't touch her."

Mila nodded and, before leaving the room, bent over Debby's corpse to slip from her wrist the bracelet with the little key dangling from it. That object, along with the information that the little girl had not been raped, would be the only gift that she could bring to the Gordons.

As soon as she said good-bye to Chang and Goran, Mila became aware of an urgent need to remove her clean gown. Because at that moment she felt dirty. Passing through the changing room, she stopped by the big ceramic basin. She turned on the hot water and slipped in her hands, beginning to rub them hard.

Still frantically washing, she looked up at the mirror in front of her. She imagined little Debby's reflection as she came into the changing room, with her green skirt, her blue blazer and the clasp in her hair. And she imagined her supporting herself on her one remaining arm and going to sit on the bench by the wall. And beginning to look at her, her feet dangling. Debby opened her mouth wide and then closed it again, as if trying to communicate with her. But no words came out. And Mila so wanted to ask her about her blood sister. The one they all knew only as child number six.

Then she woke from her vision.

The water was pouring from the tap. Steam rose in wide swirls, and had covered almost the whole surface of the mirror.

It was only then that Mila became aware of the pain.

She looked down and instinctively pulled her hands from the jet of boiling water. The skin on the back of her hands was red, while blisters were already appearing on her fingers. Mila immediately wiped them with a towel, then went to the first-aid cupboard in search of bandages.

No one must ever know what had happened to her.

* * *

When she opened her eyes, the first thing she remembered was the burn on her hands. She sat bolt upright, abruptly becoming aware of the bedroom that surrounded her. The wardrobe in front of her, with its framed mirror, the cupboard on its left and the window with the lowered shutter that let in a few lines of bluish light. Mila had gone to sleep with her clothes on, because the sheets and blankets of that squalid motel room were stained and dirty.

Why had she woken up? Perhaps someone had knocked. Or perhaps she had only dreamed it.

There was another knock. She got up and walked over to the door, opening it a few centimeters.

"Who is it?" she asked pointlessly as she saw Boris's smiling face.

"I've come to get you. They start searching Bermann's house in an hour. The others are waiting for us there…and I thought I'd bring you breakfast." He waved beneath her nose a paper bag that probably contained coffee and a croissant.

Mila quickly glanced at herself. She wasn't actually presentable, but perhaps that was a good thing: it would discourage her colleague's hormones. She invited him in.

Boris took a few steps inside the room, looked around, puzzled, as Mila walked over to the basin in a corner to splash her face but, more importantly, to hide her bandaged hands.

"This place is even worse than I remembered." He sniffed the air. "And there's always the same smell."

"I think it's an insect repellent."

"When I joined the unit, I spent almost a month here before finding myself an apartment…you know every key here opens all the rooms? The customers have a habit of leaving without paying, and the owner got tired of constantly having to replace the locks. At night you're best off blocking the door with the wardrobe."

Mila looked at him in the mirror over the basin. "Thanks for the advice."

"No, seriously. If you need a better place to live, I can give you a hand."

Mila glanced at him quizzically. "You wouldn't by any chance be inviting me to stay at yours, officer?"

Boris, embarrassed, quickly backtracked. "No, I didn't mean that. It's more that I could ask around and see if there's a colleague who might want to share her apartment, that's all."

"I hope I won't be staying here long enough to need it," she observed with a shrug. After drying her face, she spotted the bag he had brought her. She almost snatched it from his hands and went and sat cross-legged on the bed to inspect its contents.

Coffee and croissants, as she had hoped.

Boris was caught off guard by her movements, all the more so when he saw her hands covered with bandages. But he said nothing. "Hungry?" he asked instead, shyly.

She answered with her mouth full. "I haven't had a bite for two days. If you hadn't come this morning, I don't think I'd have had the strength to get out the door."

Mila knew she shouldn't have said anything like that, it sounded too much like encouragement. But she couldn't find another way of thanking him, and besides, she really was hungry. Boris smiled at her proudly.

"So, how are you getting on?" he asked her.

"I'm pretty adaptable, so, OK."

Apart from the fact that your friend Sarah Rosa practically hates me, she thought.

"I liked your intuition about the blood sisters…"

"A stroke of luck: I just fished among my adolescent experiences. You must have done stupid things when you were twelve, didn't you?"

As she noticed the bafflement of her colleague, who was trying helplessly to think of a reply, she couldn't help smiling.

"I was joking, Boris…"

"Oh, of course," he said, blushing.

Mila swallowed down the last mouthful, licked her fingers and threw herself on the second croissant in the bag, which was meant for Boris, although in the face of such ravenous hunger he didn't have the courage to say anything.

"Boris, tell me one thing…why did you call him Albert?"

"It's a very interesting story," he said. He cautiously moved to sit beside her. "Five years ago a really strange thing happened to us. There's this serial killer abducting women, raping them, strangling them and then letting us find the corpses with their right feet missing."

"Their right feet?"

"Exactly. No one can understand it because when he acts this guy is very precise and clean, he leaves no clues. He just does this amputation thing. And he strikes at complete random... So, we're already at the fifth corpse and we can't stop him. At this point Dr. Gavila has an idea..."

Mila had finished the second croissant as well and moved on to the coffee. "What kind of idea?"

"He asks us to go through the archives for all cases concerning feet, even the most petty and trivial."

Mila looked more than puzzled.

Then she emptied three sachets of sugar into the polystyrene cup. Boris noticed and pulled a disgusted face; he was about to say something about it but instead went on with his story. "It struck me as ridiculous too, at first. So, instead we start looking and it turns out that a little while ago there was a thief going around the area stealing women's shoes from the stands outside shoe shops. They only have one shoe per size and model—you know, to stop them being stolen—and usually it's the right one, to make it easier for the customers to try them on."

Mila froze, holding her cup of coffee in midair, and thought for a moment, delightedly, about the originality of that investigative hunch. "So you kept an eye on the shoe shops and caught the thief..."

"Albert Finley. A thirty-eight-year-old engineer, married, two young sons. A little house in the country and a camper van for holidays."

"Normal guy."

"In the garage at his home we find a freezer and inside it, carefully wrapped in cellophane, five women's right feet. He enjoyed making them wear the shoes he stole. It was a kind of fetishist obsession."

"Right foot, left arm. Hence Albert!"

"Exactly!" said Boris, putting a hand on her shoulder in a gesture of approval. Mila abruptly moved aside, jumping off the bed. The young policeman was hurt.

"Sorry," she said.

"No problem."

It wasn't true, and Mila didn't believe him. But she decided to pretend that it was as he said. She turned her back on him and went back towards the basin. "I'll just get myself ready, then we can go."

Boris got up and went to the door. "That's fine. I'll wait for you outside."

Mila saw him leaving the room. Then she looked up at the mirror. *Oh God, when will it end?* she wondered. *When am I going to let anyone touch me again?*

All the way to Bermann's house they had hardly exchanged a word. In fact, as she got into the car, Mila had found the radio on and immediately understood that this was a declaration of intent about how the journey was to be. Boris had been hurt, and perhaps now she had another enemy within the unit.

They got there in just under an hour and a half. Alexander Bermann had lived in a small villa surrounded by trees, in a quiet residential area.

The street in front had been screened off. Beyond that boundary there was a crowd of onlookers, neighbors and journalists. Mila, looking at them, thought it had begun. As they arrived, they had listened to a radio news item about the discovery of little Debby's corpse, and Bermann's name had also come out.

The reason for so much media euphoria was simple. The graveyard of arms had been a public relations disaster, but now at last they had a name to give the nightmare.

Mila had seen it happen on other occasions. The press had clung tenaciously to the story and in a very short time they would be trampling indiscriminately over every aspect of Bermann's life. His suicide amounted to an admission of guilt. For that reason the media would insist on their version. They would put him in the role of monster without allowing any contradiction, trusting solely in the force of their unanimity. They would cruelly tear him to pieces, just as he was supposed to have done to his little victims, but without seeing the irony of the parallel. They would extract liters of blood from the whole business, just to spice up the headlines and make them more enticing. Without respect, without fairness. And even when someone was bold enough to point it out, they would take refuge behind the handy idea of "press freedom" to conceal their unnatural prurience.

Mila and Boris made their way through the little crowd, entered the exclusion zone set up by the law-enforcement officers and walked quickly along the drive to the front door of the house, unable to avoid being dazzled by a few camera flashes. At that moment Mila caught Goran's eyes on the other side of the window. She felt absurdly guilty because he had seen her arriving with Boris. And then stupid for having thought such a thing.

Goran turned his attention back to the inside of the house. Shortly afterwards, Mila stepped through the door.

Stern and Sarah Rosa, with the help of other detectives, had already been there for a while, and were bustling around like worker ants. Everything had been turned upside down. The officers were painstakingly examining furniture, walls and anything else that might be able to reveal a clue to the mystery.

Once again, Mila had been unable to join in the search. Besides, Sarah Rosa had immediately barked in her face that she had only observation rights. So she started looking around, keeping her hands in her pockets so that she didn't have to justify the bandages wrapped around them.

What attracted her attention were the photographs.

There were dozens of them arranged around the place on tables and chests of drawers, in elegant walnut or silver frames. They showed Bermann and his wife in happy times. A life that now seemed far away and impossible. They had done a lot of traveling, Mila noticed. There were pictures from all over the world. But as the pictures became more recent and their faces older, their expressions seemed veiled. There was something in those photographs, Mila was sure of it. But she couldn't say what it was. She had had a strange feeling as she walked into that house. Now she thought she had a clearer sense of what it might be.

A presence.

Amidst all the comings and goings of the police officers, there was another spectator. Mila recognized the woman in the photographs: Veronica Bermann, the wife of the alleged murderer. She could tell immediately that the woman was proud by nature. She maintained an attitude of decorous detachment as those strangers touched her things without asking her permission, violating the intimacy of those objects, those memories, with their invasive presence. She seemed not so much resigned as consenting. She had offered to cooperate with Chief Inspector Roche, confidently asserting that her husband had nothing to do with those terrible accusations.

Mila was still watching her when, turning round, she found herself confronted with an unexpected spectacle.

There was an entire wall covered with *preserved butterflies*.

They were in glass frames. There were strange ones and beautiful ones. Some of them had exotic names, which were quoted along with the place of origin on a bronze plate. The most fascinating ones came from Africa and Japan.

"They're beautiful because they're dead."

It was Goran who said it. The criminologist was wearing a black jumper and wool trousers. Part of his shirt collar stuck out of the neck of his pullover. He came and stood next to her to get a better look at the butterfly wall.

"When we see something like this we forget the most important and most obvious thing...those butterflies will never fly again."

"It's unnatural," Mila agreed. "And yet it's so seductive..."

"That's exactly the effect that death has on some individuals. That's why serial killers exist."

Goran made a small gesture. That was all it took for all the members of the team to gather around him immediately. A sign that even if they seemed entirely absorbed in their own tasks, they were really still looking at him, waiting for him to say or do something.

Mila had confirmation of the great trust that they placed in his hunches. Goran guided them. It was very strange, because he wasn't a police officer, and cops—at least the ones she knew—had always resisted putting their trust in civilians. It would have been more accurate for the group to call themselves "the Gavila team" than "the Roche team," particularly since Roche, as usual, wasn't there. He would only appear if incontestable evidence appeared that would nail Bermann once and for all.

Stern, Boris and Rosa took up their positions around the criminologist, according to their usual pattern. Mila remained a step behind: afraid of feeling excluded, she excluded herself.

Goran spoke in a low voice, immediately catching the tone with which he wanted the conversation to proceed. He probably didn't want to disturb Veronica Bermann.

"So, what have we got?"

Stern was the first to reply with a shake of his head: "There's nothing in the house to link Bermann to the six little girls."

"His wife seems to be in the dark about everything. I asked her a few questions, and I didn't have the feeling that she was lying," added Boris.

"Our men are going over the garden with the corpse dogs," said Rosa. "But there's nothing so far."

"We'll have to reconstruct all of Bermann's movements over the past six weeks," observed Goran and everyone agreed, even though they knew it would be an almost impossible task.

"Stern, is there anything else?"

"No strange movements of money in his account. The biggest bill that Bermann has had to foot over the past year was a course of artificial insemination for his wife, which set him back a fair bit."

Listening to Stern's words, Mila realized what it was that she had felt just before entering the house and then looking at the photographs. Not a presence, as she had thought at first. She had been wrong.

It was more of an *absence*.

What she had noticed was the lack of children in this house, which, with its expensive and impersonal furnishings, was a house created for two individuals who feel destined to remain alone. That was why the course of artificial insemination mentioned by Officer Stern seemed contradictory, since in that place you couldn't even feel the anxiety of someone expecting the gift of a child.

Stern concluded his exposition with a quick sketch of Bermann's private life. "He didn't use drugs, he didn't drink and he didn't smoke. He had a card for a gym and one for a video store, but he only rented documentaries about insects. He went to the local Lutheran church and, twice a month, worked as a volunteer at a rest home."

"A saintly man," said Boris sarcastically.

Goran turned towards Veronica Bermann to check if she had heard that last remark. Then he turned to look at Rosa: "Is there anything else?"

"I've scanned the hard disk of the home and office computers. I've also recovered all deleted files. But there was nothing of interest. Just work, work, work. The guy was fixated on his job."

Mila noticed that Goran had suddenly become distracted. It didn't last long, and he soon returned to concentrate on the conversation. "What do we know about his Internet use?"

"I called his web server and they gave me a list of the web pages he had visited over the last six months. Nothing there, either... It seems he has a passion for sites dedicated to nature, travel and animals. And he bought antiques online and, on eBay, mostly collectible butterflies." When Rosa had finished her report, Goran folded his arms again and started looking at his colleagues, one by one. That brief look took in Mila, too, and at last she felt involved.

"So, what do you think?" he asked.

"I feel as if I've been dazzled," Boris said suddenly, emphatically underlining the phrase with a hand screening his eyes. "He's too *clean*." The others nodded.

Mila didn't know what he was referring to, but she didn't want to ask. Goran slid a hand over his forehead and rubbed his weary eyes. Then that *distraction* appeared on his face once again... it was a thought that took him elsewhere for a second or two, and suggested that the criminologist was filing something away for future reference. "What's the first reason for investigating a suspect?"

"We all have secrets," said the diligent Boris.

"Exactly," said Goran. "We all have a weakness, at least once in our lives. Each of us has one secret, big or small, that we can't own up to...and yet look around: that man is the prototype of the good husband, the good believer, the great worker," he said, marking out each word on his fingers. "He's a philanthropist, a health fanatic, he only rents documentaries, he has no vices of any kind, he *collects butterflies*...Can you believe in a man like that?"

This time the reply was taken for granted. No, you couldn't.

"So what's a man like that doing with the corpse of a little girl in his boot?"

Stern cut in: "He's having a cleanup..."

Goran agreed: "He casts a spell on us with all this perfection to keep us from looking elsewhere...and where are we not looking at this moment?"

"So what do we have to do?" asked Rosa.

"Start from the beginning. The answer is there, among the things you've already examined. Go through everything again. You've got to remove that brilliant coating covering it all. Don't be deceived by the glare of the perfect life: that glitter is only there to distract us and muddle our ideas. And then you've got to..."

Goran wandered off again. *His attention was elsewhere.* This time they all noticed. Something was finally materializing in his head, and growing.

Mila decided to follow the criminologist's eyes as they moved around the room. They weren't simply lost in the void. She noticed that he was looking at something...

The little red LED flashed intermittently, marking out a rhythm of its own as a way of attracting attention.

Gavila asked in a loud voice: "Has anyone listened to the messages on the answering machine?"

The room instantly froze. They stared at the phone, winking its red eye at everyone, and immediately felt guilty, exposed by that glaring oversight. Goran paid no attention, and simply went and pressed the button that activated the little digital recorder.

A moment later, the darkness regurgitated a dead man's words.

And Alexander Bermann entered his house for the last time.

"Erm... It's me... Erm... I haven't much time... But I wanted to tell you I'm sorry... I'm sorry, for everything... I should have done it before, but I didn't... Try to forgive me. It was all my fault..."

The communication broke off and a stony silence fell over the room. Everyone's eyes, inevitably, came to rest on Veronica Bermann, who was as impassive as a statue.

Goran Gavila was the only one who moved. He walked towards her and gripped her shoulders, entrusting her to a policewoman to lead her into another room.

It was Stern who spoke for everyone: "Well, ladies and gentlemen, we would seem to have a confession."

8.

She would call her *Priscilla*.

She would adopt the method used by Goran Gavila, who gave an identity to the murderers he was hunting down. To humanize them, to make them more real in his eyes, more than just fleeting shadows. So Mila would christen victim number six, giving her the name of a luckier little girl who was now—somewhere, who knows where—going on being a little girl like so many others, unaware of what she had escaped.

Mila took the decision on the way back to the motel. An officer had been given the task of taking her there. Boris hadn't offered his services this time, and Mila didn't blame him, having rejected him so abruptly that morning.

The choice of the name Priscilla for the sixth child was not due solely to the need to give her a sense of humanity. There was another reason, too: Mila couldn't go on referring to her with a number. Now she felt she was the only one who still had the girl's identity at heart, because after hearing Bermann's phone call, finding her was no longer a priority.

They had a corpse in a car and, on a telephone voice-mail tape, what sounded to all intents and purposes like a confession. There was no need to take any further trouble. All that had to be done was to link the sales rep to the other victims. And then come up with a motive. But perhaps there already was one…

The victims aren't the children. They are the families…

It was Goran who had given her this explanation as they studied the little girls' families from behind the glass in the morgue. Parents who, for various reasons, had had only one child. A mother long past forty and hence no longer biologically capable of hoping for another pregnancy…*They are his true victims. He studied them, he chose them.* And then: *An only daughter. He wanted to strip them of all hope of getting over their grief, of trying to forget their loss. They will have to remember what he did to them for the rest of their days…*

Alexander Bermann had no children. He had tried to have them, but it hadn't worked. Perhaps that was why he had wanted to unleash his rage on those poor families. Perhaps he had used them to take his revenge on his fate of infertility.

No, it wasn't revenge, Mila thought. *There's something else…*She wasn't giving up, but she didn't know where that feeling came from.

The car arrived near the motel and Mila got out, saying good-bye to the officer who had been her driver. He exchanged a nod with her and turned his car before heading back, leaving her alone in the middle of the big gravel yard, a strip of forest behind her with bungalows poking out of it here and there. It was cold, and the only light came from the neon sign announcing vacancies and pay TV. Mila headed towards her room. All the windows were in darkness.

She was the only guest.

She walked past the porter's office, which was plunged in the bluish darkness of a flickering television set. The sound was turned off and the man wasn't there. Perhaps he had gone to the toilet, Mila thought, and continued on her way. Luckily she had kept the key, or else she would have had to wait for the porter to come back.

She had a paper bag containing a fizzy drink and two cheese toasted sandwiches—her dinner for the evening—and a tub of ointment that she would later spread on the little burns on her hands. Her breath condensed in the cold air. Mila quickened her pace; she was starving. Her footsteps on the gravel were the only sound that filled the night. Her bungalow was the last in the row.

Priscilla, she thought as she walked. And she remembered the words spoken by Chang, the medical examiner: that it had been even worse for the sixth one…

That phrase was what had obsessed Mila.

But not just because of the idea that the sixth girl had had to pay a higher price than the others—*He slowed down the bleeding to make her die more slowly…He wanted to enjoy the show*…—No, there was something else. Why had the murderer changed his modus operandi? As she had during her meeting with Chang, Mila felt a tickle at the base of her neck.

By now her room was only a few meters away, and she was concentrating on that sensation, sure this time that she would be able to grasp its cause. A little dip in the ground nearly made her trip.

It was then that she heard it.

The brief sound behind her swept her thoughts away in an instant. Steps on the gravel. Someone was "copying" her walk. He was coordinating his footsteps with hers to get close to her without her noticing. When she had tripped, her pursuer had lost the rhythm, thus revealing his presence.

Mila didn't get flustered, she didn't slow down. Her pursuer's footsteps were lost once more in hers. She calculated that he was about ten meters behind her. Meanwhile she started trying to come up with possible solutions. No point drawing the gun she wore behind her back—if the person behind her was armed they would have plenty of time to shoot first. *The porter,* she thought. The television left on in the empty office. *He's killed him already. Now it's my turn*. By now it wasn't far to the door of the bungalow. She had to make her mind up. And she did. She had no other choice.

She rummaged in her pocket for her key, and quickly climbed the three steps leading to the porch. She opened the door after turning the key a couple of times, her heart thumping in her chest, and slipped into the room. She drew her gun and reached her other hand towards the light switch. Her bedside light came on. Mila didn't move from her position, frozen, her back flattened against the door and her ears pricked. *He hasn't attacked me,* she thought. Then she heard footsteps moving on the planks of the porch.

Boris had told her the keys of the motel were all skeleton keys, since the owner had got fed up replacing them because guests took them with them when they left without paying. *Does the person who's following me know that? He's probably got a key like mine.* And she thought that if he tried to get in she could take him by surprise from behind.

She fell onto her knees and slid along the stained carpet until she reached the window. She flattened herself against the wall and raised her hand to open it. It was so cold that the hinges stuck. With a bit of effort she opened one of the panels. She got to her feet, took a jump and found herself outside, back in the dark.

In front of her was the forest. The high treetops swayed rhythmically together. To the rear of the motel there was a concrete platform connecting all the bungalows. Mila crept over to it, keeping low to the ground and trying to catch every movement, every sound around her. She quickly reached the bungalow next to hers, and the one next to that. Then she stopped and entered the narrow gap that separated one from the other.

At that point she could have leaned out to get a glimpse of the porch of the bungalow. But it would have been a risk. She wrapped the fingers of both hands around her pistol to improve her grip, forgetting the pain of her burns. She quickly counted to three, taking three big breaths as well, and sprang around the corner with her weapon raised. No one. It couldn't have been her imagination. She was convinced that someone had been following her. Someone perfectly capable of moving behind his target, concealing the acoustic shadow of his footsteps.

A predator.

Mila searched for some sign of the enemy in the square. He seemed to have vanished into the wind, to the repetitive concert of the yielding trees surrounding the motel.

"Excuse me..."

Mila leapt back and looked at the man without raising her pistol, paralyzed by those two simple words. It took her a few seconds to work out that it was the porter. He realized that he had frightened her and repeated, "Excuse me," this time only by way of apology.

"What's going on?" asked Mila, who still hadn't managed to get her heart rate back to normal.

"There's a call for you..."

The man pointed to his booth and Mila set off in that direction without waiting for him to show her the way.

"Mila Vasquez," she said into the receiver.

"Hi, Stern here...Dr. Gavila wants to see you."

"Me?" she asked, surprised but with a hint of pride.

"Yes. We called the officer who drove you there, he's coming back to pick you up."

"Fine." Mila was puzzled Stern said nothing more, so she ventured to ask, "Has anything turned up?"

"Alexander Bermann was hiding something from us."

Boris tried to set the SatNav without taking his eyes off the road. Mila stared straight ahead without saying anything. Gavila was in the backseat, huddled in his crumpled coat, eyes closed. They had been sent to the house of Veronica Bermann's sister, where Veronica had sought refuge from the journalists.

Goran had reached the conclusion that Bermann had been trying to cover something up. Everything on the basis of that message on the answering machine: *Erm...It's me...Erm...I haven't much time...But I wanted to tell you I'm sorry...I'm sorry, for everything...I should have done it before, but I didn't...Try to forgive me. It was all my fault...*

They had established from the phone records that Bermann had made the call when they were at the traffic police station, more or less at the same time as the corpse of little Debby Gordon had been found.

Goran wondered why a man in Alexander Bermann's situation—with a corpse in the boot and the intention of getting away as quickly as possible—should have made a call to his wife.

Serial killers don't apologize. If they do, it's because they want to create a different image of themselves, it's part of their mystifying nature. Their purpose is to muddy the truth, to feed the curtain of smoke that surrounds them. But with Bermann it seemed different. There was an urgency in his voice. There was something he had to finish before it was too late.

What did Alexander Bermann want to be forgiven for?

Goran was convinced that it had something to do with his wife, with their relationship as a couple.

"Could you repeat that for me, please, Dr. Gavila…?"

Goran opened his eyes and saw Mila turned in her seat, staring at him as she waited for a reply.

"Veronica Bermann may have discovered something. That probably caused arguments between her and her husband. I reckon he wanted to ask her forgiveness for that."

"And what makes that information so important for us?"

"I don't know if it really is…but a man in his situation doesn't waste time resolving a simple marital row if he doesn't have an ulterior motive."

"And what might that be?"

"Perhaps his wife isn't entirely aware of what she knows."

"And with that phone call he wanted to damp down the situation, to stop her getting to the bottom of it. Or telling us…"

"Yes, that's what I think…Veronica Bermann has been very cooperative until now, there would be no point in her hiding anything from us if she thought the information had nothing to do with the crimes, but concerned only the two of them."

Now Mila was quite clear about everything. Dr. Gavila's hunch would inevitably lead to a change of direction for the investigation. But first it had to be checked. That was why Goran hadn't yet spoken to Roche.

They hoped to extract significant clues from the meeting with Veronica Bermann. Boris, as an expert in the interrogation of witnesses and people with information about particular crimes, would have had to have a kind of informal chat with her. But Goran had decided that only he and Mila would meet with Bermann's wife. Boris had agreed as if the order had come from a superior and not a civilian adviser. But his hostility towards Mila had grown. He didn't see why she had to be present.

Mila was aware of the tension and, in reality, she herself didn't fully understand what it was that had led Gavila to prefer her. Boris had been left only with the task of instructing her in how to guide the conversation. And that was exactly what he had done, before fiddling with the SatNav in search of their destination.

Mila remembered Boris's comment as Stern and Rosa drew a portrait of Alexander Bermann: *I feel as if I've been dazzled. He's too* clean.

That perfection was hardly credible. It seemed to have been prepared for someone.

We all have a secret, Mila repeated to herself. *Even me.*

There's always something to hide. Her father had said to her when she was young: "We all stick our fingers in our noses. We might do it when no one else is watching, but we do do it."

So what was Alexander Bermann's secret?

What did his wife know?

What was the name of child number six?

It was almost dawn when they got there. The village lay behind a church, on the curve of an embankment overlooking the river.

Veronica Bermann's sister lived in a flat over a pub. Sarah Rosa had phoned Veronica to tell her about the visit she was about to receive. Predictably enough, she hadn't objected, and had shown no unwillingness to talk. The fact that she had been given notice was intended to make it clear to her that she wasn't going to face an interrogation. But Veronica Bermann wasn't interested in Special Agent Rosa's precautions, she would probably have agreed to a grilling.

It was almost seven o'clock in the morning when the woman welcomed Mila and Goran, perfectly at ease in dressing gown and slippers. She invited them into the living room, with visible beams in the ceiling and carved furniture, and offered them some freshly made coffee. Mila took time to savor her coffee. She was in no hurry, she wanted the woman to lower her defenses completely before she began. Boris had warned her: in some cases it only takes a word out of place for the other person to close up and refuse to go on cooperating.

"Mrs. Bermann, all this must be very hard, and we're sorry to descend on you so early."

"Don't worry, I always get up early."

"We need to find out more about your husband, not least because it's only by knowing him better that we'll be able to establish how deeply involved he really was. And believe me, there are still plenty of dark sides to this business. Could you tell us about him...?"

Veronica's face didn't move a muscle, but her eyes grew more intense. Then she began: "Alexander and I had known each other since high school. He was two years older than me, he was on the hockey team. He wasn't a great player, but they were all very fond of him. We started going out together, but in a group, just friends; nothing was going on yet, and it didn't even occur to us that something else might bring us together. To tell the truth, I don't think he ever 'saw' me like that...as a possible girlfriend, I mean. And neither did I."

"It happened later..."

"Yes, isn't that strange? After high school I lost track of him and we didn't see each other for many years. Mutual friends told me he'd gone to university. Then one day he reappeared in my life: he called me, saying he'd found my number in the phone book. Then I found out from friends that in fact, when he'd come back after graduating, he'd asked around about me and wanted to know what had become of me..."

Listening to her, Goran had a sense that Veronica Bermann wasn't just abandoning herself to nostalgia, but that in some way her story had a precise purpose. As if she was deliberately guiding him somewhere, far away in time, where they would find what they had come looking for.

"It was then that you started seeing each other again..." said Mila. And Goran noticed with satisfaction that the officer, following Boris's advice, had decided not to ask Veronica Bermann any questions, but to suggest sentences that she would then complete, so that it seemed more like a conversation than an interrogation.

"It was then that we started seeing each other again," repeated Mrs. Bermann. "Alexander started pressing me to marry him. And in the end I accepted."

Goran concentrated on that last sentence. It sounded wrong, like a proud lie hastily added to the discussion in the hope that it might pass unobserved. And he remembered what he had noticed the first time he saw the woman: Veronica wasn't pretty, she probably never had been. A mediocre, undramatic kind of femininity. While Alexander Bermann was a handsome man. Pale blue eyes, the dark smile of someone who knows he can exert a certain fascination. It was hard for the criminologist to believe that it had taken such persistence to persuade her to marry him.

Mila resumed control of the conversation: "But lately your relationship hadn't been going very well…"

Veronica paused. For quite a long time, thought Goran. Maybe Mila had cast her bait too soon.

"We had problems," she admitted at last.

"You tried to have children in the past…"

"I took some hormonal treatment for a while. Then we tried insemination as well."

"I imagine you both really wanted a baby…"

"It was Alexander who was keenest on the idea…"

She said it defensively, a sign that that might have been the reason for the greater friction between the couple.

They were getting close to their goal. Goran was satisfied. He had wanted Mila there to talk to Mrs. Bermann because he was sure a female presence would be the ideal way of striking a sympathetic bond, and break down any possible resistance on the woman's part. He could, of course, have chosen Sarah Rosa, and perhaps that wouldn't have upset Boris's susceptibilities. But Mila had struck him as more suitable, and he hadn't been wrong.

The policewoman leaned over the little table that separated the sofa from the place where Veronica Bermann was sitting, to set down her coffee cup. It was a way of meeting Goran's eye without letting the woman see. Goran nodded slightly: it was a sign that the time had come to stop beating about the bush and try for the all-out attack.

"Mrs. Bermann, why, in your husband's answering machine message, did he ask you to forgive him?"

Veronica turned her head away to hide a tear that was threatening to break through the barrier she had created for her emotion.

"Mrs. Bermann, your confidences are safe with us. I'm going to be frank with you: no policeman or lawyer or judge will ever be able to force you to answer this question, because the fact is that it has no relevance to the investigation. But it's important that we know, because it's quite possible that your husband is innocent..."

Hearing those last words, Veronica Bermann turned to face her.

"Innocent? Alexander didn't kill anyone...but that doesn't mean he was faultless!"

She said this with a dark rage that had appeared without warning and distorted her voice. Goran had the confirmation he had been waiting for. Mila understood it too: Veronica Bermann had wanted this. She had been waiting for their visit, their questions camouflaged by innocuous phrases scattered here and there in the conversation. They had imagined that they were leading the dialogue, but this woman had prepared her story to bring them to this precise result. She had to tell someone.

"I suspected that Alexander had a lover. A wife always takes this kind of eventuality into account, and at that moment she also decides whether or not she'll be able to forgive. But sooner or later a wife also wants to know. And that's why one day I started going through his things. I didn't know exactly what I was looking for, and I couldn't predict how I would react if I found any proof."

"What did you find?"

"Confirmation. Alexander was hiding an electronic diary identical to the one that he usually used for work. Why take two the same except to use the first to conceal the second? That's how I found out the name of his lover: he marked all their appointments! I confronted him with the facts: he denied everything, and immediately made the second diary disappear. But I wouldn't leave it there: I followed him to that woman's house, to that squalid place. I didn't have the courage to go any further, though. I stopped at the door. I didn't even want to look her in the face, in reality."

Was that Alexander Bermann's unmentionable secret? Goran wondered. A lover? They'd gone to all that trouble for so little?

Luckily he hadn't informed Roche of his initiative, or else he would also have had to face the mockery of the chief inspector, who would by now have closed the case. Meanwhile Veronica Bermann was a river in full spate and had no intention of letting them go any further before giving vent to her grievances about her husband. Her husband's attitude of resolute self-defense after the discovery of the corpse was plainly nothing but a shrewd facade. A way of escaping the weight of accusation, to dodge the sprays of mud. Now that she had found the courage to free herself from the pact of conjugal solidarity, she too had begun to dig Alexander Bermann into a hole from which he would never be able to escape.

Goran tried to catch Mila's eye to get her to bring the conversation to an end as soon as possible. It was at that moment that the criminologist noticed a sudden change in the policewoman's features, which now revealed an expression somewhere between astonishment and uncertainty.

In the many years of his career, Goran had learned to recognize the effects of fear on other people's faces. He could tell that something had deeply disturbed Mila.

It was a name.

He heard her ask Veronica Bermann, "Could you repeat the name of your husband's lover for me?"

"I told you: that whore's name is *Priscilla*."

9.

It couldn't just be a coincidence.

Mila recalled, for the benefit of those present, the most salient aspects of the last case she had dealt with. The case of the music teacher. As she reported what Sergeant Morexu had said about finding that name—Priscilla—in one of the diaries belonging to the "monster," Sarah Rosa raised her eyes to the sky, and Stern echoed her gesture with a shake of the head.

They didn't believe her. That was understandable. And yet Mila couldn't stop thinking that there was a connection. Only Goran indulged her. No one knew what the criminologist was hoping to achieve, but Mila wanted to explore that quirk of fate at all costs. Veronica Bermann had said she had followed her husband to his lover's house, and that was where they were headed now. It was possible that other horrors were hidden there. Perhaps even the bodies of the missing children.

And the answer to the question of number six.

Mila wanted to tell the others, "I called her Priscilla..." But she didn't. It felt almost like blasphemy now. It was as if the name had been chosen by Bermann himself, the girl's killer.

The structure of the little building was typical of a place on the outskirts of town. They were in the classic ghetto area, built in the sixties as the natural adjunct to a new industrial area. It was made up of gray buildings which had over time been coated by the reddish dust from a nearby steelworks. Buildings of little commercial value, in urgent need of repair. A transient population lived there, chiefly immigrants, the unemployed and people who got by on state benefits.

"Why would anyone come and live in a place like this?" Boris wondered, looking around disgustedly.

The house number they were looking for was at the end of the block. It was a basement flat reached by an external staircase. The door was made of iron. The three windows at street level were protected by grilles and boarded off on the inside.

Stern tried to look through them, bent into a ridiculous position, hands cupped around his eyes and hips jutting backwards so he didn't get his trousers dirty.

"You can't see anything from here."

Boris, Stern and Rosa nodded to one another and arranged themselves around the entrance. Stern gestured to Goran and Mila to stay back.

It was Boris who stepped forward. There was no bell, so he knocked. He did so energetically, with the palm of his hand. The noise was intimidating, while Boris's tone remained deliberately calm.

"This is the police. Open up, please, madam."

It was a technique of psychological pressure to make the other party lose their bearings: addressing them with fake patience and at the same time asking them to hurry. But in this case it didn't work, because there didn't seem to be anyone in the house.

"OK, then: let's go in," suggested Rosa, who was the most impatient to check.

"We have to wait for Roche to call and tell us he's got a warrant," Boris replied and looked at the time. "We shouldn't take too long..."

"Roche and his warrant can fuck right off!" Rosa retorted. "There could be anything in there!"

Goran said, "She's right. Let's go in."

From the way everyone accepted the decision, Mila knew that Goran carried more weight than Roche in this team.

They arranged themselves around the door. Boris took out a set of screwdrivers and started fiddling with the lock. After a few moments the mechanism clicked open. Holding the gun firmly in his fist, he pushed the iron door with his other hand.

The first impression was that the place was completely uninhabited.

A corridor, narrow and bare. The daylight couldn't get in. Rosa pointed her torch and they saw three doors. The first two on the left, the third at the end.

The third was closed.

They started to walk forward into the apartment. Boris at the front, Rosa behind him, then Stern and Goran. Mila brought up the rear. Apart from the criminologist, each was carrying a weapon. Mila was only "attached" to the unit so she couldn't, but she kept a gun slipped into her jeans, behind her back, with her fingers closed around the butt, ready to draw. That was why she had come in last.

Boris tried the switch on one of the walls. "There's no light."

He raised the torch to examine the first of the three rooms. It was empty. On the wall he noticed a damp patch rising from the foundations, eating away at the plaster like a cancer. The heating and drainage pipes crossed on the ceiling. A pool of sewage had formed on the floor.

"What a stench!" said Stern.

No one could have lived in these conditions.

"Hardly what you'd call a love nest," said Rosa.

"Then what is this place?" Boris wondered.

They reached the entrance to the second room. The door was stiff on rusted hinges, and slightly ajar: a possible attacker could easily have been hiding behind it. Boris kicked the door wide open, but there was no one there. The room was virtually identical to the first. The floor tiles had come away, revealing the concrete that covered the foundation. There was no furniture, just the steel skeleton of a sofa. They walked on.

There was one last room. The one at the end of the corridor, with the closed door.

Boris raised the first two fingers of his left hand, bringing them up to his eyes. Stern and Rosa nodded at the signal and took up position on either side of the door. Then the young officer took a step back, lifted his foot and kicked the door at handle height. The door burst open and the three officers immediately put themselves in the line of fire, at the same time illuminating all the corners with their torches. There was no one there.

Goran pushed his way among them, sliding his latex-gloved hand along the wall. He found the switch. After two brief flickers, a fluorescent light lit up on the ceiling, casting its dusty glow on the room, which was quite different from the others. First of all it was clean. The walls showed no signs of damp, because they were covered with plastic, impermeable paper. Here the floor still had its tiles, and they weren't broken. There were no windows, but an air conditioner came on after a few seconds. The electric wires weren't set into the walls, a sign that they had been added later. Plastic channels led the cables to the switch with which Goran had turned on the light, and also to a plug on the right-hand side of the wall where there was a desk and an office chair. And on the table, a personal computer that was switched off.

That was the only furniture, apart from an old leather armchair against the opposite wall, on the left.

"From the look of it, this was the only room Alexander Bermann was interested in," Stern said, turning to Goran.

Rosa stepped through the door and walked towards the computer: "I'm sure this is where we're going to find the answers we're looking for."

But Goran stopped her, holding her back with one hand. "No, we should follow procedure. Let's leave here now, so as not to alter the humidity of the atmosphere." Then he turned to Stern: "Call Krepp and tell him to come with his unit to take prints. I'll tell Roche."

Mila carefully studied the light that gleamed in the criminologist's eyes. She had a strong sense that he was close to something important.

* * *

He ran his fingers over his head, as if combing hair that he didn't have. All he had was a strip of hair at the back of his neck, from which a ponytail emerged and fell down his back. A green and red snake stretched along his forearm, its jaws opening on his hand. His other arm had a similar tattoo, and there was yet another on his chest where it was revealed under his shirt. In the middle of the various piercings that covered his face was Krepp, the scientific expert.

Mila was fascinated by his appearance, so unlike the average sixty-year-old. She thought: *This is how punks end up when they get old*. And yet, until a year before, Krepp had been a perfectly normal middle-aged man, fairly austere and rather gray in his manners. From one day to the next, a change occurred. But after everyone had checked that the man hadn't lost his senses, no one had said a word about his new look, because Krepp was the best in his field.

After thanking Goran for preserving the original humidity of the scene, Krepp had immediately set to work. He had spent an hour in the room with his team, all in overalls and with masks on their faces to protect themselves from the substances they used to take fingerprints, then he had left the basement and come over to the criminologist and Roche, who had joined them in the meantime.

"How's Krepp?" the chief inspector had said by way of greeting.

"That business about the graveyard of arms is driving me out of my mind," Krepp began. "We were still analyzing those limbs in search of useful prints when you called us."

Goran knew that taking a print from human skin was the most difficult thing in the world, because of possible contamination, or because of the sweating of the subject under examination or, in the case of a corpse, such as the arms, because of the processes of putrefaction.

"I tried using iodine fuming, kromekote paper, and even electromyography."

"What's that?" asked the criminologist.

"It's the most modern way of taking prints left on the skin: radiography in electronic emission... That bastard Albert is pretty clever at not leaving prints," said Krepp. And Mila noticed that he was the only one now who referred to the murderer by that name, because for the others he had by now assumed the identity of Alexander Bermann.

"So what have we got here, Krepp?" asked Roche, who was fed up hearing things that were of no use to him.

The technician slipped off his gloves and, still looking down, began to describe what he had done: "We used ninhydrin, but the effect wasn't entirely clear under the laser, so I improved it with zinc chloride. We took some prints on the wallpaper by the light switch and the porous covering of the table. It was harder with the computer: the prints were superimposed on one another, we would have needed cyanoacrylate, but we should take the keyboard to the atmospheric chamber and—"

"Later. We have no time to get hold of a replacement keyboard and we have to analyze the computer now," Roche broke in, desperate to know. "So: the prints belong to a single person..."

"Yes, they all belong to Alexander Bermann."

Everyone was struck by the sentence, except one person; the one who already knew the answer. And he had known it since the moment they had set foot in the basement.

"From the look of it, 'Priscilla' never existed," Gavila said.

He made the statement without looking at Mila, who felt a twinge of pride nonetheless.

"There's something else..." Krepp had started talking again. "The leather armchair."

"What?" asked Mila, emerging from the silence.

Krepp looked at her as one does when noticing something for the first time, then lowered his eyes to her bandaged hands and suddenly assumed an expression of concern. Mila couldn't help thinking it was ridiculous that Krepp, looking as he did, should have looked at *her* like that. But she maintained her composure.

"There are no prints on the armchair."

"And is that strange?" asked Mila.

"I don't know," said Krepp. "I can only say that they are everywhere else, but not there."

"But we have Bermann's prints on everything else: what does it matter?" Roche cut in. "They're enough to fix him good and proper...and if you really want to know, I'm starting to like this guy less and less."

Mila reflected that he should really have liked him quite a lot, given that he was the solution to all his problems.

"So what do we do with the chair, do we go on analyzing it?"

"Forget that damned chair and let my men take a look at the computer."

At the words "my men," the team members tried not to look at one another, to keep from laughing. Sometimes Roche's steely tone could be even more self-contradictory than Krepp's appearance.

The chief inspector walked off towards the car that waited for him at the end of the block, but not before reassuring his people with the words, "Keep at it, guys, I'm counting on you."

When he was far enough away, Goran turned to the others. "OK," he said. "Let's see what's in that computer."

They resumed possession of the room; the plastic-coated walls made it look like a huge womb. Alexander Bermann's lair was about to open itself up only to them. At least that was what they hoped. They put on their latex gloves. Then Sarah Rosa sat down at the terminal: it was her turn.

Before turning on the PC, she connected a little gadget to one of the USB ports. Stern turned on a tape recorder, setting it next to the keyboard. Rosa described the operation: "I've connected Bermann's computer to an external memory: in case the PC crashes, this will copy the whole of the hard disk in a flash."

The others were standing behind her in a silent group.

She turned on the computer.

The first electrical signal was followed by the familiar sound of the drives starting up. It all seemed normal. Slowly, the PC started to wake from its lethargy. It was an old model that was no longer produced. The data of the operating system appeared in order, followed soon after by the image of the desktop. Nothing important: just a blue screen with the icons of very common programs.

"It looks like my PC at home," Boris ventured, but no one laughed.

"OK...let's see what Mr. Bermann has in his documents folder."

"There are no text files...that's strange," observed Goran.

"Maybe he chucked everything away at the end of each session," Stern suggested.

"If that's the case, I can try to get them back," Rosa said confidently. Then she put a CD in the disk drive and quickly uploaded some software capable of restoring any deleted files.

The computer memory never empties completely, and it's almost impossible to erase certain data, all of which are indelibly stamped there. Mila remembered someone telling her that the silicone composite imprisoned in every computer works a little like the human brain. Even when it seems that we've forgotten something, somewhere in our heads there's actually a group of cells that preserves the information, and it may give it back to us, if not in the form of images, then as instinct. We don't necessarily have to remember the first time we were burnt by fire as children. What matters is that that awareness, stripped of all the biographical circumstances in which it was formed, remains stamped on our minds to reappear every time we approach anything hot. Mila glanced down at her bandaged hands. Apparently the wrong information was stored in some part of her.

"There's nothing here."

Rosa's disconsolate observation brought Mila back to reality. The computer was completely empty.

But Goran wasn't convinced. "There's a web browser."

"But the computer isn't connected to the Internet," Boris pointed out.

Sarah Rosa had worked out what the criminologist was getting at. She picked up her mobile and checked the display: "There's a signal...he could have been connected by mobile phone."

She immediately opened the browser screen and checked the list of addresses in its history. There was only one.

"That's what Bermann was doing in here!"

There was a sequence of numbers. The address was a code.

http://4589278497.89474525.com

"It's probably the address of a restricted server," Rosa suggested.

"What does that mean?" Boris asked.

"That you can't get to it via a search engine and you have to have a key to get in. It's probably contained inside the computer. But if it isn't, we risk denying ourselves access forever."

"Then we've got to be careful and do exactly what Bermann did..." said Goran before turning towards Stern: "Do we have his mobile phone?"

"Yes, I've got it in the car with his home computer."

"Then go and get it..."

When Stern got back, he found them in silence. They were waiting for him with ill-disguised impatience. The officer passed Bermann's mobile phone to Rosa, who connected it to the computer and switched it on. The server took a moment to recognize the call. It was processing the data. Then it quickly started loading.

"Apparently we can get in without any difficulty."

Eyes fixed on the screen, they waited for the image that would appear in a few minutes. It could be anything, Mila thought. A powerful tension united the members of the team, like a charge of energy crackling from one body to the next. She could feel it in the air.

The monitor began to settle into an arrangement of pixels arranged in order across the screen like little pieces of a jigsaw puzzle. But what they saw wasn't what they were expecting. The energy that had filled the room until a moment before drained away in an instant and the enthusiasm vanished.

The screen was blank.

"It must be a firewall," Rosa announced. "It interpreted our attempt as an intrusion."

"Did you hide the signal?" asked Boris uneasily.

"Of course I did!" the woman snapped. "Do you think I'm an idiot? There's probably a code or something..."

"Some sort of log-in and password?" asked Goran, wanting to know more about it.

"Something like that," Rosa replied distractedly. "What we had was an address for a direct connection. Log-in and password are old-fashioned mechanisms: they leave traces and they can always lead you to someone. Anyone who enters this site wants to remain anonymous."

Mila still hadn't said a word and the conversation was making her nervous. She breathed deeply and clenched her fists until her fingers cracked. There was something that didn't tally, but she couldn't work out what it was. Goran turned towards her for a moment, as if stung by her gaze. Mila pretended not to notice.

Meanwhile the atmosphere in the room was overheating. Boris had decided to unleash on Sarah Rosa his frustration at this failure. "If you thought the site might be blocked, why didn't you follow a parallel connection procedure?"

"Why didn't you suggest it?"

"Why, what happens in cases like that?" asked Goran.

"What happens is that when a system like this is blocked there's no way of penetrating it!"

"We could try to come up with a new code and have another go," Sarah Rosa suggested.

"Really? There will be millions of combinations," Boris scoffed.

"Oh, piss off! Are you trying to put all the blame on me?"

Mila went on watching this curious exchange in silence.

"If anyone had any ideas to put forward, or any advice to give, they could have done it before!"

"But you jump down our throats every time we open our mouths!"

"Boris, just leave me alone! I could also point out that—"

"What's this?"

Goran's phrase fell between the adversaries like a barrier. His tone wasn't alarmed, or impatient, as Mila might have expected, but still made them fall silent at last.

The criminologist was pointing at something in front of him. Following the line of his outstretched arm, they found themselves studying the computer screen again.

It wasn't black anymore.

In the upper part, by the left-hand edge, some writing had appeared.

- r u there?

"Oh, Christ!" exclaimed Boris.

"So, what is it? Can any of you tell me?" Goran asked again.

Rosa sat down at the monitor again, with her hands outstretched towards the keyboard. "We're in," she announced.

The others gathered around her to get a better view.

The cursor under the phrase went on flashing, waiting for an answer, one that didn't come for the time being.

- that u?

"Look, could someone please explain to me what's going on?" Goran was losing patience now.

Rosa quickly delivered an explanation. "It's a 'door.'"

"Which is?"

"It's a means of access. It seems to me that we're inside a complex system. And this is a dialogue window: a kind of chat…there's someone at the other end."

"And they want to talk to us…" added Boris.

"Or to Alexander Bermann," Mila corrected him.

"So what are we waiting for? Let's answer!" said Stern, with a note of urgency in his voice.

Gavila looked at Boris: he was the communication expert. The young officer nodded and took his place behind Sarah Rosa, so that he could suggest what she should write.

"Tell them you're here."

And she wrote:

- Yes, I'm here.

They waited a few moments and then another phrase appeared on the monitor.

- i hadn't hrd from u i was worried.

Boris dictated the next reply to Sarah Rosa. But he recommended using only lower-case letters, like the person at the other end, and then explained that some people feel intimidated by the use of capitals. And they really wanted the other person to feel at ease.

- ive been v busy, how u?
- ive been askt loads of qstions but said 0

Someone had been asking questions? About what? Everyone, and Goran in particular, immediately had a sense that the person they were talking to was involved in something shady.

"Maybe he's been interrogated by the police, but they didn't think it was advisable to hold him," suggested Rosa.

"Or perhaps they didn't have sufficient proof," Stern said, backing her up.

The figure of an accomplice of Bermann's started forming in their minds. Mila thought back to what had happened in the motel, when she had thought someone was following her on the gravel. She hadn't mentioned it to anyone, for fear that she'd only been imagining it.

- who asked u questions?

A pause.

- them
- them who?

There was no reply. Boris tried to get round the obstacle by asking something else.

- what did you tell them?
- i told them the story you said an it workd

More than the obscurity of the words, it was the grammatical mistakes that worried Goran.

"It might be a code of recognition," he explained. "He might be waiting for us to make some mistakes as well. And if we don't, he might terminate the communication."

"You're right. Then copy the language and put in your own mistakes," Boris suggested to Rosa.

Meanwhile some more words appeared on the screen:

- ive prepard everything as u wantd i cant wait will you tell me wen?

The conversation wasn't getting them anywhere. Then Boris asked Sarah Rosa to reply that soon they would know "when," but for the time being it was better to recapitulate the whole plan, to be sure that the other person knew it.

Mila thought that was an excellent idea; that way they would have an advantage over whoever it was at the other end. A moment later, the reply came:

- the plan is: leve at night cos then no one will c me. at 2 go to end of street. hide in bushes. wait. the car lights will come on 3 times. then I can apear.

No one understood a thing. Boris looked round, in search of suggestions. He caught Gavila's eye: "What do you think, Dr. Gavila?"

The criminologist was thinking. "I don't know...there's something I'm not getting. I can't quite put my finger on it."

"I had the same feeling," said Boris. "The guy who's speaking seems...seems either to be retarded or to have some sort of psychological deficiency."

Goran came closer to Boris: "You've got to bring him out into the open."

"How?"

"I don't know...tell him you're safer than him, and that you're thinking of calling the whole thing off. Tell him 'they' are on your tail as well, and then ask him to give you some proof...that's it: ask him to call you on a secure number!"

Rosa hurried to tap in the question. But for a long time there was nothing in the space for the answer but the blinking cursor.

Then something began to appear on the screen.

- i cant speak on the phone. theyre lisning to me.

It was quite plain: either he was very cunning or he really was afraid of being spied on.

"Insist. Get round it. I want to know who 'they' are," said Goran. "Ask him where they are right now..."

The answer came quickly.

- theyre close.

"Ask him how close," insisted Goran.

- theyre here bside me.

"And what the hell does that mean?" Boris snorted, bringing his hands behind his neck in a gesture of exasperation.

Rosa slumped against the back of the chair and shook her head, disheartened. "If 'they' are so close and they're keeping an eye on him, how come they can't see what he's writing?"

"Because he can't see what we're seeing."

It was Mila who said it. And she was pleased to notice that they hadn't turned to look at her as if a ghost had just spoken. Instead, her remark sparked the group's interest.

"What do you mean?" asked Gavila.

"We've been taking it for granted that he has a blank screen in front of him just like we do. But I think his dialogue window is inserted in a web page that contains other elements: perhaps graphic animations, words or images of some kind... That's why even though they're close to him 'they' can't tell that he's communicating with us."

"She's right!" said Stern.

The room filled once more with a tentative euphoria. Goran turned to Sarah Rosa: "Can we see what he's seeing?"

"Of course," she said. "I'll send him a recognition signal and, when his computer bounces it back to me, we'll have the Internet address that he's logged on to." As she was explaining all this, the officer was already opening her notebook to create a second Internet connection.

A moment later the words appeared on the main screen:

- R u still there?

Boris looked at Goran: "What should we say?"

"Take your time. But don't arouse his suspicions."

Boris wrote to wait a few seconds, because there was someone at the door and he had to go and get it.

Meanwhile, in the notebook, Sarah Rosa managed to copy the Internet address from which the other person was communicating. "There, got it..." she announced.

She inserted the data in the URL bar and pressed enter.

A few seconds later a web page appeared.

It would have been impossible to say whether it was astonishment or horror that left her speechless.

On the screen, bears were dancing with giraffes, hippopotami were beating out the rhythm on bongos and a chimpanzee was playing the ukulele. The room filled with music. And as the jungle came to life all around them, a brightly colored butterfly welcomed them to the site.

Its name was Priscilla.

They were stunned with disbelief. Then Boris looked at the main screen where the question still shone out:

- R u still there?

It was only then that the officer managed to utter those four painful words:

"Fuck...it's a child."

10.

The word most frequently entered in search engines is *sex*. The second is *God*. Every time Goran thought about it, he wondered why anyone would try to find God on the Internet, of all places. In third place, there are actually two words: *Britney Spears*. And joint third is *death*.

Sex, *God*, *death* and *Britney Spears*.

The first time Goran had entered his wife's name in a search engine had been just three months before. He didn't know why he had done it. The idea had just come to him, instinctively. He hadn't been sure he would find her, and he actually hadn't found her. But that was officially the last place he would have thought of looking for her. Was it possible that he knew so little about her? From that moment something had snapped within him.

He had worked out why he was following her.

In reality, he didn't want to know where she was. Deep down, he didn't really care. What he really wanted to know was whether she was *happy* right then. Because that was what made him angry: that she had left him and Tommy so that she could be happy somewhere else. Can a person be capable of hurting someone so deeply in order to follow a selfish desire for happiness? Obviously they could. She had done it and, what was worse, she hadn't come back to repair things, to heal the wound, that tear in the flesh of the man with whom she had chosen to share her life, and in the flesh of his flesh. Because you *can* come back, you have to. There's always a moment when, walking along, looking straight ahead, you hear something—a cry—and you turn a bit to see if everything's still as it was, or whether something has changed in the people we left behind us, and in ourselves. That moment comes, for everyone. Why not for her? Because she hadn't even tried? No silent phone call in the dead of night. No wordless card. How many times had Goran stood and waited outside Tommy's school hoping to catch her secretly spying on her son? And yet there was nothing. She hadn't even gone to check that he was all right. Goran had started wondering about the person he had thought he would be able to keep by his side for his whole life.

What, really, made him so different from Veronica Bermann?

That woman had been tricked. Her husband had used her to create a respectable facade, so that she would look after his possessions: his name, his house, his belongings, everything. Because, in the end, what he wanted was somewhere else. But unlike Goran, Mrs. Bermann sensed the abyss that gaped beneath her perfect life, she had sniffed out its rotten smell. And had said nothing. She had joined in with the deception, even without taking part in it. She had been an accomplice in the silence, a companion in the performance, a wife for good or ill.

Goran, on the other hand, had never suspected that his wife might abandon him. Not a clue, not a sign, not even a sign of decay that one might remember and say, "Yes! It was so obvious and like an idiot I didn't notice." He would rather have discovered that he was a terrible husband so that he could blame himself, his carelessness, his lack of attention. He wished he could find the reasons within himself: that way at least he would have had some. And there was nothing, just silence. And doubts. He had given the rest of the world the crudest version of the facts: she had walked out, full stop. Because Goran knew that everyone would see what he wanted them to see. Someone would see the poor husband. Someone else, the man who must have done something to her to make her run away. And he had immediately identified himself in those roles, passing freely from one to the other. Because every pain is ordinary in its own way.

And what about her? For how long had she pretended? Who could say how long the idea had been maturing. Who knows how much it had taken to enrich it with unmentionable dreams, with thoughts hidden under the pillow every evening, as she slept next to him. Weaving that desire with the everyday gestures of a mother, of a wife. Until those fantasies became a project, a plan. A *design*. Who could say when she had convinced herself or worked out that what she imagined could be realized. The pupa contained the secret of its metamorphosis and meanwhile she went on living alongside them, alongside him and Tommy, silently preparing for change.

And where was she now? In a parallel universe, made up of men and women like the ones Goran met every day, made of houses to run, husbands to support, children to nurture. A world identical and banal, but far removed from him and from Tommy, with new colors, new friends, new faces, new names. What was she looking for in that world? Basically we are all in search of answers in a parallel universe, Goran thought. Like the people who use the web to look up *sex, God, death* and *Britney Spears*.

Alexander Bermann, on the other hand, went on the Internet in search of children.

It had all come out at once. From the opening of the website *Priscilla the Butterfly* on Bermann's computer to the identification of the international server that managed that system, everything had begun to come into shape.

It was a pedophile network with branches in various different states.

Mila was right: "her" music teacher was on there too.

The special unit for Internet crimes had identified almost a hundred subscribers. The first arrests had taken place, others would be happening in the next few hours. A small but well-selected number of subscribers. All professional people beyond suspicion, affluent and hence willing to pay large sums to preserve their anonymity.

Among them, Alexander Bermann.

On his way home that night, Goran thought again of the mild-mannered man, always smiling and morally upright in the descriptions of Bermann's friends and acquaintances. A perfect mask. Who could say what had made him connect the idea of Bermann with the idea of his wife. Or perhaps he knew but didn't want to admit it. At any rate, once the threshold had been crossed he would set those reflections aside and dedicate himself completely to Tommy, as he had promised him on the phone, when he had told him he would be coming home soon. His son had received the news enthusiastically and asked him if they could send out for pizza. Goran had agreed easily, knowing that that small concession would be enough to keep him happy. Children are always able to draw some kind of happiness from the things that happen to them.

So Goran had found himself getting pizza with pepperoni for himself and double mozzarella for Tommy. They had ordered the pizza together on the phone, because ordering pizzas was a shared ritual. Tommy had dialed the number and Goran had made the request. Then they had got out the big plates bought specially for the purpose. Tommy would drink fruit juice, Goran had allowed himself a beer. Before bringing them to the table, they had put their glasses in the freezer, so that they would be opaque with frost and cold enough to receive their drinks.

But Goran was far from peaceful. His mind was still running to that perfect organization. The officers in the special web-crime unit had unearthed a database containing more than three thousand children's names, linked with addresses and photographs. The network used fake domains for children to lure victims into the trap…so like the ones in the cartoons that Goran and Tommy had watched together after dinner on a satellite channel. The blue tiger and the white lion. As his son had cuddled up against him, concentrating completely on the two jungle friends, Goran had watched him.

I have to protect him, he thought.

And the thought had given him a strange fear deep in his chest, a dark, sticky knot. The dread of not doing enough, of not being enough. Because a single parent can't be enough. Even if Tommy and he basically managed. But what would have happened if, behind Bermann's blank computer screen, rather than that unknown child, it had been his Tommy? Would he have been capable of noticing that someone was trying to enter his son's mind, his son's life?

As Tommy finished his homework, Goran had hidden himself away in his study. It wasn't yet seven o'clock, so he had started flicking through Bermann's file again, finding various bits of food for thought that might be useful to the investigation.

First of all, that leather armchair in the basement, the one on which Krepp had found no fingerprints.

On everything else, but not there... why?

He was sure there was a reason for that, too. And yet, every time he thought he had grasped a concept, his mind slipped elsewhere. To the dangers surrounding the life of his son.

Goran was a criminologist, he knew what evil was made of. But he had always observed it from a distance, as an academic. He had never been corrupted by the idea that the same evil might somehow stretch out its bony finger until it touched him. Now, though, he was thinking about it.

When do you become a "monster"?

That term, which he had officially banned, now returned to the deepest recess of his mind. Because he wanted to know how it happens. When you realize you have crossed that boundary.

Bermann belonged to a perfect organization, with a related hierarchy and status system. The sales representative had joined it while at university. In those days the Internet was not yet seen as a hunting ground, and it took a considerable effort to stay in the shadows and not arouse suspicion. That was why followers were advised to create a safe and exemplary life for themselves in which they could hide their own true nature and conceal their own impulses. Blend in, and disappear; those were the key words of the strategy.

Bermann had come back from university with a crystal clear idea of what he would do. First of all he had traced an old school friend that he hadn't seen for years. Veronica, who had never been pretty enough for the boys—himself included—to take an interest in her. He had led her to believe that his was a love that he had nurtured for years and shyly concealed. And she, as predicted, had immediately agreed to marry him. The first years of marriage had passed as they do for all couples, with highs and lows. He frequently traveled for work. In reality he was often taking advantage of his travels to meet others like himself or to groom his young prey.

With the advent of the Internet things had got much easier. Pedophiles had immediately started making use of that incredible instrument that not only let them act under cover of anonymity, but also set up ingenious traps to manipulate their victims.

But Alexander Bermann couldn't complete his perfectly planned disguise, because Veronica couldn't give him an heir. That was the missing piece, the detail that would truly have put him beyond suspicion: because a father isn't interested in other people's children.

The criminologist brushed aside the fury that had risen up in his throat and closed the file that had been getting fatter and fatter over the last few hours. He didn't want to read it anymore. In fact he wanted only to go to bed and dull himself with sleep.

Who could Albert be but Bermann? Even if they had yet to link him to the graveyard of arms and the disappearance of all six little girls, and find the missing corpses, no one more than he would deserve to wear the executioner's garb.

But the more Goran thought about it the less convinced he was.

At eight o'clock Roche would officially announce the capture of the guilty man at a packed press conference. Goran realized that the idea tormenting him now had started buzzing around in his head soon after he had discovered Bermann's secret. Lingering behind, foggily indistinct, the idea had squatted in a corner of his mind all afternoon. But in the shadows where it had taken refuge it went on pulsing, to show him it was there, and it was alive. Only now, in the peace of his room, Goran had decided to concentrate on it fully.

There's something in this business that doesn't add up…

You don't think Bermann's guilty?

Oh, of course I do: the man was a pedophile. But he didn't kill the six little girls. He has nothing to do with it…

How can you be so sure?

Because if Alexander Bermann really was our Albert, we would have found the last *little girl in his boot—number six—and not Debby, the first. She would already have been rotting for some time…*

And just as he was becoming aware of this deduction, the criminologist looked at his watch: a few minutes till the press conference at eight.

He had to stop Roche.

The chief inspector had summoned the main newspapers as soon as information about developments in the Bermann case had started circulating. The official pretext was that he didn't want the journalists to get hold of the information secondhand, perhaps badly filtered by some confidential source. In reality, he was worried that the story could trickle away in different directions, excluding him from the limelight.

Roche was good at handling events like this, he knew how to gauge the wait and he derived a certain pleasure from leaving the press dangling. That was why he started those meetings a few minutes late, letting it be known that as head of the team he was always delayed by last-minute developments.

The inspector enjoyed the murmur coming from the press room next to his office: it was like energy that fed on his ego. Meanwhile he sat there calmly, with his feet on the desk that he had inherited from his predecessor, whose vice inspector he had been for a long time—too long, he thought, and had had no compunction about firing eight years before.

The lines on his phone had gone on lighting up uninterruptedly. But he had no intention of replying: he wanted to let the tension mount.

There was a knock at the door.

"Come in," said Roche.

As soon as she entered, Mila noticed a smug grin on the chief inspector's face. She had wondered why on earth he wanted to see her.

"Officer Vasquez, I wanted to thank you personally for the invaluable contribution that you have made to this investigation."

Mila would have blushed if she hadn't understood that this was only the calculated prelude to getting rid of her. "I don't think I did much, sir."

Roche picked up a letter opener and went on cleaning his nails with the tip. Then, distractedly, he went on: "No, it was extremely useful."

"We don't yet know the identity of the sixth girl."

"It will come out, like everything else."

"Sir, I would like to ask your permission to complete my work, at least for a few days. I'm sure I can get a result…"

Roche dropped the letter opener, took his feet off the desk and got up to walk towards Mila. With the most brilliant of smiles, he took her right hand, still bandaged, and shook it, without noticing that he was hurting her. "I've talked to your superior: Sergeant Morexu assured me that you will receive a commendation for this case."

Then he walked her to the door.

"Safe home, officer. And think of us from time to time."

Mila nodded, because there was nothing else to say. A few seconds later she found herself outside, watching the office door as it closed.

She would have liked to discuss the question with Goran Gavila, because she was sure he knew nothing about her sudden dismissal. But he had already gone home. A few hours before she had heard him on the phone, agreeing to dinner. Judging by the tone he was using, the person on the other end couldn't have been more than eight or nine years old. They were going to order a pizza.

Mila had worked out that Goran had a son. Perhaps there was also a woman in his life, and she too would be sharing the pleasant evening that father and son were preparing. Mila had felt a twinge of envy, without knowing why.

She handed in her badge at the door and was given an envelope with a railway ticket to take her home. This time no one would take her to the station. She would have to call a taxi, in the hope that her own police headquarters would reimburse the expense, and drop by at the motel to pick up her things.

Once she was in the street, though, Mila discovered that she wasn't in a hurry. She looked around, breathed in air that suddenly struck her as clear and peaceful. The city looked as if it was immersed in an unnatural bubble of cold, balanced on the edge of a meteorological event. One degree more or less and everything would change. The rarefied atmosphere contained the premature promise of a snowstorm. Or else everything would stay as it was now, motionless.

She took the ticket from the envelope. There were still three hours till her train. But she was thinking about something else. Would that be long enough to do what she had to do? There was no way of knowing, except having a go. Basically, if she drew a blank, no one would know. And she couldn't leave with that doubt.

Three hours. They would have to do.

She had hired a car and had been traveling for around an hour. The mountain tops carved out the sky in front of her. Log cabins, with sloping roofs. Gray smoke, scented with resin, rose from the chimneys. Wood stacked up in the yards. From the windows, a comforting, ocher light.

Driving along Highway 115, Mila had taken exit 25. She was heading for the boarding school that Debby Gordon had attended. She wanted to see her room. She was sure she would find something there that would take her to child number six, to her name. Even if she was of practically no use to Chief Inspector Roche by now, Mila couldn't leave that undiscovered identity behind her. It was a little gesture of pity. The news had not yet been broadcast that there had been more than five girls, because no one had yet had the opportunity to mourn the sixth victim. And they wouldn't be able to do it without a name, Mila knew that. She would become the white mark on a tombstone, the silent pause at the end of a brief list of names, just one number to add to the cold accountancy of death. And she absolutely couldn't allow that to happen.

In fact there was another idea that obsessed her, for which she had traveled so many miles. It was that tickle at the base of her neck…

The policewoman reached her destination just after nine. The boarding school was in a pretty village twelve hundred meters up the hill. The streets at that time of day were deserted. The school building was just outside the village, surrounded by a pretty park, with a riding school and tennis and netball courts. It was reached by a long drive on which students walked slowly back from their sports activities. The girls' crystalline laughter violated the instructions that they walk in silence.

Mila passed them and parked in the area in front of the school. A little while later she turned up at the office to ask if she could visit Debby's room, hoping that no one would cause any problems. After consulting with a superior, the assistant came back to her and told her she could go. Luckily, after their discussion, Debby's mother had phoned to tell them Mila was on her way. The assistant gave her a pass with "visitor" on it, and showed her the way.

Mila walked down the corridors until she reached the wing where the pupils had their rooms. It wasn't hard to find Debby's. Her classmates had covered her door with colored ribbons and notes. They said they would never stop missing her, they would never forget her. And there was the inevitable "You will always stay in our hearts."

She thought once more of Debby, of the phone calls she had made to her family desperate for them to take her home, the isolation that a child of her age, shy and self-conscious, can suffer at the hands of her schoolmates in a place like that. And that was why she found those notes in bad taste, the hypocritical manifestation of belated emotion. *You could have noticed her when she was here,* she thought. *Or when someone took her away from under your noses.*

Shrieks and delighted squawks reached her from the end of the corridor. Stepping over the stumps of the now extinguished candles that someone had arranged along the threshold as a sign of remembrance, Mila entered Debby's refuge.

She closed the door behind her and everything was suddenly silent. She stretched a hand out towards a lamp and lit it. The room was small. Outside it there was a window that looked out directly over the park. Resting against the wall, a very tidy desk stood below shelves packed with books. Debby liked reading. On the right was the bathroom door, closed, and Mila decided she would leave it till last. On the bed were a few cuddly toys that scrutinized the policewoman with their cold, useless eyes, making her feel like an intruder. The room was entirely covered with posters and photographs showing Debby at home, with her classmates from her old school, her girlfriends and her dog Sting. All the things that had been taken from her so that she could attend that exclusive boarding school.

Debby was a girl with the potential to be a beautiful woman, Mila observed. Her contemporaries would have noticed the fact too late, sorry not to have glimpsed the swan hidden in that bewildered duckling sooner. But at that point she would have wisely ignored them.

She cast her mind back to the autopsy that she had witnessed, to when Chang had freed her face from the plastic, and the grip with the white lily had appeared in her hair. Her murderer had combed it and Mila remembered thinking that he had made her beautiful for them.

No, though, she was beautiful for Alexander Bermann…

Her eye was drawn to an area of wall that had remained strangely empty. She approached it and discovered that at various points the plaster had flaked away. As if something had been stuck to it that was no longer there. Other hands, other eyes had touched Debby's world, her things, her memories. Perhaps it had been her mother who had taken the pictures off the wall; she would have to check.

She was still thinking about that when she was startled by a sound. It came from outside. Not from the corridor, but from behind the bathroom door.

She instinctively brought her hand to her belt, in search of her gun. When she had taken it out and leveled it, she rose and walked over to the bathroom door. Another sound. Clearer this time. Yes, there was someone in there. Someone who hadn't noticed she was there. Someone who, like herself, had thought that this would be the best time to enter Debby's room undisturbed and take something away…clues? Her heart was thumping madly. She wouldn't go in, she would wait.

Suddenly the door opened. Mila moved her finger to the safety catch. Then, luckily, she froze. The little girl spread her arms wide with terror, dropping what she held in her hands.

"Who are you?" Mila asked her.

The girl stammered: "I'm a friend of Debby's."

She was lying. Mila was perfectly well aware of it. She put her gun back in her belt and looked at the ground, at the things the girl had dropped. They were a bottle of perfume, some bottles of shampoo and a wide-brimmed red hat.

"I came to get the things I lent her," but it sounded more like an excuse. "The others came here before me..."

Mila recognized the red hat from one of the photographs on the wall. Debby was wearing it. And she realized that she was witness to an act of looting that had probably been going on for several days, the work of some of Debby's schoolmates. It wouldn't have been strange if one of them had taken the photographs from the wall.

"Fine," she said crisply. "Now get out of here."

The girl hesitated for a moment, then picked up the things she had dropped and ran from the room. Mila let her go. Debby would have liked that. The things would have been no use to her mother, who would blame herself for the rest of her life for sending her there. Compared to the other parents, Mrs. Gordon was "lucky"—if you could talk of luck in such cases—to have her daughter's body to mourn.

Mila started rummaging among the papers and books. She wanted a name and she would get one. Of course, it would have been easier to find Debby's diary. She was sure she must have had something to confide her miseries in. And, like all twelve-year-olds, she would have kept it in a secret place. A place not too far from her heart, however. Where she could have gone and got it as soon as she needed it. And when do we have the greatest need to take refuge in what is dearest to us? At night. Mila knelt down beside the bed, reached under the mattress, and felt around until she found something.

It was a tin box decorated with little silver rabbits, closed with a miniature padlock.

She set it down on the bed and looked around in search of the place where the key might be hidden. Then she suddenly remembered the bracelet dangling from Debby's right wrist at the autopsy. With a tiny key on it.

She had given it back to Debby's mother and there was no time to get the key back. So Mila decided to force the box open. Using a ballpoint pen as a lever, she managed to dislodge the rings that held the padlock. Then she lifted the lid. Inside was a potpourri of spices, dried flowers and scented wood. A red-stained safety pin that must have been used for the blood-sisters ritual. An embroidered silk handkerchief. A rubber bear with chewed ears. Birthday candles. A teenager's treasure trove of memories.

But no diary.

Strange, Mila said to herself. The size of the box and the meagerness of its remaining contents suggested the presence of something else. And also the fact that Debby felt the need to protect it all with a padlock. Or perhaps there really wasn't a diary.

Disappointed to have drawn a blank, she looked at her watch: she'd missed the train. She might as well stay there and look for something that might lead her to Debby's mysterious friend. Even before, as she was looking through the girl's things, that sensation had floated back to the surface, the one that she had already felt several times without ever managing to grasp it.

Tickle at the base of the neck.

She couldn't leave there without first understanding what it was. But she needed someone or something that might back up her fleeting thoughts, give them a direction. In spite of the late hour, Mila took a decision that was difficult but necessary.

She dialed Goran Gavila's number.

"Dr. Gavila, it's Mila…"

The criminologist was startled, and didn't say a word for a few seconds.

"How can I help you, Mila?"

Did he sound irritated? No, it was just a sense she had. Mila began by telling him she should already have been on a train, and instead she was in Debby Gordon's room at the boarding school. She preferred to tell him the whole truth, and Goran listened to her without comment. When she had finished there was a long silence at the other end.

Mila couldn't have known, but Goran was staring at his kitchen cupboards, holding a cup of steaming coffee. The criminologist was still awake because he had been trying to contact Roche to halt his media suicide, but without success.

"We might have been a bit hasty with Alexander Bermann."

Mila noticed that Gavila had spoken in a faint voice, as if the words had had to struggle up from his lungs.

"That's what I think too," she said. "How did you get there?"

"Because he had Debby Gordon in the boot. Why not the last child?"

Mila remembered Stern's explanation of that curious circumstance: "Perhaps Bermann had made mistakes when hiding the corpse, some false steps that might have given him away, so he was moving her to a place where he could hide her better."

Goran listened, puzzled. His breathing at the other end was measured.

"What's the matter, have I said something wrong?"

"No. But you didn't sound very convinced as you were saying it."

Mila considered this for a moment. "No, you're right," she admitted.

"There's something missing. Or rather, there's something that isn't *in harmony* with everything else."

Mila knew that a good policeman lives on perceptions. He never mentions them in official reports: all that matters there is an account of the "facts." But since it was Gavila who had introduced the subject, Mila ventured to talk to him about her two sensations. "The first time it happened was during the medical examiner's report. It was like a wrong note. But I didn't manage to catch it, I lost it almost immediately."

Tickle at the base of the neck.

She heard Goran moving a chair at his house, and she sat down too. Then he spoke: "Let's try, hypothetically, to rule out Bermann..."

"OK."

"Let's imagine that someone else was behind all this. Let's say that this guy appeared out of nowhere and slipped a little girl with a severed arm into Bermann's boot..."

"Bermann would have said so, to shift suspicion from himself," Mila said.

"I don't think so," Goran replied, confidently. "Bermann was a pedophile: he wouldn't have shifted a thing. He knew he was finished. He killed himself because he had no way out, and to cover up for the organization to which he belonged."

Mila remembered that the music teacher had killed himself as well.

"So what do we do?"

"We go back to Albert, the neutral and impersonal profile we'd developed originally."

For the first time Mila felt truly involved in the case. Teamwork was a new experience for her. And she didn't mind working with Dr. Gavila. She hadn't known him for long, but she'd already learned to trust him.

"The assumption is that there's a reason for the abduction of the little girls and the graveyard of arms. It may be absurd, but it exists. And to explain it we have to know our man. The better we know him, the more we'll be able to understand. The better we understand, the closer we'll get to him. Is that clear?"

"Yes... but what's my role exactly?" she asked.

Goran's voice was low and full of energy: "He's a predator, isn't he? So teach me how he hunts..."

Mila opened the notebook she had brought with her. At the other end he heard her flicking through the pages. She started reading from her notes about the victims: "Debby, twelve. Disappeared at school. Her classmates remember seeing her coming out at the end of lessons. They didn't notice she was missing from the school until the evening register."

Goran took a long sip of his coffee and said, "Now tell me about the second one..."

"Anneke, ten. At first everyone thinks she's lost in the woods... Number three was called Sabine, she was the youngest: nine. It happened on Saturday evening when she was at the fair with her mother and father."

"She's the one he took from the merry-go-round, right from under her parents' noses. And that's when alarms went off all over the country. Our team was called in, and that was when the fourth girl disappeared."

"Melissa. The oldest: thirteen. Her parents had given her a curfew, but on her birthday she broke it to go and celebrate with her friends at the bowling alley."

"They all showed up except Melissa," the criminologist remembered.

"Caroline was taken from her bed, which means he got into her house…and then there's number six."

"Later. Let's stick with the others for now."

Goran felt incredibly in tune with the policewoman. It was something he hadn't felt for a long time.

"Now I need you to talk to me, Mila. Tell me: how does our Albert behave?"

"First he kidnaps a little girl who's far from home and who doesn't socialize much. So no one notices anything and he'll have time…"

"Time to do what?"

"It's a test: he wants to be sure that he'll succeed in what he does. And with time at his disposal he can always get rid of the victim and disappear."

"With Anneke he's already more relaxed, but even so he decides to abduct her in the woods, far from any witnesses…And how does he act with Sabine?"

"He takes her from under everyone's noses: at the funfair."

"Why?" Goran cut in.

"For the same reason that he abducts Melissa when everyone's already on the alert, or Caroline in her house."

"What's the motive for that?"

"He feels strong, he's become confident."

"Fine," said Goran. "Go on…now tell me about this blood-sisters business, from the beginning."

"It's something you do when you're very young. You prick your index finger with a safety pin and then bring your fingertips together while reciting a nursery rhyme."

"Who are the two girls?"

"Debby and number six."

"Why does Albert choose her?" Goran wondered. "It's ludicrous. The authorities are in a state of alarm, they're all looking for Debby already, and back he comes to take her best friend! Why run a risk of that kind? Why?"

Mila knew what the criminologist was getting at, but even if she was the one who said it, he was the one who had taken her there. "I think it's about *challenge*..."

The last word uttered by Mila opened a closed door in the head of the criminologist, who rose from his chair and started walking through the kitchen.

"Go on..."

"He wanted to demonstrate something. That he was the most cunning, for example."

"The best of all. He's plainly egocentric, a man afflicted with a narcissistic personality disorder...let's talk about number six."

"We know nothing about her."

"Talk to me about her anyway. Do it with what we've got..."

Mila set the notebook down, now she was forced to improvise. "Fine, let's see...she's approximately the same age as Debby, because they were friends. So about twelve. That's confirmed by the Barr body tests."

"Fine...and?"

"According to the autopsy she died in a different way."

"Meaning? Remind me..."

She tried to find the answer in the notebook. "He cut off her arm, as he did to the others. Except that her blood and tissues contained traces of a drug cocktail."

Goran asked her to repeat Chang's list of medicines. Antiarrhythmics like disopyramide, ACE inhibitors, and atenolol which is a beta-blocker...

He wasn't convinced by that.

"I'm not convinced by that," said Mila. And for a moment Goran Gavila was struck by the suspicion that the woman could read his mind.

"During the meeting he said that was how Albert reduced her heartbeats, lowering the pressure," Mila pointed out. "And Dr. Chang added that the purpose was to slow the bleeding, to make her die more slowly."

Slow the bleeding. Make her die more slowly.

"OK, fine, now tell me about her parents..."

"Which parents?" asked Mila, trying to keep up.

"I don't care if it isn't written in your bloody notes! I want your thoughts, damn it!"

How did he know about her notes? she wondered, shaken by his reaction. "The parents of the sixth child have not presented themselves like the others for the DNA test. We don't know who they are, because they haven't reported her disappearance."

"Why haven't they reported it? Perhaps they don't know yet?"

"Unlikely."

Slow the bleeding.

"Perhaps she didn't have any parents! Perhaps she was alone in the world! Perhaps none of them gives a damn about her!" Goran was losing his temper.

"No, she has a family. She's got to be like all the others, remember? Only daughter, mother over the age of forty, a couple who decided to have only one child. He doesn't change, because they are his true victims: they probably won't have any more children. *He chose the families, not the girls.*"

"Right," said Goran, to her gratification. "Then what?"

Mila thought for a moment. "He likes to *challenge us*. He likes a challenge. Like the little blood sisters. This is a puzzle... he's testing us."

Make her die more slowly.

"If there are parents, and they know, why haven't they reported the disappearance?" Goran pressed her, letting his gaze wander around the kitchen floor. He felt as if they were close to something. Perhaps an answer.

"Because they're scared."

Mila's words illuminated all the dark corners of the room. And she felt an itch at the base of her neck, a tickle...

"Scared of what?"

They wanted the idea to assume the form of words, so that they could grasp it and make sure it didn't dissolve.

"Her parents are scared that Albert might hurt her..."

"How, if she's already dead?"

Slow the bleeding. Make her die more slowly.

Goran stopped, kneeling. Mila rose to her feet.

"He didn't slow the bleeding...*he stopped it.*"

They got there at the same time.

"Oh, my God..." she said.

"Yes...she's still alive."

11.

The little girl opens her eyes.

She takes a deep breath, as if reemerging from a liquid abyss, with lots of tiny, invisible hands dragging her back down. But she struggles to keep her balance, to stay awake.

The pain is searing, but it gives her some lucidity. She tries to remember where she is. She has lost her bearings. She is lying on her back, she knows that. Her head spins and she is surrounded by a curtain of darkness. She definitely has a fever and she can't move. Only two other sensations can pierce the fog of her half-sleep. The smell of damp and rocks, like the smell of a cave. And the repeated, enervating sound of dripping.

What has happened?

The memories return one at a time, around her. Then she feels like weeping. Hot tears start flowing down her cheeks, wetting her dry lips. That's how she discovers she is thirsty.

They were supposed to go to the lake that weekend. She, Dad and Mum. There were days when she couldn't think of anything else. The outing when her dad was going to teach her to fish. She had collected earthworms in the garden, putting them in a tin. They moved, they were alive. But she didn't care about that. Or rather, she thought that detail was irrelevant. Because she took it for granted that earthworms have no feelings. She hadn't wondered what it felt like for them to be trapped in there. But now she wonders. Because that's what she is feeling now. She feels sorry for them, and for herself. And shame for having been bad. And she hopes with all her heart that whoever has taken her, dragging her from her life, is better than she is.

She doesn't remember much of what happened.

She had woken early to go to school, even earlier than usual, because it was Thursday, and like every Thursday, her father couldn't take her because he was seeing his clients. He sold hairdressing products and, in anticipation of an increase in regular customers at the weekend, supplied them with hair lacquer and shampoo as well as cosmetics. That was why she had to go to school on her own. She had been doing it now since she was nine. She still remembered the first time he had walked her the short distance to the bus stop. She held his hand, paying attention to his instructions, such as looking both ways before crossing the road, or not being late because the driver wouldn't wait, or not stopping to talk to strangers because it could be dangerous. Over time, she had interiorized that advice to such an extent that she no longer felt she was hearing her father's voice saying them in her head. She had become an expert.

That Thursday morning she had got up with new joy in her heart. Apart from the imminent trip to the lake, there was another reason to be happy. The plaster she had on her finger. In the bath she had lifted a flap off it in the hot water and looked at her fingertip with a mixture of pride and pain.

She had a blood sister.

She couldn't wait to see her again. But that wouldn't happen before the evening, since they went to different schools. In the usual place they would tell each other the latest news, because they hadn't seen each other for some days. Then they would play and make plans, and before parting they would make a solemn pledge to stay friends forever.

Yes, it was going to be a great day.

She had slipped her algebra book into her rucksack. It was her favorite subject, and her marks said as much. At eleven they had PE, so she had taken a leotard from one of the drawers and put her gym shoes and white socks in a carrier bag. As she was making the bed, her mother had called her down for breakfast. They were always in a great hurry at the breakfast table. That morning had been no different from the others. Her father, who usually had only a coffee, was standing by the table reading the paper. He held it in front of his face in one hand, while the other gripped the cup that went back and forth from his lips. Her mother was already on the phone to a colleague and she had made fried eggs without missing a word of the conversation. Houdini was curled up in his basket and hadn't deigned to glance at her since she had come downstairs. Her grandfather said that, like himself, the cat suffered from low blood pressure, so he needed some time to get his act together in the morning. For a while now she had stopped being hurt by Houdini's indifference. They had reached a tacit pact whereby they respected one another's space, and that would have to do.

After breakfast, she had put her dirty plate in the sink and walked around the kitchen for a kiss from each of her parents. Then she had left the house.

In the wind she could still feel on her cheek the damp imprint of coffee from her father's lips. The day was bright. There was nothing threatening about the few clouds that sullied the sky. The forecasts said the weather would stay like that all weekend. "All the better for a fishing trip," her father had remarked. And with that promise in her heart she had walked along the pavement, straight to the bus stop. It was three hundred and twenty-nine steps in all. She had counted them. From time to time she counted them again. As she did that morning. And when she was about to get to the three hundred and tenth step, someone had called her.

She would never forget that number. The precise point at which her life had broken into pieces.

She had turned round and seen him. That smiling man walking towards her didn't have a familiar face. But she had heard him calling her name, and had immediately thought, "If he knows me he can't be dangerous." As he came towards her she tried to get a better look at him to work out who he was. He had speeded up his footsteps to catch up with her, she had waited for him. His hair... was strange. Like the hair of a doll she had when she was little. It looked fake. By the time she had worked out that the man was wearing a wig it was too late. She hadn't even noticed the parked white van. He had grabbed her, opening the door at the same time and getting inside with her. She had tried to cry out, but he had a hand over her mouth.

The wig had slipped from his head and he had pressed a wet handkerchief against her face for a long time. Then the sudden, unstoppable tears, black dots and red patches over her eyes, stripping the world of its color. Finally, darkness.

Who is this man? What does he want from her? Why has he brought her here? Where is he now?

The questions come quickly, and leave again unanswered. The images of her last morning as a little girl fade away and she finds herself in that cave once more—the damp belly of the monster who swallowed her up. On the other hand, that comfortable sense of torpor is returning. Anything, as long as I don't have to think about all that, she thinks. She closes her eyes, plunging once again into the sea of shadows that surrounds her.

She hasn't even noticed that one of those shadows is watching her.

12.

Snow had fallen heavily during the night, settling like silence on the world.

The temperature had grown milder, and a pale breeze swept the streets. While the long-awaited meteorological event slowed everything down, a new frenzy had taken hold of the team.

They had a purpose, at last. A way of making up for all the evil that had occurred, if only partially. Find the sixth girl, save her. And save themselves at the same time.

"As long as she's still alive," Goran kept on repeating to himself, somewhat dampening the enthusiasm of the others.

After the discovery, Chang had been hung out to dry by Roche for not reaching the same conclusion before. The press still hadn't been informed of the existence of the sixth abducted child, but in anticipation the chief inspector was coming up with an excuse for the media, and he needed a scapegoat.

In the meantime, Roche had called together a team of medics—each with a different specialization—to answer a single, fundamental question.

"How long could a child survive in those conditions?"

There had been no unequivocal answer. The more optimistic maintained that with appropriate medical treatment and without the development of infections, she would be able to survive between ten and twenty days. The pessimists thought that in spite of her young age, with an amputation like that her life expectancy would inevitably diminish by the hour and in fact it was very likely that the girl was already dead.

Roche wasn't satisfied, and decided to go on maintaining publicly that Alexander Bermann was still the main suspect. Even though he was convinced that the sales rep had nothing to do with the disappearance of the girls, Goran would not deny the chief's official version. The truth wasn't the issue. He knew that Roche couldn't afford to lose face by taking back his previous declarations about Bermann's guilt. It would be damaging to him, but also to the credibility of their investigative methods.

The criminologist's conviction, however, was that the man had been somehow "chosen" by the real perpetrator.

Albert was suddenly at the center of their attention again.

"He knew that Bermann was a pedophile," said Goran when they were all in the operations room. "We underestimated him for a moment."

A new element had entered Albert's profile. They had first guessed as much when Chang had described the lesions on the recovered arms, using the word "surgical" for the precision with which the murderer had inflicted the fatal blow. The use of drugs to slow the blood pressure of the sixth child confirmed their man's clinical abilities. Finally, the fact that he was probably keeping her alive led them to think that he had a remarkable knowledge of reanimation techniques and the protocols of intensive therapy.

"He could be a doctor, or perhaps he used to be one," Goran reflected.

"I'll do some research into the professional registers. He might have been struck off," Stern said suddenly.

It was a good start.

"How would he get hold of the medicine to keep her alive?"

"Excellent question, Boris. Let's check the pharmacies, the private ones and the ones in the hospitals, to see if anyone's requested those drugs."

"He might have got hold of them months ago," Rosa observed.

"Especially antibiotics: he might need them to avoid infections… what else?"

Apparently there was nothing else. Now it was just a question of finding out where the little girl was, dead or alive.

In the operations room everyone looked at Mila. She was the expert, the person to consult to reach the goal that would give a meaning to their work.

"We have to find a way of communicating with the family."

Everyone looked at each other, until Stern asked, "Why? Now we have the edge over Albert: he doesn't yet know that we know."

"Do you really think a mind capable of imagining all this wouldn't have predicted our actions long ago?"

"If our hypothesis is correct, he's keeping her alive for us."

Gavila had intervened in support of Mila, bringing her the gift of his new theory.

"He's the one controlling the game, and the girl is the final prize. It's a competition to see who's the more clever."

"So he's not going to kill her?" Boris asked.

"He isn't going to kill her. We are."

The statement was hard to digest, but it was the essence of the challenge.

"If we take too long to find her, the girl will die. If we irritate him in any way, the girl will die. If we don't stick to the rules, the girl will die."

"The rules? What rules?" asked Rosa, her anxiety ill concealed.

"The ones he has established, and we unfortunately don't know. The tracks along which his mind works are obscure to us, but very clear to him. In the light of which, every one of our actions can be interpreted as breaking the rules of the game."

Stern nodded thoughtfully. "So going straight to the family of the sixth child is a bit like playing along with his game."

"Yes," said Mila. "That's what Albert expects of us right now. He has taken it into account. But he's also convinced that we'll fail, because the parents are too scared to come out into the open or they would have done so already. He wants to show us that his force of persuasion is more powerful than any attempt on our part. Paradoxically, he's trying to come across as the 'hero' of the story in their eyes. It's as if he was saying to them, 'I'm the only one who can save your child, you can trust no one but me'...Do you realize how much psychological pressure he can exert? If we can persuade those parents to contact us we will have scored a point in our favor."

"But there's a danger of causing him offense," protested Sarah Rosa, who didn't seem to agree.

"That's a risk we have to take. But I don't think he'll hurt the girl because of that. He'll punish us, he may make us lose some time. He won't kill her now: first he has to show us the finished job."

Goran thought it was extraordinary the way Mila had mastered the mechanisms of the investigation so quickly. She was good at setting out precise guidelines. Still, even if the others were listening to her at last, she wouldn't find it easy to be accepted once and for all by her colleagues. They had immediately identified her as an alien presence, one that they didn't need. And their opinion certainly wouldn't change quickly.

At that moment Roche decided he had had enough and decided to intervene: "We'll do as Officer Vasquez suggests: we'll spread the news of the existence of a sixth abducted girl and, in the meantime, we'll publicly address her family. Christ! Let's show some balls here! I'm tired of waiting for things to happen, as if this monster was really making all the decisions!"

Some people were startled by the chief inspector's new attitude. Not Goran. Without noticing, Roche was merely using their serial killer's technique of reversing roles and, consequently, responsibility: if they didn't find the child, it would only be because her parents hadn't trusted the investigators, and had stayed in the shadows.

And yet there was a hint of truth in what he was saying: the time had come to try and anticipate events.

"You heard those quacks, didn't you? The sixth girl has ten days at the most!" Then Roche studied the members of the unit one by one and announced in a serious voice: "I've decided: we're reopening the Studio."

At dinnertime, on the evening news, the face of a famous actor appeared on the screen. They had chosen him to announce the appeal to the parents of the sixth child. He was a familiar face, and he would bring the right dose of emotional involvement to the subject. The idea had plainly been Roche's. Mila thought it was just right: it would discourage time wasters and compulsive liars from calling the superimposed number.

More or less at the same time as the public found out, with a mixture of horror and hope, about the existence of the sixth still-living child, the team took possession of the "Studio."

It was an apartment on the fourth floor of an anonymous building near the center. It was mostly home to secondary offices of the Federal Police, the ones that dealt with administration and accounts, and the outmoded paper archives that hadn't yet been digitized for the new databases.

The apartment had previously been used by the witness protection program to accommodate people who needed to be hidden. The Studio was set perfectly between two other identical apartments. That was why it had no windows. The air conditioning was always running and the only means of access was the front door. The walls were very thick and there were various security devices. Given that the apartment was no longer used for its original purpose, the devices had been deactivated. All that remained was a heavy armored door.

Goran had been the one who had wanted this place, since the establishment of the violent crimes investigation unit. It hadn't taken much for Roche to make him happy: he had simply remembered that safe house that hadn't been used for years. The criminologist maintained the need to live shoulder to shoulder while the case continued. That way ideas could circulate more easily, and be shared and processed instantly. Their forced cohabitation would yield cooperation, and that in turn would serve to feed a single pulsing brain. Dr. Gavila had borrowed from the "new economy" the methods for setting up the work environment, made up of common spaces and with a "horizontal" distribution of functions, as opposed to the vertical division that normally prevails in the police, linked to divisions of rank, which often generates conflict and competition. In the Studio, on the other hand, differences were erased, solutions evolved and everyone's contribution was requested, listened to and considered.

When Mila crossed the threshold, she thought immediately that *this* was the place where serial killers were caught. It didn't happen in the real world, but in here, between these walls.

At the center of it all there was a simple manhunt, but also the effort to understand the motive behind an apparently incomprehensible sequence of horrific crimes. The distorted vision of a sick mind.

Mila was aware that that step would be the harbinger of a new phase of the investigation.

Stern was carrying the brown fake leather bag that his wife had prepared for him, and stepped aside to let the others in. Boris, with his rucksack on his back. Then Rosa and, last of all, Mila.

Beyond the armored door there was a booth covered with bulletproof glass that had once housed the security guards. Inside, the dead monitors of the video system, a few revolving chairs and a rack for weapons, empty. A second security threshold, with an electric gate, separated that passageway from the rest of the house. Once the guards had had to activate it, but now it was wide open.

Mila noticed that it smelled stuffy in there, a smell of damp and stale smoke, and the incessant hum of the air conditioning. It wouldn't be easy to sleep; they would have to get hold of some earplugs.

A long corridor cut the apartment in two. On the walls, sheets of paper and photographs from a previous case.

The face of a girl, young and beautiful.

From the glances the others were exchanging, Mila understood that the case hadn't ended well, and that they probably hadn't set foot in that place since then.

No one spoke, no one explained anything to her. Only Boris exploded, "Fucking hell, they could at least have taken her face off the walls!"

The rooms were furnished with old office furniture, from which wardrobes and sideboards had been fashioned with a great deal of imagination. In the kitchen, a desk acted as a dining table. The fridge was the old-fashioned kind that uses CFCs and damages the ozone layer. Someone had had the sense to unplug it and leave it open, but they hadn't freed from it the blackened remains of a Chinese meal. There was a common room, with a few sofas, a TV and a place for plugging in notebooks and peripherals. In one corner there was a coffee machine. Here and there, dirty ashtrays and all kinds of rubbish, especially cardboard cups from a fast-food restaurant. There was only one bathroom, small and malodorous. Next to the shower someone had put an old filing cabinet, on which lived half-empty bottles of liquid soap and shampoo, and a pack of five toilet rolls. Two closed rooms were reserved for interrogations.

At the end of the apartment was the guest accommodation. Three bunk beds and two camp beds against the wall. A chair for each bed, to put suitcases or personal effects on. They were all sleeping together. Mila waited for the others to take possession of the beds, imagining that each of them had had their own for some time. As the last to arrive, she would take the one that remained. In the end she opted for one of the camp beds. The furthest away from Rosa.

Boris had been the only one to take the top bed of one of the three bunks. "Stern snores," he warned her under his breath as he passed her. The amused tone and the smile with which he had accompanied this impertinent confidence made Mila think that perhaps his rage with her had subsided. Better that way: it would make it less difficult for them to live together. She had shared spaces with colleagues before, but in the end socializing with them had always been rather awkward. Even with members of her own sex. While a natural camaraderie had soon established itself among the others, she remained aloof, unable to close up the distance between them. At first it was very difficult for her. Then she had learned to create a "bubble of survival" around herself, a portion of space that sounds and noises, including the remarks of the people who stayed outside it, could only enter if she allowed it.

Goran's things were already arranged on the second camp bed in the guest accommodation. He was waiting for them in the main room. The one that Boris had, on his own initiative, christened the "Thinking Room."

They entered in silence and found him behind them, busy writing on the board: *familiar with reanimation techniques and protocols of intensive therapy: probable doctor*.

Stuck to the walls were the photographs of the five little girls, the snapshots of the graveyard of arms and Bermann's car, as well as copies of all the reports on the case. In a box placed in a corner, Mila recognized the face of the beautiful young girl: the criminologist must have taken those pictures down from the wall to replace them with the new ones.

In the middle of the room, five chairs arranged in a circle.

The *Thinking Room*.

Goran noticed the way Mila glanced at the sparse furniture and immediately explained: "It helps us to focus. We have to concentrate on what we've got. I've arranged everything according to a method that seemed right to me. But as I always say, if you don't like it you can change it. Put them wherever you want. In this room we're free to do whatever comes to mind. The chairs are a small concession, but coffee and the toilet will be a special reward, so we've got to deserve them."

"Perfect," said Mila. "What do we have to do?"

Goran clapped his hands once and pointed to the board where he had already started to jot down the characteristics of their serial murderer. "We have to understand Albert's personality. Each time we discover a new detail about him, we'll write it down here…Can you imagine what goes into the heads of serial killers, and try to think the way they do?"

"Yes, of course."

"Well, forget that; it's nonsense. You can't. Our man Albert has an intimate justification for what he does, perfectly structured in his psyche. It's a process constructed through years of experiences, of traumas or fantasies. That's why we mustn't try and imagine what he's going to do, but force ourselves to understand *how* he came to do what he's done. Hoping to get to him that way."

Mila thought that in any case the path of clues traced by the killer had been interrupted by the Bermann discovery.

"He's going to make us find another corpse."

"That's what I think too, Stern. But at the moment there's something missing, don't you think?"

"What?" asked Boris who, like the others, still didn't understand where the criminologist was taking things. But Goran Gavila wasn't a man for easy, direct answers. He preferred to reason with them up to a certain point and allow the rest to reconstruct itself.

"A serial killer moves in a world of symbols. He treads an esoteric path, begun many years before in the depths of his heart, and which he now pursues in the real world. The abducted children are only a way of reaching a destination, a goal."

"It's a search for happiness," said Mila.

Goran looked at her. "Exactly. Albert is looking for a kind of payment, a retribution not only for *what he does,* but above all for *what he is*. His nature suggests an impulse to him, and he's just following it. And with what he does he's also trying to communicate something to us..."

That was what was missing. A sign was missing. Something that would take them *beyond* the exploration of Albert's very personal world.

Sarah Rosa spoke: "There were no clues on the corpse of the first child."

"That's a reasonable observation," Goran agreed. "In the literature on serial killers—including the film versions—it's well-known that the serial killer always tends to "trace" his own journey, leaving investigators with some trails to follow...but Albert hasn't done that."

"Or else he has and we haven't noticed."

"Perhaps because we're not able to read the signs," Goran conceded. "We probably don't know enough yet. That's why the time has come to reconstruct the *stages*..."

There were five stages that criminologists used to mark out the action of serial murderers. The starting point is the assumption that the serial killer isn't born that way, but passively accumulates experiences while incubating the homicidal personality that will later flow into violence.

The first stage of this process is "fantasy."

"What is Albert's fantasy?" Stern asked as he slipped his umpteenth mint into his mouth. "What fascinates him?"

"It's the challenge that fascinates him," said Mila.

"Maybe he was, or felt he was, underestimated for a long time. Now he wants to demonstrate to us that he's better than the others…and better than us."

"But Albert has gone further: he's planned every move, predicting our reaction. He's in 'control.' That's what he's telling us: he knows himself very well, but he knows us well too," said Goran. "This phase is in the past."

The second stage is "organization" or "planning." When the fantasy matures, he moves on to an executive phase, which inevitably began with the choice of the victim.

"We already know that he doesn't choose the children, but the families. The parents are his real target, the ones who wanted only one child. He wants to punish them for their selfishness…The symbolism of the victim isn't apparent here. The girls are all different from one another, they're different ages, although not very far apart. Physically they don't have any features in common, like blond hair or freckles, for example."

"That's why he doesn't touch them," said Boris. "He's not interested in them in that way."

"Why girls, then, and not boys too?" Mila asked.

No one could answer the question. Goran nodded, pondering the detail.

"That's occurred to me, too. But the problem is that we don't know where his fantasy originated. The explanation is often much more banal than we can imagine. It could be because he was humiliated by a girl at school, who knows…It would be very interesting to know the answer. But there are no more clues, so we have to make do with what we've got."

Mila was still convinced that the criminologist was annoyed with her. It was as if he were somehow frustrated that she didn't know all the answers.

The third phase is "deception."

"How are the victims lured away? What trick does Albert use to abduct them?"

"Debby, out of school. Anneke, in the woods where she'd gone on her mountain bike."

"He took Sabine from a merry-go-round, from under everyone's noses," said Stern.

"Because everyone was looking only at their own children," added Rosa with a sharp edge to her voice. "People don't give a damn, that's the truth of it."

"At any rate he did it in front of lots of people. He's tremendously skillful, the bastard!"

Goran nodded to Stern to calm down; he didn't want his anger to take the upper hand.

"He abducted the first two in isolated places. They were a kind of dress rehearsal. When he became confident, he took Sabine."

"And with her he raised the level of the challenge."

"Let's not forget that no one was looking for him at that time: it was only with Sabine that the disappearances were linked and the fear began..."

"Yes, but the fact remains that Albert managed to take her in front of her parents. He made her disappear as if in a conjuring trick. And I'm not convinced, as Rosa says, that the people there didn't care...he tricked *those* people as well."

"Well done, Stern, that's what we've got to work on," said Goran. "How did Albert do that?"

"Got it: he's invisible!"

Boris's joke got a brief smile from the others. But for Gavila it contained a grain of truth.

"That tells us that he's like an ordinary man, that he has excellent camouflage qualities: he looked just like any other dad when he slipped Sabine off the merry-go-round horse to take her away. The whole thing taking what, four seconds?"

"He got away immediately, mingling with the crowd."

"And the girl didn't cry? She didn't protest?" Boris snorted with disbelief.

"Do you know lots of seven-year-olds who don't throw tantrums on merry-go-rounds?" asked Mila.

"Even if she cried, it looked like a perfectly normal scene to everyone there," said Goran, picking up the thread of the discussion. "Then Melissa came..."

"There was already a state of high alert. She had been given a curfew, but she wanted to go out anyway, to meet her friends at the bowling alley."

Stern got up from his chair and walked over to Melissa's smiling photograph on the wall. The picture had been taken from the school yearbook. Even though she was the oldest, her still immature physique had preserved its childhood features, and she was not very tall. Soon she would have crossed the threshold of puberty, her body would have revealed unexpected softnesses and the boys would finally have noticed her. For now, the caption beside the yearbook photograph only praised her gifts as an athlete and her involvement with the student newspaper as chief editor. Her dream was to become a reporter, and it would never come true.

"Albert was waiting for her. The bastard..."

Mila looked at him: the special agent seemed upset by his own words.

"But he abducted Caroline from her bed, in her house."

"All calculated..."

Goran walked over to the board, took a pen and began quickly jotting down some points.

"The first two he simply whisks away. The fact that dozens of children run away from home every day because they got a bad mark or argued with their parents works in his favor. So there's nothing to link the two disappearances...The third must clearly look like an abduction, so that the alarm bells ring... In the case of the fourth, he already knew that Melissa wouldn't have resisted the impulse to go and celebrate with her friends... And finally, for the fifth, he had spent a long time studying the places and habits of the family so that he could enter their house undisturbed... What do we deduce from that?"

"That he is using sophisticated forms of deception. Aimed less at the victims than their guardians: their parents, or the forces of law and order," said Mila. "You don't need stage directions to win the trust of little girls: you take them away by force, and that's it."

Mila remembered that Ted Bundy had worn a fake plaster to inspire trust in the students that he lured away. It was a way of seeming vulnerable in their eyes. He asked them to help him carry heavy objects and persuaded them into his VW Beetle. They all noticed too late that there was no handle on their side...

When Goran had finished writing, he announced the fourth stage. The "killing."

"There's a ritual in the bringing of death that the serial killer repeats every time. He can perfect it over time, but broadly it remains the same. It's his trademark. And every ritual is accompanied by a particular symbolism."

"For now we've got six arms and one corpse. He kills them by cleanly severing the limb, apart from the last one, as we know," added Sarah Rosa.

Boris picked up the pathologist's report. "Chang says he killed them all immediately after abducting them."

"Why such a hurry?" Stern wondered.

"Because he isn't interested in the girls, so there was no point in keeping them alive."

"He doesn't see them as human beings," Mila broke in. "For Albert they're just objects."

Even number six, they all thought. But no one had the courage to say so. It was plain that Albert didn't care whether she suffered or not. She just had to stay alive until he had achieved his goal.

The last stage is the "arrangement of the remains."

"First the graveyard of arms, then Albert puts a corpse in the boot of a pedophile's car. Is he sending us a message?"

Goran looked quizzically at the others.

"He's telling us that he isn't like Alexander Bermann," said Sarah Rosa. "In fact, he might be trying to suggest to us that he was a victim of abuse when he was young. It's as if he was saying, 'Look, I'm the way I am because someone turned me into a monster!'"

Stern shook his head. "He enjoys challenging us, giving us a show. But today the first pages of the newspapers deal only with Bermann. I doubt that he wants to share the glory with anyone else. He didn't choose a pedophile for revenge, he must have had other motives..."

"There's another thing that I find curious..." Goran was recalling the autopsy he had witnessed. "He washed and rearranged Debby Gordon's body, dressing her in her own clothes."

He made her pretty for Bermann, thought Mila.

"We don't know whether he did this with all of them, and whether it has become part of his ritual. But it's strange..."

The strangeness to which Dr. Gavila was referring—and Mila, even though she wasn't an expert, knew this very well—was that serial killers often take something away from their victims. A fetish, or a souvenir, to relive the experience in private.

Owning the object is the equivalent, for them, of owning the person.

"He didn't take anything from Debby Gordon."

As soon as Goran had uttered the words, Mila suddenly remembered the key dangling from Debby's bracelet, which opened the tin box.

"That son of a bitch..." she exclaimed, almost without noticing. Once again, she was suddenly the center of attention.

"Do you want to tell us as well?"

Mila looked up at Goran. "When I was in Debby's room at the boarding school, I found a tin box hidden under her mattress: I thought her diary would be in it, but it wasn't."

"So?" Rosa asked smugly.

"The box was closed with a padlock. The key was on Debby's wrist, so it was natural to think that if only she could open it, the diary didn't really exist...but I was wrong: the diary should have been there."

Boris leapt to his feet. "It *was* there! The bastard went to the girl's room!"

"Why would he have taken such a risk?" objected Sarah Rosa, who didn't want to say Mila was right.

"Because he always takes risks. It excites him," Goran explained.

"But there's another reason too," added Mila, feeling more and more confident about her theory. "I noticed that some photographs had disappeared from the walls: they probably showed Debby with child number six. He wants to keep us from finding out who she is at all costs!"

"That's why he took the diary away too...and he closed the box with the padlock again...Why?" Stern was troubled.

But for Boris it was all clear. "Don't you get it? The diary has disappeared but the box is locked, and the key is still on Debby's wrist...He's telling us: 'Only I could have taken it.'"

"Why does he want us to know?"

"Because he has left us with something...something for us!"

The "sign" that they were looking for.

Once again the Thinking Room had borne fruit.

The criminologist turned to Mila: "You've been there, you've seen what there was in that room..."

She tried to concentrate, but she couldn't think of anything that rang a bell.

"But there must be something!" Goran pressed her. "We're right about this."

"I looked in every corner of that room and nothing attracted my attention."

"It must be something obvious, you can't have missed it!"

But Mila shook her head. Stern decided they would all go back to the place for a more accurate examination. Boris picked up the phone to tell the boarding school they were on their way, while Sarah Rosa instructed Krepp to join them as soon as possible to take prints.

It was at that moment that Mila had her little epiphany.

"That's why I didn't see it," she announced, finding all the confidence that she seemed to have lost a little while before. "Whatever it is, it isn't in that room anymore."

When they got to the school, Debby's classmates were gathered in the hall that was normally used for assemblies and the official award of diplomas. The walls were covered with carved mahogany. The severe faces of the teachers who had made the school illustrious over the years looked down on the scene from their gilded frames, their expressions frozen in the portraits that imprisoned them.

It was Mila who spoke. She tried to be as nice as she could because the girls were already scared enough. The headmistress had assured them all of complete impunity. And yet, from the fear that flickered across their faces, it was clear that they didn't much trust her promise.

"We know that some of you visited Debby's room after her death. I'm sure you did it mostly because you wanted to own a memory of your friend who died so tragically."

As she said it, Mila met the eyes of the student she had surprised in the bathroom with her hands full of things. If that hadn't happened, it would never have occurred to her to do what she was doing.

Sarah Rosa watched her from a corner of the room, certain that she wouldn't get anything. But both Boris and Stern trusted her. Goran merely waited.

"I'd really rather not ask, but I know how fond you were of Debby. So I need you to bring those things to me here, now."

Mila tried to be firm about her request.

"Please don't forget anything, even the most insignificant object could turn out to be useful. We're sure that among those things there's a clue that our investigations have missed. I'm sure that each of you wants Debby's murderer to be caught. And since I also know that none of you would risk being charged with removing evidence, I trust that you will do your duty."

Mila had used that last threat, which was impossible given the young age of the girls, to stress the gravity of their actions. And also to give a small revenge to Debby, so little valued in life, but suddenly the focus of so much attention after her death just because of some ruthless looting.

Mila waited, gauging the length of the pause to give each of them the chance to think. Silence would be her best instrument of persuasion, and she knew they felt more awkward with each passing second. She noticed some girls swapping glances. None of them wanted to be the first, which was normal. Then a couple of them agreed with a gesture to leave the ranks, which they did almost simultaneously. Another five did the same. The rest remained motionless in their places.

Mila let another minute pass, studying the girls' faces in search of an individualistic vulture who might have gone against the herd. No luck. She hoped the seven who had left were the ones responsible.

"Fine, the rest of you can go."

The girls took their leave without delay, and ran off. Mila turned towards her colleagues and met Goran's impassive eye. But suddenly he did something that caught her off guard: he winked. She wanted to smile at him, but she didn't, because all eyes were fixed on her.

After about quarter of an hour, the seven girls came back to the hall. Each one brought several objects. They laid them down on the long table where the cloaked teachers usually sat during ceremonies. Then they waited for Mila and the others to examine the items.

Most of them were clothes and accessories, childish objects like dolls and cuddly toys. There was a pink MP3 player, a pair of sunglasses, some perfume, some bath salts, a makeup bag shaped like a ladybird, Debby's red hat and a video game.

"I didn't break it…"

Mila looked up at the chubby girl who had spoken. She was the youngest of them all, she couldn't have been more than eight. She had long blond hair in a plait and sky-blue eyes barely holding back tears. The policewoman smiled to comfort her, then looked more closely at the console. Then she took it and passed it to Boris.

"What is it?"

He turned it around in his hands.

"It doesn't look like a video game…"

He turned it on.

A red light started flashing on the screen, making a brief sound at regular intervals.

"I told you it was broken. The game doesn't do anything," the chubby girl hurried to explain.

Mila noticed that Boris had suddenly turned white.

"I know what this is... fuck."

Hearing Boris's swear word the chubby girl opened her eyes wide, incredulous and amused that someone could have desecrated that austere place.

But Boris didn't even notice her, he was so intent on the working of the object in his hands.

"It's a GPS receiver. Somewhere, someone is sending us a signal..."

13.

The appeal to the family of the sixth little girl wasn't bearing any fruit.

Most of the calls were from people expressing their sympathy and, in fact, merely blocking the lines. An anxious grandmother of five grandchildren had called seven times asking for "news of the poor little girl." When the umpteenth call came in, one of the officers on duty asked her as politely as possible not to call back and, by way of reply, had been told to go to hell.

"If you try and tell them they're not being helpful, they tell you you're insensitive," Goran observed when Stern told him what was happening.

They were in the mobile unit, tracing the GPS signal.

In front of them, the armored vehicles of the special unit, who were in the driver's seat this time—as Roche had colorfully put it a little while earlier.

They still didn't know where Albert was taking them. It could have been a trap. But Goran was of an entirely different opinion.

"He wants to show us something. Something he's plainly very proud of."

The GPS signal had been narrowed down to a vast area of several square kilometers. At that distance you couldn't identify the transmitter. They would have to go there in person.

The tension in the mobile unit was palpable. Goran swapped a few words with Stern. Boris took out his gun to check its efficiency, then checked again that his bulletproof jacket fitted closely to his ribs. Mila looked out the window at the area close to the motorway junction, a tangle of bridges and tarmac tongues.

The GPS receiver had been given to the captain of the special unit, but on her computer screen Sarah Rosa was able to follow what their colleagues in the car ahead were seeing.

A voice announced via radio: "We're getting close to it. The signal seems to be coming from a point a kilometer ahead of us. Over."

They all leaned in to look.

"What kind of place is this?" Rosa wondered.

In the distance Mila saw a massive red brick building, made up of several interconnecting blocks arranged in the form of a cross. The style was the reinvented gothic of the 1930s, grim and severe, typical of the church-run buildings of the period. A bell tower emerged from one of the sides. Beside it, a church.

The armored vehicles drove in single file down the beaten-earth drive leading to the central body. Reaching the area in front of it, the men prepared to break into the building.

Mila got out with the others and looked up at the imposing facade, blackened by time. Above the door were some words in bas-relief. *Visitare Pupillos In Tribulatione Eorum Et Immaculatum Se Custodire Ab Hoc Saeculo.*

"Help the orphans in their tribulation and remain uncontaminated by this world," Goran translated for her.

It had once been an orphanage. Now it was closed.

The captain nodded and the operative units split up, entering the building by the side doors.

They waited for about a minute, then Mila and the others entered by the main door, along with the captain.

The first room was huge. Ahead of them were two interlinking stairways leading to the upper floors. A high window filtered a foggy light. The only owners of the place now were a few doves which, frightened by the alien presence, stirred and flapped their wings around the skylight, casting fleeting shadows on the ground. The building echoed with the noise of the boots of the men from the special units inspecting room after room.

"Empty!" they called each time a room was secured.

Taking in the unreal atmosphere, Mila looked round. Once again a boarding school was part of Albert's plan. But very different from Debby Gordon's exclusive institution.

"An orphanage. Here at least they had a home and a guaranteed education," Stern remarked.

But Boris explained: "This is where they sent the ones who would never be adopted: the children of prisoners, and the orphans of parents who had killed themselves."

They were all waiting for a revelation. Anything to break the spell of horror would have been welcome. As long as it finally revealed the reason that had brought them all there. The echo of the footsteps suddenly stopped. After a few seconds, a voice broke through on the radio.

"Sir, there's something here..."

The GPS transmitter was in the basement. Mila found herself running in that direction with the others, through the school kitchens with their big iron cauldrons, then a vast refectory, with chairs and tables covered with blue Formica. She went down a narrow spiral staircase until she found herself in a wide, low-ceilinged room whose light came from a row of air vents. The floor was made of marble and sloped towards a central corridor where the drains appeared. The huge basins along the wall were also made of marble.

"This must have been the laundry," said Stern.

The men from the special units had thrown up a cordon around the basins, keeping a good distance away so as not to contaminate the scene. One of them slipped off his helmet and knelt down to vomit. No one wanted to look.

Boris was the first to break through the barrier, and he stopped sharply, bringing a hand to his mouth. Sarah Rosa looked away. Stern said only, "May God forgive us..."

Dr. Gavila remained impassive. Then it was Mila's turn.

Anneke.

The body lay in a few centimeters of murky liquid.

Her complexion was waxy and already showed the first signs of post-mortem decay. And she was naked. In her right hand she gripped the GPS transmitter, still pulsing, an absurd ray of light in that square of death.

Anneke's left arm had been severed as well, and its absence dislocated the posture of the torso. But it wasn't that detail that disturbed them all, or the state of preservation of the corpse, or the fact of being confronted by the display of an innocent obscenity. The reaction had been provoked by something quite different.

The corpse was smiling.

14.

His name was Father Timothy. He looked about thirty-five. Soft, blond hair, parted at the side. And he was shivering.

He was the place's sole inhabitant.

He lived in the priest's house next to the little church: the only buildings in the vast complex that were still used. The rest had been abandoned years before.

"I'm here because the church is still consecrated," the young priest explained. Even though Father Timothy now served mass exclusively for himself. "No one comes here. The edge of town is too far away, and the motorway has completely cut us off."

He had been there for just six months. He had taken the place of a certain Father Rolf when the priest had retired and, obviously, he knew nothing about what had happened in the institute.

"I never set foot in there," he admitted. "Why would I?"

Sarah Rosa and Mila had told him the reason for their raid. And what they had found there. When he had learned of the existence of Father Timothy, Goran had preferred to send the two of them to talk to him. Rosa pretended to take notes in a notebook, but it was obvious that she didn't care in the slightest what the priest had to say. Mila tried to reassure him by telling him that no one expected anything from him, and that he wasn't to blame for what had happened.

"That poor unfortunate child," the priest had exclaimed, before bursting into tears. He was devastated.

"When you feel you're ready, we'd like you to join us in the laundry," said Sarah Rosa, reigniting his dismay.

"Why?"

"Because we might need to ask you some questions about the location: this place is like a maze."

"But I just told you I've hardly ever been in there, and I don't think—"

Mila interrupted him: "It'll only take a few minutes, and we'll have removed the corpse."

She made sure that she reassured him on this point, because she had worked out that Father Timothy didn't want the image of the tortured body of a child to be imprinted on his memory. After all, he had to keep on living in that gloomy place.

"As you wish," he finally agreed, with a nod of his head.

He walked them to the door, repeating his promise to remain available.

Returning to the others, Rosa deliberately remained a few steps ahead of Mila, to stress the distance that existed between them. At any other time, Mila would have reacted to the provocation. But now she was part of a team and had to respect different rules if she wanted to take her work to its conclusion.

I'll sort you out afterwards, Mila brooded.

But as she was formulating that thought she realized she had taken it for granted that there would be an end. That in some way they would put the horror behind them.

It's part of human nature, she thought. You've got to carry on with your own life. The dead would be buried, and over time everything would be absorbed. All that remained would be a vague memory in their souls, the waste left by an inevitable process of self-preservation.

For everyone. But not for her, because that very evening would render that memory indelible.

* * *

It's possible to get lots of information from the scene of the crime, both about the dynamic of events and the personality of the murderer.

While in the case of the first corpse, Bermann's car couldn't be considered a proper crime scene, in the case of the second you could work out a lot about Albert.

In spite of Sarah Rosa's attempts to keep her out of the meeting, Mila had finally won a place in that chain of energy—as she had christened the team's gathering after the finding of Debby's body—and now even Boris and Stern thought she was one of them.

Once they had dismissed the special forces officers, Goran and his men had taken over the laundry.

The scene had been frozen by halogen lights planted on four tripods and connected to a generator, since there was no electricity in the building.

They hadn't found anything yet. Dr. Chang was already at work on the corpse, however. He had brought a strange piece of equipment in a little case, consisting of test tubes, chemical reagents and a microscope. Right now he was taking a sample of the murky water in which the corpse was partially immersed. Soon Krepp would be coming too, for the prints.

They had about half an hour before leaving the field open to the scientists.

"Obviously we aren't looking at a primary crime scene," Goran began, meaning that this was a secondary scene because the death of the child had clearly happened elsewhere. In the case of serial killers, the place where the victims are found is much more important than the place where they were killed. Because, while the killing is always an act that the murderer reserves for himself, everything that comes afterwards becomes a way of sharing the experience. Through the corpse of the victim, the murderer establishes a kind of communication with the investigators.

From that point of view, Albert was certainly no slouch.

"We have to read the scene. Understand the message that it contains, and who it's meant for. Who'd like to start? I should remind you that no opinion will be rejected out of hand, so please feel free to say what's going through your mind."

No one wanted to go first. There were too many doubts piling up in their heads.

"Maybe our man spent his childhood in this institute. Maybe this is where his hatred, his rancor come from. We should look through the archives."

"Frankly, Mila, I don't think Albert is trying to give us information about himself."

"Why?"

"Because I don't think he wants to be caught…at least for now. After all, we've only found the second corpse."

"I could be wrong, but don't serial killers sometimes want to be caught by the police because they can't stop killing?"

"That's bollocks," said Sarah Rosa with her usual arrogance.

And Goran added: "It's true that often the ultimate aspiration of a serial killer is to be stopped. Not because he can't control himself, but because when he's captured he can finally come out into the open. Especially if he has a narcissistic personality, he wants to be recognized for the greatness of his work. And while his identity remains a mystery, he can't reach his goal."

Mila nodded, but she wasn't entirely convinced. Goran noticed, and turned to the others.

"Perhaps we should recapitulate how we're going to go about reconstructing the relationship that exists between the crime scene and the serial killer's organizational behavior."

This was a lesson for Mila's benefit. But she wasn't annoyed about it. It was a way of putting her on a par with the others. And from Boris and Stern's reaction, it seriously looked as if they didn't want her to be left behind.

It was the oldest of the officers who spoke. He did so without looking directly at Mila, not wanting to embarrass her.

"According to the state of the crime scene, we subdivide serial killers into two major categories: 'disorganized' and 'organized.'"

Boris continued: "A member of the first group is, as you might think, disorganized in all aspects of his own life. He is an individual who has failed in his human contacts. He is reclusive. His intelligence is lower than the average, he has a limited education and pursues a job that doesn't require any particular skill. He isn't sexually competent. From this point of view he has only had hasty and clumsy experiences."

Goran continued: "Usually he's a person who was severely disciplined in childhood. For that reason, many criminologists maintain that he tends to inflict the same amount of pain and suffering on his victims that he received as a child. For that reason, he hides a feeling of rage and hostility that isn't necessarily manifested externally to the people he normally consorts with."

"The disorganized serial killer doesn't plan: he acts spontaneously," said Rosa, who didn't like to be excluded.

And Goran clarified: "The lack of organization of the crime makes the killer anxious at the moment of its perpetration. For that reason he tends to act close to places familiar to him, places where he feels at ease. Anxiety and the fact that he doesn't travel far lead him to commit errors, for example leaving clues that often betray him."

"His victims, generally speaking, are just people who happen to be in the wrong place at the wrong time. And he kills because that is the only way he knows of having relationships with other people," Stern concluded.

"And how does the organized one behave?" asked Mila.

"Well, first of all he's very cunning," said Goran. "It can be extremely hard to identify him because of his perfect disguise: he looks like a normal, law-abiding individual. He has a high IQ. He is good at his work. He often occupies an important position within the community that he lives in. He didn't suffer any particular traumas in childhood. He has a family that loves him. He is sexually competent and has no problems getting on with the opposite sex. He just kills for pure pleasure."

This last assertion made Mila shiver. She was not the only one to be struck by these words because, for the first time, Chang took his eyes away from his microscope to look at them. Perhaps he too was wondering how a human being can derive satisfaction from the pain he inflicts on his fellow man.

"He's a predator. He selects his victims accurately, generally looking for them in places far from where he lives. He is astute and prudent. He is capable of predicting the development of the investigations into him, thus anticipating the movements of the investigators. That's why it's hard to catch him: he learns from experience. The organized killer tails, waits and kills. His actions can be planned out for days, or weeks. He chooses his victim with the greatest care. He observes them. He slips into their lives, collecting information and carefully recording their habits. He's constantly trying to find a contact, faking certain types of behavior or certain affinities to win their trust. To gain control over them, he prefers words to physical force. His work is one of *seduction*."

Mila turned to look at the spectacle of death that had been staged in the room. Then she said: "His crime scene will always be clean. Because his watchword is 'control.'"

Goran nodded. "You seem to have given us a portrait of Albert."

Boris and Stern smiled at her. Sarah Rosa carefully avoided her eye and pretended to look at her watch, snorting at this pointless waste of time.

"Gentlemen, ladies, we have some information…"

The silent member of that little assembly had spoken: Chang rose to his feet, holding a slide that he had just taken from the eye of his microscope.

"What is it, Chang?" Dr. Gavila asked impatiently.

But the legal examiner wanted to savor the moment. His eye burned with the light of a small triumph.

"When I saw the body, I wondered how it could have been submerged in those two inches of water…"

"We're in a laundry," said Boris, as if it was the most obvious thing in the world.

"Yes, but like the electrical system in this building, the water supply hasn't worked for years."

The revelation took them all by surprise. Especially Goran.

"So what's that liquid?"

"Brace yourself, doctor... it's *tears*."

15.

Man is the only being in nature capable of laughter or tears.

Mila knew that. What she didn't know, on the other hand, is that the human eye produces three types of tears. Basal tears, which continuously moisten and feed the eyeball. Reflex tears, which are produced when a foreign body enters the eye. And psychic tears, associated with pain or emotion. These have a different chemical composition. They contain very high percentages of manganese and a hormone, prolactin.

In the world of natural phenomena, every single thing can be reduced to a formula, but explaining why tears of pain are physiologically different from the others is practically impossible.

Mila's tears contained no prolactin.

That was her unmentionable secret.

She wasn't capable of suffering. Of feeling the *empathy* necessary to understand other people and thus not feel alone amidst the human race.

Had it always been that way? Or had something or someone eradicated that ability ?

She had noticed it when her father died. She was fourteen years old.

She was the one who had found him, one afternoon, lifeless on the sofa in the sitting room. He looked as if he was sleeping. At least that was how she told the story when people asked her why she didn't immediately call for help, instead staying by his side for almost an hour. The truth was that Mila had immediately understood that there was nothing to be done. But she was more startled by her inability to feel anything emotionally than she was by the actual death. Her father—the most important man in her life, the one who had taught her everything, her role model—would no longer be there. Forever. And yet her heart wasn't broken.

She had cried at the funeral. Not because the idea of the ineluctable had planted despair in her soul, but only because that was what was expected of a daughter. Those salt tears had been the result of an enormous effort.

"It's a block," she said. "Just a block. It's stress. I'm in shock. It must have happened to other people too." She tried everything. She tortured herself with memories at least to feel guilty. Nothing.

She couldn't explain it to herself. Then she closed herself away in an impenetrable silence, without letting anyone ask her about her state of mind. Her mother, too, after a few attempts, had resigned herself to being cut off from that very private elaboration of grief.

The world thought she was broken, destroyed. But Mila, closed away in her room, wondered why she felt only the desire to return to her normal life, burying the man in her heart as well.

With time, things didn't change. The pain of loss never came. There were other occasions to mourn. Her grandmother, a classmate, other relatives. In those cases too, Mila could feel nothing but a clean impulse to finish with death as quickly as possible.

Who could she tell? They would look on her as a heartless monster, unworthy of membership in the human race. Only her mother, on her deathbed, had for a moment seen the indifference in Mila's expression, and had slipped her hand from hers, as if she felt suddenly cold.

Once the occasion for mourning in her family had passed, it had become easier for her to simulate with strangers things that she did not feel. Having reached the age when we begin to need human contact, especially with the opposite sex, she had encountered a problem. "I can't start a relationship with a boy if I can't feel empathy for him," she told herself over and over again. Mila had started to define her problem after she had learned the dictionary definition of "empathy": "ability to project one's own emotions on a subject to identify with him."

It was then that she started consulting psychoanalysts. Some of them couldn't give her any answers, others told her that the therapy would be long and difficult, that they would have to do a fair amount of digging to find her "emotional roots" and work out where the flow of emotions had been interrupted.

They had all agreed on one thing: they had to remove the block.

She had been in analysis for years, without ever getting anything out of it. She had changed doctors frequently, and would have gone on to infinity if one—the most cynical, to whom she could never be grateful enough—had not clearly told her: "Grief doesn't exist. Like the whole range of other human emotions. It's just a matter of chemistry. Love is just a question of endorphins. With a syringe full of pentothal I can take away all emotional demands. We are all nothing but machines made of flesh."

Finally she had felt relieved. Not satisfied, but definitely relieved. She couldn't do anything about it: her body had gone into "protected" mode, as happens to certain electrical devices when there's a power surge and they have to preserve their own circuits. That doctor had also said that there are people who, at a given moment of their existence, feel a great deal of grief, too much, far more than a human being can bear in a lifetime. And at that point, either they stop living or they become desensitized to it.

Mila didn't know whether to see her desensitization as a piece of luck, but it was thanks to it that she had become what she was. A seeker of missing children. Healing the suffering of others compensated her for what she would never feel. So her curse had suddenly become her gift.

She saved them. She brought them home. They thanked her. She grew fond of some of them and they sought her out and asked her to tell their story.

"If you hadn't been there to think of me..." they said to her.

And she certainly couldn't reveal what that "thought" had consisted of, the same thought for each child she tried to find. She could feel anger for what had happened to them—as for child number six—but she never felt "compassion."

She had accepted her fate. But she also asked herself a question.

Would she ever be capable of loving someone?

Not knowing how to answer, Mila had emptied her mind and her heart long ago. She would never have love, a husband or a boyfriend, or children, or even an animal. Because the secret is to have nothing to lose. Nothing that anyone could take away. That was the only way she could enter the minds of the people she was searching for.

By creating around herself the same void as they had around them.

Until the day she had released a boy from the clutches of a pedophile who had abducted him just to have a bit of fun over the weekend. He was going to free him after three days because, in his sick mind, he had "borrowed him." He didn't care about the state into which he had thrown the boy's family and his life. He justified himself by saying he would never have hurt him.

And what about everything else? What did he call the shock of the abduction? The imprisonment? The violence?

It wasn't a desperate attempt to find a legitimation, however feeble, for what he had done. He really believed it. Because he was unable to imagine his victim's feelings. In the end, Mila knew: the man was the same as her.

From that day onwards she had decided she would no longer allow her soul to deprive itself of the fundamental measure of others and life that was compassion. Even if she couldn't find it within herself, she would provoke it artificially.

Mila had lied to the team and to Dr. Gavila. In fact, she already had a very clear awareness of what serial killers were. Or at least one aspect of their behavior.

Sadism.

Almost always, at the bottom of a serial killer's behavior there were marked and deeply rooted sadistic components. Victims were seen as "objects" from whose suffering, from whose use, they could draw a personal advantage.

The serial killer manages to feel pleasure through the sadistic use of his victim.

Often the killer is unable to attain a mature and complete relationship with others, who are degraded from people to objects in his eyes. Violence then is his only contact with the rest of the world.

I don't want the same thing to happen to me, Mila had said to herself. The idea of having something in common with those murderers, who were incapable of pity, filled her with repulsion.

After the discovery of Anneke's corpse, as she was leaving Father Timothy's house with Rosa, Mila had promised herself that she would make what had happened to that child indelible in her memory. So at the end of the day, while the others were going back to the Studio to sum up what had happened and put the results of the investigation in order, she had taken her leave for a few hours.

Then, as she had done many times, she had gone to a chemist's. She had bought what she needed: disinfectant, plasters, cotton wool, a roll of sterile bandage, needles and surgical thread.

And a razor blade.

With a very clear idea in her mind, she had gone back to the motel, to her old room. She hadn't checked out, and was still paying for it with this very occasion in mind. She drew the curtains. She only left the light on beside one of the two beds. She sat down and emptied the contents of the little paper bag onto the mattress.

She slipped off her jeans.

After pouring a little disinfectant over her hands and rubbing it in, she soaked a wad of cotton wool in more of the same liquid and dabbed the skin of her inside right leg. Further up was the wound that had already healed, produced by her earlier clumsy attempt. But this time she wouldn't make a mess of it, she would do it properly. With her lips she pulled off the tissue paper around the razor. She held it tightly between her fingers. She closed her eyes and lowered her hand. She counted to three, then stroked the skin on the inside of her leg.

She felt the blade sliding into the living flesh, and running along it, creating a warm aperture.

The physical pain erupted with a silent roar. It rose up through her body from the wound. It reached its apex in her head, cleansing it of images of death.

"This is for you, Anneke," Mila said to the silence.

Then, at last, she wept.

A smile among the tears.

That was the symbolic image of the crime scene. Then there was the far from trifling detail that the body of the second child had been found naked in a laundry.

"Might the intention be to purify creation in a flood of tears?" Roche had wondered.

But Goran Gavila, as usual, didn't believe in those simplistic explanations. Until then, Albert's model murderer had proved too refined to lapse into such banality. He considered himself superior to the serial killers who had come before him.

At the Studio the weariness was already palpable. Mila had come back from the motel at about nine in the evening, with red eyes and a slight limp in her right leg. She had immediately gone to lie down in the guest accommodation and rest for a while, without unmaking the camp bed or even taking off her clothes. At about eleven she had been woken by Goran talking on his mobile in the corridor. She stayed motionless, pretending to be asleep. She guessed that the person at the other end wasn't his wife, but a nurse or perhaps a nanny. At one point he called her "Mrs. Runa." He asked her about Tommy—so that was the boy's name—whether he had eaten and finished his homework, and whether by any chance he had thrown any tantrums. Goran murmured a few times as Mrs. Runa brought him up to date. The conversation ended with the criminologist promising to pass by the house the following day, to see Tommy again at least for a few hours.

Mila, curled up with her back to the door, didn't move. But when Goran started talking again, she felt as if he had stopped on the threshold of the guest room, and that he was actually looking at her. She could see part of his shadow projected on the wall in front of her. What would happen if she turned round? Their eyes would meet in the gloom. Perhaps the initial embarrassment would make way for something else. A mute dialogue. But was that really what Mila really felt she needed? This man held a strange attraction for her. She couldn't say what the appeal was exactly. In the end she decided to turn round. But Goran wasn't there anymore.

A little while later she went back to sleep.

Mila... Mila...

Like a whisper, Boris's voice had slipped into a dream of black trees and endless roads. Mila opened her eyes and saw him beside her camp bed. He hadn't touched her to wake her up. He had only called her by name. But he was smiling.

"What time is it? Did I sleep too long?"

"No, it's six o'clock... I'm going out, Gavila wants me to interview some former inmates of the orphanage. I was wondering if you felt like coming with me..."

Boris's embarrassment told her that it hadn't been his idea.

"Fine, I'm coming."

The young man nodded, grateful that she'd spared him any further urging.

About a quarter of an hour later they met up in the car park outside the building. The car engine was already turned on and Boris was waiting for her outside it, leaning on the bodywork with a cigarette between his lips. He was wearing a worn parka that reached almost to his knees. Mila had on her usual leather jacket. When she was packing she hadn't predicted that it would be so cold in these parts. A timid sun peeping through the buildings had begun to warm the piles of dirty snow in the corners of the street, but it wouldn't last much longer: a storm was predicted for that afternoon.

"You should cover yourself up a bit, you know that?" said Boris, glancing anxiously at her clothes. "It freezes here at this time of year."

The inside of the car was warm and welcoming. A plastic cup and a paper bag rested on the dashboard.

"Warm croissants and coffee?"

"And all for you!" he replied, having remembered how greedy she was.

It was a peace offering. Mila accepted it without comment. With her mouth full she asked, "Where are we going exactly?"

"I told you: we have to listen to some of the people who used to live at the institute. Gavila is convinced that the arrangement of the corpse in the laundry wasn't just a spectacle meant for us."

"Perhaps he's calling up something from the past."

"The distant past, if he is. Places like this stopped existing almost twenty-eight years ago. Since they changed the law, abolishing orphanages once and for all."

There was something pained in Boris's tone, which he immediately voiced: "I was in a place like that, did you know that? I was about ten. I never knew my father, and my mother couldn't bring me up on her own. So they parked me there for a bit."

Mila didn't know what to say, startled as she was by such a personal revelation. Boris guessed.

"You don't have to say anything, don't worry. In fact, I don't even know why I told you."

"Sorry, but I'm not a very expansive person. Many people think I'm cold."

"Not me."

Boris was looking at the road. The traffic was going slowly because of the ice that still covered the tarmac. The exhaust fumes hung in the middle of the air. The people on the footpaths walked quickly.

"Stern—may God always keep him the way he is—managed to track down a dozen ex-inmates of the institute. We'll be dealing with half of those. He and Rosa will be looking after the others."

"Only twelve?"

"In the area. I don't know exactly what the doctor has in mind, but if he thinks we can get anything out of it…"

That morning they interviewed four of the former orphanage boys. They were all over twenty-eight, with more or less the same criminal pedigrees. Orphanage, reform school, jail, conditional release, jail again, probation. Only one of them had managed to wash his hands of it all thanks to his church: he had become pastor of one of the many Protestant communities in the area. Two others lived on handouts. The fourth was under house arrest for dealing. But when each of them spoke of their time in the institution, Mila and Boris noted a sudden agitation. They were people who had gone on to know prison, real prison, and yet they would never forget that place.

"Did you see their faces?" Mila asked her colleague after the fourth visit. "Do you think something bad happened in that place?"

"It was no different from others like it, believe me. But I think it's something connected to his childhood. As you grow up, experiences slide off you, even the worst ones. But when you're that age memories really imprint themselves on your flesh and don't go away."

Every time they told—with all due care—the story of finding the corpse in the laundry, the interviewees merely shook their heads. That obscure symbolism meant nothing to them.

At around midday, Mila and Boris stopped at a café where they quickly had some tuna sandwiches and a couple of cappuccinos.

The sky was heavy now. The weathermen hadn't been mistaken: soon it would start snowing again.

They still had another two orphans to meet before the weather got too bad and stopped them from going back. They decided to start with the one who lived furthest away.

"His name's Feldher. He lives about thirty kilometers away."

Boris was in a good mood. Mila would have liked to take advantage of that to ask him more about Goran. He aroused her curiosity: it didn't seem possible that he had a private life, a partner, a child. His wife, in particular, was a mystery. Especially after the phone call that Mila had caught the previous evening. Where was the woman? Why wasn't she at home looking after little Tommy? Because "Mrs. Runa" was there instead? Maybe Boris could answer her questions. But in the end, not knowing how to introduce the subject, Mila gave up.

When they got to Feldher's house it was almost two in the afternoon. They had tried to call ahead to say they were coming, but the recorded voice of a telephone company had told them the number was no longer available.

"It looks like our friend isn't doing very well," Boris had remarked.

Seeing where he lived confirmed this. The house—if you could call it that—was in the middle of a field of rubble, surrounded by the carcasses of automobiles. A red-haired dog, which seemed to be rusting slowly like everything else, welcomed them with raucous barking. Soon afterward a man of about forty appeared in the doorway. He was wearing only a filthy T-shirt and jeans, in spite of the cold.

"Are you Mr. Feldher?"

"Yes... who are you?"

Boris just raised his hand with his card: "Can we talk to you?"

Feldher didn't seem too pleased by their visit, but he beckoned them in.

He had a huge belly and his fingers were yellowed with nicotine. The interior of the house looked like him: filthy and chaotic. He served cold tea in unmatched glasses, lit a cigarette and went and sat down on a creaking deck chair, leaving the sofa to them.

"You were lucky to find me. Usually I'm working..."

"Why not today?" asked Mila.

The man looked outside: "The snow. No one takes on laborers in weather like this. And I'm losing a whole load of days."

Mila and Boris held the tea in their hands, but neither of them drank. Feldher didn't seem to take offense.

"So why don't you try to change your job?" Mila ventured, to pretend an interest and establish contact.

Feldher snorted. "I've tried! Do you think I haven't tried? But that went all to hell too, like my marriage. That whore was after something better. She told me every damned day that I was worthless. Now she's a two-bit waitress and shares an apartment with two tramps like herself. I've seen it. It's managed by the church she's joined. They told her even a good-for-nothing like her has a place in heaven! What do you think of that?"

Mila remembered that they had passed at least a dozen of those new churches along the road. They all displayed big neon signs showing the name of the congregation and also the slogan that summed them up. For a few years they had been proliferating around here, welcoming converts among those laid off by the big factories, single mothers and people disillusioned by traditional faiths. Even though the various denominations liked to seem different from one another, what they had in common was their unconditional adherence to creationist theories, homophobia, opposition to abortion, the affirmation of the principle according to which each individual has the right to bear arms and complete support for the death penalty.

It would be impossible to know how Feldher would react, Mila thought, if she had told him that one of his fellow inmates at the institute had become a pastor in one of those churches.

"When you arrived I mistook you for two of them: they come here to preach their gospel. Last month that whore I used to be with sent a couple of them here to convert me!" He laughed, showing two rows of rotten teeth.

Mila tried to move away from the conjugal theme and asked casually, "What did you do before your laboring jobs, Mr. Feldher?"

"You won't believe it..." The man smiled, glancing at the filth that surrounded him. "I'd set up a little laundry."

The two officers tried not to look at each other so as not to show Feldher how interesting this statement was. Mila couldn't help noticing that Boris let his hand slide to his hip, revealing his holster and gun. She remembered that when they got to this place their mobiles had no signal. They didn't know much about this man, and they had to be careful.

"Have you ever been in jail, Mr. Feldher?"

"Only for small misdemeanors, nothing that would keep an honest man awake at night."

Boris visibly made a mental note of that information. He stared at Feldher, making him uneasy.

"So what can I do for you, *officers?*" said the man, without concealing a certain irritation.

"As far as we can tell, you spent your childhood and much of your adolescence in an institution run by priests," Boris went on cautiously.

Feldher stared at him suspiciously: like the others, he wondered what the cops were leading up to. "The best years of my life," he said mischievously.

Boris told him what had brought them there. Feldher seemed pleased to have been told the facts before they were made public.

"I could make a lot of money telling the papers this stuff, couldn't I?" was his only comment.

Boris stared at him. "You try that and I'll arrest you."

The smile vanished from Feldher's face. The officer leaned towards him. It was an interrogation technique, Mila knew it too. People speaking to one another, unless bound by particular emotional or intimate relations, always tend to respect an invisible boundary. In this case, however, the interrogator was approaching the interrogatee in order to invade his personal space and make him feel uncomfortable.

"Mr. Feldher, I'm sure you think it's pretty funny to welcome the cops who come to see you, giving them tea you've probably pissed in, to enjoy their faces as they sit there like morons with glasses in their hands without having the courage to drink."

Feldher said nothing. Mila looked at Boris: she wondered if that had been a good move, given the situation. They would find out soon enough. The officer calmly set the tea down on the table and went back to staring the man in the eyes.

"Now I hope you'd like to tell us a bit about your stay in the orphanage..."

Feldher looked down, his voice a whisper: "You could say I was born there. I never knew my parents. They brought me there as soon as my mother spewed me out. I was given my name by Father Rolf, he said it belonged to someone he had known, who'd died young in the war. Maybe that crazy priest thought the name had brought lousy luck to the other guy, so it might bring good luck to me!"

The dog outside started barking again and Feldher broke off to shout at it: "Shut up, Koch!" Then he turned back to his guests. "I had more dogs many years ago. This place was a dumping ground. When I bought it, they assured me it had been drained. But every now and again stuff comes up: shit and various kinds of filth, especially when it rains. The dogs drink that stuff, their bellies swell up and after a few days they croak. Koch's the only one I have left, but I think he's on the way out, too."

Feldher was rambling. He didn't like going back with them to the places that had probably shaped his destiny. By talking about the dead dogs he was trying to negotiate with the officers so that they would leave him in peace. But they couldn't relax their hold.

Mila tried to be convincing when she said, "I'd like you to make an effort, Mr. Feldher."

"OK: shoot."

"I'd like you to tell us what you would connect with the image of 'a smile among the tears.'"

"It's like that stuff psychiatrists do, is that it? A kind of free association?"

"Something like that," she agreed.

Feldher started to think about it. He did it melodramatically, staring at the ceiling and with one hand scratching his chin. Maybe he wanted to give the impression of helping them, or maybe he had worked out that they couldn't charge him with "failure of memory," and he was just playing around with them. But then he said, "Billy Moore."

"Who was that, a friend of yours?"

"Oh, that kid was extraordinary! He was seven when he arrived. He was always cheerful, always smiling. He immediately became everyone's mascot…At that time they were about to shut the place down: there were only sixteen of us left."

"That whole institution for so few of you?"

"The priests had gone too. The only one left was Father Rolf…I was one of the oldest boys, I was fifteen, more or less…Billy's story was incredibly sad: his parents had hanged themselves. He had found the bodies. He hadn't screamed or gone for help: instead, he'd got up on a chair and, holding on to them, untied them from the ceiling."

"That kind of experience marks you for life."

"Not Billy. He was always happy. He adapted to the worst. As far as he was concerned everything was a game. We had never seen anything like it. For us, that place was a jail, but Billy paid us no attention. He had an energy, I don't know how to put it…he had two obsessions: those damned roller-skates that he used to ride up and down the empty corridors, and football. But he didn't like playing. He preferred to stand on the sidelines doing the radio commentary…'This is Billy Moore from the Aztec Stadium in Mexico City for the World Cup Final…' For his birthday we did a whip-round and bought him this tape recorder. It was amazing: he spent hours and hours recording stuff on that thing and listening to it over again!"

Feldher was going on a bit now; the conversation was derailing. Mila tried to bring it back on its original track. "Can you tell us something about the last few months at the institution?"

"As I've told you, they were about to close it and us boys had only two possibilities: either get adopted or end up in other institutions, like care homes. But we were grade B orphans, no one would take us. It was different for Billy, though: they were queuing up! Everyone immediately fell in love with him, they all wanted him."

"And how did that end up? Did Billy find a good family?"

"Billy died, miss."

He said it with such disappointment in his voice that it sounded as if the fate had been his own. And perhaps in a way it had been, as if the boy had represented a kind of ransom for the rest of his friends. The one who could have made it, in the end.

"How did it happen?" asked Boris.

"Meningitis."

The man sniffed, his eyes gleaming. He turned towards the window, because he didn't want these two strangers to see him so vulnerable. Mila was sure that once they had left, Billy's memory would go on floating around him like an old ghost in that house. But with his tears, Feldher had won their trust: Mila saw Boris taking his hand away from his holster. He was harmless.

"Billy was the only one who got meningitis. But being afraid of a pandemic they cleared us all out of that place in a flash…stroke of luck, eh?" He struggled to smile. "Well, they granted us a reprieve, they certainly did that. And the shithole was closed down six months earlier than predicted."

As they were getting up to leave, Boris asked again, "Did you ever see any of your classmates again?"

"No, but a few years ago I did run into Father Rolf again."

"He's retired now."

"I was kind of hoping he'd kicked the bucket."

"Why?" asked Mila, imagining the worst. "Did he hurt you?"

"Never. But when you spend your childhood in a place like that, you learn to hate what you remember because you're there."

A thought much the same as the one expressed by Boris, who found himself nodding involuntarily.

Feldher didn't walk them to the door. Instead he leaned over the table and picked up the glass of cold tea that Boris hadn't drunk. He brought it to his lips and drank it down in one go.

Then he stared at them again, defiantly: "Have a nice day."

An old group photograph—the boys who had lived in the orphanage just before it was closed—taken from what had once been Father Rolf's office.

Sixteen little boys posed around the old priest, only one smiling at the lens.

A smile among the tears.

Eyes bright, hair tousled, one incisor missing, a visible grease stain on his green pullover, displayed as if it were a badge of honor.

Billy Moore rested forever in that photograph and in the little graveyard next to the orphanage church. He wasn't the only child buried there, but his grave was the loveliest. With a stone angel spreading its wings in a protective gesture.

After listening to the story from Mila and Boris, Gavila asked Stern to get hold of all documents relating to Billy's death. The officer complied with his usual zeal, and when they were confronted with the papers they were immediately struck by a curious coincidence.

"In the case of potentially infectious diseases like meningitis, the health authorities must be informed. The doctor who received the report from Father Rolf is the same one who then drew up the death certificate. The two documents have the same date."

Goran tried to think this through: "The nearest hospital is twenty miles away. He probably didn't even take the trouble to check the identity."

"He trusted the priest's words," added Boris, "because priests don't usually tell lies..."

"Not always," thought Mila.

Gavila had no doubts on the matter: "We've got to exhume the corpse."

The snow had started falling in small, hard grains, as if to prepare the ground for the flakes that would come afterwards. Soon it would be evening, so they would have to get a move on.

Chang's gravediggers were at work and were using a little bulldozer to dig the frost-hardened ground. As the team waited, no one spoke.

Chief Inspector Roche had been informed about the developments and was staving off the press, which had suddenly whipped itself up into a state of great excitement. Maybe Feldher really had tried to speculate on what the two officers had told him without giving too much away. Besides, Roche always said, "What the media doesn't know, they make up."

So they had to get a move on before someone decided to fill that silence with some well-crafted nonsense. It would be hard to deny everything.

There was a dull thud. Finally, the bulldozer had touched something.

Chang's men climbed into the hole and started digging by hand. A plastic cloth covered the box to slow down its decomposition. It was cut away to reveal the lid of a small white coffin.

"It's all rotten here," said the medical examiner after a quick glance. "If we pull it up, we risk breaking everything. And this snow is messing everything up," added Chang, speaking to Goran, from whom he awaited the final decision.

"Fine… open it up."

No one had expected the criminologist to organize an exhumation on the spot. Chang's men stretched a tarpaulin over the hole, supporting it on poles like a big umbrella, to shelter the site.

The pathologist put on a waistcoat with a lamp on the back, then went down into the hole beneath the eyes of the stone angel. In front of him, a technician with an oxyhydrogen flame began to melt the zinc soldering of the coffin and the lid began to move.

How do you wake up a child who's been dead for eighteen years? Mila wondered. Billy Moore would probably have deserved a short ceremony, or a prayer. But no one had the desire or the time to do it.

When Chang opened the coffin, Billy's wretched remains appeared, still wearing what was left of a first communion suit. Smart, with a clip-on tie and trousers with turn-ups. In a corner of the casket were the rusted skates and an old tape recorder.

Mila remembered Feldher's story: *He had two obsessions: those damned roller-skates that he used to ride up and down the empty corridors, and football. But he didn't like playing. He preferred to stand on the sidelines doing the radio commentary.*

They were Billy's only belongings.

Chang slowly began to cut away parts of the fabric of the suit with a scalpel and, even in that awkward position, his movements were quick and precise. He checked the state of conservation of the skeleton. Then, turning to the rest of the team, he announced: "There are a number of fractures. I can't be one hundred percent certain about when they happened… but in my view this child definitely didn't die of meningitis."

16.

Sarah Rosa brought Father Timothy into the mobile unit's camper, where Goran was waiting for him with the others. The priest still looked anxious.

"We have a favor to ask you," Stern began. "We urgently need to talk to Father Rolf."

"I told you: he's retired. I don't know where he is now. When I got here six months ago I only met him for a few hours. Just long enough to do the handover. He explained a few things to me, he gave me a few documents and the keys and then he left."

Boris turned back to Stern. "Perhaps we ought to speak directly to the Curia. Do you happen to know where they send retired priests?"

"I've heard there's a kind of rest home."

"Could be, but..."

They turned back to look at Father Timothy.

"What?" asked Stern.

"I seem to remember that Father Rolf planned to go and live with his sister... Yes, he told me she was more or less the same age as him, and she'd never married."

The priest seemed pleased to have made a contribution to the investigation at last. And he had managed to offer the help he had previously denied.

"I'll talk to the Curia, if you like. Thinking about it, it shouldn't be too hard to find out where Father Rolf is. And I'll probably think of something else."

The young priest seemed calmer now.

Then Goran said, "It would be a great help to us, and we would avoid a lot of pointless publicity about what's happening here. I don't think the Curia would mind."

"I think you're right," Father Timothy agreed.

When the priest left the camper, Sarah Rosa turned back to Goran, visibly vexed.

"If we're all agreed that Billy's death wasn't an accident, why don't we put out a warrant for Father Rolf? He clearly has something to do with it!"

"Yes, but he wasn't responsible for the murder of the little boy."

Mila was struck by the word "murder," which Goran was uttering for the first time. Billy's fractures might be indications of a violent death, but there was no proof that anyone else had been involved.

"And how can you be so sure that the priest isn't guilty?" Rosa went on.

"Father Rolf only covered the thing up. He came up with the story of Billy's meningitis, so that no one would risk delving any deeper for fear of infection. And then the outside world did the rest: no one cared about those orphans, you can see that too, can't you?"

"And the orphanage was about to close anyway," Mila added.

"Father Rolf is the only one who knows the truth, that's why we have to question him. But I'm worried that if we put out a warrant…well, we still mightn't find him. He's old, and he might be determined to take this story to the grave."

"So, what do we do?" Boris was impatient. "Should we wait for the priest to get in touch?"

"Certainly not," replied the criminologist. Then he returned his attention to the plan of the orphanage that Stern had brought back from the local land registry office. He pointed out an area to Boris and Rosa.

"You have to go to the eastern pavilion. You see? The archive is there, with all the files on the boys who lived in the orphanage until it closed. Obviously we're only interested in the last sixteen children."

Goran handed them the group photograph with Billy Moore's smile. He turned it over: on the other side were the signatures of all the little boys in the picture.

"Compare the names: we need the one with the only missing file..."

Boris and Rosa looked at him, puzzled.

"How do you know there's one missing?"

"Because Billy Moore was killed by one of his schoolmates."

In the same group picture that showed Billy Moore smiling, Ronald Dermis was standing third from the left. He was eight. That meant he must have been the institution's mascot before Billy arrived.

For a child, jealousy can be reason enough for wishing someone dead.

When he left the orphanage with the others, the bureaucracy had lost track of him. Had he been adopted? Unlikely. He might have ended up in a care home. It was a mystery. Almost certainly, the hand of Father Rolf was behind that gap in information.

It was absolutely necessary to find the priest.

Father Timothy had assured them that the Curia was taking care of it: "His sister died, and he asked to be reduced to lay status." So he had left the priesthood. Perhaps it had been his sense of guilt for covering up a murder, perhaps it was the unbearable discovery that evil can be very well concealed even by the appearance of a child.

The team was troubled by this and other hypotheses.

"I still haven't worked out whether I should launch the manhunt of the century, or wait for you to deign to come up with some kind of reply!"

The plasterboard walls of Roche's office trembled at the sound of his voice. But the chief inspector's anxiety bounced off Goran's stubborn calm.

"They're chasing me for the story of the sixth child: they say we're not doing enough!"

"We won't find her until Albert decides to give us a clue. I've just had Krepp on the line, he says that crime scene's clean as well."

"At least tell me if you think Ronald Dermis and Albert are the same person!"

"We've already made the same mistake with Alexander Bermann. For the time being I wouldn't rush to hasty conclusions."

Roche wasn't used to taking advice about how to conduct his cases. But this time he accepted it.

"But we can't sit here waiting for that psychopath to take us wherever he wants to. We'll never save the girl that way! Especially given that she's still alive."

"There's only one person who can save her. And that's him."

"Do you really expect him to hand her over, just like that?"

"I'm just saying that at a certain point he might want to make a mistake himself."

"Damn it to hell! Do you think I can live on hope while those people out there just want me to look ridiculous? I need results, Dr. Gavila!"

Goran was used to Roche's temper tantrums. They weren't directed at him in particular. The chief inspector had them with the whole world. It was a side effect of the job: when you're too high up, there's always someone wanting to drag you down.

"I've taken a ton of crap over the last little while, and it wasn't all directed at me."

Goran knew how to be patient, but he was aware that that didn't always work with Roche. So he tried to take the initiative, to get him off his back.

"Do you want me to tell you one thing that's driving me mad?"

"Anything to get me out of this impasse, please."

"I haven't mentioned it till now... the tears."

"And?"

"There were at least five liters around the corpse of the second girl. However, tears are saline, that's why they tend to dry straightaway. But these didn't. I wondered why—"

"And why, if I may ask?"

"They're artificial: they precisely reproduce the chemical composition of human tears, but it's a trick. That's why they don't dry...do you know how tears are re-created artificially?"

"I have no idea."

"That's the point: Albert does. And he did it, he devoted some time to it. Do you know what that means?"

"You tell me."

Roche sat back in his armchair, staring into the void.

"What can we expect, in your view?"

"Frankly, I fear the worst is yet to come."

Mila went down into the basement of the Institute of Legal Medicine. She had acquired some figurines of famous footballers—or at least that was what they had told her when they had sold them to her. That little gesture was part of a farewell ritual. In the morgue, Chang had reassembled Billy Moore's corpse to bury it again beneath the stone angel.

The pathologist was completing the post-mortem, and had X-rayed the fractures. The boards were exposed on a light panel which Boris was standing next to. Mila wasn't surprised to find him there.

When he became aware of her, he felt the need to justify himself. "I came by to see if there was any news."

"And is there?" asked Mila, going along with his story so as not to make him feel embarrassed. Boris was clearly there for personal reasons.

Chang broke off his work to answer the question from Mila.

"The body had dropped a long way. From the seriousness and number of fractures that I have found on the skeleton, we may deduce that death was almost instantaneous."

That "almost" contained hope and, at the same time, anguish.

"Obviously no one can say whether Billy jumped, or whether he was pushed..."

"Obviously."

Mila noticed that on the chair there was a brochure for a company of funeral directors, certainly not a service supplied by the police. It must have been Boris's idea: paying his own money to ensure that Billy received a decent burial. On a shelf were Billy's skates, perfectly polished, and the tape recorder, a birthday present from which the boy was never separated.

"Maybe Chang has worked out where the death occurred," said Boris.

And the medical examiner walked towards some enlarged photographs of the boarding school.

"Bodies fall freely, and gain weight along with their velocity: it's an effect of the force of gravity. In the end it's as if you're being squashed against the ground by an invisible hand. So, if we combine the data concerning the age of the victim—readings of bone calcification—with those of the extent of the fractures, we can estimate the height from which the fall occurred. In this case, more than forty feet. Thus, taking into consideration the average elevation of the building and the inclination of the ground, we may assert with almost one hundred percent certainty that the child fell from the tower, at this point here...do you see?"

Another "almost" mixed in among Chang's words as he pointed to the exact spot in the photograph. At that moment an assistant appeared at the doorway.

"Dr. Vross, you're wanted..."

For a moment Mila couldn't connect the medical examiner with his real name. Plainly none of his subordinates dared to call him Chang.

"Excuse me," he said, leaving them on their own.

"I have to go too," said Mila, and Boris nodded.

As she left, she passed close to the shelf with Billy's skates and tape recorder on it, and set down the figurines she had bought. Boris noticed.

"His voice is on it..."

"What?" she asked, not understanding.

Boris nodded at the tape recorder, and repeated: "Billy's voice. His made-up news reports..."

He smiled. But it was a sad smile.

"Have you managed to listen to them?"

Boris nodded. "Yes, only the first bit, then I couldn't go any further..."

"I understand..." Mila said simply.

"The tape is almost perfectly preserved, do you know that? The acids produced by the"—he couldn't bring himself to say it—"decomposition process haven't damaged it. Chang says that's pretty rare. Maybe it depended on the nature of the ground he was buried in. There were no batteries, I put them in myself."

Mila pretended to be surprised, to ease Boris's tension. "So the tape recorder works."

"Of course it does. It's Japanese!"

They both laughed.

"Do you want to listen to the whole thing with me?"

Mila thought for a moment before replying. She didn't really want to. *There are things that should be allowed to rest in peace,* she thought. But in this case it was Boris who needed to listen, and she didn't want to tell him he couldn't.

"OK, then, turn it on."

Boris walked over to the tape recorder, pressed play and, in that cold morgue, Billy Moore came back to life.

"...We're in the legendary Wembley Stadium, sports listeners! The match is one that will go down in the history of the game: England v. Germany!"

He had a lively voice, with a sibilant "*s*" on which his sentences frequently stumbled. His words contained the sound of a smile, and Mila thought she could actually see Billy, young and carefree, trying to give the world some of his distinctive joy.

Mila and Boris smiled with him.

"The temperature is mild, and even though it's late autumn, no rain is forecast. The teams are already lined up in the center circle to hear the national anthems... The terraces are packed with fans! What a sight, ladies and gentlemen! We will shortly witness a great football clash! But first the list of players who will be taking part in today's—Oh my Lord, I am sorry and I repent with all my heart for my sins, because by sinning I have deserved your punishment, and much more because I have

offended you, who are infinitely good and worthy of love beyond all things."

Mila and Boris looked at one another uncomprehendingly. The voice that had been superimposed over the first recording was much feebler.

"It's a prayer."

"But that's not Billy…"

"…I propose with your holy assistance never to offend you again, and to shun all opportunities for sin. Lord of mercy, forgive me."

"That's fine."

A man's voice.

"What do you want to say to me?"

"I have said many bad words recently. And three days ago I stole some biscuits from the larder, but Jonathan ate them with me…And also…also I copied my maths homework."

"Nothing else?"

"That must be Father Rolf," said Mila.

"…"

"Think very carefully, Ron."

The name chilled the silence in the room. And Ronald Dermis, too, returned to his childhood.

"Actually…there is something…"

"And do you want to talk to me about it?"

"…No."

"If you don't talk to me, how can I give you absolution?"

"…I don't know."

"You know what happened to Billy, don't you, Ron?"

"God took him away."

"It wasn't God, Ron. You know who it was?"

"He fell. He fell from the tower."

"But you were with him…"

"…Yes."

"Whose idea was it to go up there?"

"…Someone had hidden his skates in the tower."

"Was it you?"

"...Yes."

"And did you push him as well?"

"..."

"No one will punish you if you tell us what happened. That is a promise."

"He told me to."

"Who's he? Billy? Did Billy ask you to push him?"

"No."

"So was it one of the other boys?"

"No."

"Who, then?"

"..."

"Ron."

"Yes."

"Come on, answer me. This person you're talking about doesn't exist, does he? He's just a figment of your imagination..."

"No."

"There's no one else here. Just me and your companions."

"He only comes for me."

"Listen to me, Ron: I want you to say you're very sorry for what happened to Billy."

"...I'm very sorry for what happened to Billy."

"I hope you mean that...At any rate, this will remain a secret between me, you and the Lord."

"OK."

"You mustn't speak of it to anyone else."

"OK."

"I absolve you of your sins. In the name of the Father, the Son and the Holy Ghost. Amen."

"Amen."

17.

We're looking for an individual by the name of Ronald Dermis," Roche announced to the packed audience, speaking into flashes and microphones. "He is about thirty-six years old. Brown hair, brown eyes, light complexion."

He showed an image based on the photograph in which he had posed with his companions, showing a hypothetical adult Ron. He held the image up as the flashes went off.

"We have reason to believe that this man was involved in the abduction of the missing girls. Anyone who knows him, who has any information about him or who has had contact with him over the last thirty years is requested to inform the police. Thank you."

The last word set off a chorus of questions and pleas from the journalists. "Mr. Roche!... Chief Inspector!... A question!..."

Roche ignored them, leaving the room by a back door.

It had been an inevitable move. They had to set alarm bells ringing.

Boris and Mila's discovery had been followed by two feverish hours. The situation was clear now.

Father Rolf had recorded Ron's confession on Billy's tape recorder. Then he had buried it with him, like someone planting a seed knowing that it will sooner or later bear fruit, in the hope that the truth would one day redeem everyone. The one who, in spite of his innocent years, had committed this terrible crime. The one who had been its victim. And the one who had taken the trouble to bury it under six feet of earth.

...At any rate, this will remain a secret between me, you and the Lord...

Goran said, "How did Albert know about all this? Father Rolf and Ron were the only ones who were aware of the secret. So the only possible explanation is that Ron and Albert are one and the same person."

Perhaps the decision to involve Alexander Bermann also needed to be read in that context. The criminologist couldn't remember who it was who had told him that their serial killer had chosen a pedophile because he had probably been abused as a child. Perhaps it had been Sarah Rosa. But Stern had immediately dismissed the hypothesis, and Gavila had agreed with him. Now he had to admit that he might have been wrong.

"The preferred victims of pedophiles are orphans and stray children, because they have no one to defend them."

Goran was angry with himself for not having reached that answer sooner. And yet he had all the pieces of the puzzle in front of his eyes from the start. Instead he had allowed himself to be seduced by the idea that Albert was a subtle strategist.

"Serial killers are telling us a story with what they do: the story of their inner conflict," he constantly repeated to his students.

So why had he been misled by a different hypothesis?

"He used my pride to trick me. I could only see that he was trying to challenge us. And I liked thinking we faced an adversary who was trying to be smarter than me."

After watching Roche's press conference on television, the criminologist had once again assembled the team in the laundry room at the orphanage, where Anneke's body had been found. It struck him as the most suitable place to relaunch the investigation. His brief *mea culpa* had served to dispel all doubts about the idea that they were still a team and not just a laboratory for Dr. Gavila's experiments.

The corpse of the second girl had been removed some time before, the marble basin had been drained of its tears. All that remained was the halogen lamps and the generator hum. Soon they would be taken away too.

Goran had requested the presence of Father Timothy. The priest arrived breathless and in a clear state of agitation: even though there was nothing in the room that recalled the crime scene, he still felt terribly ill at ease.

"There's no sign of Father Rolf," the young priest began. "And I really think that—"

"Father Rolf must be dead by now," Goran interrupted him curtly. "Otherwise we would have heard from him after Roche's appeal."

Father Timothy looked shocked. "So what can I do for you?"

Goran took a moment to choose his words. Then, turning towards everyone, he said, "It might seem unusual to you, I know...but I would like us to say a prayer."

Rosa couldn't conceal her astonishment. Nor could Boris, who immediately exchanged a glance with her. Mila was baffled. Not so Stern, who was very religious. He was the first to welcome Goran's suggestion. He placed himself at the center of the room and held his arms out by his side to take the hands of the others and form a circle. Mila was the next to approach. Rosa followed her unwillingly. Boris was the most reluctant, but he couldn't refuse Dr. Gavila's request. Father Timothy nodded, serene at last, before taking his place among them. Goran didn't know how to pray, and perhaps there weren't even any prayers appropriate to the occasion. But he tried anyway, in a sad voice.

"In recent times we have witnessed terrible things. What has happened here is unspeakable. I don't know if a God exists. But I have always wished it so. I know for certain that evil exists. Because evil can be *demonstrated*. Good can only be witnessed. But this isn't enough for us, who need concrete proof..." Goran paused. "If there were a God I would like to ask him...Why did Billy Moore have to die? Where did Ronald Dermis's hatred come from? What happened to him during those years? How did he learn to kill? What led him to choose evil? And why does He not put an end to all this horror?"

Goran's questions hung in the silence that surrounded them.

"When you wish, Father..." said the irreproachable Stern after a while.

And Father Timothy took control of the little gathering. He clasped his hands together and began to intone a sacred hymn. His voice—confident and beautiful—took possession of the echoing space, and began to swirl around it. Mila closed her eyes and allowed herself to be transported by his words. They were in Latin, but their meaning would have been obvious even to the deafest of men. With that chant, Father Timothy was bringing peace to where there had been chaos, cleansing everything of the defilement of evil.

The letter was addressed to the Department of Behavioral Sciences. It would have been classified as the work of a pathological liar had the handwriting not shown some similarities with a piece of homework that Ronald Dermis had done as a child.

It had been written on the page of an exercise book, with a perfectly normal ballpoint pen. The sender hadn't worried about leaving fingerprints on the page.

Apparently Albert had no need of contrivances.

for those who are hunting me billy was a bastard. a BASTARD! and i was right to kill him i hated him he would have hurt us because he would have had a family and we wouldn't what was done to me was worse and NOBODY came to save me NOBODY. i have always been here in front of your eyes and you didn't see me then HE came. HE understood me. HE taught me it was you who wanted me like this you didn't see me now do you see me? worse for you in the end it will all be your fault i am what i am. NOBODY can prevent all this NOBODY.

RONALD

Goran had made a copy of the letter so that he could study it more closely. He would spend that night at home, with Tommy. He really wanted an evening with his son. There were days when he didn't see him at all.

He stepped into the apartment and immediately heard him coming.

"How was it, Dad?"

Goran grabbed him and pulled him up in a hearty hug.

"I can't complain. What about you?"

"I'm fine."

They were magic words. His son had learned to use them when the two of them had been left alone. As if to say that Goran had no reason to worry, because he was "fine." He didn't miss Mum. They were learning not to miss her.

But that was also as far as it went. The subject was closed with those simple words. Everything was reconciled. *There, we've remembered how much it hurts to be without her. Now we can get on with our lives.*

And that was what happened.

Goran had brought a bag that Tommy impatiently explored.

"Oh wow! Chinese food!"

"I thought you might like to vary Signora Runa's menu a bit."

Tommy pulled a disgusted face. "I hate her meatballs! She puts too much mint in them, they taste of toothpaste!"

Goran laughed: the boy was actually right.

"OK, off you go and wash your hands."

Tommy ran to the bathroom. When he came back he started to get things ready. Goran had moved lots of the kitchen equipment down from shelves higher than the boy could reach: he wanted to make him feel he was part of their new family arrangement. Doing things together meant that they now had to look after one another, so neither of them could give up. Neither of them was allowed to yield to sadness.

Tommy picked up a plate, on which he put the fried wontons and sweet and sour sauce, while his father poured Cantonese rice into two bowls. They also had chopsticks and, instead of fried ice-cream Goran had bought a tub of chocolate and vanilla.

As they had their dinner they talked about the day. Tommy told him how his plans for summer camp were going. Goran asked him about school and was proud to discover that his son had got outstanding marks in gymnastics.

"I was lousy at almost all sports," Goran admitted.

"Which one were you good at?"

"Chess."

"Chess isn't a sport!"

"What do you mean? They play it in the Olympics, don't they?"

Tommy didn't seem entirely convinced. But he had learned that his father never told lies. That had been a hard lesson, in fact. Because the first time he had asked him about his mother, Goran had told him the whole truth. No beating around the bush. "No funny business," as Tommy always said when claiming someone's loyalty. And his father had immediately agreed. Not out of revenge or to punish his mother. Lies—or, worse, half-truths—would only have increased the boy's anxiety. He would have found himself on his own, facing big lies: the lie of his mother who had left, and his father who didn't have the courage to tell him.

"Will you teach me to play chess one day?"

"Of course."

With that solemn promise, Goran put him to bed. Then he went and closed himself away in his study. He picked up Ronald's letter and read it for the umpteenth time. One thing had struck him about the text since he first read it. The phrase: *then HE came. HE understood me. HE taught me.*

The word "HE" had been deliberately written in capitals. Goran had heard that strange reference once before. It was on the tape of Ronald's confession to Father Rolf.

He comes only for me.

It was a clear example of personality dissociation, in which the negative *I* is always separated from the acting *I*. And becomes *He*.

"It was ME. But HE told me to do it. It's HIS fault I'm what I am."

In that context, everyone else became "NOBODY." That too written in capitals.

NOBODY came to save me. NOBODY can prevent all this.

Ron wanted to be saved. But everyone had forgotten him and the fact that he was, in the end, only a child.

She had gone out to get something to eat. And after wandering pointlessly among shops and restaurants that had closed early because of the weather, Mila had had to settle for some ready-made soup from a grocery store. She thought she would heat it up in the microwave she had noticed in the Studio kitchen. But she had remembered too late that she wasn't even sure it worked.

She went back to the apartment before the searing cold of the evening paralyzed her muscles, keeping her from walking. She wished she had her tracksuit and jogging shoes there: she spent whole days not moving much and the lactic acid building up around her joints made moving more difficult.

As she prepared to climb the stairs, she saw Sarah Rosa on the pavement outside, in animated conversation with a man. He was trying to calm her down, but without apparent success. Mila thought it must be her husband, and felt a great deal of sympathy for him. Before the harpy could spot her and thus have one more reason to hate her, Mila entered the building.

On the stairs she bumped into Boris and Stern who were coming down.

"Where are you going?"

"We're calling in at the Department to check how the manhunt's going," Boris replied, putting a cigarette in his mouth. "Want to come?"

"No, thanks."

Boris noticed the soup. "Then *bon appétit.*"

Mila continued on her way upstairs, and heard him addressing his older colleague. "You should take up smoking again."

"You'd be better off taking up these..."

Mila recognized the sound of Stern's box of mints, and smiled.

She was alone in the Studio now. Goran was going to spend the evening at home with his son. She was slightly disappointed. She had got used to him being there, and found his investigative methods interesting.

Apart from the daily prayer. If her mother had been alive and had seen her taking part in that ritual, she wouldn't have believed her eyes.

The microwave worked. And the soup wasn't too bad. Or perhaps it was her hunger that made it seem better than it was. With the bowl and a spoon, Mila went and sat in the guest accommodation, happy to have a bit of time for herself.

She sat down cross-legged on the camp bed. The wound on her left thigh felt a bit tight, but it was getting better. *Everything always gets better,* she thought. Between one mouthful and another, she took a photocopy of Dermis's letter and put it in front of her. She studied it as she went on eating. Of course Ronald had chosen a very strange moment to reappear in this business. But there was something about his words that wasn't quite in tune. Mila hadn't had the courage to talk to Goran about it, because she didn't think he could offer any advice. But the idea had tormented her all afternoon.

The letter had also been made available to the press, quite unusually. Clearly, Gavila had decided to stroke their serial killer's ego. It was as if he were saying, "You see? We're paying attention to you!" when in fact he only wanted to distract him from the little girl he was keeping prisoner.

"I don't know how long he'll be able to resist the impulse to kill her," he had said a few hours before.

Mila tried to banish that thought from her mind, and focused on the letter once again. She was irritated by Ronald's chosen form for the missive. That was what she found discordant. She couldn't have said why, but the text centered on the page, in a kind of single unbroken line, prevented her from fully grasping its contents.

She decided to break it down. She set down the bowl and picked up a notebook and pencil.

for those who are hunting me:

–billy was a bastard a BASTARD! and i was right to kill him. i hated him. he would have hurt us. because he would have had a family and we wouldn't.

–what was done to me was worse! and NOBODY came to save me! NOBODY.

–i have always been here in front of your eyes and you didn't see me

–then HE came. HE understood me. HE taught me

–it was you who wanted me like this you didn't see me now do you see me? worse for you in the end it will all be your fault

–i am what i am. NOBODY can prevent all this NOBODY.

–RONALD

Mila reread the sentences, one at a time. It was a rant, full of hatred and rancor. It was aimed at everyone, without distinction. Because Billy, in his murderer's mind, represented something big and all-absorbing. Something that Ron would never be able to have.

Happiness.

Billy was cheerful, even though he had witnessed his parents' suicide. Billy would have been adopted, even though he was a grade B orphan. Billy was loved by everyone, even though he had nothing to offer in return.

By killing him, Ronald would erase his smile forever from the hypocritical face of the world.

But the more she reread those words, the more Mila realized that the sentences in the letter weren't a confession or a challenge, they were *answers*. As if someone were questioning Ronald, and he couldn't wait to leave the silence in which he had been imprisoned for so long, to free himself from the secret imposed on him by Father Rolf.

But what were those questions? And who was asking them?

Mila thought again of what Goran had said during the prayer. About the fact that good is not demonstrable, while we constantly have examples of evil right in front of our eyes. *Proof*. Ronald maintained that he had performed a positive, necessary action by killing his fellow-orphan. For him, Billy represented evil. And who could show that he had not done something good? His logic was perfect. Because Billy Moore, as he grew up, might well have become a very bad man. Who could truly say?

Going to Sunday School as a little girl, there was one question that Mila had always asked herself. As she had grown up, the question had stayed with her.

If God is good, why does he let children die?

If you thought about it, it did contrast with the ideal of love and justice that filled the Gospels.

But the fate of dying young is perhaps the one that God reserves for his worst children. And perhaps the children she saved could turn into murderers, or serial killers. In all likelihood what she was doing was wrong. If someone had killed Adolf Hitler or Jeffrey Dahmer or Charles Manson when they were still in nappies, would that have been a good or a bad deed? But their murderers would have been punished and condemned, certainly not celebrated as saviors of humanity!

She concluded that good and evil are often jumbled up. That the one is sometimes the instrument of the other, and vice versa.

Just as the words of a prayer can be jumbled up with the ravings of a murderer, she thought.

Suddenly there was that familiar tickle at the base of her neck. Like someone emerging from a hiding place behind her. Then she repeated the last thought to herself, and realized at that moment that she knew the questions that Ronald had tried to answer in his letter.

They were contained in Goran's prayer.

She struggled to remember them, even though she had heard them only once. She made various attempts in her notebook. She got the order wrong and had to start again, but finally there they were, right before her eyes.

Then she tried to match them up with the sentences in the letter. Reassembling that long-distance dialogue.

At last she reread everything…

And it was all quite clear from the very first sentence.

For those who are hunting me.

Those words were aimed at them, at the police. To answer the questions that the criminologist had spoken into the silence…

–Why did Billy Moore have to die?

billy was a bastard a BASTARD! and i was right to kill him. i hated him. he would have hurt us because he would have had a family and we wouldn't.

–Where did Ronald Dermis's hatred come from?

what was done to me was worse! and NOBODY came to save me! NOBODY.

–What happened to him during those years?

i have always been here in front of your eyes and you didn't see me.

–How did he learn to kill?

then HE came. HE understood me. HE taught me.

–What led him to choose evil?

it was you who wanted me like this. you didn't see me. now do you see me? worse for you in the end it will all be your fault.

–And why does he not put an end to all this horror?

i am what i am. NOBODY can prevent all this. NOBODY.

Mila didn't know what to think. But perhaps the answer to her question lay at the bottom of the letter.

A name.

RONALD

She would have to test her hypothesis straightaway.

18.

Snow fell from purple clouds in a heavy sky.

Mila managed to find a taxi only after waiting in the street for more than forty minutes. When he learned where she was going, the taxi driver protested. He said it was too far away, and at night, with that awful weather, he would never find another passenger to bring back. It was only when Mila offered to pay him twice the going rate that he changed his mind.

Several centimeters of snow had already accumulated on the road, making salt-scattering pointless. It was only possible to drive with chains, and the gears plainly resented it. The taxi smelled of stale air, and Mila noticed the remains of a kebab with onions on the passenger seat. The smell mingled with that of a pine air freshener right over the heating vents. It really wasn't a nice way to receive customers.

As they crossed the city, Mila put her ideas in order. She was sure her theory held and, as they approached the place where they were headed, her conviction grew even stronger. She thought of calling Gavila for confirmation, but her phone was almost out of battery. So she postponed the call until she had found what she was looking for.

When they reached the motorway tollbooths the police were sending the traffic back.

"There's too much snow, it's dangerous!" the officers were telling the drivers.

Some articulated lorries were parked on the edge of the road, in the hope of continuing their journey the following morning.

The taxi passed the roadblock and set off along a secondary road. The orphanage could be reached without taking the motorway. In the past this had probably been the only way, and luckily the taxi driver knew it.

She asked him to drop her off near the gate. Mila didn't even think of asking him to wait for her and offering him money again. She was sure she wasn't wrong, and that soon the place would be full of her colleagues again.

"Don't you want me to stay here till you've done what you have to do?" the man asked when he saw the dilapidated state of the building.

"No, thanks, just go."

The taxi driver didn't press the point, but turned round and changed into first, leaving a faint whiff of kebab and onions.

Mila climbed over the gate and walked up the dirt path, her feet sinking into the muddy snow. She knew that the police, following Roche's orders, had removed their patrol. Even the mobile unit's camper had been taken away. There was nothing there that could be of interest to the investigation.

Until tonight, she thought.

She reached the front of the building, but the door, after being forced open by the special units, had had its lock replaced. She turned towards the priest's house, wondering whether Father Timothy was still awake.

She had come all that way, and she had no choice.

She headed towards the priest's dwelling. She knocked several times, until a second-floor window lit up. Father Timothy appeared a moment later.

"Who is it?"

"Father, I'm Officer Vasquez. We've met before, do you remember?"

The cleric tried to focus his eyes on her in the middle of the dense snow.

"Yes, of course. What do you want at this time of night? I thought you'd finished your work here..."

"I know, but I'm sorry, there's something I need to check in the laundry room. Could you let me have the keys, please?"

"Fine, I'll come down."

Mila was already starting to wonder why it was taking him so long, when a few moments later she heard the sound of rattling behind the door as he undid the bolts. She saw him appear, wrapped in a threadbare cardigan with holes at the elbows, and with the usual mild expression on his face.

"You're shivering."

"Don't worry, Father."

"Come in and dry yourself for a moment while I look for the keys. You know, you lot left a terrible mess behind."

Mila followed him into the house. The sudden warmth produced an immediate effect of well-being.

"I was about to go to bed."

"I'm sorry."

"That's OK. Can I get you some tea? I always have some before I go to sleep, I find it relaxes me."

"No, thanks. I'd like to get back as soon as possible."

"Drink it, it'll do you good. I've already made some, you'll just have to pour it. In the meantime, I'll get the keys."

He came out of the room and she headed towards the little kitchen that the priest had pointed towards. The teapot was on the table. Its scented steam wafted over to her, and Mila couldn't resist. She poured herself a cup and added a large amount of sugar. She remembered the squalid cold tea that Feldher had tried to get her and Boris to drink in his house on the dump. God knows where he got the water to make it.

Father Timothy came back with a big bunch of keys. He was still trying to find the right one.

"Feeling better now, aren't you?" smiled the priest, pleased to have insisted.

Mila returned his smile: "Yes, much better."

"Here we are: this should be the one that opens the main door...do you want me to come with you?"

"No, thanks," and she immediately saw the priest relaxing. "But you could do me a favor."

"Tell me."

She handed him a piece of paper. "If I'm not back in an hour, call this number and ask for help."

Father Timothy turned white. "I thought the danger had passed."

"It's just a precaution. I don't think anything's going to happen to me. It's just that I don't know how to get about in this building: I could even have an accident...and there's no light in there."

As she said those last words, she realized it was a detail she had never considered. How did she think she would do it? There was no electricity, and the generator used for the halogen lamps would certainly have been dismantled and taken away along with the rest of the equipment.

"Damn!" she said. "You haven't got a torch, by any chance?"

"I'm sorry, officer...But if you've got a mobile phone, you might be able to use the display light."

She hadn't thought of that.

"Thanks for the tip."

"You're quite welcome."

A moment later, Mila went back out into the cold night, while the priest slid the bolts of the door shut, one by one.

She walked down the slope until she reached the front door of the orphanage. She slipped the key into the lock and heard the echo of the clicks disappearing into the space beyond. She pushed the enormous door and closed it behind her again.

She was in.

The doves gathered around the skylight greeted her presence with a frantic beating of their wings. The display of her phone gave off a faint green glow, revealing only a very small portion of what she had in front of her. A dense darkness lay in wait on the edge of that bubble of light, ready to invade and attack her at any moment.

Mila tried to remember how to get to the laundry. And she set off.

The sound of her footsteps violated the silence. Her breath condensed in the cold air. Soon she found herself back in the kitchens, and recognized the outline of the big iron cauldrons. Then she passed into the refectory, where she had to be careful not to crash into the Formica tables. She bumped into one with her hip, knocking over one of the chairs that had been placed on top of it. The noise, amplified by the echo, was almost deafening. As she was putting it back, Mila saw the opening that led to the lower floor via the narrow spiral staircase. She entered the stone intestine and slowly went down the stairs, made slippery by the wearing of the years.

She reached the laundry.

She moved her phone to look around her. In the marble basin in which Anneke's body had been found someone had left a flower. Mila also remembered the prayer that they had all recited together in that room.

And she started looking.

First of all she looked along the outline of the walls, then she ran her fingers around the baseboard. Nothing. She tried not to wonder how long it would be before her phone ran out of battery. Less because of the prospect of finding herself in the dark again, than because of the idea that without that light, however small, it would take her much longer. After an hour, Father Timothy would come for help, and she would cut a very sorry figure. She would have to hurry.

Where is it? she thought. *I know it's here somewhere . . .*

A very loud and sudden noise made her heart leap in her chest. It was a few minutes before she realized it was only her phone ringing.

She turned the display around and read: *Goran.*

She put on her hands-free and replied.

"Is there no one at the Studio? I've called at least ten times in the last hour."

"Boris and Stern have gone out, but Sarah Rosa should be there."

"And where are you?"

Mila thought there was no point telling a lie. Even though she wasn't at all sure about her hypothesis, she decided to let him know.

"I think Ronald was listening to us the other evening."

"What makes you think that?"

"I compared his letter with the questions that you asked yourself during our prayer. They seem like answers…"

"That's an excellent deduction."

The criminologist didn't seem very surprised. Maybe he had reached the same conclusion. Mila felt a bit stupid for thinking she could surprise him.

"But you haven't answered my question: where are you now?"

"I'm looking for the microphone."

"Which microphone?"

"The one Ronald put in the laundry."

"Are you at the orphanage?"

Goran's voice was suddenly alarmed.

"Yes."

"You've got to get out of there straightaway!"

"Why?"

"Mila, there's no microphone!"

"I'm sure there—"

Goran interrupted: "Listen, the officers scoured the whole area, they would have found it!"

She immediately felt really stupid. The criminologist was right: could she really have been so foolish not to consider that? What was she thinking of?

"Then how did…" She didn't finish her sentence. An imaginary drop of icy water slipped down her spine. "He was here."

"The prayer was just a trick to bring him out into the open!"

"Why didn't I think of that before?"

"Mila, for the love of God get out of there!"

At that moment she realized what a risk she was taking. She took out her gun and walked quickly towards the exit, which was at least two hundred meters from where she was. A vast distance to cover with that "presence" in the orphanage.

"Who could it be?" Mila wondered as she climbed the spiral staircase to the refectory.

As she noticed that her legs were giving way, she worked out the answer.

"The tea..."

There were disturbances on the line. She heard Goran on the headphones, asking her, "What?"

"Father Timothy is Ronald, isn't he?"

Disturbances. Noise. More disturbances.

"Yes! After Billy Moore's death, Father Rolf sent everyone away from the orphanage before the real date of closure. Except Ronald. He kept him with him because he feared his nature and hoped he could keep him under control."

"I think he's drugged me..."

Goran's voice was irregular. "...you said? I don't...erstand..."

"I think..." Mila tried to repeat, but the words thickened in her mouth.

She fell forward.

The hands-free slipped out of her ear. The phone fell from her hand, sliding under one of the tables. Her heartbeats were getting faster with terror, speeding the drug through her body. Her senses grew dull. But she managed to hear Goran's voice coming from the hands-free, saying, "Mila! Mila...ay something!...oing on?"

She closed her eyes, afraid that she wouldn't be able to open them again. Then she told herself that she didn't want to die in a place like that.

"Adrenaline...I need adrenaline..."

She knew how to get some. She was still holding the gun tightly in her right hand. She aimed it so that the barrel brushed her deltoid. And fired. The bullet ripped through the leather of her jacket and pierced her flesh, powerfully echoing around the abyss that surrounded her. She screamed through the noise. But she regained consciousness.

Goran clearly called her name: "Mila!"

She crept towards the light on her phone display. She picked it up and replied to Gavila.

"All OK."

She got back to her feet and started walking again. It took a huge effort to move as much as a step. She felt as if she was in one of those dreams when someone's chasing you and you can't run because your legs are heavy, as if you were up to your knees in a dense liquid.

The wound pulsed, but it wasn't losing much blood. She had gauged the shot well. She gritted her teeth and, step by step, she felt as if the exit was getting closer and closer.

"If you knew everything, why didn't you arrest that bastard straightaway?" she yelled into her phone. "And why wasn't I informed?"

The criminologist's voice was clear again. "Sorry, Mila. We wanted you to go on acting naturally with him, so as not to arouse his suspicions. We're monitoring him from a distance. We've put signal tracers in his car. We hoped he could lead us to the sixth child…"

"But he didn't…"

"Because he's not Albert, Mila."

"But he's still dangerous, isn't he?"

Goran stayed silent for a moment too long. He was.

"I've raised the alarm, they're on their way to you. But it'll take some time; the control cordon has a radius of several kilometers."

Whatever they do, it'll be too late, thought Mila. In that weather and with the drug circulating around her body, draining her strength, she hadn't a hope. And she knew it. She should have listened to that stupid taxi driver when he'd tried to discourage her from coming here! And—damn it—why hadn't she agreed when he'd offered to wait for her until she'd finished? And now here she was, in a trap. She had chased herself right into it, perhaps because unconsciously part of her wanted it to happen. She was seduced by the idea of taking risks. Even of dying!

No, she insisted to herself. *I want to live*.

Ronald—alias Father Timothy—still hadn't made his move. But she was sure she wouldn't have long to wait.

Three short sounds in sequence brought her back to her senses.

"Fuck," she said, as her phone battery abandoned her once and for all.

The darkness closed over her like the fingers of a hand.

How many times had she found herself in a mess? After all it had happened before. In the music teacher's house, for example. But how many times had she found herself in a mess like this? The answer she gave herself caught her off guard.

Never.

Drugged, injured, without her strength and without her mobile phone. That last lack made her feel like laughing: what could she have done with the telephone? Perhaps call some old friend. Graciela, for example. And ask her, "How are you? I'm about to die!"

The darkness was the worst thing. But she had to see it as an advantage: if she couldn't see Ronald, he couldn't see her either.

He's expecting me to head for the exit...

She really did want to leave this place behind her. But she was aware that she mustn't follow her instinct, or she would die.

I've got to hide and wait for reinforcements to arrive.

She established that this was the wise decision. Because sleep could have come for her at any moment. She still had the gun, and that reassured her. Perhaps he was armed too. Ronald didn't look like someone who was good with guns, but then she wasn't good with them either. But Father Timothy had been good at acting shy and apprehensive. Basically, Mila reflected, he might be able to hide lots of other skills.

She crouched under one of the tables in the huge refectory, and listened. The echo didn't help: it amplified useless noises, obscure creaks, far off and deceptive, that she couldn't interpret. Her eyelids closed, inexorably.

He can't see me. He can't see me, she repeated constantly to herself. *He knows I'm armed: if he makes a noise or uses the torch to look for me, he's a dead man.*

Unlikely colors started floating in front of her eyes.

It must be the drugs...she said to herself.

The colors turned into faces, and grew animated just for her. It couldn't only be her imagination. Suddenly, flashes were going off at various points in the room.

That bastard's in here and he's using a camera flash!

Mila tried to aim her gun. But those blinding lights, distorted by the hallucinogenic effect of the drug, made him impossible to locate.

She was imprisoned in a huge kaleidoscope.

She shook her head, but she was no longer in control of herself. A moment later she felt a tremor running through the muscles of her arms and legs, like an uncontrollable convulsion. However much she tried to banish it, the idea of death kept seducing her with the promise that, if she closed her eyes, everything would stop. Stop forever.

How much time had passed? Half an hour? Ten minutes? And how much time did she have left?

And at that moment she heard him.

He was close. Very close. No more than four or five meters away from her.

Then she saw him.

It only lasted a fraction of a second. In the halo of light surrounding him, she spotted the sinister smile that oozed from his face.

Mila knew he would find her at any moment, and she wouldn't have enough energy to shoot at him. So she had to do it first, even if it meant revealing her position.

She aimed into the darkness, pointing her weapon in the direction in which she saw him reappearing from one moment to the next in the halo of the flash. It was risky, but she had no alternative.

She was about to pull the trigger when Ronald started singing.

The same beautiful voice as when Father Timothy had intoned his hymn of prayer in front of the team. It was a contradiction in terms, a freak of nature that such a gift should have been stored in the unfeeling heart of a murderer. And it was from that heart that the song of death, high and dismayed, rose up.

It could have been sweet and touching. Instead, what Mila felt was terror. Her legs were finally giving, as were the muscles of her arms. And she let herself slip to the floor.

The glare of a flash.

Torpor wrapped around her like a cold blanket. She heard Ronald's footsteps getting more distinct as he approached to flush her out.

Another flash.

It's over. Now he's going to see me.

It didn't really matter how he killed her. She abandoned herself to death's flatteries with unexpected calm. Her last thought went to child number six.

I'll never know who you were...

A faint flow enwrapped her completely.

The butt of her pistol slipped from her palm. Two hands gripping her. She felt herself being lifted up. She tried to say something, but the sounds remained stuck in her throat.

She lost her senses.

As she awoke she was aware of a springy gait: Ronald was carrying her over his shoulder, they were climbing the stairs.

She lost consciousness again.

A very strong smell of ammonia sucked her from her artificial sleep. Ronald was holding a small bottle to her nose. He had tied her hands, but he wanted her to be alert.

She was buffeted by an icy wind. They were outside. Where were they? Mila sensed that they were somewhere high up. Then she remembered the enlarged photograph of the orphanage that Chang had produced to show her the spot from which Billy Moore had fallen.

The tower. We're on the tower!

Ronald lost interest in her for a moment. She saw him walking towards the parapet and looking over the edge.

He wants to throw me down.

Then he came back and grabbed her by the legs, dragging her to the cornice. With the little strength remaining to her, Mila tried to kick out, but without success.

She screamed. She struggled. A blind desperation filled her heart. He lifted her torso onto the parapet. With her head thrown back, Mila looked at the chasm below her. And then, through the curtain of snow, she made out in the distance the gleaming lights of the police cars approaching along the highway.

Ronald leaned over. She felt his hot breath as he whispered, "It's too late, they won't get here in time..."

Then he started to push her. Even with her hands tied behind her back, she managed to grip the slippery edge of the cornice. She battled with all her strength, but she couldn't resist for long. Her only ally was the ice that covered the floor of the tower, making Ronald's foot slip every time he tried to give her the final push. She saw his face distorting with the effort, and losing his calm because of her stubborn resistance. Then Ronald changed his technique. He decided to lift her legs beyond the parapet. He planted himself in front of her. And at that precise moment a desperate survival instinct made her put all her remaining strength into her knee, which she landed in his lower abdomen.

Ronald staggered backwards, bending breathlessly over, his hands clamped over his crotch. Mila worked out that this was her only chance before he recovered.

Without her strength, gravity was her only ally.

The wound to her shoulder was on fire, but Mila ignored the pain. She straightened up: now the slippery ice was against her, but she still took a run and hurled herself towards him. Ronald saw her suddenly pouncing at him and lost his balance. He waved his arm around in search of a handhold, but by now he was halfway over the cornice.

When he worked out that he wasn't going to make it, Ronald stretched out a hand to grab Mila and drag her with him into the chasm that gaped below him. She saw his fingers claw at the hem of her leather jacket in one last terrible caress. She saw him plunge in slow motion, the white flakes seeming to break his fall.

The dark received him.

19.

The deepest darkness.

A perfect barrier between sleep and waking. The fever has increased. She feels it on her reddened cheeks, on her aching legs, in her churning stomach.

She doesn't know when her days start and finish. Whether she has been lying there for hours or weeks. Time doesn't exist in the belly of the monster that has swallowed her: it dilates and contracts, like a stomach slowly digesting its food. And it's no use. Here time is no use for anything. Because she can't answer the most important question.

When will it end?

The deprivation of time is the worst of her punishments. More than the pain in her left arm, which sometimes spreads towards her neck and presses on her temples until it makes her feel ill. Because one thing is clear to her now.

This is all a punishment.

But she doesn't know exactly what sin she must be punished for.

Maybe I was bad to my mother or father, I've thrown too many tantrums, I never want to drink milk at the table, and I secretly throw it away when they aren't looking, I insisted that they bought me a cat, promising that I would look after it forever, but after I met Houdini I asked for a dog and they got very angry and said we couldn't get rid of the cat, and I tried to make them understand that Houdini doesn't like me at all, or perhaps it's because I got bad marks at school, this year my first report was half a disaster, and I have to get better at geography and drawing, or maybe it was the three cigarettes I smoked secretly on the roof of the gym with my cousin, but I didn't inhale, no, in fact maybe it's the ladybird-shaped hair grips that I stole from the mall, I swear I only did it that one time, and I'm very stubborn, specially with Mom who always wants to decide what clothes I have to wear, and she hasn't worked out that I'm a big girl now and I don't like the things she buys for me because we've got different tastes…

When she's awake, she goes on thinking of an explanation, trying to find a motive that would justify what's happening to her. So she ends up imagining the silliest things. But every time she seems to have identified a reason at last, it collapses like a house of cards because her pain outweighs her guilt.

Other times, though, she gets angry because her father and mother haven't yet come to get her.

What are they waiting for? Have they forgotten they have a daughter?

Then she regrets it. And she starts calling out to them in her mind, hoping she has some kind of telepathic power. It is the last resource remaining to her.

There are also times when she is convinced she is dead.

Yes, I'm dead and they've buried me down here. I can't move because I'm in a coffin. I'll be here forever…

But then the pain reminds her she is alive. The pain is both a sentence and a liberation. It drags her from her sleep and brings her back to reality. As it's doing now.

A hot liquid slides into her right arm. She feels it. It's nice. It smells like medicine. Someone is taking care of her. She doesn't know whether to be happy about it or not. Because it means two things. The first is that she isn't alone. The second is that she doesn't know if the presence near her is good or bad.

She has learned to wait. She knows when it will manifest itself. For example, she has understood that the weariness filling her at all times and the sleep into which she suddenly plunges are not autonomously decided by her body. It's a drug that dulls her senses.

Only when the drug takes effect does the presence come.

It sits down next to her and feeds her patiently with a spoon. The taste is sweet, there's no need to chew. Then it gives her water to drink. It never touches her, never says anything. She would like to speak, but her lips refuse to form the words and her throat won't make the necessary sounds. Sometimes, she feels that presence moving around her. Sometimes she feels as if it's there, motionlessly watching her.

A new stab of pain. A strangled scream that bounces off the walls of her prison. And brings her back to her senses.

It's then that she notices.

In the darkness now a small light has appeared, far away. A little red dot has suddenly appeared, to limit her small horizon. What is it? She tries to get a better look, but she can't. Then she feels something under her hand. Something that wasn't there before. An object with a rough and irregular consistency. It seems to be scaly. It's disgusting. It's stiff. It must be a dead animal. It's stiff because it's made of plastic. It's fixed to her palm with sticky tape. And those aren't scales, they're keys.

It's a remote control.

Suddenly everything's clear to her. She just has to lift her wrist a little and point the object towards the little red light, and press a key at random. The sequence of noises that follows tells her she isn't mistaken. First a gap. Then the tape quickly rewinding. The familiar sound of the mechanism of a video tape recorder. At the same time, a screen lights up in front of her.

For the first time, light illuminates the room.

She is surrounded by high walls of dark rock. And she is lying in what looks like a hospital bed, with handles and a steel head and foot. Beside her there's a stand with a drip feed ending in a needle in her right arm. The left is completely hidden by very tight bandages that hold her whole torso immobile. On a table there are jars of baby food. And lots and lots of medicine. Beyond the television, though, there is still impenetrable darkness.

Finally the video tape finishes rewinding. It suddenly stops. And then it starts again, but slower this time. The rustle of the audio heralds the beginning of a film. A moment later some cheerful, strident music starts up—the sound track is slightly distorted. Then the screen fills with blurred colors. A little man appears in dungarees and a cowboy hat. There's also a horse with very long legs. And the man tries to get on, but can't. His attempts repeat and always end in the same way: with the man tumbling to the ground and the horse laughing at him. It goes on like that for about ten minutes. Then the cartoon finishes without end titles. But the video cassette goes on playing static. When it reaches the end, the tape rewinds automatically. And starts again from the beginning. Always the little man. Always the horse he will never be able to climb up on. And yet she goes on watching him. Even though she knows how things are going to go with the scornful animal.

She hopes.

Because that is the only thing left to her. Hope. The ability not to abandon herself completely to horror. Perhaps whoever chose that cartoon for her had an opposite intent. But the fact that the little man won't give up and keeps on trying in spite of the tumbles and the pain gives her courage.

Go on, climb back in the saddle! she tells him in her head every time. Before sleep overwhelms her once more.

District of ■■■■■■
Office of the District Attorney
J. B. Marin
Dic. 11—c.a.

For the Attention of the Director, Dr. Alphonse Bérenger.
c/o Prison of ■■■■■.
Penitential District No. 45.
Subject: in reply to the "confidential" report of 23 November.

Dear Dr. Bérenger,

I am writing in reply to your request for additional investigations into the individual imprisoned in your penitentiary and so far identified only as prisoner number RK-357/9. I regret to inform you that the latest research into the man's identity has produced no results.

I agree with you when you state that the suspicion exists that prisoner RK-357/9 may have committed some serious crime in the past, and is doing everything he can to keep it in the dark. At this point, DNA examination is the only instrument at our disposal to confirm or deny it.

However, as you know very well, we cannot force prisoner RK-357/9 to carry out the test. In fact, this would expose us to a serious violation of his rights with regard to the crime for which he has been sentenced (refusing to supply identification to public officials).

This would be a different matter if there were "substantial" and "unequivocal" indications that prisoner RK-357/9 was responsible for a serious crime, or if there were "serious motives for thinking him a danger to society."

At present, however, this is not the case.

In the light of this, the only way we have of getting hold of his DNA is to take it directly from matter of organic origin, with the sole condition that this has been casually lost or left spontaneously by the subject in the course of his normal daily activities.

Taking into account the hygienic obsession of prisoner RK-357/9, this Office authorizes prison guards to enter his cell without warning to inspect it with a view to retrieving the said organic material.

In the hope that this expedient is adequate for the achievement of the purpose, I remain yours sincerely,

Vice District Attorney

Matthew Sedris

20.

Military Hospital of R.
16 February

"Let them say what they like, but you just drop it! You're a good police officer, OK?"

Sergeant Morexu summoned all his gypsy spirit to express his sympathy with her. Never before had he spoken to her in that sad tone. It was almost fatherly. And yet Mila felt she didn't deserve his defense. The phone call from her superior had reached her unexpectedly, just as news of her nocturnal trip to the orphanage had emerged. They would blame her for the death of Ronald Dermis, she was sure of it, even though it had only been self-defense.

She had recuperated in a military hospital. A civilian establishment had not been chosen because Roche had wisely decided to take her away from the curious eyes of the press. That was why she had a whole ward to herself. And when she asked why on earth there were no other patients there, the concise reply had been that the complex had been planned to quarantine people affected in a possible bacteriological attack.

The beds were remade every week, the sheets washed and ironed. In the pharmacy, the medicines that went out of date were promptly replaced. And all this waste of resources solely for the remote possibility that someone might decide to unleash a genetically modified virus or bacteria that would leave no survivors.

The craziest thing in the world, thought Mila.

The wound in her arm had been sewn up with about forty stitches by a kind surgeon who, when he had examined her, hadn't mentioned the other scars. He had only said, "You couldn't have ended up in a better place for a firearms injury."

"What do viruses and bacteria have to do with bullets?" she had asked provocatively. He had laughed.

Then another doctor had examined her a few times, measuring her blood pressure and taking her temperature. The effects of the powerful sleeping pills that Father Timothy had administered had vanished of their own accord in a few hours. A diuretic had done the rest.

Mila had had lots of time to think.

She couldn't help thinking about child number six. She didn't have a whole hospital at her disposal. The greatest hope was that Albert was keeping her constantly sedated. The specialists that Roche had called in to give their thoughts about the likelihood of survival had taken into account not only the serious physical damage but also the shock and stress to which the girl had been subjected.

She may not even have noticed that her arm is missing, Mila thought. That often happened to people who had suffered an amputation. She had heard it mentioned with reference to people who had suffered war injuries—even though they've lost a limb, they still feel a residual sensitivity in that part of the body, have a sense of movement beyond the pain and sometimes even a tickling sensation. Doctors call it "perception of the phantom limb."

Those thoughts profoundly disturbed her, amplified by the oppressive silence of the ward. Perhaps for the first time in many years she found herself wishing she had company. Before Morexu's phone call no one had come. Not Goran or Boris or Stern, let alone Rosa. Which could mean only one thing: they were taking a decision about her, and about whether or not to keep her in the team. Even though the last word would go to Roche.

She was angry with herself for having been so naive. Perhaps she really did deserve their mistrust. The only thought that consoled her was Goran's certainty that Ronald Dermis couldn't be Albert. Otherwise there would be nothing to be done for the sixth child.

Isolated in that place, she knew nothing of the developments in the case. She asked for updates from the nurse who served her breakfast, and who showed up again with a newspaper a short time later.

The case filled the first six pages. The small amount of information that had filtered through was repeated several times and inflated beyond measure. People were greedy for news. Once the public had found out about the existence of a sixth child, the country had reacquired a sense of solidarity that prompted everyone to do things that would have been unthinkable shortly before, like organizing prayer vigils or support groups. An initiative had been launched: "A candle for every window." Those little flames would mark the wait for the "miracle," and would be extinguished only when the sixth child returned home. People used to ignoring each other for a lifetime were encountering a new kind of experience thanks to this tragedy: human contact. They no longer had to wear themselves out trying to find pretexts for having relationships with each other. Because it was taken for granted that they now had something in common: pity for that creature. And that helped them to communicate. They did it everywhere. At the supermarket, in the bar, at work, on the subway. The television programs spoke of nothing else.

But amongst all the initiatives, one in particular had created a sensation, embarrassing even the investigators.

A reward.

Ten million to anyone who provided information useful to the rescue of the sixth child. A big sum that had prompted fierce polemics. Some people maintained that it had polluted the spontaneity of people's solidarity. Others claimed it was a fair idea that would finally get things moving because, beyond the feel-good facade, selfishness still ruled, and could be harnessed only by the promise of profit.

So, without noticing, the country had divided itself once again.

The initiative for the reward came from the Rockford Foundation. When Mila asked the nurse who was behind the charity, the woman opened her eyes wide with surprise.

"Everyone knows it's Joseph B. Rockford."

Her reaction told Mila how much, absorbed in the hunt for missing children and her own personal problems, she had cut herself off from the real world.

"Sorry, I don't," she replied. And she thought about the absurdity of a situation in which the life of a magnate was fatally interwoven with that of an unknown child. Two human beings who, until now, must have led very different lives, and they would probably have continued like that until the end of their days if Albert hadn't thought of bringing them together.

She went to sleep with those thoughts, and was finally able to benefit from a dreamless sleep that cleansed her mind of the waste of those days of horror. When she woke, restored, she was not alone.

Gavila was sitting beside her on the next bed.

Mila sat up, wondering how long he had been there. He calmed her down: "I chose to wait rather than wake you. You looked so serene. Did I do the wrong thing?"

"No," she lied. It was as if he had caught her at a moment when she was entirely defenseless and, before he noticed her embarrassment, she hurried to change the subject: "They want to keep me under observation here. But I told them I'm getting out this afternoon."

Goran looked at his watch: "Then you'll have to get a move on: it's almost evening."

Mila was surprised she had slept so long.

"Is there any news?"

"I'm just back from a long meeting with Chief Inspector Roche."

That's why he's here, she thought. *He wanted to tell me in person that I'm out.* But she was wrong.

"We've found Father Rolf."

Mila felt a contraction in her stomach, imagining the worst.

"He died about a year ago, of natural causes."

"Where was he buried?"

From that question, Goran knew that Mila had already guessed everything.

"Behind the church. There were other graves, too, containing animal carcasses."

"Father Rolf was keeping him on a short rein."

"It seems to have gone like this. Ronald had a borderline personality disorder. He was a serial killer in the making, and the priest had understood that. The killing of animals is typical in these cases. It always starts like that; then when the subject gets no more satisfaction from it, he shifts his attention to his peers. Ronald, too, would have moved on to kill other humans. Basically that experience had been part of his emotional baggage since childhood."

"We've stopped him now."

Goran shook his head seriously. "In fact, it was Albert who stopped him."

It was paradoxical, but it was also the truth.

"But Roche would have a heart attack rather than admit anything of the kind!"

Mila thought that by saying these things Goran was just trying to postpone the news that she was off the case, and decided to get to the nub.

"I'm out, aren't I?"

He looked startled. "Why do you say that?"

"Because I fucked up."

"We all do that."

"I caused Ronald Dermis's death: so we'll never know how Albert found out about his story..."

"First of all, I think Ronald took his own death into account: he wanted to end the doubts that had troubled him for many years. Father Rolf had turned him into a fake priest, convincing him that he could live like a man dedicated to God and his fellowman. But he didn't want to love his fellowman, he wanted to kill him for his own pleasure."

"And how did Albert find out about that?"

Goran's face darkened. "He must have come into contact with Ronald at some point in his life. I can't think of any other explanation. He understood what Father Rolf understood before him. And he got there because they are similar, he and Ronald. In some way they found one another, and recognized one another too."

Mila took a deep breath as she thought about fate. Ronald Dermis had been understood by only two people in his life. A priest who had found no better solution for him than hiding him from the world. And someone like himself, who had probably revealed his own nature to him.

"You would have been the second..."

Goran's words brought her back to reality.

"What?"

"If you hadn't stopped him, Ronald would have killed you as he did Billy Moore many years ago."

At that point he drew an envelope from the inside pocket of his coat and handed it to her.

"I thought you had a right to see them..."

Mila took the envelope and opened it. Inside were the photographs that Ronald had taken as he pursued her in the refectory. In a corner of one of those pictures, there she was. Crouching under the table, eyes wide with fear.

"I'm not very photogenic," she said, trying to play it down. But Goran noticed that she was shaken.

"This morning Roche announced that you're dismissed for twenty-four hours...or at least until the next corpse is found."

"I don't want a holiday, we have to find the sixth child," protested Mila. "She can't wait!"

"I think the chief inspector knows that...but I fear he's trying to play another card."

"The reward," Mila said immediately.

"It might yield unexpected fruits."

"And what about research into the professional registers of doctors? And the theory that Albert might be one who's been struck off?"

"A feeble track. No one really believed in that from the start. Just as I don't think anything can come out of investigating the drugs he's probably using to keep the girl alive. Our man could have got hold of them in lots of ways. He's cunning and he's prepared, don't forget it."

"Much more than we are, by the look of it," was Mila's piqued reply.

Goran took no offense. "I came here to collect you, not to argue."

"To collect me? What do you have in mind, Dr. Gavila?"

"I'm taking you to dinner... And by the way, I'd like you to start calling me Goran."

Once they were out of the hospital, Mila had insisted on calling in at the Studio: she wanted to wash and change her clothes. She went on telling herself that if her sweater hadn't been torn by the bullet, and if the rest of her clothes hadn't been bloody from her wound, she would have worn the ones she had on. In fact that unexpected invitation to dinner had made her agitated, and she didn't want to stink of sweat and iodine.

The tacit agreement with Dr. Gavila—even if she now had to call him by his first name—was that she shouldn't see it as an excursion, and that after dinner she would come back to the Studio straightaway to resume her work. But—even though she felt guilty towards the sixth child—she couldn't help feeling slightly smug about the invitation.

She couldn't shower because of her wound. So she washed herself carefully bit by bit, until she exhausted the supply of hot water in the little boiler.

She put on a black polo-neck. The only spare jeans she had were too provocatively tight at the rear, but she had no choice. Her leather jacket was torn at the left shoulder, where she had shot it with her gun, so she couldn't use it. To her great surprise, however, an army-green parka lay on the camp bed in the guest room, with a note beside it: "The cold here is deadlier than any bullets. Welcome back. Your friend, Boris."

She felt full of affection and gratitude. Most of all because Boris had signed himself her "friend." That stripped her of any doubts about him. There was also a box of mints on the jacket: Stern's contribution to that gesture of friendship.

It had been years since she had worn a color other than black. But the green parka suited her. Even the size was right. When he saw her coming out of the Studio, Goran didn't seem to notice her new look. He had always been too distracted, he probably didn't pay any attention to other people's appearance.

They walked to the restaurant. It was a pleasant stroll and, thanks to Boris's present, Mila didn't feel the cold.

The steakhouse sign promised juicy Argentinean Angus steaks. They sat down at a table for two, by the window. Outside, the snow covered everything, and a reddish, smoky sky promised more that night. In the restaurant people chatted and smiled, cheerfully.

Everything on the menu looked good, and Mila took a while to make her mind up. In the end she chose a well-done steak with roast potatoes and lots of rosemary. Goran had an entrecôte and tomato salad. They both drank only sparkling mineral water.

Mila had no idea what they would talk about: whether it would be work or their lives. The second option, interesting though it was, made her uneasy. But first there was something she was curious about.

"What really happened?"

"What do you mean?"

"Roche wanted to throw me off the case, but then he changed his mind…why?"

Goran hesitated for a moment, but finally decided to tell her.

"We put it to a vote."

"A vote?" she said, surprised. "So it was a yes."

"By some margin."

"But…how?"

"Even Sarah Rosa voted in favor of your staying," he said, guessing the reason for her reaction.

Mila was thunderstruck. "My worst enemy, of all people!"

"You shouldn't be too hard on her."

"I really thought it was the other way around…"

"Rosa's going through a bad patch: she's splitting up from her husband."

Mila wanted to say she had seen them arguing below the Studio the night before, but she kept quiet to avoid seeming too indiscreet.

"That's a shame."

"It's never easy when there are children involved."

Mila thought this was a reference that went beyond Sarah Rosa, and possibly involved Goran himself.

"Rosa's daughter has developed an eating disorder in reaction to it all. With the result that her parents still share a roof, but you can imagine the effects of that situation."

"And that means she can take it out on me?"

"As a new arrival, and the only other female on the team, you're the easiest target for her. She certainly can't take it out on Boris or Stern, people she's known for years..."

Mila poured herself some mineral water, then turned her attention to her other colleagues.

"I'd like to know them well enough to know how to behave with them," was her excuse.

"Well, it seems to me that with Boris it's pretty easy: what you see is what you get."

"Yeah," agreed Mila.

"I could tell you that he was in the army, where he became an expert in interrogation techniques. I've often seen him at work, but he boggles my mind every time. He can get inside people's heads."

"I didn't think he was as clever as that."

"No, he is. A few years ago they arrested a guy because he was suspected of killing and hiding the corpses of his aunt and uncle, who he was living with. You should have seen him; he was cold, extremely calm. After eighteen hours of serious interrogation in which five officers had taken turns to grill him, he hadn't admitted a thing. Then Boris arrives, goes into the room, spends twenty minutes with him and he confesses to everything."

"Goodness! And Stern?"

"Stern is a good man. In fact the expression could have been coined specifically for him. He's been married for twenty-six years. He has two sons, twins, both in the navy."

"He seems a bit quiet. I noticed he's very religious as well."

"He goes to mass every Sunday, and he also sings in the choir."

"I can't believe his suits, they make him look like someone in a seventies cop show!"

Goran laughed and agreed. Then he grew serious again when he added, "His wife, Marie, was on dialysis for five years, waiting for a kidney that didn't come. Two years ago, Stern donated one of his."

Surprised and admiring, Mila didn't know what to say.

Goran went on: "He gave up a good half of the time left to him so that she had at least a hope."

"He must be very much in love."

"Yes, I think he is..." said Goran, with a hint of bitterness that she couldn't help noticing.

At that moment their orders arrived. They ate in silence, the lack of conversation not oppressive in the slightest, like two people who know each other so well that they don't constantly need to fill the gaps with words to keep from feeling embarrassed.

"I have to tell you one thing," she continued towards the end. "It happened when I got here, the second evening I set foot in the motel where I was staying before I moved to the Studio."

"I'm listening..."

"It might have been nothing, or perhaps it was just a feeling, but...I felt as if someone was following me as I crossed the area outside."

"What do you mean you *felt?*"

"That he was copying my footsteps."

"Why should anyone have been following you?"

"That's why I haven't mentioned it to anyone. It struck me as absurd. It was probably just my imagination..."

Goran registered the information and said nothing.

When coffee came, Mila looked at her watch.

"There's a place I'd like to go," she said.

"At this time of night?"

"Yes."

"OK. Then I'll ask for the bill."

Mila offered to split it, but he insisted on his obligation to pay since he was the one who had invited her. With his typical—and almost picturesque—disorder, along with banknotes, coins and business cards, he took some colored balloons out of his pocket.

"They're my son Tommy's, he puts them in my pocket."

"Oh, I didn't know you were..." she pretended.

"No, I'm not," he said hastily, lowering his eyes. Then he added, "Not anymore."

Mila had never been to a funeral at night before. Ronald Dermis's was the first. It had been decided to hold it then for reasons of public order. For her, the idea that someone could take out their revenge on a coffin was at least as gloomy as the event itself.

The undertakers were at work around the grave. They didn't have a digger. The ground was icy, and moving it was both difficult and tiring. There were four of them, and they took turns every five minutes, two to dig and two more to light the scene with their torches. Every now and again one of them cursed the damned cold and, to warm themselves up, they passed around a bottle of Wild Turkey.

Goran and Mila watched the scene in silence. The coffin containing Ronald's remains was still in the van. A little further on was the stone that would be put there at the end: no name, no date, just a serial number. And a small cross.

At that moment, the scene of Ronald's fall from the tower reappeared in Mila's head. As he plunged, she had seen no fear, no alarm on his face. It was as if he was undaunted by death. Perhaps, like Alexander Bermann, he preferred that solution. Yielding to the desire to erase himself forever.

"Everything all right?" Goran asked her, penetrating her silence.

Mila turned towards him. "Everything's fine."

At that moment she thought she noticed someone behind a tree in the cemetery. She took a better look and recognized Feldher. Apparently Ronald's secret funeral wasn't as secret as all that.

The laborer was wearing a checked woolen jacket and holding a can of beer, as though raising a toast to his old childhood friend, even though he probably hadn't seen him for years. Mila thought this might be a positive thing: even in a place where evil is buried, there can still be room for pity.

If it hadn't been for Feldher, for his involuntary help, they wouldn't have been there. And it was thanks to him that she had stopped that serial killer in the making—as Goran had called him.

When she caught his eye he crushed the tin and headed towards his pickup, parked not far away. He would return to the solitude of his house on the dump, to cold tea in mismatching glasses, to the rust-colored dog, to wait for that same anonymous death to turn up at his door one day.

Mila's decision to attend Ronald's hurried funeral was probably linked to something Goran had said in the hospital: "If you hadn't stopped him, Ronald would have killed you as he did Billy Moore many years ago."

And who knows, perhaps he would have gone on killing after her.

"People don't know, but according to our statistics, between six and eight serial killers are currently active in this country. But no one has identified them yet," said Goran as the gravediggers lowered the wooden box into the hole.

Mila was shocked. "How is that possible?"

"Because they strike at random, without a pattern. Or because no one has managed to link murders that look very different to one another. Or perhaps because the victims aren't worthy of a large-scale investigation…maybe, for example, a prostitute is found in a ditch. In most cases it's drugs, or her pimp, or a customer. Bearing in mind the risks of the profession, ten murdered prostitutes are considered an acceptable average, and they don't end up on a serial killer case list. It's hard to accept, I know, but sadly that's how it is."

A gust of wind threw up little whirlwinds of snow and dust. Mila shivered and huddled even deeper into her parka.

"What's the point of it all?" she asked. But the question had nothing to do with the case they were dealing with, or with her chosen profession. It was a prayer, a way to surrender to her inability to understand certain dynamics of evil, and also a sad request for salvation. And she certainly didn't expect a reply.

But Goran spoke. "God is silent. The devil whispers..."

Neither of them said anything more.

The gravediggers were beginning to fill in the hole with icy earth. The graveyard rang with the sound of spades. Then Goran's mobile phone rang. He hadn't had time to take it from his coat pocket when Mila's phone rang as well.

They didn't have to answer to know that the third girl had been found.

21.

The Kobashi family—father, mother and two children, a boy of fifteen and a girl of twelve—lived in the prestigious complex of Capo Alto. Sixty hectares plunged in greenery, with a swimming pool, a riding school, a golf course and a clubhouse reserved for the owners of the forty villas of which it was composed. A refuge of the haute bourgeoisie, made up for the most part of specialist doctors, architects and lawyers.

A two-meter wall, cleverly masked by a hedge, separated this paradise of the elite from the rest of the world. The place was guarded twenty-four hours a day. The electronic eyes of seventy CCTV cameras that kept the whole perimeter under surveillance and a private police force guaranteed the safety of the residents.

Kobashi was a dentist. A high salary, a Maserati in the drive and a Mercedes in the garage, a second home in the mountains, a yacht and an enviable collection of wines in the cellar. His wife brought up the children and furnished the house with unique and wildly expensive objects.

"They were in the tropics for three weeks, they came back last night," Stern announced as Goran and Mila reached the villa. "The reason for the trip was the business of the kidnapped girls. The daughter is more or less the same age, so they thought it was a good idea to send the servants on holiday and get a change of air."

"Where are they now?"

"In a hotel. We've put them there for their safety. The wife needed a few Valiums. Not to put too fine a point on it, they're devastated."

Stern's last words helped to prepare them for what they were about to see.

The house was no longer a house. Now it was definitely a "crime scene." It had been entirely enclosed by a tape to keep away the neighbors who were crowding around to see what had happened.

"At least the press won't be able to get in," Goran remarked.

They walked along the lawn that separated the villa from the street. The garden was well tended and splendid winter plants decorated the beds where Mrs. Kobashi would grow her prize roses in summer.

An officer had been placed at the door to let in only authorized personnel. Both Krepp and Chang were at work with their respective teams. Shortly before Goran and Mila prepared to cross the threshold, Chief Inspector Roche came out.

"You can't imagine…" he said in a deathly voice, holding a handkerchief over his mouth. "This business is taking an increasingly horrible turn. I wish we had been able to prevent this slaughter…they're only children, for God's sake!"

Roche's fury sounded genuine.

"As if that weren't enough, the residents have already complained about our presence, and they're pressuring their political acquaintances to have us sent away as soon as possible! Can you imagine? Now I have to call some fucking senator to reassure him that we'll be quick!"

Mila looked around the little crowd of residents assembled in front of the villa. It was in their private Eden, and they saw them as invaders.

But in their corner of paradise, an unexpected gateway to hell had opened up.

Stern passed Mila the jar of camphor paste to put under her nostrils.

She completed the ritual of being introduced to death by putting on plastic shoe covers and latex gloves. The officer at the door stepped aside to let them pass.

The holiday suitcases and the bags of souvenirs were still by the door. The flight that had brought the Kobashis back from the tropical sun to that February chill had landed at about ten o'clock at night. Then home as quickly as possible, to get back to the old habits and comfort of the place that would never be the same for them. The servants would only return from leave the following day, so they were the first to step across the threshold.

The stench fouled the air.

"This is what the Kobashis smelt as soon as they opened the door," Goran said immediately.

"For a moment or two they must have wondered what it was," said Mila. "Then they turned the light on..."

In the big sitting room, the scientific technicians and the pathology staff coordinated their gestures as they moved, as if guided by a mysterious and invisible choreographer. The precious marble floor pitilessly reflected the light from the halogen lamps. Modern furniture alternated with antiques. Three dust-colored sofas bounded three sides of a square in front of a huge pink stone fireplace.

On the middle sofa sat the body of the little girl.

Her eyes were open—veined blue. *And she was looking at them.*

The fixed stare was the last sign of humanity in that ravaged face. The processes of decomposition were already at an advanced stage. The lack of the left arm gave her a slanted posture. As if she was going to slip to one side at any moment. Instead she remained seated.

She was wearing a blue floral dress. The stitching and cut suggested that it was homemade, and that it had probably been made to measure. Mila also noticed the crocheting of her white socks, the satin belt fastened at the waist with a mother-of-pearl button.

She was dressed like a doll. *A broken doll.*

Mila couldn't look at her for more than a few seconds. She looked down and noticed for the first time the silk rug between the sofas. It showed Persian roses and multicolored waves. She had the impression that the figures were moving. Then she looked more closely.

The rug was completely covered with little insects that swarmed and clambered over each other.

Mila instinctively brought a hand to the wound in her arm, and squeezed it. Anyone watching her would have thought that it hurt. In fact it was the opposite.

As usual, she was seeking comfort in pain.

It didn't last long, but it gave her the strength to be a careful witness to that obscene display. When she had had enough of the spasm, she stopped squeezing. She heard Dr. Chang saying to Goran: "They're larvae of *Sarcophaga carnaria*. Their biological cycle is quite quick and they're in the warm. And they're very greedy."

Mila knew what the doctor was referring to, because her missing-person cases were often solved with the finding of a corpse. Often it was necessary to proceed not only to the pitiful rite of recognition, but also to the more prosaic one of dating the remains. Different insects participate in the different phases that follow death, especially when the remains are exposed. The *Sarcophaga carnaria* was a viviparous fly, and had to be part of the second group, because Mila heard the pathologist saying that the corpse must have been there for at least a week.

"Albert had a lot of time to act, while the owners were away."

"But there's something I really don't understand..." Chang added. "How did the bastard manage to get the body here with seventy surveillance cameras and thirty private guards checking the area twenty-four hours a day?"

22.

"We've had a problem with energy surges crashing the system," the Commander of the Capo Alto private guard had said when Sarah Rosa had asked him to explain the three-hour blackout of TV cameras that had happened the previous week, when it was assumed that Albert had taken the little girl into the Kobashis' house.

"And doesn't something like that put you on a state of alert?"

"Well—no, miss..."

"I understand," and she hadn't said anything else, merely looked at the captain's stripes on his uniform. A rank as fake as his function. The guards who should have been guaranteeing the safety of the residents were really just uniformed bodybuilders. Their only training consisted of a three-month paid course held by retired police officers at the offices of the company that had taken them on. Their equipment consisted of a hands-free connected to a walkie-talkie and a pepper spray. So it hadn't been too hard for Albert to get round them. A breach a meter and a half across had also been made in the perimeter barrier, hidden by the hedge that covered the whole of the surrounding wall. That aesthetic whim now made Capo Alto's one true security measure look ridiculous.

Now it was a matter of working out why Albert had chosen this particular place and this particular family.

The fear of facing a new Alexander Bermann had led Roche to permit all kinds of investigation, even the most invasive, into Kobashi and his wife.

Boris had been given the task of quizzing the dentist.

The man probably had no idea of the special treatment reserved for him over the next few hours. Being questioned by a professional interrogator isn't the same as the methods in police stations over most of the world, where everything is based on the process of wearing down the suspect through hours and hours of psychological pressure and forced wakefulness, answering the same questions over and over again.

Boris hardly ever tried to catch out the people he was interrogating, because he knew that stress often produces negative effects on the deposition, which then becomes vulnerable to attacks from a good attorney in the courtroom. Neither was he interested in half-confessions or attempts at negotiation that the suspects often brought into play when they felt they were on the ropes.

No. Special Agent Klaus Boris only tried to get a full confession.

Mila saw him in the Studio kitchen, preparing to come onstage. Because that, in the end, was what it was all about: a performance in which the parts are often reversed. By using lies, Boris would break down Kobashi's defenses.

His shirt sleeves were rolled up, he held a little bottle of water in one hand and walked back and forth to stretch his legs: unlike Kobashi, Boris would never sit down, always intimidating the other man with his build.

Meanwhile Stern was updating him about what he had so far managed to discover about the suspect.

"The dentist evades part of his taxes. He has an off-shore account to which he sends the untaxed income from his clinic and the prizes from the golf tournaments that he plays almost every weekend...Mrs. Kobashi, on the other hand, has a different kind of hobby: every Wednesday afternoon she meets a well-known lawyer in a hotel in the center. Of course the lawyer plays golf with her husband every weekend…"

That information would constitute the key to the interrogation. Boris would measure it out, using it at the right moment to bring the dentist down.

The interrogation room in the Studio had been set up a long time ago, next to the guest room. It was narrow, almost suffocating, with no windows and only one doorway that Boris would lock as soon as he had gone inside with the suspect. Then he would slip the key into his pocket, as he always did: a simple gesture that assured him of his position of strength.

The neon light was powerful, and the lamp gave off an irritating hum; that sound was also one of Boris's tools. He would mitigate its effects by stuffing cotton wool in his ears.

A fake mirror separated the room from another, with a different doorway, so that the others could witness the interrogation. It was very important that the man under questioning was always positioned in profile with regard to the mirror and never head-on: he had to feel he was being observed without ever returning that invisible gaze.

Both the table and the walls were painted white: the monochrome effect meant that he had no point to concentrate upon so that he could reflect on his answers. One leg of his chair was shorter than the others, and it would rock constantly to irritate him.

Mila came into the other room as Sarah Rosa prepared the Voice Stress Analyzer, or VSA—an apparatus that would allow them to measure the stress in the variations of the man's voice. When someone lies, the amount of blood in their vocal cords diminishes as a result of the tension, consequently reducing the normal vibration. A computer would analyze the micro-variations in Kobashi's words, revealing his lies.

But the most important technique that Klaus Boris would use—the one in which he was practically a master—was *observation of behavior*.

Kobashi was led into the interrogation room after being politely invited—albeit with no preliminary warning—to help the police with their inquiries. The officers whose task it was to escort him there from the hotel in which he was staying with his family had made him sit on his own on the backseat of the car and taken a longer route than usual to bring him to the Studio, to intensify his state of doubt and uncertainty.

Given that this was only an informal discussion, Kobashi hadn't asked for the presence of a lawyer. He was afraid that such a request would expose him to suspicions of guilt. That was exactly what Boris was hoping for.

In the room, the dentist looked drawn. Mila studied him. He was wearing yellow summer trousers. They were probably part of one of the golfing suits he had brought with him on his trip to the tropics, which now constituted the entirety of his wardrobe. He had on a fuchsia-colored cashmere sweater and, poking from its collar, a white polo-neck.

He had been told that an investigator would shortly be arriving to ask him some questions. Kobashi had nodded, putting his hands in his lap in a defensive position.

Meanwhile Boris watched him from the other side of the mirror, allowing himself a long wait to study him properly.

Kobashi noticed a file on the table, with his name on it. Boris had put it there. The dentist would never touch it, just as he would never look in the direction of the mirror, even though he knew very well that he was being observed.

The file was actually empty.

"It looks like a dentist's waiting room, doesn't it?" joked Sarah Rosa, staring at the unfortunate man behind the glass.

Then Boris announced: "Right: let's get started."

A moment later he entered the interrogation room. He greeted Kobashi, locked the door and apologized for his lateness. He made it clear once again that the questions he was going to ask him were only requests for clarification, then took the file from the table and opened it, pretending to read something.

"Dr. Kobashi, you're forty-three, is that right?"

"Exactly."

"For how long have you been working as a dentist?"

"I'm an orthodontic surgeon," he explained. "But I've been doing that for fifteen years."

Boris took some time to examine the invisible papers.

"Can I ask you what your income was last year?"

The man started slightly. Boris had delivered his first blow: the reference to income was an indirect allusion to taxes.

As predicted, the dentist lied shamelessly about his financial situation, and Mila couldn't help noticing how naively he went about it. The conversation was about a murder, and any fiscal information that might emerge would have no relevance, and couldn't be passed on to the tax office.

The man also lied about his personal details, thinking that he could easily control his replies. And for a while Boris let him get on with it.

Mila knew Boris's game. She had seen other old-school colleagues doing something similar, although the special agent practiced it at indubitably higher levels.

Whenever Kobashi relied upon his own imagination, Boris knew straightaway. The increase in anxiety generates anomalous microactions, like bending one's back, rubbing one's hands, massaging one's temples or wrists. These actions are often accompanied by physiological alterations like an increase in sweating, a rise in the tone of the voice and uncontrolled eye movements.

But a well-trained specialist like Boris also knew that these are only suggestions of lies, and they must be treated as such. To prove that the subject is lying he has to admit his own responsibility.

When Boris sensed that Kobashi felt confident enough, he moved into the counterattack, insinuating into his questions clues to do with Albert and the disappearance of the six little girls.

Two hours later, Kobashi had been worn out by a barrage of increasingly intimate questions. By now the dentist had abandoned any notion of calling a lawyer, he just wanted to get out of there as quickly as possible. He was in such a state of psychological collapse that he would have said anything just to have his freedom back. He might even have admitted to being Albert.

Except that it wouldn't have been true.

When Boris realized that, he left the room, on the pretext of getting a glass of water, and rejoined Goran and the others in the room behind the mirror.

"He has nothing to do with it," he said. "And he doesn't know a thing."

Goran nodded.

Sarah Rosa had recently come back with the results of the analyses of the computers and the use of mobile phones owned by the Kobashi family, which had not provided a shred of evidence. And there were no interesting leads to be found among their friends and acquaintances.

"Which means it must be the house," the criminologist concluded.

Had the Kobashis' house been the scene—as in the case of the orphanage—of something terrible that had never come to light?

But that theory didn't work, either.

"The villa was the last to be built on the only free lot of the complex. It was finished about three months ago, and the Kobashis have been its first and only owners," said Stern.

But Goran refused to give up: "The house hides a secret."

Stern immediately understood and asked, "Where do we start?"

Goran thought for a moment, then issued the order: "Start by digging up the garden."

First the corpse dogs were brought in, capable of sniffing out human remains to a great depth. Then came special radar equipment to scan under the ground, but nothing suspicious appeared on the screens.

Mila watched the various attempts take place; she was still waiting for Chang to give her the identity of the child found in the house by comparing her DNA with that of the parents of the victims.

They started digging at about three in the afternoon. The little diggers shifted the earth in the garden, destroying the masterly external architecture that must have cost a great deal of trouble and a great deal of money. Now it was carried away and dumped carelessly on the trucks.

The noise of the diesel engines disturbed the peace of Capo Alto.

As if that weren't enough, the vibrations produced by the diggers constantly set off the alarm on Kobashi's Maserati.

After the garden, the search moved inside the villa. A specialist company was called in to remove the heavy marble slabs from the sitting room. The internal walls were sounded for gaps, which were then brought to light with picks. The furniture also suffered an unhappy fate: dismantled and dissected, now fit only for the rubbish dump. There had also been digging in the cellar and the foundations.

Roche had authorized that destruction. The Department couldn't afford to fail again, even at the cost of causing millions worth of damage. But the Kobashis had no intention of coming back and living there. Everything that belonged to them had been irredeemably polluted by horror. They would sell the property at a lower price than they had paid for it, because their gilded life would never be the same with the memory of what had happened.

At about six p.m., the nervous tension of the people in charge of work on the crime scene was palpable.

"Could somebody turn off that damned alarm?" Roche yelled, pointing at Kobashi's Maserati.

"We can't find the car remotes," Boris replied.

"Call the dentist and tell him to give them to us! Do I have to tell you everything?"

They were going around in circles. Rather than uniting them, the tension was turning them against one another, frustrating them with their inability to solve the problem that Albert had devised for them.

"Why did he dress the child as a doll?"

The question was driving Goran mad. Mila had never seen him like this. There was something personal in this challenge. Something that perhaps even the criminologist wasn't aware of, which was interfering with his ability to reason lucidly.

Mila kept her distance, unnerved by the wait. What was the meaning of Albert's behavior?

At midnight Kobashi's car alarm still marked the passing of time, inexorably reminding everyone that their attempts so far had been pretty well useless.

Nothing new had emerged from under the ground. The villa had been practically gutted, but the walls had revealed no secrets.

As Mila had been sitting on the pavement in front of the house, Boris had come over, holding a mobile phone.

"I'm trying to make a call but there's no signal..."

Mila checked her phone as well. "Maybe that's why Chang still hasn't called to give me the outcome of the DNA test."

Boris gestured around him. "Well, it's some consolation to know that rich people lack something too, don't you think?"

He smiled, put his phone back in his pocket and sat down next to her. Mila still hadn't thanked him for the present of the parka, so she did so now.

"It's nothing," he replied.

At that moment they noticed that the private guards of Capo Alto were arranging themselves around the villa to form a security cordon.

"What's going on?"

"The press are coming," Boris told her. "Roche has decided to authorize pictures of the villa: a few minutes for the television news to show that we're doing everything possible."

She watched the fake policemen taking up position: they were ridiculous in their blue and orange uniforms, made to measure to display their muscular physiques, with hard expressions on their faces and their walkie-talkies that were supposed to give them a very professional appearance.

Albert made you look like idiots by blowing your cameras with a simple short-circuit! she thought.

"After all this time and still no answers, Roche will be foaming at the mouth..."

"He always finds a way to come out smelling of roses, don't worry."

Boris took out his papers and a packet of tobacco and started silently rolling himself a cigarette. Mila had the distinct sense that he wanted to ask her something, but not directly. And if she stayed silent she wouldn't help him.

She decided to give him a hand: "What did you do with the twenty-four hours of freedom that Roche allowed you?"

Boris was evasive. "I slept and thought about the case. Sometimes you need to clear your head...I know you went out with Gavila last night."

Hey, he's finally said it! But Mila was wrong in thinking that Boris's reference was motivated by jealousy. His intentions were quite different, as she discovered from what he said next.

"I think he's suffered a lot."

He was talking about Goran's wife. And he did so in such a sad voice that it made her think that whatever had happened to the couple, it had indirectly involved the team as well.

"I really don't know anything about it," she said. "He didn't talk to me about it. Just a hint at the end of the evening."

"Then perhaps it's better if you know now..."

Before going on, Boris lit the cigarette, dragged deeply on it and breathed out the smoke. He was searching for words.

"Dr. Gavila's wife was a fantastic woman, not just beautiful but nice, too. I've lost count of the times we all ate at their house. She was part of us, as if she was on the team as well. When we had a difficult case on our hands, those dinners were the only relief after a day among blood and corpses. A reconciliation with life, if you know what I mean..."

"And then what happened?"

"It happened a year and a half ago. With no warning, without so much as a hint, she walked out."

"She left him?"

"Not just Gavila, but Tommy too, their only son. He's a lovely boy, he's lived with his father since then."

Mila had guessed that the criminologist was weighed down by the sadness of a separation, but she'd never imagined anything like that. *How can a mother abandon a son?* she wondered.

"Why did she leave?"

"No one ever worked it out. Perhaps she had someone else, perhaps she got tired of that life, who knows...She didn't leave so much as a note. She just packed her bags and left. End of."

"I wouldn't have given up without knowing why she did it."

"The strange thing is that he never asked me to find out where she was." Boris's tone changed, he looked around before going on, checking that Goran was nowhere around. "And there's something that Gavila doesn't know and mustn't know..."

Mila nodded to show him that he could trust her.

"Well...a few months later, Stern and I tracked her down. She was living in a town on the coast. We didn't go to her directly, we just let her spot us in the street in the hope that she might come over and talk to us."

"And did she?"

"She was surprised to see us. But then she just waved, lowered her eyes and walked on."

This was followed by a silence that Mila couldn't interpret. Boris tossed his cigarette butt away, careless of the furious glance from one of the private security guards who immediately came and picked it up off the lawn.

"Why did you tell me that, Boris?"

"Because Dr. Gavila is my friend. And so are you, although I haven't known you as long."

Boris must have understood something that neither she nor Goran had yet managed to get into focus. Something about them. He was only trying to protect them both.

"When his wife walked out, Gavila kept going. He had to, especially because of the boy. Nothing changed with us. He still seemed exactly the same: precise, punctual, efficient. He just stopped dressing quite so smartly. That wasn't important, it was nothing to worry about. But then came the 'Wilson Pickett' case..."

"Like the singer?"

"Yes, that's what we called it." Boris clearly regretted having mentioned it. He said tersely, "It went badly. There were mistakes, and someone threatened to dissolve the team and dismiss Dr. Gavila. It was Roche who defended us and insisted that we keep our jobs."

Mila was about to ask what happened, sure that Boris would tell her in the end, when the alarm on Kobashi's Maserati went off again.

"Damn, that noise blows a hole in your brain!"

At that moment Mila happened to glance towards the house and in a moment she cataloged a series of images that drew her attention: the same expression of annoyance had appeared on the faces of the security guards, and they had all put their hands to their walkie-talkie headpieces as if there had been some sudden and unbearable interference.

Mila looked at the Maserati again. Then she slipped her mobile phone from her pocket: there was still no signal. She had an idea.

"There's one place we haven't looked yet..." she said to Boris.

"What place is that?"

Mila pointed upwards.

"In the ether."

Less than half an hour later, in the cold of night, the experts from the electronics team had already started to sound out the area. Each one wore headphones and held a little device aimed at the sky. They walked around—very slowly, silent as ghosts—trying to pick up possible radio signals or suspect frequencies, just in case the air contained some kind of message.

Which it did.

That was what was interfering with the alarm on Kobashi's Maserati and inhibiting phone reception. And had got into the walkie-talkies of the security guards in the form of an unbearable whistle.

A little while later the transmission was transferred to a receiver.

They gathered around the apparatus, to hear what the darkness had to tell them.

Not words, but sounds.

They were plunged into a sea of rustling from time to time, but there was a harmony in the precise sequence of notes. Short, then longer.

"Three dots, three lines and three dots again," Goran translated for the benefit of the others. In the language of the most famous radio code in the world, those elementary sounds had an unequivocal meaning.

SOS.

"Where's it coming from?" asked the criminologist.

The technician studied the signal as it appeared on his screen. Then he looked towards the street and pointed: "From the house opposite."

23.

It had been in front of their eyes all the time.

The house opposite had been watching their strenuous efforts silently all day. It was there, a few feet away, calling them, repeating its curious and anachronistic request for help.

The two-story villa belonged to Yvonne Gress. The painter, as the neighbors called her. She lived there with her two children, a boy of eleven and a girl of sixteen. They had moved to Capo Alto after Yvonne's divorce, and she had returned to her passion for art, which she had abandoned as a girl to marry the promising young lawyer, Gress.

At first Yvonne's abstract paintings hadn't been well received. The gallery that showed them had closed her solo show without a single piece sold. But Yvonne, convinced of her talent, hadn't let go. And when a friend had commissioned a portrait in oils of her family to hang over the mantelpiece, Yvonne had discovered her forte. Within a very short space of time she had become the most hotly desired portrait-painter among people weary of the usual photographs, who wanted to immortalize their own clans on canvas.

When the Morse code message drew attention to the house on the other side of the street, one of the guards remarked that Yvonne Gress and her kids hadn't been around for a while.

The curtains were drawn, which made it impossible to look inside.

Before Roche gave the order to enter the villa, Goran tried to call the woman's phone number. A moment later, in the general silence of the street, a ringing sound was heard coming faintly but clearly from the inside of the house. No one answered.

They also tried to contact her ex-husband, in the hope that at least the children were there. When they managed to track him down he said he hadn't heard from the children for ages. That wasn't strange, since he had abandoned his family for a model in her twenties, and thought he fulfilled his paternal duty by paying regular maintenance money to see that they were fed.

The technicians placed thermal sensors around the perimeter of the villa, to trace any sources of heat inside.

"If there's anyone alive in that house we'll soon know," said Roche, who had blind confidence in the efficiency of technology.

Meanwhile electricity, gas and water had also been checked. The respective connections had not been cut off because the bills were paid by direct debit, but the meters had stopped three months before: a sign that for almost ninety days no one in there had turned a light on.

"That's more or less since the Kobashis' villa was finished and the dentist moved here with his family," Stern remarked.

Goran asked, "Rosa, I want you to examine the CCTV camera recordings: there's obviously a connection here."

"Let's hope there are no more blackouts on the system," she said.

"We're preparing to go in," announced Gavila.

Meanwhile Boris put on his Kevlar protection in the mobile unit. "I want to go in," he declared when he saw Mila appearing on the threshold of the camper. "They can't stop me—I want to go too." He couldn't stomach the idea that Roche might ask the special units to go in first. "They'll only make a mess. They'll have to move about in the dark once they get in..."

"Well, I suspect they'll manage," observed Mila, without intending to contradict him too much.

"And will they also be able to guarantee their evidence?" he asked sarcastically.

"Then I want to be in there too."

Boris stopped for a moment and looked down at her without saying a word.

"I think I've deserved it—after all, I was the one who worked out that the message was—"

He interrupted her by throwing her a second bulletproof jacket.

A little while later they left the camper to join Goran and Roche, reasserting to them their reasons for going in.

"Out of the question," the chief inspector said immediately. "This is an operation for special forces. I can't afford such recklessness."

"Listen, Inspector..." Boris went and planted himself in front of Roche so that he couldn't ignore him. "Send Mila and me in on reconnaissance. The others will only go in if they really need to." Roche refused to yield. "I've been in the army, I'm trained for these things. Stern has twenty years' experience in the field as I can confirm, and if he hadn't lost a kidney he'd be volunteering with me, as he knows very well. As for officer Mila Vasquez; she went alone into the house of a maniac who was holding a little boy and a girl prisoner."

If Boris had known what had really happened when she had put her own life on the line as well as her hostages' lives, he wouldn't have supported her candidacy quite so stoutly, Mila thought bitterly.

"So think about it: there's a girl still alive somewhere, but she won't be for long. Every crime scene tells us more about her kidnapper." Then Boris pointed to Yvonne Gress's house: "If there's anything in there that can bring us to Albert, we need to find it before it gets destroyed. And the only way is to send us in."

"I don't think so, Special Agent," Roche replied serenely.

Boris came a step towards him, looking him straight in the eye. "Do you want any more complications? It's hard enough as it is..."

A guarded threat, Mila thought. She was surprised that Boris would address his superior in that tone. But it seemed like a matter between the two of them.

Roche looked at Gavila for a moment too long: was he after advice, or did he just want someone to share responsibility for the decision?

But the criminologist didn't try to exploit the situation, and just nodded.

"I hope we won't regret it." The chief inspector deliberately used the plural to stress Goran's share of responsibility.

At that moment a technician came over with a monitor for the thermal data. "Mr. Roche, the sensors have found something on the second floor…something alive."

Everyone looked back at the house.

"The subject is still on the second floor, and isn't moving from there," Stern announced on the radio.

Boris silently counted backwards before turning the front door handle. The spare key had been given to him by the commander of the security guards: there was a copy for every villa, they kept them in case of emergency.

Mila studied Boris's concentration. Behind them, the men of the special unit were ready to intervene. The special agent was the first to step inside, and she followed him. Their guns were leveled and apart from their Kevlar protection they wore caps with an earpiece, a microphone and a little torch by the right temple. From outside, Stern guided them by radio, while watching, on a screen, the movements of the outline found by the thermal sensors. The figure showed numerous fluctuating colors indicating the various temperatures of the body, from blue, to yellow, to red. It wasn't possible to make out its shape.

But it looked like a body lying on the ground.

It might be someone who'd been injured. But before they found out, Boris and Mila would have to carry out an accurate search in line with security procedures.

Outside the villa, two huge, powerful reflectors had been set up, illuminating both facades. But because of the drawn curtains the light fell only faintly on the interior. Mila tried to get her eyes accustomed to the dark.

"All OK?" Boris asked her in a whisper.

"All OK," she confirmed.

Meanwhile, where the Kobashis' lawn had once been, Goran Gavila now stood, more desperate for a cigarette than he had been for years. He was worried. Particularly for Mila. Beside him, Sarah Rosa was watching the CCTV recordings, sitting in front of four monitors. If there really was a link between the two houses that stood opposite one another, they would soon know.

The first thing Mila noticed in Yvonne Gress's house was the chaos.

From the door she had a complete view of the sitting room on her left and the kitchen on her right. The table was piled high with open cereal boxes, half-empty bottles of orange juice and cartons of rancid milk. There were also empty beer cans. The larder had been opened, and some of the food was scattered on the floor.

The table had four chairs. *But only one had been moved.*

The sink was full of dirty plates and pots with encrusted food remains. Mila aimed the light of her torch at the fridge: under a tortoise-shaped magnet she saw the picture of a blond woman in her forties, smiling as she hugged a little boy and a slightly older girl.

In the sitting room, the low table in front of a huge plasma screen was covered with empty bottles of spirits, more beer cans and ashtrays spilling over with butts. An armchair had been dragged into the middle of the room, and there were muddy boot prints on the carpet.

Boris attracted Mila's attention and showed her the map of the house, suggesting that they should split up before meeting again at the bottom of the stairs leading to the floor above. He pointed to the area behind the kitchen, keeping the library and the study for himself.

"Stern, everything still OK on the first floor?" Boris whispered into his radio.

"It's not moving," was the reply.

They nodded to one another, and Mila set off in the direction assigned to her.

"We've got it," Sarah Rosa said to the monitor at that same moment. "Look…"

Goran leaned on her shoulder: according to the date in the corner of the screen, these images dated from nine months before. The

Kobashis' villa was just a building site. In the speeded-up shot, the workers scuttled around the unfinished facade like frantic ants.

"Now watch..."

Rosa sped through the recording until it reached sunset, when everyone left the building site to go home and come back the following day. Then she put the video back to normal speed.

At that moment there was a glimpse of something in the shot of the Kobashis' front door.

It was a shadow, motionless, waiting. And it was smoking.

The intermittent glow of the cigarette revealed its presence. The man was inside the dentist's villa, waiting for evening to fall. When it was dark enough, he came outside. He looked round, then walked the few yards that separated him from the house opposite and entered without knocking.

"Listen..."

Mila was in Yvonne Gress's studio, where canvases were stacked in every corner, easels and paints scattered here and there; when she heard Goran's voice in the earpiece she stopped.

"We've probably worked out what happened in that house."

Mila waited.

"We're dealing with a *parasite*."

Mila didn't understand, but Goran explained the term.

"Every evening, one of the workers employed on the Kobashi villa waited for the building site to close before immediately letting himself into the house opposite. We fear he may have"—the criminologist paused before defining such a chilling idea—"kidnapped the family in their own home."

The guest takes possession of the nest, convincing himself that he is part of the family's life. He justifies everything with his supposed love. But when he tires of that fiction, he gets rid of his new family and seeks another nest to infest.

As she observed the putrid signs of his passage in Yvonne's studio, Mila remembered the *Sarcophaga carnaria* larvae banqueting on the Kobashis' rug.

Then she heard Stern asking, "For how long?"

"Six months," was Goran's reply.

Mila felt a tightness in her stomach. For six months Yvonne and her children had been the prisoners of a psychopath who had been able to do whatever he liked with them. And, what was more, he did it in the middle of dozens of other houses, where other families, isolated in this affluent place, imagined they could flee the horrors of the world, trusting in an absurd ideal of security.

Six months. And no one had noticed anything.

The lawn had been mown every week and the roses in the beds had continued to receive the loving care of the gardeners of the residential complex. The porch lights were turned on every evening, with a timer synchronized to the timetable indicated by the rules of the condominium. The children had played on bikes or with balls in the drive in front of the house, ladies had walked by chattering about this and that and exchanging recipes for desserts, the men had gone jogging on Sunday morning and washed the car in front of their garages.

Six months. And *no one had seen.*

They hadn't wondered why the curtains were drawn even by day. They hadn't noticed the mail that was accumulating in the letter box. No one had paid any attention to the absence of Yvonne and her children at social occasions in the clubhouse, like the autumn dance and the tombola on 23 December. The Christmas tree decorations—the same for the whole complex—had been arranged as usual by the management, and then removed after the holiday. The phone had gone unanswered, Yvonne and the children hadn't come to open the door when people had knocked, and yet no one's suspicions had been roused.

Yvonne Gress's only relatives lived a long way away. But even they didn't seem to have thought there was anything strange about that silence that had been protracted for so long.

Throughout that long, long time, the little family had wished, hoped, prayed every day for help or attention that had never come.

"He's probably a sadist. And this is his game, his entertainment."

His doll's house, the words ran through Mila's mind, as she thought about the clothes worn by the corpse that Albert had left on the Kobashis' sofa.

She thought of the countless violations that Yvonne and her children had undergone in that endless period of time. Six months of torment. Six months of torture. Six months of agony. But thinking about it, it had taken less than that for the whole world to forget about them.

And even the "guardians of the law" hadn't noticed anything, even though they were stationed twenty-four hours a day—in a state of alert!—right in front of the house. They too were somehow guilty, complicit. And so was she.

Once again, Mila reflected, Albert had shone a light on the hypocrisy of that portion of the human race that feels "normal" just because it doesn't go around killing innocent children by severing one of their arms. But it is capable of an equally serious crime: indifference.

Boris interrupted Mila's train of thought.

"Stern, how are things going up there?"

"Nothing there."

"Fine, then let's move."

They met as agreed at the bottom of the stairs leading to the second floor, where the bedrooms were.

Boris nodded to Mila to cover him. From that moment they would observe the most complete radio silence so as not to reveal their positions. Stern was authorized to break it only to warn them if the living outline showed any movement.

They began to climb the stairs. The carpet that covered the steps was dotted with stains: footprints and leftover food. On the wall next to the stairs were photographs of holidays, birthdays and family parties, and at the top there was a portrait in oils of Yvonne and her children. Someone had dug out the eyes in the painting, perhaps irritated by that insistent gaze.

When they reached the landing, Boris stepped aside to let Mila catch up with him. Then he led the way forward: various half-opened doors led onto the corridor, which turned off to the left at the end.

Behind that last corner was the last living presence in the whole house.

Boris and Mila started walking slowly in that direction. They passed one of the doors that stood ajar. Mila recognized the rhythmical sound of the Morse code that had been sent into the ether. She gently opened the door and found herself looking at the eleven-year-old boy's room. There were posters of planets on the walls and astronomy books on the shelves. A telescope was set up by the barred window.

On the little desk there was a science diorama: the scale reproduction of a nineteenth-century telegraph station. It consisted of a little wooden board with two dry batteries connected, through electrodes and copper wire, to a perforated disk that rotated on a sprocket at regular intervals—*three dots, three lines, three dots.* The whole thing had then been linked by a small cable to a walkie-talkie in the shape of a dinosaur. The diorama bore a bronze plate bearing the inscription FIRST PRIZE.

That was where the signal had been coming from.

The eleven-year-old boy had turned his homework into a transmitter, evading the checks and restrictions of the man who was keeping them prisoner.

Mila moved the beam of the torch over the unmade bed. Under it was a dirty plastic bucket. She also noticed signs of rubbing at the edges of the bed head.

On the opposite side of the corridor was the room of the sixteen-year-old girl. On the door, colored letters composed a name: Keira. Mila quickly glanced at the room from the doorway. The sheets were piled up on the floor. An underwear drawer had been tipped up on the floor. The mirror from the chest of drawers had been moved in front of the bed. It wasn't hard to imagine why. Here too there were signs of rubbing on the struts.

Handcuffs, thought Mila. *He kept them tied to their beds during the day.*

This time the dirty plastic bucket was in a corner. It must have been used for bodily functions.

A few yards away was Yvonne's room. The mattress was grimy, and there was only one sheet. There were stains of vomit on the carpet, and tissues were scattered around the place. On one wall there was a nail which might once have held a painting, but from which a leather belt now hung in full view, a reminder of who was in charge and how.

This was your games room, you bastard! And I expect you paid the little girl a visit every now and again, too! And when you tired of them, you went into the eleven-year-old's bedroom, even if it was just to beat him…

Anger was the only emotion she had been granted in this life. And Mila took advantage of it, greedily drinking from that dark well.

There was no way of knowing how many times Yvonne Gress had forced herself to be "nice" to that monster, just to keep him with her in that room, and avoid him taking it out on her children.

"Guys, there's something moving." Stern's voice was alarmed.

Boris and Mila turned simultaneously towards the corner at the end of the corridor. There was no more time to inspect the place. They aimed their guns and torches in that precise direction, waiting to see something appear at any moment.

"Don't move!" said Boris.

"It's coming towards you."

Mila moved her index finger on the trigger and began to exert light pressure on it. She heard her heart thumping in a crescendo in her ears.

"It's behind the corner."

The presence announced itself with a faint groan. A hairy muzzle appeared, and looked at them. It was a Newfoundland dog. Mila raised her weapon and saw Boris doing the same.

"All OK," she said to the radio. "It's just a dog."

Its fur was rough and sticky, its eyes red, and it was injured in one paw.

He didn't kill it, thought Mila, approaching it.

"Come on, boy, come here…"

"He's survived on his own here for at least three months: how did he do that?" Boris wondered.

As Mila stepped towards him, the dog retreated.

"Careful, he's frightened, he might bite you."

Mila paid no heed to Boris's suggestions and went on slowly approaching the Newfoundland. She knelt down to reassure him, and called to him. "Come on, boy, come to me."

When she was close enough, she saw that he had a nameplate hanging from his collar. She read his name in the torchlight.

"Newfie, come to me, come on..."

At last the dog allowed her to reach him. Mila held a hand in front of his muzzle, so that he could sniff it.

By now Boris was impatient. "OK, let's stop checking the map and then bring the others in."

The dog lifted a paw towards Mila, as if trying to show her something.

"Wait..."

"What?"

Mila didn't reply, but got up and saw that the Newfoundland had gone back towards the dark corner of the corridor.

"He wants us to follow him."

They walked behind him. They turned the corner and saw that the corridor ended a few yards further on. At the end, on the right, there was one last room.

Boris checked on the map. "It faces towards the back, but I don't know what it is."

The door was closed. Some things were piled up in front of it. A quilt printed with a pattern of bones, a bowl, a colored ball, a lead and the remains of some food.

"That's who's been raiding the larder."

"I wonder why he brought his things up here..."

The Newfoundland approached the door as if to confirm that this was now his bed.

"Are you saying he brought everything up here all by himself? Why?"

As if to answer Mila's question, the dog started scratching the wood of the door and whimpering.

"He wants us to go in..."

Mila took the lead and tied the dog to one of the radiators.

"You be good, Newfie."

The Newfoundland barked, as if he had understood. They shifted the things from the doorway, and Mila gripped the handle as Boris leveled his gun at the door: the thermal sensors hadn't revealed any other presences in the house, but you never knew. But they were both convinced that this thin barrier concealed the tragic epilogue to what had been happening there for so many months.

Mila lowered her hand to click the lock open, then pushed. The light from the torches pierced the darkness. The beams moved from one side to the other.

The room was empty.

It was about twenty feet by ten. There was no carpet on the floor, and the walls were painted white. The window was closed with a heavy curtain. A lamp hung from the ceiling. It was as if the room had never been used.

"Why has he brought us here?" Mila asked, more to herself than to Boris. "And where are Yvonne and her children?"

She avoided the real question: Where did the bodies end up?

"Stern."

"Yes?"

"Bring in the scientists, we've finished here."

Mila went back to the corridor and freed the dog, which ran away from her, into the room. Mila watched him settle in a corner.

"Newfie, you can't stay here!"

But the dog didn't move. Then she approached him with the lead in her hand. The animal barked again, but didn't seem threatening. Then he started sniffing the floor by the skirting board. Mila bent down beside him, pushed his muzzle aside and moved her torch to get a better view. No, there was nothing there. Then she saw it.

A brown stain.

It was less than three millimeters across. She came closer and saw that it was rectangular and with a slightly puckered surface.

Mila had no doubt what it was. "This is where it happened," she said.

Boris didn't understand.

Then Mila turned towards him: "This is where he killed them."

"We actually had noticed someone going into the house...but, you know, Yvonne Gress was an attractive woman living on her own...so she sometimes received visits from men in the neighborhood late in the evening."

The commander of the security guards gave a meaningful nod, to which Goran reacted by standing on tiptoe to stare him in the eyes.

"Don't you dare insinuate anything of that kind."

He said it in a neutral voice, but one which contained a threat.

The security chief should have been trying to justify this serious breach on the part of himself and his underlings. But he'd been briefed by the lawyers of the Capo Alto complex. Their strategy consisted in making Yvonne Gress look like an easy woman, just because she was single and independent.

Goran remarked that the *creature*—because he could think of no other name for him—who had come and gone from her house for six months had taken advantage of the same excuse to do as he pleased.

The criminologist and Rosa viewed lots of the film from that long period of time. They had to speed up the recording, but more or less the same scene was repeated over and over again. Sometimes the man didn't come, and Goran imagined that those nights were the best for the segregated family. But perhaps, too, they were the worst, since it meant they couldn't be untied from their beds, and they couldn't get any food or water if he didn't look after them.

Being raped meant surviving, in the perennial quest for the lesser evil.

The films also showed the man by day, working on the building site. He always wore a cap with a visor, which prevented the cameras from recording his facial features.

Stern questioned the owner of the building firm that had taken him on as a seasonal worker. They said the man's name was Lebrinsky, but the name turned out to be false. That often happened, mostly because foreign workers without residence permits were taken on at the building sites. By law, the employer was only obliged to ask them for their papers, not to check that they were genuine.

Some laborers who had worked at the Kobashis' villa during that time said "Lebrinsky" was a taciturn character who kept himself to himself. They gave remembered descriptions of him to create an identikit. But in the end the reconstructions were too different to be useful.

When he had finished with the head of the security guards, Goran joined the others inside Yvonne Gress's villa, which was by now the exclusive domain of Krepp and his men.

The piercings of the fingerprint expert jangled cheerfully on his face as he moved around the place like an elf in an enchanted wood. The house had a surreal look: the carpet had been completely covered with plastic sheets and there were halogen lamps set up around the place to highlight various areas or even just a detail. Men in white overalls and protective Perspex goggles dusted every surface.

"OK, our man isn't very clever," Krepp began. "Apart from the mess that the dog has made, he's left all kinds of rubbish around here: cans, cigarette stubs, used glasses. There's enough of his DNA to clone him!"

"Fingerprints?" asked Sarah Rosa.

"Tons! But he has never been a guest of our prison system, sad to say, and there's no record of him."

Goran shook his head; a pile of clues like that and still it wasn't possible to find a suspect. Certainly the parasite had been much less cautious than Albert, who had taken care to black out the security cameras before getting into the Kobashis' house with the girl. Precisely for that reason, there was one thing that didn't make sense to Goran.

"What can you tell me about the bodies? We've viewed the films and the parasite has never taken anything out of the house."

"Because they didn't leave by the door..."

They all looked at each other, trying to work out what the sentence could mean. Krepp added, "We're going through the drains, I think he got rid of them like that."

He had chopped them up, Goran concluded. That maniac had

acted out the part of the loving husband and the adored dad. And then one day he had tired of them, or maybe he had just finished work on the house opposite, and come in for the last time. Perhaps Yvonne and her children had had a sense that the end was approaching.

"But I've saved the strangest thing till last..." said Krepp.

"What might that be?"

"The empty room on the floor above, the one in which our policewoman friend found that small bloodstain."

Goran saw Mila stiffen, on the defensive. The expert had that effect on lots of people.

"The room on the second floor will be my 'Sistine Chapel,'" Krepp stressed. "That stain suggests to us that it was there that the massacre took place. And that afterwards he cleaned everything, although he missed that detail. But he did more than that: he actually repainted the walls."

"Why would he do that?" asked Boris.

"Because he's stupid, that much is obvious. After leaving such a mess and so many clues, and flushing the remains down the sewer, he had already earned himself a life sentence. So why bother to freshen up a room?"

For Goran, too, the motive was obscure. "So how do you proceed from here?"

"We'll take off the paint and see what's underneath. It'll take us a while, but with new techniques we can recover all the bloodstains that that idiot tried to hide so childishly."

Goran wasn't convinced. "All we have for now is false imprisonment and the concealment of bodies. He would get jail, but that doesn't mean justice will have been done. To get the truth out, and arrest him for homicide, we need that blood as well."

"You'll have it, Dr. Gavila."

For the time being they had a very brief description of the subject they were looking for. They compared it with the data gathered by Krepp.

"I'd say he's a man between forty and fifty," Rosa began. "Well-built, and about five foot eleven."

"The shoe prints on the carpet are a size nine, so I'd say that's about right."

"A smoker."

"He rolls his own cigarettes with tobacco and papers."

"Like me," said Boris. "I'm always glad to have something in common with guys like that."

"And I'd say he likes dogs," Krepp concluded.

"Just because he left the Newfoundland alive?" asked Mila.

"No, my dear. We've found some mongrel hairs."

"But who says the man brought them into the house?"

"They were in the mud of the shoe prints that he left on the carpet. Obviously there was material from the building site—cement, gums, solvents—which acted as glue for the rest. Including the stuff that the guy brought in from his own house."

Krepp looked at Mila like someone who has been unwisely challenged, and who has finally prevailed with dazzling brilliance. After that brief interval of glory, he looked away from her and went back to being the cold professional they all knew.

"And there's one more thing, but I haven't yet worked out if it's worth mentioning."

"Tell us anyway," broke in Goran. He knew how much Krepp liked being asked.

"In that mud under his shoes there was a high concentration of bacteria. I asked the opinion of my most trusted chemist..."

"Why a chemist and not a biologist?"

"Because I guessed that they were 'refuse-eating' bacteria, which exist in nature but are used for various purposes, such as devouring plastic and petroleum derivatives." Then he became specific: "They don't eat anything, in fact, they just produce an enzyme. They're used for cleaning up former dumps..."

At those words, Goran noticed that Mila had suddenly glanced towards Boris, and that he had done the same.

"Former dumps? Holy shit...we know this guy!"

24.

Feldher was waiting for them.

The parasite had withdrawn into his cocoon, at the top of the hill of refuse.

He had all kinds of weapons, which he had been piling up for months in preparation for the final showdown. He hadn't actually done very much about hiding. He knew that sooner or later someone would come to ask him for explanations.

Mila arrived with the rest of the team, followed by the special units which placed themselves around the property.

From his lofty position, Feldher could check the streets leading to the former dump. He had also cut down the trees that blocked his view. But he didn't start firing straightaway. He waited until they were in position before beginning his target practice.

First he aimed at his dog, Koch, the rusty mongrel that wandered about the scrap iron. He killed it with a single shot, to the head. He wanted to show the men out there that he was serious. And perhaps spare the animal a worse death, thought Mila.

Crouching behind one of the armored vehicles, the policewoman observed the scene. How much time had passed since the day she had set foot in that house with Boris? They had gone there to ask Feldher about the religious institution he had grown up in, while he himself concealed a secret much worse than Ronald Dermis's.

He had lied about lots of things.

When Boris had asked him if he had ever been in jail, he had answered in the affirmative. And in fact it wasn't true. That was why they hadn't found a match for the prints left in Yvonne Gress's house. But he had been able to use that lie to be certain that the two officers knew almost nothing about him. And Boris hadn't noticed anything, because you don't usually lie to give a negative image of yourself.

Feldher had done it. He had been quite crafty, Mila thought.

He had sized them up, and he had started playing with them, certain that they would have no clues to link him to Yvonne's house. If he had suspected the opposite, they probably wouldn't have left that house alive.

Mila had been tricked for a second time by his presence at Ronald's nocturnal funeral. She had thought it was a gesture of pity, when in fact Feldher was checking out the situation.

"Come on, you bastards, come and get me!"

Machine-gun bullets rattled through the air, some thudding dully against the armored vehicles, others echoing off the scrap metal.

"Sons of bitches! You won't get me alive!"

No one replied, no one tried to strike a deal with him. Mila looked round: there was no negotiator anywhere around with a megaphone, ready to tell him to drop his weapons. Feldher had already signed his own death warrant. None of the men out there was interested in saving his life.

They were only waiting for one false move to wipe him off the face of the earth.

A few snipers were already in place, ready to fire as soon as he moved. For the moment, they were letting him rant. That made it more likely that he would make a mistake.

"She was mine, you bastards! Mine! I just gave her what she wanted!"

He was provoking them. And to judge from the faces staring at him, the attempt was successful.

"We've got to take him alive," said Goran eventually. "It's the only way we'll find out the link between him and Albert."

"I don't think the guys in the special units agree with you, Doctor," said Stern.

"Then we've got to talk to Roche: he has to give the order to call in a negotiator."

"Feldher isn't going to be taken: he's already predicted everything, including his own death," observed Sarah Rosa. "He's trying to think up a coup de théâtre so that he can go out with a bang."

She wasn't mistaken. The pyrotechnicians who had just arrived had identified some variations in the terrain surrounding the house. "Land mines," one of them said to Roche, coming over to join him.

"With all the shit that's under there, this could be the end of the world."

A geologist was consulted, and she confirmed that the dump forming the hill could contain tons of methane produced by the decomposition of refuse.

"You've got to get out of here straightaway: a fire could be devastating."

Goran insisted that they should at least try to negotiate with Feldher. In the end, Roche allowed him half an hour.

The criminologist thought about using the phone, but Mila remembered that the line had been cut off for nonpayment because when he and Boris had tried to contact Feldher some days before, they'd got a recorded voice. The phone company took seven minutes to reestablish contact. They only had twenty-three to persuade the man to give himself up. But when his home phone started ringing, Feldher reacted by firing at them.

Goran didn't throw in the towel. He picked up a megaphone and planted himself behind the armored vehicle nearest the house.

"Feldher, it's Goran Gavila!"

"Fuck off!" Followed by a shot.

"Listen to me: I despise you, like all the other people here."

Mila understood that Goran didn't want to barter with Feldher by making him believe things that weren't true, because there would be no point. The man had already chosen his own fate. That was why the criminologist had immediately put his cards on the table.

"You piece of shit, I don't want to listen to you!" Another shot, this time a few inches away from where Goran was standing. Although he was well protected, Goran gave a start.

"But you will, because I've got something to tell you!"

What kind of offer could he make him when they'd reached this point? Mila had no sense of Goran's strategy.

"We need you, Feldher, because you probably know who's keeping the sixth child prisoner. We call him Albert, but I'm sure you know his real name."

"I don't give a fuck!"

"You do, because there's a price on the information right now!"

The reward.

So that was Goran's game. The ten million offered by the Rockford Foundation to anyone who provided information useful to the rescue of child number six.

Some might also have wondered what advantage the sum might hold for a man who was sure he was going to jail. Mila understood. The criminologist had been trying to plant in Feldher's mind the idea that he might get away with it, that he might be able to "screw the system." The same system that had persecuted him all his life, making him what he was. A miserable wretch, a loser. With that money he could afford a big lawyer, who might be able to reduce the charge on the grounds of diminished responsibility, a legal option usually reserved for wealthy defendants because it was difficult to sustain and demonstrate without adequate funds. Feldher could have hoped for a lower sentence—maybe as little as twenty years—to be spent not in prison but among the patients of a judicial psychiatric hospital. Then, once he was out, he would enjoy the rest of his wealth. As a free man.

Goran had hit the target. Because Feldher had always wanted to be something more. That was why he had gone into Yvonne Gress's house. To know, at least once, what it feels like to live a privileged life, in a rich area, with a beautiful wife and beautiful children, and beautiful things.

Now he had the chance of getting a double result: winning that money and getting away with what he'd done.

He would walk right out of that house, smiling his way past a hundred police officers who wanted him dead. But above all, he would come out a rich man. In many ways as an actual *hero*.

There were no insults, no shots from Feldher in reply. He was thinking.

Goran took advantage of that silence to add to his expectations.

"Mr. Feldher, no one can take away what you've earned. And even though I don't like to admit it, a lot of people will have to thank you. So put down your weapons now, come outside and give yourself up..."

Once again, evil in the service of good, Mila thought. Goran was using the same technique for good.

A few seemingly interminable seconds passed. But Goran knew that the more seconds passed, the more hope there was that his plan might succeed. From behind the armored vehicle that sheltered him, he saw one of the men from the special units extending a pole with a little mirror to check Feldher's position in the house.

A moment later he spotted him in the reflection.

They could only see his shoulder and the back of his neck. He was wearing a camouflage jacket and a hunting cap. Then for a moment he had a glimpse of his profile, his chin and his untended beard.

It took only a split second. Feldher raised his rifle, perhaps to shoot or as a sign of surrender.

The muffled whistle passed quickly over their heads.

Before Mila realized what was happening, the first bullet had already struck Feldher in the neck. Then came the second, from another direction.

"No!" cried Goran. "Stop! Don't shoot!"

Mila saw the elite marksmen of the special units emerging from their hiding places, the better to take aim.

The two holes that Feldher had taken to his neck sprayed vaporized blood to the rhythm of his carotid artery. He was dragging himself along on one leg, his mouth wide open. With one hand he tried desperately to plug his wounds, while with the other he tried to hold the rifle raised to return fire.

Goran, careless of the danger, came out into the open in a desperate attempt to stop time.

At that moment, a third shot, more accurate than the others, struck its target in the neck.

The parasite had been exterminated.

25.

Sabine likes dogs, did you know that?"

She'd said it in the present tense, thought Mila. That was normal: that mother had not yet come to terms with her grief. Soon it would begin. And for some days she would have neither peace nor sleep.

But not now, it was too soon.

Sometimes in cases like this, for some reason, grief leaves a space, a barrier between you and the information, an elastic barrier that stretches out and shrinks in again, without letting the words "we've found your daughter's body" bring their message to its destination. The words bounce off that strange sense of tranquility. A brief pause of resignation before the collapse.

A few hours before, Chang had given Mila an envelope containing the results of the DNA comparison. The child on the Kobashis' sofa was Sabine.

The third to be abducted.

And the third to be found.

It was now a consolidated program. A modus operandi, Goran would have said. Even though no one had ventured any hypotheses on the identity of the corpse, everyone had expected it to be her.

Mila had left her colleagues to wonder about the sudden defeat of Feldher at his home, and try to search that mountain of refuse for possible clues that might lead to Albert. She had asked the Department for a car and now she was in the sitting room in the house of Sabine's parents, in a part of the countryside inhabited chiefly by horse breeders and people who had chosen to live close to nature. She had traveled almost three hundred miles to get there. The sun was setting and she had been able to enjoy the wooded landscape crisscrossed with streams that fed into amber-colored pools. She thought that for Sabine's parents, receiving a visit from her, even at such an unusual time of day, might be reassuring, a sign that someone had taken care of their daughter. She wasn't mistaken.

Sabine's mother was tiny and lean, her face covered with little lines that emanated a sense of strength. Mila looked at the photographs that the woman had put in her hands, listened to her talking about the first and only seven years of Sabine's life. Her father stood in a corner of the room, leaning against the wall with his eyes downcast and his hands behind his back: he was swaying back and forth, concentrating only on his breathing. Mila was sure his wife ruled the roost in this house.

"Sabine was premature: eight weeks early. We told ourselves it had happened because she had this crazy desire to come into the world. And there's some truth in that..." She smiled and looked at her husband, who nodded. "The doctors told us straightaway that she wouldn't survive, because her heart was too weak. But contrary to all predictions, Sabine survived. She was the size of my hand and weighed barely a pound, but she fought tenaciously in the incubator. And week after week, her heart grew stronger and stronger...Then the doctors had to change their minds, and told us she would probably survive, but that her life would be one of hospitals, medicine and operations. All in all, that we would have been better off if she had died..." She paused for a moment. "At one point I was so convinced that my daughter would suffer for the rest of her days that I prayed that her heart would stop. Sabine was even stronger than my prayers: she developed like a normal child and, eight months after she was born, we brought her home."

The woman broke off. For a moment, her expression changed. It got ugly.

"That son of a bitch wrecked all her efforts!"

Sabine was the youngest of Albert's victims. She had been taken off a merry-go-round. On a Saturday evening. In front of her mother and father, and in front of the eyes of all the other parents.

Everyone was looking at their own child, Sarah Rosa had said at the first meeting in the Thinking Room. And Mila remembered her adding, *People don't care, that's the reality.*

Mila hadn't gone to that house just to console Sabine's parents, but also to ask them a few questions. She knew she had to take advantage of those moments before suffering crashed into their temporary refuge and erased everything once and for all. She was aware of the fact that the couple had been questioned dozens of times about the circumstances of the little girl's disappearance. But perhaps her questioners didn't have her experience of missing children.

"The fact is," she began, "that you are the only ones who might have seen or noticed something. All the other times, the kidnapper acted in isolated places, or when he was alone with his victims. In this case he took a risk. And it's also possible that something went wrong."

"Do you want me to tell you everything from the start?"

"Yes, please."

The woman collected her thoughts, then began: "That was a special evening for us. You must know that when my daughter turned three, we decided to leave our jobs in the city to move here. We were drawn by the landscape and the chance to bring up our daughter far from the noise and smog."

"You said the evening of your daughter's abduction was a special one for you..."

"That's right." The woman tried to catch her husband's eye, then continued: "We won the lottery. A large sum. Not enough to make us rich, exactly, but enough to give Sabine and her children a comfortable future... I'd never really done it before. But one morning I bought a ticket and it happened."

The woman forced a smile.

"I bet you've always wondered what you would do if you won the lottery."

Mila nodded. "So you went to the fair to celebrate, right?"

"Right."

"I'd like you to reconstruct the exact moments when Sabine was on that merry-go-round."

"We'd chosen the blue horse together. During the first two turns her father stayed with her. Then Sabine had insisted on doing the third on her own. She was very stubborn, so we let her do it."

"I can see that, it's quite natural with children," said Mila to absolve her in advance of any sense of guilt.

The woman raised her eyes to her, then said confidently: "There were other parents on the merry-go-round, each beside their own child. My eyes were fixed on mine. I swear I didn't miss a single second of that turn. Except for the moments when Sabine was on the opposite side to us."

He made her disappear like a conjuring trick, Stern had said in the Thinking Room.

Mila explained: "Our hypothesis is that the kidnapper was already on the merry-go-round: one parent among many others. That made us think that he must look like an ordinary man: he managed to pass for a father, immediately making off with the little girl and vanishing into the crowd. Sabine might have cried or protested. But no one paid any attention because in everyone's eyes she just looked like a little girl throwing a tantrum."

Probably the idea that Albert had passed for Sabine's father hurt more than anything else.

"I assure you, Officer Vasquez, that if there had been a strange man on that merry-go-round, I would have noticed. A mother has a sixth sense for these things."

She said it with such conviction that Mila didn't feel like contradicting her.

Albert had managed to give himself a perfect disguise.

Twenty-five police officers, closed in a room for ten days, had carefully examined hundreds of photographs taken at the fair that evening. They had also viewed the amateur films shot on family video cameras. Not a single shot had immortalized Sabine with her abductor, not even fleeing. They didn't appear in a single photograph, not even as colorless shadows in the background.

She had no other questions, so Mila took her leave. Before she left, Sabine's mother insisted that she take away a photograph of her daughter.

"So you won't forget her," she said, unaware that Mila wouldn't forget her anyway, and that in a few hours' time she would bear a tribute to that death in the form of a new scar. "You'll take it, won't you?"

She wasn't surprised by Sabine's father's question, in fact she expected it. Everyone asked it. "You will catch the murderer?"

And she gave the reply she always gave in such cases.

"We'll do all we can."

Sabine's mother had wished her daughter dead. Her wish had come true seven years later. Mila couldn't help thinking about it as she drove back to the Studio. The woods that had cheered her journey on the way there were now dark fingers that climbed towards the wind-stirred sky.

She had programmed her SatNav to take her back the shortest possible way. Then she had switched the display to night mode. The blue light was relaxing.

The car radio only picked up AM stations and, after wandering through the frequencies, she had found one that played old classics. Mila kept Sabine's photograph on the seat beside her. Thank heavens, her parents had been spared the painful process of the identification of the body, when her remains were already prey to *fauna cadaverica*. For that reason she blessed the breakthroughs in DNA extraction.

That brief chat had given her a sense of incompleteness. There was something wrong, something that hadn't worked, that had got in her way. It was a simple consideration. One day that woman had bought a lottery ticket and won. Her daughter had fallen victim to a serial killer.

Two unlikely events in a single life.

The terrible thing, however, was that the two events were linked.

If they hadn't won the lottery, they would never have gone to the fair to celebrate. And Sabine wouldn't have been abducted and brutally killed. The retribution for that stroke of luck had been death.

That's not true, she thought to herself. *He chose the families, not the children. He would have taken her anyway.*

But the thought made her uneasy, and she couldn't wait to get to the Studio to relax and chase it from her mind.

The road curved among the hills. Every now and again there were signs for horse ranches. They weren't far away from one another, and to reach them you had to take secondary roads that often ran for miles through the middle of nothing. Throughout the journey Mila had seen only a few cars coming in the opposite direction, and a combine harvester with flashing lights to warn of its slow progress.

The station played an old hit by Wilson Pickett, "You Can't Stand Alone."

It took her a few seconds to link the artist with the name of the case that Boris had mentioned when talking about Goran and his wife. *It went badly. There were mistakes, and someone threatened to dissolve the team and dismiss Dr. Gavila. It was Roche who defended us and insisted that we keep our jobs,* he had explained.

What had happened? Perhaps it had something to do with the pictures of the beautiful girl she had glimpsed at the Studio? Had her new colleagues set foot in the apartment since then?

But these were questions she couldn't have answered. She dismissed them from her mind. Then she turned up the heating a little: outside it was minus three, but inside the car it was fine. She had even taken off her parka before sitting down at the wheel, and waited for the car to warm up gradually. That passage from intense cold to heat had calmed her nerves.

She yielded pleasurably to the weariness that was gradually taking control of her. All in all, she was enjoying the car journey. In a corner of the windscreen, the sky, which had been covered by a thick layer of cloud for days, suddenly opened up. Like someone had cut out a scrap of it, revealing a multitude of scattered stars and letting the moonlight through.

At that moment, in the solitude of those forests, Mila felt privileged. As if that unexpected spectacle were only for her. As the road curved round, the tear of light moved over the windscreen. She followed it with her eyes. But when they settled on the rearview mirror, she saw a gleam.

The moonlight was reflected in the bodywork of the car that was following her with its lights out.

The sky closed over her. And it was dark again. Mila tried to stay calm. Once again, someone was copying her footsteps, as had happened in the gravel yard outside the motel. But if the first time she had accepted that it might be a figment of her imagination, now she was absolutely convinced of its reality.

I have to stay calm and think.

If she accelerated, she would reveal her state of alarm. And she didn't know how skilled a driver her pursuer was: on those rough roads, roads that she didn't know, an attempted escape could have proved fatal. There were no houses to be seen, and the first center of human habitation was at least twenty miles away. And besides, her nocturnal adventure at the orphanage, with Ronald Dermis and his drugged tea, had put her courage severely to the test. She hadn't admitted it until then—in fact, she had insisted to everyone that she felt well and hadn't suffered from shock. But now she wasn't so sure that she could confront another dangerous situation. The tendons in her arms stiffened, her nervous tension rose. She felt her heart speeding up, and she didn't know how to stop it. She was gripped by panic.

I must stay calm, I must stay calm and think sensibly.

She turned off the radio to help her concentration. She worked out that her pursuer was using her lights to guide him. After staring at the SatNav screen for a moment, she detached it from its fitting and put it in her lap.

Then she reached her hand towards the light switch *and turned them out.*

Suddenly she accelerated. In front of her there was nothing but a wall of darkness. Without knowing where she was going, she trusted only the trajectory indicated by the navigation device. Take a forty-degree bend to the right. She obeyed and saw the cursor on the display pointing out her journey. A straight line. Skidding slightly, she complied. She kept her hands firmly on the wheel, because without any bearings it would only have taken a tiny variation to send her off the road. A curve to the left, sixty degrees. This time she had to change down suddenly so as not to lose control, and steered into the bend. Another straight line, longer than the earlier one. How long could she go on without having to turn the lights back on? Had she managed to trick whoever was on her tail?

Taking advantage of the straight road ahead of her, she looked in the rearview mirror.

The lights of the car behind her came on.

Her pursuer had finally revealed himself, and he wasn't giving up. His headlights shone their beam on her and beyond her, on the road ahead of her. Mila steered just in time to take the bend and, at the same time, she turned her lights back on. She accelerated and traveled just over three hundred meters at full speed.

Then she abruptly braked in the middle of the carriageway and stared at the mirror again.

The ticking of her engine, along with the thumping drum in her chest, were the only sounds she could hear. The other car had stopped before the bend. Mila saw the white beam of the headlights stretching across the tarmac. The roar of the exhaust sounded like some wild beast preparing to leap and sink its teeth into its prey.

Come on, I'm waiting for you.

She took her gun and slipped a bullet into the barrel. She didn't know where she got that courage that she had felt she didn't have only a moment before. Desperation had led her into a ludicrous duel, in the middle of nowhere.

But her pursuer didn't take up the invitation. The headlights around the bend disappeared, making way for two faint red glows.

The car had turned round.

Mila didn't move. Then she started breathing normally again.

For a moment she lowered her eye to the passenger seat, seeking comfort in Sabine's smile.

Only then did she notice that there was something wrong in the picture.

It was just past midnight when she got to the Studio. Her nerves were still on edge, and for the rest of the journey she had thought only about the photograph of Sabine, looking around at the same time, waiting for whoever was following her to appear at any moment from a side road, or ambush her behind a bend.

She quickly climbed the stairs leading to the apartment. She wanted to speak to Goran straightaway, and tell the team what had happened. Perhaps that had been Albert tailing her. It must have been. But why her?

Reaching the right floor, she opened the heavy armed door with the keys Stern had given her, passed the security booth and found herself plunged in the most complete silence. The creak of her rubber soles on the linoleum floor was the only sound in those rooms that she quickly inspected. First the common area where, on the rim of an ashtray, she noticed a cigarette that had burned away in a long strip of gray ash. There were the remains of dinner on the kitchen table—a fork, resting on one side of a plate, a portion of flan that had barely been touched—as if someone had been suddenly forced to interrupt their meal. The lights were all out, even in the Thinking Room. Mila quickened her pace as she headed for the bedroom: something had plainly happened. Stern's bed was unmade, there was a box of mints on her pillow.

A beep from her phone told her that a text had come in. She read it.

We're going to the Gress house. Krepp wants to show us something. Join us. Boris

26.

When she got to Yvonne Gress's house she saw that they hadn't all gone in yet: Sarah Rosa was slipping on her overalls and plastic shoe covers by the van. Mila had noticed that Sarah had been much calmer with her over the past few days. She walked around, almost always lost in other thoughts. Perhaps it was because of her family troubles.

But now Rosa looked up at her. "Christ! You don't miss a trick, do you?"

Just leave it... thought Mila.

She ignored her, trying to get into the van to get some overalls. But Rosa planted herself on the steps, keeping her from getting past.

"Hey, I'm talking to you!"

"What do you want?"

"You really think you're quite the expert, don't you?"

She was standing only a few inches from her face. From below, Mila could smell her breath: cigarettes, gum and coffee. She wanted to push her aside, or give her a piece of her mind. But then she remembered what Goran had said about her separation from her husband and her daughter with an eating disorder, and decided to put it off for the time being.

"Why have you got it in for me, Rosa? I'm just doing my job."

"Then you'd have found child number six by now, don't you think?"

"I will."

"You know, I don't think you're going to be in this team for long. You think you've won them over for now, but sooner or later they'll work out that they can do without you."

Rosa stepped aside, but Mila stayed where she was.

"If you hate me so much, when Roche wanted to fire me, why did you vote for me to stay?"

Sarah turned towards her with an amused look on her face.

"Who told you that?"

"Dr. Gavila."

Rosa burst out laughing and shook her head.

"You see, sweetie, it's that kind of thing that means you won't last long. Because if he told you that in confidence, then you've betrayed him by telling me. And, by the way, he fooled you…because I voted against you."

And she left her there, frozen, heading resolutely towards the house. Mila watched after her, dumbfounded by her last words. Then she got into the van to change.

Krepp had guaranteed that it would be his "Sistine Chapel." The comparison with the room on the second floor of Yvonne Gress's villa wasn't as wild as all that.

In modern times, Michelangelo's masterpiece had been given a radical restoration that had given the paintings back their original splendor, freeing them of the thick layer of dust, smoke and animal glue that had accumulated over centuries of use of candles and braziers. The experts had started their work with a little detail—about the size of a stamp—to give themselves an idea of what was hidden underneath. It had come as a complete surprise: the thick layer of soot had hidden extraordinary colors that couldn't even have been imagined before.

So Krepp had begun with a simple drop of blood—the one found by Mila with the help of the Newfoundland dog—to end up making his masterpiece.

"There was no organic material," said the scientist. "But the pipes were worn, and there were traces of hydrochloric acid. Let's hypothesize that Feldher used it to dissolve the remains, to make it easier to get rid of them. Acid's even very good at getting rid of bone."

Mila only caught the last part of the sentence as she reached the second-floor landing. Krepp was in the middle of the corridor, and in front of him were Goran, Boris and Stern. Further back was Rosa, leaning against the wall.

"So the only clue we have to link the massacre to Feldher is this little blood stain?"

"Have you had it analyzed?"

"Chang says it's ninety percent likely that it belongs to the boy."

Goran turned to look at Mila, then back to Krepp: "OK, we're all here. We can start..."

They'd been waiting for her. She should have felt flattered, but she was still trying to digest Sarah Rosa's words. Who was she to believe? That hysterical madwoman who'd been abusing her since the start, or Goran?

Meanwhile Krepp, before leading them into the room, told them, "We can stay in here for a quarter of an hour at most, so if you have any questions please ask them now."

They said nothing.

"OK, let's go in."

The room was sealed off by a double glass door with a little passageway in the middle that allowed one person to enter at a time. It served to preserve the microclimate. Before going inside, one of Krepp's colleagues took everyone's body temperature with an infrared thermometer of the kind normally used with children. Then he entered the data in a computer connected to the humidifiers in the room that would correct their contribution to keep the thermal conditions constant.

The reason for these devices was explained by Krepp himself, who came into the room last.

"The main problem has been the paint used by Feldher to cover the walls. It couldn't be removed with a normal solvent without also taking away what was under it."

"So what did you do?" asked Goran.

"We analyzed it and it emerged that it's a water-based paint using a vegetable fat as a collagen. All we had to do was spray a solution of refined alcohol and leave it in suspension for a few hours to dissolve the fat. We effectively reduced the thickness of the paint on the walls. If there's any blood under there, Luminol should be able to show it up…"

3-aminophthalhydrazide, better known as Luminol. A substance that aids a great deal of the techniques of modern scientific policing. Reacting with an element in blood, it produces a blue fluorescence, visible only in the dark. There is only one problem with Luminol: the fluorescent effect lasts just thirty seconds. Which makes the test practically unrepeatable after the first time.

For that reason a series of long-exposure cameras would document each result before it vanished forever.

Krepp distributed masks with special filters and protective goggles because—even though it had not yet been demonstrated—it was feared that Luminol might be carcinogenic.

Then he turned back to Gavila: "When you're ready…"

"Let's get started."

With a walkie-talkie, Krepp transmitted the order to his men outside.

First all the lights were turned out.

It wasn't a pleasant sensation for Mila. In that claustrophobic darkness she could make out only her own short breathing which, filtered through the mask, sounded almost like a death rattle. It was superimposed over the deep, mechanical breathing of the humidifiers, incessantly pumping their vapors into the room.

She tried to stay calm, even though anxiety was rising in her chest and she couldn't wait for the experiment to finish.

A moment later the noise changed. The vents began to emit into the air the chemical solution that would make the blood on the walls visible. Shortly afterwards, the hiss of the new substance was accompanied by a thin bluish glow that started appearing all around them. It looked like sunlight filtered through the depths of the sea.

At first Mila thought it was only an optical effect, a kind of mirage created by her mind in response to a state of hyperventilation. But when the effect spread, she realized she could see her colleagues again. As if someone had turned the lights back on, but replacing the icy color of the halogens with this new indigo tone. At first she wondered how it was possible, then she got there.

There was so much blood on the walls that the Luminol effect lit them all up.

The splashes spread in various directions, but all seemed to come from the exact center of the room. As if there had been a kind of sacrificial altar there in the middle. And the ceiling looked like a layer of stars. The magnificence of the vision was broken only by the knowledge of how it was produced.

Feldher must have used a chainsaw to reduce the bodies to a mass of mangled flesh, a mush that could easily be flushed down the toilet.

Mila noticed that the others were as frozen as she was. They looked around, like robots, as the precision cameras arranged along the perimeter went on clicking relentlessly. Just fifteen seconds had passed, and the Luminol was still showing up new and increasingly latent stains.

They stared at that horror.

Then Boris raised his arm towards a side of the room, showing the others what was gradually appearing on the wall.

"Look..." he said.

And they saw.

In one area of the wall the Luminol did not take root, it encountered nothing, and that area remained white. It was framed by a rim of blue stains. As when you spray paint on an object on a wall and, when you remove it, an outline remains. Like an outline carved into the plaster. Like the negative of a photograph.

Each of them thought that the print looked vaguely like a human shadow.

As Feldher tore into the bodies of Yvonne and her children with chilling ferocity, someone, in one corner of the room, was impassively witnessing the spectacle.

27.

Someone has called her name.

She's sure of it. She hasn't dreamed it. That was what dragged her from her sleep this time; not fear, not the sudden awareness of where she had been for so long.

The effect of the drug that dulled her senses vanished as soon as she heard her name bouncing off the belly of the monster. Almost like an echo that had come looking for her from who knows where, and finally found her.

"I'm here!" she wants to shout, but she can't, her mouth is still furred.

And then there are the noises, too. Sounds that weren't there before. What do they sound like, footsteps? Yes, they're the footprints of heavy boots. And shoes, at the same time. There are people! Where? They're above her, around her. Everywhere, but somehow far away, too far away. What are they doing here? Have they come looking for her? Yes, that's it. They're there for her. But they can't see her in the belly of the monster. So the only option is to make them hear her.

"Help," she tries to say.

Her voice comes out in a strangled form, infected by days of induced agony, violent, cowardly sleep, administered to her at will, at random, just to keep her well-behaved as the monster digests her in its stone stomach. And the world out there slowly forgets her.

But if they are here now, it means they haven't forgotten me yet!

The thought fills her with a strength she didn't know she had. A reserve stored by her body in a deep hiding place, and to be used only for emergencies. She starts thinking hard.

How can I tell them I'm here?

Her left arm is still bandaged. Her legs are heavy. Her right arm is her only possibility, the only thing that keeps her attached to life. The remote control is still fastened to the palm of her hand. She lifts it and aims it at the screen. The volume is normal, but perhaps it can be increased. She tries to, but can't find the right button. Perhaps because they all give a single command. Meanwhile the sounds continue above her. The voice that she hears belongs to a woman. But there's a man with her. Or rather, two.

I've got to call them! I've got to make sure they notice me, or I'll die down here!

It's the first time she mentions the possibility of dying. She has always avoided the thought until now. Perhaps she did it as a kind of good-luck charm. Perhaps because a child shouldn't think of death. But now she realizes that if no one comes to rescue her, that will be her fate.

The ridiculous thing is that the one who is going to put an end to her brief existence is now looking after her. He bandaged her arm, he gives her medicine through the drip. He takes scrupulous care of her. Why does he do that, if he's going to kill her in the end anyway? The question brings her no relief. There's only one reason to keep her alive down there. And she suspects that he has plenty of other torments in store for her.

So perhaps this is the only opportunity she has to get out of here, to get back home, to see her family. Her mother, her father, her grandfather, even Houdini. She swears she will even love that damned cat if this nightmare ever ends.

She lifts her hand, and starts thumping the remote control hard against the steel edge of the bed. The sound that she makes is irritating even to her, but it is liberating. Harder and harder. Until she feels the plastic gadget beginning to break. She doesn't care. Those metallic hammering noises are getting angrier and angrier. A broken cry emerges from her throat.

"I'm here!"

The remote control comes away from her palm and she's forced to stop. But she hears something above her. It might be positive, or it might not. It's silence. Perhaps they've become aware of her and now they're trying to hear better. That's it, they can't have left already! Then she starts knocking again, even though her right arm hurts. Even though the pain runs along her shoulder and flows into her left arm. Even if that only increases her desperation. Because if by any chance no one hears her, it will be even worse afterwards, she's sure of it. Someone will avenge her. And make him pay.

Cold tears run down her cheeks. But the sounds start up again and she takes courage again.

A shadow detaches itself from the rocky wall and comes towards her.

She sees it, but goes on anyway. When the shadow is close enough, she notices its delicate hands, its little blue dress, the chestnut hair falling softly on its shoulders.

The shadow turns back towards her with a child's voice.

"That's enough now," it says. "They'll hear us."

Then it rests a hand on hers. The contact is enough to make her stop.

"Please," the shadow adds.

And its plea is so sad that she is convinced, and doesn't start again. She doesn't know why that child wants something so ridiculous as to stay in there. But she obeys anyway. She doesn't know whether to start crying over her failed escape attempt, or to be happy to discover she's no longer alone. She is so grateful that the first human presence she has been aware of is a little girl like herself, that she doesn't want to disappoint her. So she forgets she wants to leave.

The voices and sounds on the floor above have stopped. This time the silence is complete.

The little girl slips her hand from hers.

"Stay..." she pleads now.

"Don't worry, we'll see each other again."

And the girl returns to the darkness. And she lets her go. And she clutches at that small and insignificant promise to go on hoping.

28.

"Alexander Bermann's armchair."

In the Thinking Room, the team were concentrating on Gavila's words. They thought back to the ghetto district where the pedophile kept his lair, and the computer with which he went hunting on the Internet.

"Krepp found no prints on the old leather armchair in the basement!"

Goran suddenly saw this as a revelation.

"On everything else, hundreds, but not there. Why? Because someone took the trouble to wipe them off!"

The criminologist moved towards the wall where all the reports, photographs and documents about the orphanage case were pinned up with drawing pins. He took one down and started reading. It was the transcription of the recording in which Ronald Dermis, as a child, confessed to Father Rolf, found on the tape recorder in Billy Moore's coffin.

"'You know what happened to Billy, don't you, Ron?' 'God took him away.' 'It wasn't God, Ron. You know who it was?' 'He fell. He fell from the tower.' 'But you were with him…' '…Yes.' And then later the priest assures him: 'No one will punish you if you tell us what happened. That is a promise,' and you hear Ronald replying, '*He told me to*'...You understand? '*He*.'"

Goran inspected the faces that were looking at him in puzzlement.

"Now hear what Father Rolf asks: 'Who's he? Billy? Did Billy ask you to push him?' 'No,' Ronald replies. 'So was it one of the other boys?' and Ronald says, 'No.' 'Who then? Come on, answer me. This person you're talking about doesn't exist, does he? He's just a figment of your imagination...' and Ronald seems certain when he denies it again, but Father Rolf cuts in, 'There's no one else here. Just me and your companions,' and finally Ronald replies, '*He only comes for me*.'"

Gradually, they were all getting there.

Goran, as excited as a little boy, ran to the pages on the wall and took down a copy of the letter that the adult Ronald had sent the investigators.

"There was one part that struck me on that note: '*then HE came. HE understood me. HE taught me*.'"

He showed them the letter, pointing to the passage.

"You see? Here the word 'he' is deliberately written in capitals...I'd already thought about that, but the conclusion I had reached was wrong. I thought it was a clear example of personality dissociation, in which the negative *I* always appears separate from the agent *I*. And that's why it becomes *He*...'It was ME, but it was HE who told me to do it, it's HIS fault I'm what I am'...I was wrong! And I was making the same mistake that Father Rolf made thirty years before! When during Ronald's confession he mentioned 'Him,' the priest thought he was referring to himself, and that he was just trying to externalize his own guilt. That's typical of children. But the Ronald we knew was no longer a child..."

Mila saw some of the energy fading from Goran's eyes. It happened every time he got an assessment wrong.

"This 'He' that Ronald is referring to is not a projection of his own psyche, a double to hold responsible for his own actions! It's the same 'He' who made himself comfortable in Alexander Bermann's armchair every time he went on the Internet hunting for children! Feldher leaves a myriad of clues in Yvonne Gress's house, but takes care to repaint the room where the massacre happened because there on the wall is the only thing he urgently needs to hide…or highlight: the image, immortalized in blood, of the watching man! Because *'He' is Albert*."

"I'm sorry, but it doesn't work," said Sarah Rosa with a calm and confidence that startled the others. "We've watched the films from the Capo Alto surveillance system and, apart from Feldher, no one went into that house."

Goran turned towards her, pointing at her with a finger: "Exactly! Because every time he did, he blocked the cameras with a little blackout. If you think about it, you could get the same effect on the wall with a cardboard outline or a mannequin. And what does this teach us?"

"That he's an excellent creator of illusions," said Mila.

"Again, exactly! Since the start, this man has challenged us to understand his tricks. Take the abduction of Sabine from the merry-go-round, for example…brilliant! Dozens of people, dozens of pairs of eyes at the fair and no one notices a thing!"

Goran gave the impression of being really delighted by the ability of his challenger. Not because he didn't feel pity for the victims. It wasn't a demonstration of a lack of humanity on his part. Albert was his object of study. Understanding the devices that moved his mind was a fascinating challenge.

"But personally I believe Albert was *really* present in the room while Feldher was massacring his victims. I would rule out mannequins or tricks of that kind. And you know why?" For a moment the criminologist enjoyed the expression of uncertainty on their faces. "In the arrangement of the bloodstains on the wall around the outline, Krepp identified what he called 'constant variations'—that's what he called them. And it means that, whatever obstacle was placed between the blood and the wall, he wasn't motionless, but moving!"

Sarah Rosa was open-mouthed. There wasn't much to say.

"Let's be practical about this," Stern announced. "If Albert knew Ronald Dermis when he was a little boy, how old could he have been? Twenty, thirty? That would make him fifty or sixty now."

"Correct," said Boris. "And considering the dimensions of the shadow that formed on the wall in the massacre room, I would say he's about five foot three."

"Five foot two," said Sarah Rosa, who had already taken the measurement.

"We have a partial description of the man we have to look for, that's something in itself."

Goran spoke again: "Bermann, Ronald, Feldher: they're like wolves. And wolves often work in a pack. Every pack has a leader. And Albert is telling us this: he's their leader. There was a moment in the lives of those three individuals when they met, separately or together. Ronald and Feldher knew each other, they'd grown up in the same orphanage. But we can assume that they didn't know who Alexander Bermann was... The only common element is him, Albert. That's why he's left his mark on every crime scene."

"And what's going to happen now?" asked Sarah Rosa.

"You can imagine that yourselves. Two corpses of little girls are still missing and, consequently, two parts of the pack."

"There's also little girl number six," Mila pointed out.

"Yes... but Albert's keeping her for himself."

She had lingered for about half an hour on the pavement outside, without having the courage to ring. She was trying to find the right words to explain her presence. By now she was so unused to interpersonal relationships that even the simplest approaches struck her as impossible. And meanwhile she was getting cold out there without being able to make her mind up.

The next blue car, I'll move.

It was after nine and there wasn't much traffic. Goran's windows, on the third floor of the block, were lit. The slush-bathed street was a concert of metallic drips, spluttering gutters and gurgling drainpipes.

Fine: I'm going.

Mila moved from the cone of shadow that had protected her till then from the eyes of possible curious neighbors, and ran quickly to the door. It was an old building which must, in the mid-nineteenth century, have housed a factory, with its big windows, wide cornices and the chimney pots that still adorned the roof. There were several of them in the area. The whole district had probably been gentrified by the work of a few architects who had transformed the old industrial workshops into condominiums.

She rang on the entry phone, and waited for almost a minute before she heard Goran's voice.

"Who is it?"

"It's Mila. Sorry, Goran, but I needed to talk to you, and I didn't want to do it on the phone. Before, at the Studio, you were very busy, and then I thought I'd—"

"Come up. Third floor."

A brief electric tone sounded and the lock of the front door clicked open.

A goods carrier acted as a lift. To make it work you had to close the sliding doors by hand and move a lever. Mila rose slowly through the floors until she reached the third. On the landing she found a single door, half-open for her.

"Come in, sit down."

Goran's voice reached her from inside the apartment. Mila followed it. It was a wide loft, with various rooms coming off it. The floor was made of raw wood. The radiators were cast iron and ran around the pillars. A big lit fireplace filled the room with amber light. Mila closed the door behind her, wondering where Goran was. Then she saw him appearing fleetingly in the kitchen doorway.

"I'll be with you in a second."

"No rush."

She looked round. Unlike the criminologist's usual disheveled appearance, his house was very orderly. There wasn't an inch of dust around, and everything seemed to reflect the care he took to bring a little harmony into his son's life.

A moment later she saw him coming in with a glass of water.

"I'm sorry I've just turned up out of the blue."

"That's OK, I usually go to sleep late." Then, pointing to the glass: "I was putting Tommy to bed. It won't take long. Sit down, or fix yourself a drink: there's a mobile bar down at the end there."

Mila nodded and saw him heading towards one of the rooms. Partly to avoid any embarrassment, she went and made herself a vodka and ice. As she was drinking, standing by the fireside, she saw the criminologist through the half-open door of his son's bedroom. He was sitting on the boy's bed, telling him something, as he stroked his hip with one hand. In the half-darkness of that room, barely lit by a night-light in the shape of a clown, Tommy appeared as a shape under the blankets, formed by his father's caresses.

In that family context, Goran looked like someone else.

For some reason she remembered the first time when, as a girl, she had gone to see her father in his office. The man who left the house every morning in his jacket and tie was transformed there. He became a hard, serious person, so different from her gentle dad. Mila remembered being terribly distressed.

The same applied to Goran. She felt a great wave of tenderness for him as she saw him pursuing his job as a father.

For Mila that dichotomy had never occurred. There was only one version of her. There was no break to the continuity in her life. She never stopped being the policewoman who tried to find missing people. Because she was always looking for them. On her free days, when she was on leave, while she was doing her shopping. Studying the faces of strangers had become a habit.

Minors who disappear have a story, like everyone else. But at some point the story is interrupted. Mila examined their little footsteps, lost in the dark. She never forgot their faces. Years might have passed, but she would always be able to recognize them.

Because the children are among us, she thought. *Sometimes you just have to look for them in the adults they have become.*

Goran was telling his son a fairy tale. Mila didn't want to go on disturbing that scene with her gaze. It wasn't a spectacle for her eyes. She turned round, but immediately saw Tommy's smile in a picture frame. If she had met him, he would have made her uneasy, and she had turned up late in the hope of finding him already in bed.

Tommy was a part of Goran's life that she wasn't disposed to know.

A little while later he joined her and, with a smile, announced, "He's gone to sleep."

"I didn't want to disturb anyone. But I thought it was important."

"You've already apologized. But now come on, tell me what's happening..."

He sat down on one of the sofas and invited her to sit down next to him. The fire cast dancing shadows on the wall.

"It's happened again: I've been followed."

Goran frowned.

"Are you sure?"

"The last time, no, this time yes."

She told him what had happened, trying not to leave out any details. The car with its headlights turned off, the reflection of the moon on the bodywork, the fact that her pursuer had turned around and driven off once spotted.

"Why should anyone follow you, of all people?"

He had already asked her that question at the restaurant, when she had mentioned the sense of being tailed that she had felt in the yard at the motel. This time Goran seemed to be turning it on himself.

"I can't think of a valid reason," he admitted after thinking for a moment.

"There would be no point putting someone on my back at this point, trying to catch my pursuer..."

"He's aware that you know now, so he won't do it again."

Mila nodded. "But that's not the only reason I came."

Goran turned to look at her. "Have you discovered something?"

"It's more that I've worked something out. One of Albert's conjuring tricks."

"Which of the many?"

"How he managed to take the child from the merry-go-round without anyone noticing anything."

Now Goran's eyes were shining with interest.

"Go on, I'm listening..."

"We've always taken it for granted that Albert was the kidnapper. A *man,* then. But what if it was actually a woman?"

"Why do you think that?"

"It was actually Sabine's mother who made me consider that hypothesis for the first time. Even though I didn't ask her, she said that if there had been a strange man on that merry-go-round—someone who wasn't a father—she would have noticed. Also adding that a mother has a kind of sixth sense for these things. And I believe her."

"Why?"

"Because the police have viewed hundreds of pictures taken that evening, and home movies too, and no one has noticed a suspicious man. From this we too have deduced that our Albert looks entirely ordinary... Then it occurred to me that a woman would find it even easier to take the child away."

"So you think he has an accomplice." He quite liked the idea. "But we have no clues supporting a thesis of this kind."

"I know. And that's the problem."

Goran got to his feet and started pacing around the room. He rubbed his untidy beard and thought.

"It wouldn't be the first time...it's happened in the past. In Gloucester, for example, with Fred and Rosemary West."

The criminologist quickly ran through the case of the serial killer couple. He a bricklayer, she a housewife. Ten children. Together they kidnapped and killed innocent girls after forcing them to take part in their erotic parties, before burying them in the back garden at number 25 Cromwell Street. One of the girls who had ended up under the paving stones was the couple's sixteen-year-old daughter, who had probably dared to rebel. Two other victims were found in other places that could be connected to Fred. Twelve corpses in all. But the police stopped digging at the little gray house for fear that it would collapse.

"Perhaps the woman is looking after the sixth child."

Goran seemed very intrigued. But he didn't want to let himself get carried away with enthusiasm.

"Don't misunderstand me, Mila: it's an excellent hunch. But we've got to check it out."

"Will you mention it to the others?"

"We'll take it into consideration. Meanwhile I will ask one of our men to take a look at the pictures and films taken at the fair."

"I could do that."

"Fine."

"There is one more thing…It's something I'm curious about. I've tried to find the answer on my own, but I haven't got there."

"What is it?"

"In the decomposition process, a corpse's eyes undergo a transformation, don't they?"

"Well, usually the iris discolors over time…"

Goran stopped to stare at her, he couldn't work out what she was getting at.

"Why are you asking me?"

Mila took out of her pocket the picture of Sabine that her mother had given her at the end of her visit. The same one that she had kept on the passenger seat all the time while she was driving back. The one that she had found herself staring at after she had got over her fear of being followed, and which had aroused her doubt.

There was something wrong.

Goran took it and looked at it.

"The corpse of the little girl that we found in the Kobashis' house had blue eyes," Mila pointed out. "Sabine's eyes were *brown*."

In the taxi, Goran hadn't said a word. After she had told him her discovery, Mila had seen his mood suddenly change.

"We are looking at someone we think we know everything about, when we don't know anything about him at all…" He thought for a while. "He's played us for fools."

At first, she had thought the criminologist was referring to Albert. But he wasn't.

She sat through a quick sequence of phone calls to people including not only the members of the team, but also Tommy's babysitter.

"We've got to go," he had said to her, without further explanation.

"What about your son?"

"Mrs. Runa will be here in twenty minutes, he'll go on sleeping."

And they had called the taxi.

The lights were still on at Federal Police headquarters. In the building there was a bustle of policemen changing shifts. Almost all of them were busy with the case. For days now, they'd been involved in following up phone calls from eager citizens, in search of the sixth girl's prison.

After paying the taxi driver, Goran headed for the main entrance without even waiting for Mila, who had trouble keeping up with him. Climbing the stairs to the Department of Behavioral Sciences, they found Rosa, Boris and Stern waiting for them.

"What's happening?" asked Stern.

"We need clarification," Goran replied. "We have to see Roche straightaway."

He found the chief inspector in the middle of a meeting of senior Federal officers that had already been going on for a number of hours. The meeting was about the Albert case.

"We need to talk to you."

Roche got up from the armchair and introduced him to the others: "Gentlemen, you all know Dr. Gavila, who has been working with my department for years..."

Goran whispered in his ear: "Now."

The polite smile faded from Roche's face.

"You must excuse me, gentlemen, some information has come in that requires my presence elsewhere."

"This had better be important," said the chief inspector after throwing the file down on the desk in his office.

Goran waited for everyone to come into the room before closing the door and facing Roche down.

"The corpse found in the Kobashis' sitting room didn't belong to the third missing girl."

The firmness of his tone left no room for denial. The chief inspector sat down and clasped his hands in front of him.

"Go on..."

"This isn't Sabine. It's Melissa."

Mila remembered child number four. Even though she was the oldest of the six, she was physically immature for her age, which could have confused the investigation. *And she had blue eyes.*

"Go on, I'm listening..." Roche said again.

"This can mean only two things. That Albert has altered his modus operandi, because until now he's been letting us find the girls in the order in which they were abducted. Or else that Chang has made a mistake with his DNA tests. I think the first hypothesis is almost impossible...and with regard to the second, I actually think you ordered him to falsify the results before giving them to Mila!"

Roche turned purple. "Listen, Doctor, I'm not going to stay here and listen to your accusations!"

"Where was the body of child number three found?"

"What?"

The chief inspector was doing everything he could to seem surprised by this assertion.

"Because it plainly has been found, otherwise Albert wouldn't have continued with his sequence by moving straight on to number four."

"The corpse had been in the Kobashis' house for over a week! Perhaps, as you say, we should have found child number three first. Or perhaps we've simply found the fourth one first! And then Chang got muddled, what do I know?"

The criminologist stared straight into his eyes. "That's why you gave us twenty-four hours off after what happened at the orphanage. So we wouldn't be under your feet all the time!"

"Goran, I've had enough of these ridiculous accusations! You can't prove any of the things you're saying!"

"This is because of the Wilson Pickett case, isn't it?"

"What happened then has nothing to do with that, I assure you."

"But you don't trust me anymore. And perhaps you're not entirely wrong...but if you think I'm losing control of the investigation, I'd rather you said it to my face, without playing political games. You say so, and we'll all take a step back, without causing you any embarrassment, and continuing to shoulder our responsibilities."

Roche didn't reply immediately. He held his hands clasped under his chin, and rocked back and forth in his armchair. Then, very calmly, he began: "Honestly, I really don't know what you're—"

"Come on, tell him."

It was Stern who interrupted him. Roche glared at him.

"You stay right where you are!"

Goran turned to look at him. Then he stared at Boris and Rosa as well. He immediately realized that everyone knew, apart from him and Mila.

This is why Boris was so evasive when I asked him what he did with his day off, she thought. And she also remembered the slightly threatening tone her colleague had used with Roche outside Yvonne Gress's house, when he refused to send him inside before the special units. The threat implied blackmail.

"Yes, Inspector. Tell him everything and let's get it over with," Sarah Rosa cut in, backing up Stern.

"He can't be left out, it's not fair," Boris added, nodding towards the criminologist.

It was as if they wanted to apologize to him for keeping him in the dark, and that they felt guilty for obeying an order that they considered unfair.

Roche let a few more seconds pass, then looked in turn at Goran and Mila.

"Fine…but if you say a word about this, I'll ruin you."

29.

Ashy dawn was spreading across the fields.

It barely lit the outlines of the hills that followed one another like massive waves of earth. The intense green of the fields, freed from snow, stood out against the gray skies. A strip of tarmac slipped among the valleys, dancing in harmony with the movement of the landscape.

With her forehead resting against the back window of the car, Mila became aware of a strange sense of tranquility, due perhaps to fatigue, perhaps to resignation. Whatever she discovered at the end of that short journey would no longer surprise her. Roche hadn't given much away. After telling her and Goran to keep their mouths shut, he had locked himself away in his office with the criminologist for a face-to-face confrontation.

She had stayed in the corridor, where Boris had explained to her why the chief inspector had decided to exclude her and Gavila.

"He's effectively a civilian and you... well, you're something like a consultant, so..."

There wasn't much else to add. Whatever the big secret that Roche was trying to protect, the situation had to stay under control. So it was vital to avoid any leaks. He'd made sure that the only ones who knew anything were those who were directly under his command, and who could be intimidated for that reason.

Apart from that, Mila hadn't found out anything. And she hadn't asked any questions, either.

After a few hours, the door to Roche's office had opened, and the chief inspector had ordered Boris, Stern and Rosa to take Dr. Gavila to the third site. Although he didn't name her directly, he had allowed Mila to take part in the expedition as well.

They had left the building and gone to a nearby garage. They had taken two saloons with anonymous plates that couldn't be traced to the police, to avoid being followed by the journalists who were constantly parked outside the station.

Mila had got into the car with Stern and Gavila, deliberately avoiding the one in which Sarah Rosa was sitting. They had traveled several miles; she had tried to get some sleep, and had actually got some. When she woke up they were nearly there.

It wasn't a very busy road. Mila noticed three dark cars parked by the side of the carriageway, each with two men on board.

Sentries, she thought, *to keep rubberneckers away.*

They drove along a high red-brick wall for about half a mile, until they reached a heavy iron gate.

The road stopped there.

There was no bell or entry phone. There was a TV camera attached to a pole and as soon as they stopped, it sought them with its electronic eye. It remained fixed on them. At least a minute passed, and then the gate began to open. The road continued, disappearing almost immediately behind a hump. There were no other houses to be seen beyond that boundary. Just an expanse of field.

It was at least another ten minutes before they saw the spires of an old building. The house appeared in front of them as if it was emerging from the bowels of the earth. It was vast and austere. Its style was that of the early nineteenth-century country house, as built by steel or oil magnates to celebrate their own good fortune.

Mila recognized the stone coat-of-arms that dominated the facade. It contained an enormous R in bas-relief.

It was the home of Joseph B. Rockford, the president of the foundation of the same name who had put up a reward of ten million for the discovery of the sixth child.

They passed the house and parked the two saloons near some stables. To reach the third site, on the western rim of an estate of several acres, they had to take some electric cars that resembled golf carts.

Mila got into the one driven by Stern, who started explaining who Joseph B. Rockford was, his family origins and his vast wealth.

The dynasty had begun over a century before, with Joseph B. Rockford I, the grandfather. Legend had it that he was the only son of an immigrant barber. Not satisfied with scissors and razors, he had sold his father's shop to seek his fortune. While everyone at the time was investing in the new oil industry, Rockford I had had the lucky hunch of using his own savings to set up a company to drill artesian wells. Considering that oil is almost always found in the least hospitable parts of the world, Rockford had concluded that the people who were busy getting rich quick would soon lack one essential commodity: water. And the water extracted from the artesian wells, sprung from the main deposits of black gold, was sold at almost twice the price of oil.

Joseph B. Rockford I had died a billionaire. He had died shortly before his fiftieth birthday of a rare and devastating form of stomach cancer.

Joseph B. Rockford II had inherited a vast fortune from his father, which he had managed to double by speculating on everything that had come within his reach: from Indian hemp to real estate, from cattle breeding to electrical goods. To crown his rise, he had married a beauty queen who had given him two lovely children.

But shortly before he reached the age of fifty, he had showed the first symptoms of the stomach cancer that would carry him off in less than two months.

His oldest son, Joseph B. Rockford III, took over his huge empire at a very young age. His first and only act of command was to get rid of the irritating Roman numerals attached to his name. Since he had no financial goals to achieve, and since he could afford any kind of luxury, Joseph B. Rockford led a purposeless existence.

The family Foundation had been the idea of his sister Lara. The aim of the institution was to provide less fortunate children with healthy food, a roof over their heads, adequate medical care and an education. The Rockford Foundation had immediately received half of the family inheritance. In spite of the generosity of the arrangement, according to their advisers' calculations the Rockfords would have enough wealth to live comfortably for at least another century.

Lara Rockford was thirty-seven, and at the age of thirty-two she had miraculously survived a terrible car crash. Her brother Joseph was forty-nine. The genetic form of stomach cancer that had struck down first his grandfather and then his father had also appeared in him just eleven months before.

For thirty-four days, Joseph B. Rockford had been in a coma, waiting to die.

Mila carefully listened to Stern's account as the electric car bounced over the bumpy ground. They were following a path that must have formed naturally over those two days, because of the continuous passage of vehicles like these.

About half an hour later they reached the edge of the third site. In the distance, Mila made out the busy white overalls that enlivened every crime scene. Even before getting there to see with her own eyes the spectacle that Albert had prepared for them this time, it was that sight that distressed her most.

There were more than a hundred experts at work.

A tearful rain beat relentlessly down. As they made their way through the workmen removing large quantities of earth, Mila felt uneasy. As the bones were unearthed, someone cataloged them and put them in transparent bags to which labels were attached, so that they could be put in the appropriate boxes.

In one, Mila counted at least thirty femurs. In another, pelvises.

Stern turned to Goran. "The child was found around about here..."

He pointed to a fenced-off area, covered with plastic sheets to protect it against the weather. On the ground an outline of the body was drawn in latex. The white line reproduced its shape, but without its left arm.

Sabine.

"She was lying on the grass, in a state of advanced deterioration. She had been exposed for too long for the animals not to sniff out her presence."

"Who noticed she was there?"

"One of the gamekeepers who check the estate."

"Did you start digging straightaway?"

"First we brought the dogs, but they couldn't smell anything. Then we flew over the area in a helicopter to check for any irregularities in the layout of the terrain. We noticed that around the point where the body was found the vegetation was different. We showed the photographs to a botanist, and he confirmed that those variations might indicate that something was buried beneath it."

Mila had heard of this before: similar techniques had been used in Bosnia to find the common graves containing the victims of ethnic cleansing. The presence of bodies underground affects the vegetation above, because the land is enriched by organic substances produced by decomposition.

Goran looked around. "How many are there?"

"Thirty or forty bodies, who knows..."

"And how long have they been down there?"

"We found some very old bones, others seem to be more recent."

"Who did they belong to?"

"Males. Most of them young, between sixteen and twenty-two or twenty-three. In some cases this was confirmed by analysis of their dental arches."

"This puts everything else in the shade," said the criminologist, already thinking of the consequences when the story got out. "Roche won't try and cover this one up, will he? With all the people here..."

"No, the chief inspector is only trying to put off the announcement until everything's satisfactorily resolved."

"That's because no one can work out what a common grave is doing in the middle of the Rockfords' lovely estate." He said it with a hint of indignation that escaped no one present. "But I think our chief inspector has an idea... what about you?"

Stern didn't know what to say. Nor did Boris and Rosa.

"Stern, one thing... were the bodies found before or after the reward was announced?"

The officer admitted, in a faint voice: "Before."

"I suspected as much."

When they got back to the stables, they found Roche waiting for them beside the Department car that had brought him there. Goran got out of the golf cart and walked resolutely towards him.

"So, am I still involved in this investigation?"

"Of course! Do you think it's been easy for me to keep you out of things?"

"Not easy, no, given that I've discovered everything. I'd be more inclined to say it was *convenient*."

"Meaning?"

The chief inspector was starting to get annoyed.

"That I would already have identified the perpetrator."

"How can you be so sure of his identity?"

"Because if you hadn't thought Rockford was the man really behind all this, you wouldn't have gone to so much effort to keep the story hidden."

Roche took him by an arm. "Listen, Goran, you think it's all up to me. But it isn't, believe me. There's so much pressure from above, more than even you can imagine."

"Who are you trying to cover up for? How many people are involved in this filth?"

Roche turned and nodded to the driver to leave. Then he turned back towards the team.

"Fine, let's get things clear once and for all... I feel like throwing up when I think about this story. And I don't even have to threaten you to keep all this to yourselves, because if so much as a word about this comes out, you'll lose everything in an instant. Your career and your pension. And so will I."

"We understand... now, what's behind it?" Goran broke in.

"Joseph B. Rockford has never left this place, the house where he was born."

"How is that possible?" asked Boris. "Never?"

"Never," Roche confirmed. "At the start it seems he had a fixation on his mother, the former beauty queen. He had a morbid love for her that kept him from having a normal childhood and adolescence."

"But when she died..." Sarah Rosa tried to object.

"When she died it was too late: the boy wasn't able to establish any kind of human contact. Until then he had been entirely surrounded by deferential people who worked in the service of his family. And then there was the so-called Rockford curse, the fact that all the male heirs died of a stomach tumor at the age of fifty."

"Maybe his mother was unconsciously trying to save him from that fate," Goran suggested.

"And his sister?" Mila asked.

"A rebel," said Roche. "Younger than him, she was able to escape the mother fixation just in time. Then she did what she felt like with her life: she traveled the world, squandering her wealth, burning herself out on the most unlikely relationships and trying drugs and experiences of every kind. All to seem different from the brother who had remained a prisoner in this place...until the road accident five years ago effectively locked her away with him in this house."

"Joseph B. Rockford was homosexual," said Goran.

And Roche confirmed this: "Yes, he was...and the corpses found in the common grave tell the same story. All in the bloom of youth."

"Then why kill them?" asked Sarah Rosa.

It was Goran who replied. He had seen this happen before.

"The chief inspector will correct me if I'm wrong, but I think Rockford couldn't accept being the way he was. Or perhaps, when he was young someone discovered his sexual preferences and he never forgave them."

Everyone thought of his mother, even though no one mentioned her.

"So every time he repeated the act, he felt a sense of guilt. But rather than punishing himself, he punished his lovers...with death," Mila concluded.

"The corpses are here and he has never moved," said Goran. "So it was here that he killed them. Is it possible that no one—the servants, the gardeners, the gamekeepers—ever noticed anything?"

Roche had an answer, but he let them guess for themselves.

"I can't believe it," said Boris. "He paid them!"

"He bought their silence for all those years," added Stern with disgust.

What price a man's soul? thought Mila. Because that, in the end, was the issue. Sometimes a human being discovers that he has an evil nature, which means he can only find happiness by killing someone else. There's a name for him: a murderer, or serial killer. But what do you call the others, the ones around him who don't stop it happening, or who even take advantage of it?

"How did he get hold of the boys?" Goran asked.

"We don't know yet. We've put out an arrest warrant for his personal assistant, who seems to have vanished into nowhere since the body of the girl was found."

"And what will you do with the rest of the staff?"

"They're in custody until we've cleared up the issue of whether or not they took any money, and how much they knew."

"Rockford didn't stop at corrupting the people he had around him, did he?"

Goran was reading Roche's thoughts, and the chief inspector admitted: "Some years ago, a policeman's suspicions were aroused: he was investigating the disappearance of a teenage boy who had run away from home and robbed a general store. His trail brought us here. At that point, Rockford consulted some powerful friends, and the cop was transferred...Another time, a couple were parked on the road that runs along the wall surrounding the estate. They saw someone climbing over it: it was a half-naked boy, wounded in one leg and in a state of shock. They took him in their car and brought him to hospital. He only stayed there for a few hours: someone came and got him, saying they were from the police. From that point onwards nothing more was heard of the boy. The doctors and nurses were given large bribes to keep their mouths shut. The couple were illicit lovers, and all that it took was a threat to reveal all to their respective spouses."

"That's terrible," said Mila.

"I know."

"And what can you tell us about the sister?"

"I don't think Lara Rockford's quite right in the head. The traffic accident left her in a really bad way. It happened not far from here. She did it to herself: she came out into the road and drove her car into an oak tree."

"We should still talk to her. And to Rockford," said Goran. "He probably knows who Albert is."

"How on earth are you going to talk to him? He's in an irreversible coma!"

"Then he's got away with it!" Boris's face was a mask of rage. "Not only can he be no help to us, but he won't spend a day in jail for what he's done!"

"Oh, no, you're wrong," said Roche. "If there is a hell, they'll be waiting for him there. But he's going there very slowly and painfully."

"Then why are they keeping him alive?"

Roche smiled ironically, raising one eyebrow: "His sister wants them to."

The inside of the Rockfords' house was deliberately made to make you think of a castle. The interior architecture was dominated by black marble, whose veined surfaces absorbed all the light. Heavy velvet curtains obscured the windows. Most of the paintings and tapestries showed scenes of hunting and bucolic revelry. A huge crystal chandelier hung from the ceiling.

Mila felt a sudden sensation of bitter cold as soon as she passed through the doorway. However luxurious it might have been, the house had a very decadent atmosphere. If you listened carefully you could hear silences past, which had settled over time into that looming quietude.

Lara Rockford had "consented to receive them." She knew very well that she couldn't have got out of it, but the use of that phrase provided a clue to the kind of person they were about to meet.

She was waiting for them in the library. Mila, Goran and Boris would question her.

Mila saw her in profile, sitting on a leather sofa, her arm sweeping elegantly as she brought a cigarette to her lips. She was extremely beautiful. From a distance, they were all struck by the slight curve of her forehead running down the slender nose to end in a fleshy mouth. As they got closer, they saw an intense, magnetic green in her eye, framed by a long, graceful eyebrow.

But when they came in and saw her from the front, they were startled by the sight of the other half of her face. It was ravaged by an enormous scar that, starting at her hairline, dug its way down her forehead to plunge into an empty eye socket, before plummeting like the furrow of a tear to end below her chin.

Mila also noticed the woman's stiff leg, obvious despite the other leg thrown over it. Beside her, Lara held a book. The cover was turned face down and they couldn't see either the title or the author.

"Good day," she said. "To what do I owe your visit?"

She didn't invite them to sit. They stood where they were on the large rug that covered almost half the floor.

"We'd like to ask some questions," said Goran. "If possible, of course..."

"Please, I'm listening."

Lara Rockford stubbed out what was left of her cigarette in an alabaster ashtray. Then she took another from the pack in her lap, in a leather case, along with a gold lighter. As she lit it, her thin fingers trembled very slightly.

"It was you who offered the ten million reward for finding the sixth girl," said Goran.

"It seemed the least I could do."

She was challenging them on the terrain of truth. Perhaps she wanted to upset them, perhaps it was only her curious refusal to conform, as a contrast to the austerity of the house in which she was exiled.

Goran decided to rise to the challenge.

"Did you know about your brother?"

"Everyone knew. No one said anything."

"Why did they break their silence this time?"

"What do you mean?"

"The gamekeeper who found the little girl's body: I imagine he was on the payroll too…"

Mila guessed what Goran had already worked out, that Lara could easily have just hushed up the whole business. But she hadn't wanted to.

"Do you believe in the existence of the soul?"

As she asked the question, Lara stroked the cover of the book beside her.

"Do you?"

"I've been thinking about it for a while…"

"Is that why you won't let the doctors disconnect your brother from the machines that are still keeping him alive?"

The woman didn't reply immediately. Instead she raised her eyes to the ceiling. Joseph B. Rockford was on the floor above, in the bed in which he had slept since childhood. His room had been turned into an intensive care ward worthy of a modern hospital. He was connected to a machine that breathed for him, that fed him medicines and liquids, that cleansed his blood and relieved his bowels.

"Don't misunderstand me: I *want* my brother to die."

She looked sincere.

"Your brother probably knew the man who kidnapped and killed the five little girls, and now he's keeping the sixth one prisoner. You can't imagine who it could be…"

Lara turned her one eye towards Goran: at last she was looking him in the face. Or rather she was ostentatiously letting him look at her.

"Who knows, it could be a member of staff. One of the ones who are here now, or one who was here in the past. You should check."

"We're already doing that, but I fear that the man we're looking for is too clever to grant us a similar favor."

"As you will already have understood, the only people who came into this house were people whom Joseph could pay. Taken on and salaried, under his control. I've never seen strangers here."

"But you saw the boys?" Mila asked on impulse.

The woman took a long time to reply. "He paid them too. Every now and again, especially recently, he liked to give them a kind of contract with which they sold him their soul. They thought it was a game, a joke to get a little money out of a crazy billionaire. So they signed. They all signed. I found some of the parchments in the safe in his study. Their signatures are quite legible, even if what was used was not ink in the strict sense of the word."

She laughed at her macabre allusion, but it was a strange laugh that disturbed Mila. It gurgled up from the depths. As if she had chewed it for a long time in her lungs before spitting it out. It was raucous with nicotine, but also with pain. Then she picked up the book she kept by her side.

It was *Faust*.

Mila took a step towards her.

"Do you have any objections if we try to question your brother?"

Goran and Boris looked at her as if she had lost her mind.

Lara laughed again. "What do you intend to do? He's more dead than alive now." Then her face grew serious as she said, "It's too late."

But Mila insisted: "Let us try."

30.

At first sight, Nicla Papakidis looked like a frail woman.

Perhaps because she was short and disproportionately wide at the hips. Perhaps because of her eyes, which contained a sad gaiety that made her look like a song from a Fred Astaire musical, or the photograph of an old New Year's ball, or the last day of summer.

In actual fact she was very strong.

She had built up her strength a little at a time, in years of adversities great and small. She was born in a little village, the first of seven children, the only woman. She was only eleven years old when her mother died. So it was up to her to keep the household going, look after her father and bring up her brothers. She had managed to get them all through school so they would end up with decent jobs. Thanks to the money she had saved with her untiring sacrifices and severe household economies, they had never wanted for anything. She had seen them marry good girls, set up homes and provide about twenty little nieces and nephews who were her pride and joy. When even the youngest of the brothers had left the paternal home, she had stayed to look after her father in his old age, refusing to put him in a retirement home. To keep from burdening her brothers and sisters-in-law with that weight, she'd just say: "Don't worry about me. You've got your families, I'm on my own. It isn't a sacrifice."

She had tended to her father until he was over ninety, looking after him as if he was a newborn baby. When he died, she had brought all the brothers together.

"I'm forty-seven years old, and I don't think I'll ever get married. I won't have any children of my own, but I love my nieces and nephews as mine. Thank you for the invitation you have all sent me to come and live with you, but I made my choice some years ago, even if I am revealing it to you only now. We will not see each other again, dear brothers... I have decided to dedicate my life to Jesus. From tomorrow I will lock myself away in a closed convent until the end of my days."

"So she's a nun!" said Boris who had been listening in silence to Mila's story as he drove.

"Nicla isn't just a nun. She's much more than that."

"I still can't believe you managed to persuade Gavila. And not only that, but you managed to persuade Roche!"

"It's a stab in the dark—what can we lose? And I maintain that Nicla is the right person to keep this business secret."

"That's for certain!"

On the backseat there was a box with a big red bow. "Chocolates are Nicla's only weakness," Mila had said when asking Boris if they could stop at a sweet shop.

"But if she's in a closed order, she can't come with us."

"Well, it's actually a bit more complicated than that..."

"What do you mean?"

"Nicla spent some years in a convent. When they realized what she could do, they sent her back into the world."

They arrived shortly after midday. Chaos ruled in that part of the city. Traffic noise mingled with music from stereos, the screams of arguments from apartment blocks, as well as the sounds of the more or less legal activities going on in the streets. The people who lived there never moved away. The center—which was only a few subway stops away—with its smart restaurants, boutiques and tearooms, might as well have been on the planet Mars.

You were born and you died in areas like this, and you never left.

The SatNav of the car they were traveling in had stopped giving directions immediately after the highway turnoff. The only street signs were the murals that marked the borders of gang territories.

Boris turned off into a side street that ended in a blind alley. For some minutes he had been watching a car that had been given instructions to follow their movements. The fact that two police officers were driving around hadn't gone unobserved by the sentries who kept every corner of the neighborhood under constant surveillance.

"Just drive at walking pace and keep your hands in view," Mila had told him, having been in these parts before.

The building they were headed for was at the end of the street. They parked between the carcasses of two burned-out cars. They got out, and Boris started looking round. He was about to turn on the central locking when Mila stopped him.

"Don't. And leave the keys in, too. These guys would be capable of forcing the doors just out of spite."

"So what's going to stop them stealing my car?"

Mila passed by the driver's side, rummaged in her pocket and took out a red plastic rosary. She wrapped it around the mirror.

"This is the best anti-theft device around here."

Boris looked at her, puzzled. Then he followed her towards the building.

The cardboard sign at the front door announced: *Food queue starts at 11*. And since not all those for whom the message was intended knew how to read, a drawing had been added with the hands of a clock above a steaming plate.

It smelled of a mixture of cooking and disinfectant. In the hallway some mismatched plastic chairs stood around a table with some old magazines on it. There were also some brochures about various subjects, from the prevention of tooth decay in children to ways of avoiding sexually transmitted diseases. The idea was to make this place resemble a waiting room. Various handbills and leaflets spilled from a noticeboard on the wall. Voices could be heard running from one point of the building to the other, although it was impossible to know exactly where they were coming from.

Mila pulled Boris's sleeve. "Let's go, she's upstairs."

They started going up. There wasn't a single unbroken step, and the banister swung dangerously.

"What kind of place is this?" Boris avoided touching anything for fear of some kind of contagion. He went on complaining until they reached the landing.

A very pretty girl of about twenty stood by a glass door. She was handing a bottle of medicine to an old man in ragged clothes who stank of alcohol and acidic sweat.

"You have to take one a day, OK?"

The girl didn't seem bothered by the stench. She spoke in a loud, kind voice, clearly articulating her words as you do when talking to children. The old man nodded but didn't look convinced.

Then the girl pressed her point: "It's very important: you must never forget. Otherwise you'll end up like last time, when they took you away at death's door."

Then she took a handkerchief from her pocket and knotted it around his wrist.

"That way you won't forget."

The man smiled contentedly. He took the bottle and walked away, still looking at his arm with its new present.

"Can I help you?" the girl asked them.

"We're looking for Nicla Papakidis," said Mila.

Boris stared enraptured at the young woman, suddenly forgetting all the complaints he had been coming out with on the way upstairs.

"I think it's the last room at the end," she said, pointing to the corridor behind her.

When they passed beside her, Boris's gaze fell to her breasts, and encountered the gold cross the girl was wearing around her neck.

"But she's a..."

"Yes," Mila replied, trying not to laugh.

"Shame."

As they walked down the corridor, they were able to look into the rooms that appeared on either side. Steel beds, camp beds or only wheelchairs. They were all occupied by human relics, young and old, without distinction. They were suffering from AIDS; they were drug-dependent or alcoholics with their livers reduced to mush, or they were just sick and old.

They had two things in common. Weary expressions and the awareness of having made poor life choices. No hospital would have had them in that condition. And they probably didn't have a family to look after them. Or if they did, they had been banished from it.

People came to this place to die. That was what it was all about. Nicla Papakidis called it "the Port."

"This really is a wonderful day, Nora."

The nun was carefully combing the long white hair of an old woman lying on the bed facing the window, accompanying her gestures with relaxing words.

"This morning as I walked through the park I left a little bread for the birds. With all this snow they spend all their time in their nests, keeping each other warm."

Mila knocked at the already open door. Nicla turned round, and when she saw Mila her face lit up.

"My little one!" she said, coming over to hug her. "How lovely to see you again!"

She was wearing a sugar-colored sweater, with the sleeves rolled up because she always felt hot, a black skirt that reached below her knees, and trainers on her feet. Her hair was short and gray. Her very white complexion stressed her intensely blue eyes. The whole effect was one of candor and cleanliness. Boris noted that she wore a red rosary around her neck, like the one Mila had tied to the car mirror.

"This is Klaus Boris, a colleague of mine."

Boris stepped forward, somewhat uneasily. "A pleasure."

"You've just met Sister Mery, haven't you?" Nicla asked, shaking his hand.

Boris blushed. "As a matter of fact…"

"Don't worry, she has that effect on lots of people…" Then she turned to look at Mila again: "Why did you come here to the Port, little one?"

Mila grew serious. "You may have heard of the case of the missing girls."

"We pray for them here every evening. But the newsmen don't tell us much."

"I can't either."

Nicla stared at her: "You've come here about the sixth one, haven't you?"

"What can you tell me about her?"

Nicla sighed. "I'm trying to establish contact. But it isn't easy. My gift isn't what it once was: it's got a lot weaker. Perhaps I should be glad of that, since if I lost it entirely they would let me go back and join my fellow sisters in the convent."

Nicla Papakidis didn't like being called a medium. She said it wasn't the right word to describe a "gift from God." She didn't feel special. Her talent was. She was just the conduit chosen by God to bear it within her and use it for the benefit of others.

Among the many things she had said to Boris while they were heading for the Port, Mila had told him about when Nicla had discovered she had superior sensory abilities.

"At the age of six she was already famous in her village for finding missing objects: wedding rings, house keys, wills too well hidden by the deceased…One evening the chief of the local police turned up at her house: a five-year-old boy had gone missing and his mother was desperate. She was brought to the woman, who begged her to find her son. Nicla stared at her for a moment, and then said, 'This woman is lying. She buried him in the vegetable garden behind the house.' And that's exactly where they found him."

Boris was very shaken by the story. Perhaps that was partly why he went and sat a little apart from the others, letting Mila talk to the nun.

"I have to ask you something a bit different from usual," said the policewoman. "I need you to come to a place and try to make contact with a dying man."

Mila had used Nicla's visions several times in the past. Sometimes the solution to her cases had come thanks to her intervention.

"Little one, I can't move from here, you know: they always need me."

"I know, but I can't help insisting. It's the only hope we have of saving the sixth little girl."

"I told you: I'm not sure my 'gift' still works."

"I thought about you for another reason, too...there's a large sum of money available for anyone who finds the girl."

"Yes, I've heard that. But what could I do with ten million?"

Mila looked around her, as if it was natural to think of using the reward money to renovate this place. "Believe me: when you know the whole story, you'll realize that it would be the best possible use for that money. So, what do you say?"

"Vera has to come and see me today."

It was the old woman in the bed who spoke. Until then she had lain silent and motionless looking out the window.

Nicla approached her: "Yes, Nora, Vera will be coming later."

"She promised."

"Yes, I know. She promised and she will keep her word, you'll see."

"But that boy is sitting on her chair," she said, pointing to Boris, who immediately began to get up.

But Nicla stopped him: "Stay where you are." Then, in a quieter voice: "Vera was her twin. She died seventy years ago when they were still children."

The nun saw Boris blanch and smiled wryly: "No, officer, I can't contact the afterlife. But Nora likes to be told that her sister is coming to see her every now and again."

"So you'll come?" Mila pressed. "I promise someone will bring you back here before evening."

Nicla Papakidis thought about it again for a moment. "But you've brought something for me?"

A smile spread across Mila's face. "The chocolates are waiting for you down in the car."

Nicla nodded contentedly, then turned serious again. "I won't like what I see in that man, will I?"

"I really don't think so."

Nicla clutched her rosary. "Fine, let's go."

***

It's called "pareidolia": it's the instinctive tendency to find familiar shapes in chaotic images. In the clouds, in constellations or in the flakes of oatmeal floating in a bowl of milk.

In the same way, Nicla Papakidis saw things blossoming inside her. She didn't call them visions. And she liked the word *pareidolia* because—like herself—it had Greek origins.

She explained it to Boris as she sat in the back of the car gulping down one chocolate after another. What startled him wasn't so much the nun's story as the fact that he had found his own car where he had left it, without a scratch, in that rough neighborhood.

"Why do you call it the Port?"

"That depends what you believe in, Boris. Some see it only as a point of arrival. Others as one of departure."

"What about you?"

"Both."

In early afternoon the Rockford estate came into view.

Goran and Stern were waiting for them outside the house. Sarah Rosa was upstairs making arrangements with the medical staff looking after the dying man.

"You've got here just in time," said Stern. "The situation has worsened very quickly since this morning. The doctors are sure it's only a matter of hours now."

As they were leaving, Gavila introduced himself to Nicla and explained what she was to do, although he was unable to conceal all his skepticism. He had seen all kinds of mediums at work, making their own contributions to the police. Very often their interventions produced a big fat nothing, or else they muddled the investigation by creating false leads and pointless expectations.

The nun wasn't surprised by the criminologist's wariness; she had seen that expression of disbelief on people's faces many times.

Stern, being religious, wasn't convinced by Nicla's gift. As far as he was concerned, it was all mere charlatanism. But the fact that it was being practiced by a nun confused him. "At least she isn't doing it for money," he had said a little while before to an even more skeptical Sarah Rosa.

"I like that criminologist," Nicla whispered confidentially to Mila as they were going upstairs. "He has misgivings, and he doesn't try to hide them."

The comment wasn't the product of her gift. Mila understood that it came straight from her heart. Hearing those words from such a dear friend, Mila felt a surge of gratitude. The statement brushed away all the doubts that Sarah Rosa had tried to sow in her about Goran.

Joseph B. Rockford's room was at the end of a wide corridor hung with tapestries.

The big windows pointed to the west, towards the sunrise. From the balconies you could enjoy the view of the valley below.

The four-poster bed was in the middle of the room. All around it, medical apparatus accompanied the billionaire's last hours. They beat out a mechanical rhythm for him, made up of beeps from the heart rate monitor, the sighs and puffs of the respirator, repeated drips and a low and continuous electrical murmur.

Rockford's torso was raised by several pillows, his arms rested along his hips on the embroidered bedcover, his eyes were closed. He wore a pair of raw-silk pajamas, pale pink in color, open at the neck to accommodate the endotracheal tube. The little hair he had was extremely white. His face was hollow, around an aquiline nose, and the rest of his body barely formed an outline under the blankets. He looked a hundred years old, when he was barely fifty.

At that moment a nurse was tending to the wound in his neck, changing the gauze around the nozzle that helped him breathe. Of all the staff who took turns around that bed twenty-four hours a day, they had been allowed to see only his private doctor and the doctor's assistant.

When the members of the team crossed the threshold, their eyes met those of Lara Rockford, who would not have missed this scene for the world. She was sitting in an armchair, apart from the others, smoking in defiance of all hygienic rules. When the nurse had pointed out that this was perhaps not a great idea given the critical condition of her brother, she had replied simply, "It can't hurt him anyway."

Nicla walked confidently towards the bed, watching this privileged death scene. A death so different from the wretched ones that she saw every day at the Port. As she came close to Joseph B. Rockford she made the sign of the cross. Then she turned back to Goran, saying, "We can start."

They couldn't record what was about to happen. Never in a million years would a jury accept it as evidence. And neither could the press find out about this experiment. Everything had to stay within these walls.

Boris and Stern took up their positions, standing beside the closed door. Sarah Rosa went to stand in a corner and leaned against the wall with her arms crossed over her chest. Nicla went to sit in a chair beside the bed. Mila sat next to her. Facing them was Goran, who wanted to keep a close eye on both Rockford and the nun.

The medium began to concentrate.

Mila didn't know where Joseph B. Rockford really was at that moment. Perhaps he was there with them, and perhaps he could even hear them. Or else he had already gone down far enough to rid himself of his own fantasies.

But she was sure of one thing: Nicla might have to fall into a deep and treacherous abyss to find him.

"Ah, I'm beginning to feel something..."

Nicla's hands rested on her knees. Mila noticed that her fingers were beginning to contract with tension.

"Joseph is still here," the medium announced. "But he is very... far away. However, he can still perceive something of what's happening up here..."

Sarah Rosa exchanged a puzzled glance with Boris. He couldn't help giving an embarrassed half-smile, but managed to keep it in check.

"He is very disturbed. He is angry... he can't bear the fact that he's still here... he wants to go away, but he can't. Something's holding him back... he can't stand the smell."

"What smell?" asked Mila.

"The smell of rotting flowers. He says it's unbearable."

They sniffed the air, hoping for confirmation of those words, but all they could smell was a pleasant perfume: there was a big vase of fresh flowers on the windowsill.

"Try and make him speak, Nicla."

"I don't think he wants to... no, he doesn't want to talk to me..."

"You've got to persuade him."

"I'm sorry..."

"What?"

But the medium didn't finish the sentence. Instead she said: "I think he wants to show me something... yes, that's it... he's showing me a room... this room. But we aren't there. Neither are the machines that are keeping him alive right now..." Nicla stiffened: "There's someone with him."

"Who is it?"

"A woman, she's beautiful... I think it's his mother."

From the corner of her eye Mila saw Lara Rockford stirring in the armchair as she lit her umpteenth cigarette.

"What's he doing?"

"Joseph is very small... she is holding him on her knees and explaining something to him... she is telling him off and warning him... she's telling him that the world out there can only hurt him. So he's better off staying here, he will be safe. She's promising to protect him, to take care of him, never to leave him..."

Goran and Mila looked at one another. That was how Joseph's gilded prison had begun, with his mother removing him from the world.

"She's telling him that of all the world's dangers, women are the worst. The world out there is full of women who want to take everything from him... they will only love him for what he owns... they will deceive him, and take advantage of him..." Then the nun said again, "I'm sorry..."

Mila looked at Goran again. That morning the criminologist had confidently asserted, in Roche's presence, that the origin of Rockford's rage—the same rage that would in time turn him into a serial killer—lay in the fact that he couldn't accept he was the way he was.

Because someone, probably his mother, had one day discovered his sexual preferences, and had never forgiven him. Killing his partner meant erasing the guilt.

But plainly Gavila was wrong.

The medium's story partially contradicted his theory. Joseph's homosexuality could be linked to his mother's phobias. Perhaps she knew about her son and said nothing.

But in that case, why did Joseph kill his partners?

"I wasn't even allowed to invite a girlfriend..."

Everyone turned to look at Lara Rockford. The young woman gripped her cigarette between trembling fingers, and stared at the ground as she spoke.

"It was his mother who brought these boys here," said Goran.

And she confirmed his words: "Yes, and she paid them."

The tears began to pour from her one good eye, turning her face into a mask even more grotesque than before.

"My mother hated me."

"Why?" asked the criminologist.

"Because I was a woman."

"I'm sorry," Nicla said again.

"Shut up!" Lara yelled, looking at her brother.

"I'm sorry, little sister..."

"Shut up!"

She yelled it in a furious voice, rising to her feet. Her chin trembled.

"You can't imagine. You don't know what it means to turn and find those eyes on you. A gaze that follows you everywhere, and you know what it means. Even though you don't want to admit it, because the very idea disgusts you. I think he was trying to understand...why he felt attracted to me."

Nicla was in a trance, trembling violently, as Mila held her hand.

"That's why you left home, isn't it?" Goran stared at Lara Rockford, trying to win her reply at all costs. "And it was then that he began killing..."

"Yes, I think that's what happened."

"Then you came back, five years ago..."

Lara Rockford laughed. "I knew nothing about it. He tricked me, saying he felt alone and abandoned by everyone. That I was his sister and he loved me, and we had to make peace. That everything else was fixations on my part. I believed him. When I came here, he behaved normally for the first few days: he was sweet and affectionate, he paid attention to me. He didn't seem like the Joseph I'd known as a little girl. Until…"

She laughed again. And that laughter said more than words could have done about all the violence to which she had been subjected.

"It wasn't a car accident that left you like this."

Lara shook her head. "This way he could be absolutely sure that I would never leave again."

They felt terribly sorry for that young woman, a prisoner not of that house but of her own appearance.

"I'm sorry," she said as she limped towards the door, dragging her ruined leg as she did so.

Stern and Boris stepped aside to let her pass. Then they turned to look at Goran, waiting for him to take a decision.

He turned to Nicla. "Do you feel like going on?"

"Yes," replied the nun, although the effects of her exertion were clearly apparent.

The next question was the most important of all. They would have no chance to do it again. It wasn't only the survival of the sixth child that depended on it, it was theirs as well. Because if they failed to discover the meaning of what had been happening for days, they would bear the marks of events for ever.

"Nicla, make Joseph tell us when he met the man who was like him…"

31.

At night he heard her screaming.

It was the migraines that gave her no peace and didn't let her sleep. By now not even the morphine could calm her sudden twinges. She stretched out in the bed and shrieked until she lost her voice. Her former beauty, which she had tried so carefully to preserve from the inexorable withering of age, had vanished entirely. And she had become vulgar. She, who had always paid such attention to her words, who had been so measured, had become coarse and fanciful in her cursing. She had curses for everyone. For her husband, who had died too soon. For her daughter, who had run away from her. And for God who had left her like that.

He alone could placate her.

He went into her room and tied her hands to the bed with a silk scarf so that she couldn't hurt herself. She had already pulled out all her hair and her face was streaked with coagulated blood from all the times she had plunged her nails into her cheeks.

"Joseph," she called him as he stroked her forehead. "Tell me I was a good mother. Tell me, please."

And he, staring into eyes that were filling with tears, told her.

Joseph B. Rockford was thirty-two. And he was only eighteen years from his date with death. Not long before, a famous geneticist had been called in to check if Joseph would share the fate of his father and grandfather. Given the scant knowledge at the time concerning the genetic heredity of illnesses, the answer had been vague: the probability that this rare syndrome had been at work in him since birth varied between forty and seventy percent.

Since then, Joseph had lived with that one goal ahead of him. Everything else just brought him one stage closer. Like his mother's illness. The nights in the big house were shaken by her inhuman cries echoing around the big rooms. It was impossible to escape. After months of forced sleeplessness, Joseph had started putting in earplugs just to keep from hearing her agony.

But they weren't enough.

One morning, at around four o'clock, he had woken up. He was having a dream, but he couldn't remember it. But that wasn't what woke him up. He had sat up in bed, trying to work out what it had been.

There was an unusual silence in the house.

Joseph understood. He got up and put his clothes on: a pair of trousers, a high-necked jumper and his green Barbour. Then he left the room, passing by the closed door of his mother's bedroom and walking on. He came down the imposing marble stairs and, in a few minutes, he was outside.

He walked down the long avenue of the estate until he reached the west gate, which was normally used by servants and deliverymen. It was the boundary of his world. He and Lara had made their way here so many times in their childhood explorations. Even though she was much younger than him, his sister would have liked to go beyond it, demonstrating an enviable courage. But Joseph had always pulled back. Lara had left almost a year before. After she had found the strength to cross that limit, nothing more had been heard from her. He missed her terribly.

In that cold November morning, Joseph stood motionless by the gate for several minutes. Then he climbed over it. When his feet touched the ground, a new sensation took hold of him, a tickle in the middle of his chest that spread all around him. For the first time in his life he experienced the meaning of joy.

He walked along the asphalt road.

Dawn was heralded by a glow on the horizon. The landscape around him was exactly the same as the landscape of the estate, and for a moment he had a sense that he hadn't actually left the place, and that the gate was only a pretext, because the whole of creation began and ended there, and every time he passed through that boundary he would start again from the beginning, unchanged, and so on until infinity. An interminable series of identical parallel universes. Sooner or later he would see his house emerging from the path again, and he would know for certain that it had been nothing but an illusion.

But it didn't happen. As the distance grew, the awareness that he could do it came to the surface.

There was no one in sight. Not a car, not a house. The sound of his footsteps on the tarmac was the only trace of humanity amidst the song of the birds as they began to reclaim the new day. No wind stirred the trees, which seemed to stare at him as he passed, like a stranger. And he had been tempted to greet them. The air was effervescent, and it had a smell. Of frost, dry leaves and fresh green grass.

The sun was more than a promise now. It slipped across the fields, spreading and spreading like a tide of oil. Joseph couldn't have said how many miles he had walked. He was headed nowhere. But that was the great thing: he didn't care. Lactic acid pulsed through the muscles of his legs. He had never suspected that pain could be pleasant. He had energy in his body, and air to breathe. Those two variables would decide the rest. For once he didn't want to think about things. Until that day his mind had always found some new anxiety to block his way. And since the unknown still lay in wait all around him, during those few moments he had already learned that apart from danger, it could also harbor something precious. Like astonishment, like wonder.

That was exactly what he felt when he became aware of a new sound. It was low and far off, but steadily approaching, behind him.

He soon recognized it: it was the noise of a car. He turned round and saw only its roof appearing beyond a hump. Then the car went into a dip before reappearing. It was an old beige station wagon. It was coming towards him. The windscreen was so dirty that it was impossible to see the passengers. Joseph decided to ignore it, turned round and started walking again. When the car was close to him, it seemed to slow down.

"Hey!"

He hesitated to turn round. Perhaps it was someone wanting to put an end to his adventure. Yes, that was it. His mother had woken up and started shouting his name. Not finding him in bed, she had let the servants loose in and out of the estate. Perhaps the man calling out to him was one of the gardeners who had come looking for him in his own car, hoping for a handsome reward.

"Hey, you, where're you going? You want a lift?"

The question reassured him. It couldn't be someone from the house. The car pulled up beside him. Joseph couldn't see the driver. He stopped, and so did the car.

"I'm going north," said the man at the wheel. "I could save you a few miles' walk. It's not much, but you won't find many other lifts around here."

His age was indeterminable. He might have been forty, maybe less. His beard was reddish, long and disheveled, making it hard to guess. His hair was long too, and he wore it combed back with a center parting. His eyes were gray.

"So what do you want to do? Are you getting in?"

Joseph thought for a moment, then said, "Yes, thanks."

He sat down beside the stranger and the car set off. The seats were covered with brown velvet, and worn in places, revealing the canvas underneath. There was a smell that was a mix of car deodorants superimposed over one another over the years, hanging from the rearview mirror. The backseat had been lowered to make a bigger space, now occupied by cardboard boxes and plastic bags, tools and jerry cans of various sizes. Everything was perfectly arranged. There were traces of old stickers on the dashboard. The car radio, an old model with a tape machine, was playing a country music cassette. The driver, who had lowered the volume to talk to him, turned it back up again.

"Walking long?"

Joseph avoided his eye, for fear that he might notice he was lying.

"Yes, since yesterday."

"Weren't hitching?"

"Yes, I was. A truck driver gave me a lift, but he had to go in a different direction."

"Why, where're you going?"

He wasn't expecting that, and told the truth.

"I don't know."

The man started laughing.

"If you don't know, why did you let the trucker go?"

Joseph turned to look at him seriously. "Because he asked too many questions."

The man laughed even louder. "My God, I like your directness, kid."

He was wearing a red, short-sleeved windcheater. His trousers were light brown and his knitted woolen jumper had a pattern of rhomboids. He wore working boots, with a reinforced rubber sole. He gripped the wheel with both hands. On his left wrist he wore a cheap plastic quartz watch.

"Listen, I don't know what your plans are and I won't press you to tell me but, if you feel like it, I live not far from here and you could come for breakfast. What do you say?"

Joseph was about to say no. It had already been risky enough accepting a lift, now he wasn't going to follow this man somewhere to let him rob him or worse. But then he realized that he was just being influenced by another of his fears. The future was *mysterious,* not *threatening*—as he had discovered that very morning. And to savor its fruits, you had to take risks.

"OK."

"Eggs, bacon and coffee," the stranger promised.

* * *

Twenty minutes later they left the main road to go up a dirt track. They traveled slowly, with holes and bumps, until they reached a wooden house with a sloping roof. The white paint covering it had flaked off in places. The porch was dilapidated, and tufts of grass poked out here and there among the planks. They parked beside the front door.

Who is this guy? Joseph wondered when he saw where he lived, aware that the answer wouldn't be as interesting as the possibility of exploring his world.

"Welcome," said the man as soon as they crossed the threshold.

The first room was middle-sized. The furniture consisted of a table and three chairs, a sideboard with a few drawers missing and an old sofa with its upholstery torn in several places. An unframed painting showing an anonymous landscape hung from one of the walls.

Beside the only window was a soot-stained stone fireplace containing cold, blackened logs. On a stool carved from a tree trunk, several pans encrusted with burnt fat stood in a pile. At the end of the room were two closed doors.

"Sorry, there's no bathroom. But outside there's a whole load of trees," the man added, laughing.

There was no electricity or running water, either, but soon the man went out to the back of the car and took out the jerry cans that Joseph had noticed a short time before.

With some old newspapers and wood that he had collected outside, he lit the fire in the fireplace. After cleaning one of the pans as best he could, he started frying up some butter and then threw in the eggs and the bacon. Second rate it might have been, but the food gave off a smell that would have given you an appetite.

Joseph watched him curiously, tormented by questions, like the ones children ask adults when they reach the age at which they begin to discover the world. But the man didn't seem annoyed—he seemed to like talking.

"Have you been living here long?"

"For a month, but this isn't my house."

"What does that mean?"

"That thing out there is my real house," he said, pointing his chin at the car parked outside. "I travel the world."

"Why have you stopped, then?"

"Because I like this place. One day I was driving along the road and I saw the path. I turned off onto it and found myself here. The house had been abandoned for God knows how long. It probably belonged to some farm laborers: there's a tool shed out the back."

"What happened to them?"

"Oh, I don't know. They must have done the same as so many others: when there was a crisis in the country, they went in search of a better life in the city. There are plenty of abandoned farms around here."

"Why didn't they try to sell the property?"

The man laughed: "Who would buy a place like this? You can't get a cent out of land like this, my friend."

He stopped cooking and poured the contents of the pan straight onto the plates laid out on the table. Joseph, without waiting, plunged his fork into the yellow mush. He had discovered he was very hungry. The smell was terrific.

"You like it, don't you? Well, eat away, there's as much as you want."

Joseph went on greedily wolfing it down. Then, with his mouth full, he asked, "Are you going to stay here for long?"

"I thought I would go at the end of the month: the winters are hard around here. I'm getting some supplies together and then I'll go out looking for other abandoned farms, in the hope of finding some things that might still be useful in some way. This morning I found a toaster. I think it's broken, but I can fix it."

Joseph registered everything, as if putting together a kind of manual with all kinds of ideas in it: how to make an excellent breakfast with only eggs, butter and bacon, and how to get hold of drinking water. Perhaps he thought they would be useful in a new life. The stranger's life struck him as enviable. It might have been hard, but it was infinitely better than the one he had lived until then.

"You know we haven't even introduced ourselves?"

Joseph's hand, still clutching its fork, froze in midair.

"If you don't want to tell me your name, that's fine by me. I like you anyway."

Joseph went on eating. The man didn't press the point, but he felt obliged to repay him in some way for his hospitality. He decided to tell him something about himself.

"I'm almost certainly going to die when I'm fifty."

And he told him about the curse on the male heirs of his family. The man listened attentively. Without naming names, Joseph explained to the man that he was rich, and told him the origin of his wealth. Of that courageous and astute grandfather who had planted the seed of a great fortune. And he also told him about his father, who had enlarged the legacy with his entrepreneurial genius. Finally he talked about himself, about the fact that he had no other targets to reach, because everything had already been won. He had come into the world to pass on only two things: a huge fortune and an inexorably fatal gene.

"I understand that the sickness that killed your father and grandfather is inevitable, but for the money there's always a solution: why not give up your wealth if you don't feel free enough?"

"Because I grew up with money, and without it I wouldn't know how to survive for a single day. As you see, whatever change I make, I'm always destined to die."

"Balls!" said the man as he got up to wash out the pan.

Joseph tried to put it better: "I could have anything I desire. But for that very reason I don't know what desire is."

"What on earth are you talking about? Money can't buy everything."

"Oh, believe me, it can. If I wanted you dead, I could pay some men and they would kill you, and no one would ever know."

"Ever done that?" asked the other man, suddenly serious.

"What?"

"Ever paid someone to kill for you?"

"I haven't, but my father and grandfather did, I know."

There was a pause.

"But health you can't buy."

"That's true. But if you know in advance when you're going to die, the problem's solved. You see: the rich are unhappy because they know that sooner or later they're going to have to leave everything they possess. You can't take your money to the grave. I'm not condemning myself to thoughts of my own death, someone else has already done it for me."

The man stopped to think. "You're right," he said, "but it's very sad not to desire anything. There must be something you really like, isn't there? So start with that."

"Well, I like walking. And since this morning I've liked bacon and eggs. And I like boys."

"You mean you're…"

"I really don't know. I go with them, but I can't say it's something I really desire."

"So why don't you try going with a woman?"

"I probably should. But first it should be something I *desire,* you see? I can't put it better than that."

"No. I think you're clear enough already."

The man set down the pan on top of the others on the stool. Then he looked at the quartz watch on his wrist.

"It's ten o'clock, I've got to go into town: I need some parts to fix the toaster."

"Then I'll go too."

"No, why? Stay here and rest for a while if you want. I'll be back soon, maybe we could eat together again and talk some more. You're really something, you know that?"

Joseph looked at the old sofa with the torn upholstery. It looked very inviting.

"OK," he said. "I'll sleep for a while if you don't mind."

The man smiled. "Fantastic!" He was about to leave when he turned round. "By the way, what would you like for dinner?"

Joseph stared at him. "I don't know. Surprise me."

* * *

A hand shook him gently. Joseph opened his eyes and he discovered that it was already evening.

"There's tiredness for you!" said his new friend, smiling. "You've slept nine hours through!"

Joseph pulled himself up, stretching. He hadn't rested as well as that for a long time. He suddenly felt a pang of hunger.

"Is it dinnertime already?" he asked.

"Time to make the fire and I'll get it ready straightaway: I've got some chicken to cook in the embers, and some potatoes. Is that OK as a menu?"

"Fantastic, I'm starving."

"Meanwhile get yourself a beer, they're on the windowsill."

Joseph had never drunk beer, apart from the beer that his mother put in the Christmas punch. He took a tin from the six-pack and pulled the tab. He rested his lips on the aluminum rim and took a long sip. He felt the cold drink quickly going down his esophagus. It was a pleasant, thirst-quenching sensation. After the second sip, he burped.

"Bless you!" the man exclaimed.

It was cold outside, but inside the fire gave off good warmth. The light from the gas lamp in the middle of the table faintly illuminated the room.

"The ironmonger said the toaster's fixable. He also gave me some advice on how to mend it. That's great, it means I might be able to sell it again at a fair."

"So that's what you do for a living?"

"Yes, that too from time to time. People throw away a lot of things that can still be used. I take them and fix them up, and then I make some money. Some things I keep, like this painting, for example..."

He pointed at the unframed landscape on the wall.

"Why that one?" asked Joseph.

"I don't know, I like it. I think it reminds me of the place where I was born, or perhaps I've never even been there, who can say: I've traveled so much..."

"Have you really been to lots of different places?"

"Yes, loads." He seemed lost in thought for moment, but he immediately went on: "My chicken is something special, you'll see. And by the way, I've got a surprise for you."

"A surprise? What surprise?"

"Not now, after dinner."

They sat down at the table. The chicken and potatoes were perfectly cooked and delicious. Joseph filled his plate several times. The guy—that was how Joseph thought of him now—ate with his mouth open, and had already drunk three beers. After dinner he took out a hand-carved pipe and some tobacco. As he was preparing to smoke, he said, "You know, I've thought a lot about what you said to me this morning."

"What exactly?"

"What you said about 'desire.' I was struck by it."

"Really? Why?"

"You see, I don't think it's so bad to know exactly when your life is going to end. I see it as more of a privilege."

"How can you say something like that?"

"Well, of course it depends on how you look at the whole picture. Whether you're inclined to see the glass as half full or half empty. In short: you can list all the things you lack. Or you can define the rest of your life according to your deadline."

"I don't follow you."

"I think the fact you know you're going to die at fifty makes you think you have no power over your life. But you're wrong there, my friend."

"What do you mean by 'power'?"

The guy took a twig from the fire and lit his pipe with the end of it. He took a deep puff on it before he replied. "Power and desire go hand in hand. They are made from the same accursed substance. The second depends on the first, and vice versa. And that's not just philosophical crap, you can see it in nature itself. You put it well this morning: we can only desire what we don't have, you think you have the power to get anything and you desire nothing. But that happens because your power derives from money."

"Why, is there any other kind?"

"Certainly, the power of the will, for example. You have to put it to the test to understand. But I suspect you don't want to do it..."

"Why do you say that? I can do it."

The guy looked at him. "Are you sure?"

"Definitely."

"Fine. Before dinner I told you I had a surprise for you. Now I've got to show it to you. Come on."

He got up and walked towards one of the closed doors at the end of the room. Joseph unsteadily followed him to the half-open doorway.

"Look."

He took a step into the darkness, and he sensed it. There was something in the room, breathing quickly. He immediately thought of an animal and stepped backwards.

"Come on," the guy said, "take a better look."

It took Joseph a few seconds for his eyes to get accustomed to the dark. The gas lamp on the table was just bright enough to shed a faint light on the boy's face. He was lying on a bed, with his hands and feet tied to posts with thick ropes. He was wearing a checked shirt and jeans, but no shoes. A handkerchief around his mouth kept him from talking, so he just made disconnected noises, like animal cries. The hair over his forehead was drenched with sweat. He was struggling like an imprisoned animal, and his eyes were wide with terror.

"Who is he?" Joseph asked.

"A present for you."

"And what should I do with it?"

"Whatever you like."

"But I don't know who he is."

"Neither do I. He was hitchhiking. I got him into the car on the way back here."

"Perhaps we should untie him and let him go."

"If that's what you want."

"Why shouldn't it be?"

"Because this is a demonstration of what power is, and how it is linked with desire. If you want to free him, do that. But if you want anything else from him, it's up to you to choose."

"Are you talking about sex, by any chance?"

The guy shook his head, disappointed. "Your horizon is very limited, my friend. You have a human life at your disposal—the greatest, most astonishing of God's creations—and the only thing you can think of doing is fucking it..."

"What should I do with a human life?"

"You said it today: if you wanted to kill someone, you would just have to pay someone else to do it for you. But do you really think that gives you the power to take a life? *Your money* has that power, not *you*. Until you do it with your own hands, you're never going to experience what it means."

Joseph looked at the visibly terrified boy again. "But I don't want to know," he said.

"Because you're afraid. Afraid of the consequences, of the fact that you might be punished, or about your sense of guilt."

"It's normal to be afraid of certain things."

"No, it isn't, Joseph."

He didn't notice that the guy had called him by name: at that moment he was too busy looking back and forth between man and boy.

"What if I told you that you can do it, that you can take someone's life and no one will ever know?"

"No one? What about you?"

"I'm the one who kidnapped him and brought him here, remember? And I'll also be the one who will bury his body..."

Joseph lowered his head. "No one would ever know?"

"What if I told you that you would be unpunished, would that give you the *desire* to try?"

Joseph looked at his hands for a long while, and his breathing grew faster as he began to feel a strange euphoria rising up within him, something he had never felt before.

"I'd like a knife," he said.

The guy went into the kitchen. As he waited, Joseph stared at the boy who was pleading with him with his eyes and crying. At the sight of those silent tears, Joseph discovered he felt nothing. No one would mourn his death when, at the age of fifty, the disease of his father and grandfather came to claim him. For the world he would always be the rich boy, undeserving of any kind of compassion.

The guy came back to him with a long, sharp knife. He put it in his hands.

"There's nothing more gratifying than taking a life," he said. "Not a particular person's life, an enemy or someone who has hurt you. Just any human being. It gives you the same power as God."

He left him alone and walked away, closing the door behind him.

The moonlight slid between the broken blinds, making the knife in his hand gleam. The boy grew agitated, and Joseph was aware of his anxiety, his fear in the form of sounds, but also of smells. His acid breath, the sweat from his armpits. He approached the bed, slowly, his footsteps squeaking on the floor, so that even the boy must have been aware of what was happening. He put the blade of the knife flat on his chest. Should he say something? Nothing came to mind. A shiver ran through him and something happened that he really wasn't expecting: he had an erection.

He lifted the blade a few inches, running it slowly along the boy's body until it reached his stomach. He stopped. He took a breath and slowly pushed the tip of the blade through the fabric of his shirt until it touched the flesh. The boy tried to scream, but all that came out was the pitiful imitation of a cry of pain. Joseph pushed the blade even further in, and the skin parted as if it was being torn. He recognized the white of the fatty tissue. But the wound still wasn't bleeding. Then he plunged the blade in all the way until he felt the hot blood on his hand and became aware of a pungent exhalation from the intestines. The boy arched his back, involuntarily helping him with his task. He pressed again until he felt the knife tip touch the dorsal column. The boy was a tense bundle of muscle and flesh beneath him. He remained in that arched position for a few moments. Then he fell back heavily on the bed, stripped of his strength, like an inanimate object. *And at that moment, the alarms…*

…began sounding all together. The doctor and the nurse ran around the patient with the emergency trolley. Nicla, bent over, tried to get

her breath back: the shock of what she had seen had torn her violently from her trance. Mila had her hands on her back, trying to make her breathe. The doctor tore open the pajamas covering Joseph B. Rockford's chest, pulling off all the buttons, which rolled around the room. Boris nearly slipped on them as he tried to come to Mila's support. Then the doctor put the plates that the nurse had passed him on the patient's chest, shouting "now!" before the electrical discharge. Goran walked over to Mila. "Let's get her out of here," he said, going to relieve the nun. As they were leaving the room with Rosa and Stern, the policewoman turned towards Joseph B. Rockford one last time. His body was racked by the shocks but, under the blankets, she noticed what looked like an erection.

You complete bastard, she thought.

The beep of the heart monitor stabilized into a single peremptory note. But at that moment Joseph B. Rockford opened his eyes.

His lips began moving without being able to make a sound. His vocal cords had been damaged when they had given him the tracheotomy to enable him to breathe.

He should have been dead by now. The machines around him said that he was now just a lifeless piece of meat. And yet he was trying to communicate. His groans made him sound like a man drowning and trying to catch one last desperate breath of air.

It didn't take long.

In the end, an invisible hand dragged him down again, and it was as if Joseph B. Rockford's soul had been swallowed up by his deathbed, leaving nothing but an empty, discarded body.

32.

As soon as she recovered, Nicla Papakidis made herself available to a Federal Police draftsman to draw the identikit of the man she had seen with Joseph.

The stranger whom he had christened "the guy," and who was presumed to be Albert.

The long beard and the curly mane of hair prevented her from giving a precise description of the man's salient features. She didn't know what his jaw was like, and his nose was just a vague shadow on his face. She couldn't catch the exact shape of his eyes.

All she could say with any certainty was that they were gray.

But the result would be sent out to all police cars, to the ports and airports and border patrols. Roche was trying to decide whether to have copies in the press as well, although that would have involved an explanation of how they had ended up with the identikit. If he revealed that there was a medium behind it, the media would deduce that the police had nothing to work with, that they were stumbling around in the dark and that they had turned to a psychic out of desperation.

"That's a risk you have to take," Goran suggested.

The chief inspector had joined the team at the Rockfords' house again. He hadn't wanted to meet the nun, because he had made it clear from the start that he didn't want anything to do with their experiment: as always, all the responsibility would fall on Goran. The criminologist had willingly accepted, because he had come to trust Mila's hunches.

"Little one, one thing has occurred to me," said Nicla to her favorite as they sat in the mobile unit camper watching Gavila and the chief inspector talking on the lawn in front of the house.

"What?"

"That I don't want the reward."

"But if this is the man we're looking for, it will go to you by right."

"I don't want it."

"Just think of all the things you could do for the people you look after every day."

"And what do they need that they don't have already? They have our love, our care and, believe me, when one of God's creatures reaches the end of his days, he doesn't need anything else."

"If you took that money, I could think that something good had come out of all this..."

"Evil generates only more evil. That has always been its chief characteristic."

"Once I heard someone say that evil can always be demonstrated. Good can't. Because evil leaves traces of its passing. While you can only bear witness to good."

Nicla smiled, finally. "It's odd," she said suddenly. "You see, Mila, the fact is that good is too fleeting to be recorded in any way. And as it passes it doesn't leave a trail. Good is clean, evil is dirty...But I can prove that good exists, because I see it every day. When one of my poor people is approaching the end, I try and stay with them as much as possible. I hold their hand, listen to the things they have to say to me; if they tell me their sins I don't judge them. When they understand what is happening to them, whether they have led a good life and done no evil, or whether they have done evil and repented...well, they're always smiling. I don't know why but it happens, I assure you. So the proof of good is the smile with which they challenge death."

Comforted, Mila nodded. She wouldn't insist that Nicla accept the reward. Perhaps she was right.

It was almost five in the evening, the nun was tired. But there was one more thing to do.

"Are you sure you would recognize the abandoned house?" she asked.

"Yes, I know where it is."

They just had to perform a routine inspection before going back to the Studio. It was required for positive proof of the medium's information.

But they all went anyway.

In the car, Sarah Rosa followed Nicla's directions, and turned where she said. The weather report said there was more snow on the way. On one side, the sky was clear and the sun was setting quickly. On the other, the clouds were already gathering on the horizon, and there were flashes of approaching lightning.

They were bang in the middle.

"We've got to get a move on," said Stern. "It will soon be dark."

They reached the dirt road and turned down it. The stones rattled under their tires. After all those years, the wooden house was still standing. The white paint had flaked off completely, and only remained in a few distinct patches. The planks exposed to the weather were rotting, making the house look like a rotten tooth.

They got out of the car and headed towards the porch.

"Careful, it could collapse," Boris warned.

Goran climbed the first step. The place matched the nun's description. The door was open, the criminologist barely had to push it. Inside, the floor was covered with a layer of soil, and rats could be heard moving under the tables, disturbed by their presence. Gavila recognized the sofa, even though nothing was left of it now but a skeleton of rusty springs. The dresser was still there. The stone fireplace had partly collapsed. Goran took a little torch from his pocket to examine the two back rooms. Meanwhile Boris and Stern had come in and were looking around.

Goran opened the first door. "This is the bedroom."

But the bed was no longer there. In its place was a lighter shadow on the floor. It was there that Joseph B. Rockford had received his blood baptism. God knows who the boy was who had been killed in that room almost twenty years before.

"We'll have to dig around here for human remains," said Gavila.

"I'll call the gravediggers and Chang's men as soon as we've finished checking the place," Stern said.

Meanwhile, outside the house, Sarah Rosa was walking nervously back and forth, her hands in her pockets to protect them against the cold. Nicla and Mila watched her from inside the car.

"You don't like that woman," said the nun.

"It would be more accurate to say that she doesn't like me."

"Have you tried to work out why?"

Mila looked at her sideways. "Are you trying to tell me it's my fault?"

"No, I'm just saying that before making accusations we should always be sure."

"She's been on my back ever since I got here."

Nicla raised her hands in a gesture of surrender. "Then don't rise to her bait. It will all pass as soon as you have gone."

Mila shook her head. Sometimes the nun's good sense was unbearable.

Inside, Goran left the bedroom and turned automatically towards the other closed door.

The medium hadn't mentioned that second room.

He aimed the light at the handle and opened the door.

It was exactly the same size as the one next to it. And it was empty. The damp had attacked the walls and a patina of mildew already nestled in the corners. Goran shone his torch beam around. As it passed across one of the walls, he noticed that something was reflecting the light.

He held the torch steady and saw that there were five gleaming squares, each about six inches across. He stepped closer, then froze. Fixed to the walls with simple drawing pins was a series of snapshots.

Debby. Anneke. Sabine. Melissa. Caroline.

In the pictures they were still alive. Albert had brought them here before killing them. And he had immortalized them in that very room, in front of that wall. Their hair was disheveled, their clothes a mess. A merciless flash had surprised them with their eyes red from crying, their faces filled with terror.

They were smiling and waving.

He had forced them to assume that grotesque pose in front of the lens. That cheerfulness, forced by fear, was horrifying.

Debby's lips were twisted into a grimace of unnatural contentment, and she looked as if she might burst into tears again at any moment.

Anneke held one arm raised, the other dangling along her hips, in a gesture of resignation and defeat.

Sabine had been captured as she was looking round, trying to understand what her childish heart could not grasp.

Melissa was tense and combative. But it was plain that she too would soon give in.

Caroline was motionless, eyes wide above her smile of disbelief.

It was only after studying them all that Goran called in the others.

Absurd. Incomprehensible. Pointlessly cruel.

There were no other terms for it. They all maintained the silence that had taken hold of them on their way back to the Studio.

It was going to be a long night. No one was confident of finding sleep after a day like that. Mila had held out for forty-eight uninterrupted hours, during which too many things had happened.

Albert's outline being found on the wall of Yvonne Gress's villa. Her evening chat at Goran's house, when she had told him she had been followed, as well as revealing her theory that their man had an accomplice. Then there had been that question about the color of Sabine's eyes that had led to the discovery of Roche's deception. The visit to the Rockfords' ghostly house. The common grave. Lara

Rockford. The intervention of Nicla Papakidis. The exploration of the mind of a serial killer.

And last of all, those photographs.

Mila had seen many photographs in the course of her work. Pictures of minors, taken by the sea or at school concerts. She was shown them by parents or relations when she went to see them. Children who disappeared before reappearing in other photographs—often naked, or wearing grown-up clothes—in the collections of pedophiles, or in mortuary files.

But in the five pictures found in the abandoned house there was something more.

Albert knew they would find their way there. And he was waiting for them.

Had he even predicted that they would investigate his pupil Joseph with a medium?

"He's been watching us from the start," had been Gavila's laconic comment. "He's always a step ahead of us."

Mila reflected that their every move had been circumspect, elusive and neutralized. And now they had to watch their backs, too. That was the burden that weighed upon her companions in the car as they returned to their headquarters.

And there were still two bodies to discover.

The first was definitely a corpse. The second would be with the passing of time. No one was brave enough to admit it, but now they despaired of preventing the murder of child number six.

As for little Caroline, who could say what horror would be revealed. Could there be anything worse than all that they had already discovered? Albert was preparing for a grand finale with the sixth.

It was after eleven when Boris parked the minivan below the Studio. He let everyone out, locked the car and noticed that they were waiting for him to go up.

They didn't want to leave him behind.

The horror that they had witnessed had left them more united than before. Because all they had left was their colleagues. Even Mila was part of that fellowship. And so was Goran. They had been shut out for a while, but it hadn't lasted for long, and it had only happened because of Roche's desire to control everything. They had been allowed back in again. That wrong had been forgiven.

They slowly climbed the stairs of the building. Stern put an arm around Rosa's shoulders. "Go home to your family tonight," he said to her. But she merely shook her head. Mila had understood. Rosa couldn't break the chain. Otherwise the whole world would fall apart, and the gates that still protected it would be thrown wide open to the Champion of evil, and he would come flooding in. They were the last vanguard in this struggle, and even if they were losing they had no intention of letting go.

They all crossed the threshold of the Studio at the same time. Boris waited to close the door, then joined them and found them standing in the corridor, as though hypnotized. He didn't understand what was happening until he glimpsed, in a gap between their shoulders, the body lying on the ground. Sarah Rosa screamed. Mila turned away, unable to look. Stern crossed himself. Gavila couldn't speak.

Caroline, the fifth girl.

■■■■■■ Prison
Penitential district no. 45
Report No. 2 the Director, Alphonse Bérenger
23 Nov
For the attention of the Office of the General Prosecutor
J. B. Marin
In the person of the Vice Prosecutor
Matthew Sedris
Subject: OUTCOME OF INSPECTION—CONFIDENTIAL

Dear Mr. Sedris,

We wish to inform you that the inspection of the isolation cell of prisoner RK-357/9 was made by surprise last night.

The prison guards burst in to take away organic material "lost by chance or left spontaneously by the individual" with a view to identifying his genetic imprint, all following your office's recommendations to the letter.

I must inform you that, to their great astonishment, my men found themselves faced with an immaculate cell. Which makes us think that prisoner RK-357/9 was expecting us. I can only reason that the prisoner keeps himself in a constant state of alert, and that he predicted and calculated our every move.

I fear that, without an error on the part of the inmate or a change in the incidental circumstances, it will be difficult to achieve concrete results.

Perhaps we still have one chance of getting to the heart of the mystery. We have noticed that prisoner RK-357/9 sometimes, perhaps because of his isolation, talks to himself. They seem to be ravings, and uttered in a low voice, but at all events we consider it appropriate, with your agreement, to place a bug in his cell to record his words.

Obviously we will also repeat our surprise inspections designed to secure his DNA.

I present one last observation for your attention: the subject is always calm and accommodating. He never complains and does not seem annoyed by our attempts to lead him into error.

We have little time left. In 86 days we will have no other choice but to set him free.

Yours sincerely,

Director

Dr. Alphonse Bérenger

33.

Apartment known as the "Studio,"
now renamed "site 5"
22 February

It would never be the same again.

With that shadow hanging over them, they had confined themselves to the guest room, waiting for Chang and Krepp's teams to examine the apartment. Roche, who had been informed immediately, had been talking to Goran for over an hour.

Stern was lying on his camp bed, with one arm behind his neck and his eyes fixed on the ceiling. He looked like a cowboy. The perfect crease of his suit had been unaffected by the knot of his tie. Boris had turned onto one side, but he clearly wasn't sleeping. His left foot went on nervously tapping the bedcover. Rosa was trying to contact someone on her mobile phone, but the signal was weak.

Mila regarded her silent companions one by one before returning her gaze to the laptop on her knees. She had requested the files with the amateur photographs taken at the fair on the evening of Sabine's abduction. They had already been viewed to no effect, but she wanted to see them in the light of the theory she had already expounded to Goran, that the perpetrator might be a woman.

"I'd like to know how the hell he managed to get Caroline's corpse in here..." Stern admitted, expressing the question that troubled them all.

"Yeah, I'd like to know that too..." Rosa agreed.

The office block that housed the Studio was no longer guarded as it had once been, when witnesses had been brought there for their own protection. The building was practically empty and the security systems had been deactivated, but the only access to the apartment was the front door, and it was armored.

"He came in through the front door," Boris said laconically, emerging from his feigned lethargy.

But there was another thing that made them nervous more than anything else. What was Albert's message this time? Why had he decided to cast such a heavy shadow over his pursuers?

"If you ask me, he's just trying to slow us down," Rosa suggested. "We're getting too close to him, so he's shuffled the cards."

"No, Albert doesn't do things by chance," Mila cut in. "He has taught us that every move is carefully premeditated."

Sarah Rosa fixed her eye on her: "So? What the hell are you saying? That one of us is a fucking monster?"

"That's not what she meant," said Stern. "She's just saying that it must be a reason connected with Albert's plan: it's part of the game he's been playing with us since the start. It might also have something to do with this place, and what it was used for in the past."

"It might involve an old case," Mila added, noticing that the suggestion had fallen on deaf ears.

Before the dialogue could resume, Goran came into the room, leaving the door ajar behind him.

"I need your attention."

He sounded urgent. Mila took her eyes off her laptop. They all looked at him.

"In theory, we're still in charge of the investigation, but things are getting complicated."

"What does that mean?" Boris shouted.

"You'll understand in a few moments, but for the time being I advise you to stay calm. I'll explain afterwards..."

"After what?"

Goran had no time to answer before the door opened and Chief Inspector Roche stepped in. With him was a stoutly built man of about fifty, in a crumpled suit and with a tie too thin for his bull-like neck and an unlit cigar between his teeth.

"Sit down, sit down..." said Roche, even though no one had given any kind of greeting. The chief inspector wore a forced smile of the kind that is supposed to inspire calm and instead produces anxiety.

"Gentlemen, the situation is confused but we will come out of it: I certainly won't let some psychopath cast doubts about my men!"

As always, he underlined the last phrase too emphatically.

"So I have taken some precautions entirely in your interest, and I'm adding an extra colleague to your investigation." He announced this without mentioning the man standing beside him. "This is nothing short of embarrassing: we can't find this Albert, and he comes and finds us! So, in agreement with Dr. Gavila, I have entrusted Captain Mosca here with the task of assisting you until the closure of the case."

No one breathed, even though they had already understood what the "assistance" would consist of. Mosca would assume control, giving them only one option: to stand by him and try and regain a little credibility, or get out.

Terence Mosca was very well known in police circles. He owed his fame to an operation lasting more than six years, in which a drug-trafficking organization had been infiltrated. He was responsible for hundreds of arrests and various undercover operations. But he had never worked on serial murders or pathological crimes.

Roche had brought him in for only one reason: years before, Mosca had competed with him for the post of chief inspector. The way things were going, it had struck him as appropriate to involve his worst rival in the case to make him shoulder part of the weight of a failure that he now considered more than likely. A risky move, which showed the extent to which he felt he was on the ropes: if Terence Mosca now solved the Albert case, Roche would have to make way for him at the top of the command hierarchy.

Before Mosca began speaking, he took one step ahead of Roche as a way of stressing his autonomy.

"The pathologist and the scientific expert have not yet produced anything significant. The only thing we know is that to get into the apartment the subject tampered with the armored door."

When he had opened the door on their return, Boris had not noticed any signs of a break-in.

"He's very careful to leave no clues: he didn't want to spoil your surprise."

Mosca went on chewing on his cigar and staring at everyone with his hands in his pockets.

"I've instructed some officers to go around the neighborhood in the hope of finding a witness. We might even get a number plate…as to what it was that led the subject to put the corpse here of all places, we are obliged to improvise. If anything comes to mind, please let me know. That's all for now."

Terence Mosca turned on his heels and, without giving anyone a chance to reply or add anything, he returned to the crime scene.

But Roche stopped. "You haven't much time. We need an idea, and we need it quickly."

Then the chief inspector left the room as well. Goran closed the door and the others immediately came to stand around him.

"What on earth's going on?" Boris asked huffily.

"Why do we need a guard dog now?" Rosa echoed.

"Calm down, you haven't understood," said Goran. "Captain Mosca is the most appropriate person right now. I was the one who requested his intervention."

The others were startled.

"I know what you're thinking, but it let me give Roche an escape route and I saved our role in the investigation."

"Officially we're still involved, but everyone knows that Terence Mosca likes to be a maverick," Stern observed.

"That's exactly why I suggested him: if I know him, he won't want us under his feet, so he won't care what we do. We just have to tell him how we're getting on, that's all."

It seemed like the best possible solution, but it didn't lift the burden of suspicion that weighed on each of them.

"They'll all have their eyes on us." Stern shook his head irritably.

"So we'll let Mosca go after Albert while we dedicate ourselves to child number six..."

It seemed like a good strategy: if they found her alive, they would sweep away that atmosphere of suspicion that had formed around them.

"I think Albert left Caroline's body here to trick us. Because even if nothing is ever proved against us, a doubt about us will always remain."

Even though he was doing everything he could to seem calm, Goran was well aware that his statements were still not enough to lighten the mood. Because since the fifth corpse had been found, each of them had begun to look differently at the others. They had known each other a lifetime, but none of them could have ruled out the possibility that each of them had a secret of some kind. That was Albert's true purpose: to divide them. The criminologist wondered how long it would be before the seed of mistrust began to germinate among them.

"The last child doesn't have much time left," he said confidently. "Albert has almost accomplished his plan. He's just preparing for the finale. But he needed a free hand, and he has ruled us out of the competition. That's why we have only one chance of finding her, and that's through the only one of us who is free of all suspicion, since she didn't join the team until Albert had already planned everything."

Suddenly feeling their eyes upon her, Mila felt uneasy.

"You'll be able to move much more freely than us," Stern said encouragingly. "If you had to act entirely on your own initiative, what would you do?"

In fact Mila did have an idea. But she had kept it to herself until then.

"I know why he only chose girls."

They had asked themselves that question in the Thinking Room, when the case was still in its early stages. Why had Albert not kidnapped boys as well? There was no sexual intent behind his behavior, since he didn't touch the girls.

Mila thought she had come up with an explanation. "They all had to be girls because of number six. I'm almost convinced that he chose her *first,* not last as he wants to make us believe. The others were girls only to conceal that detail. But she was the first object of his fantasy. We don't know why. Perhaps she has some special quality, something that distinguishes her from the others. That's why he *has* to keep her identity secret from us until the end. It wasn't enough for him to let us know that one of the kidnapped girls was still alive. No, we could absolutely on no account know who it was."

"Because that could lead us to him," Goran concluded.

But these were merely fascinating conjectures that were no help to anyone.

"Unless…" said Mila, guessing what the others were thinking, and repeated: "Unless there's always been a link between us and Albert."

Now they didn't have much to lose, and Mila no longer had any qualms about telling everyone the story of how she had been followed.

"It's happened twice. Even though it's only the second time I'm absolutely sure about. While outside the motel it was more a feeling than anything else…"

"So?" Stern asked curiously. "What's it got to do with anything?"

"Someone has followed me. It may have happened other times too, I couldn't swear, I didn't notice…But why? To check on me? What for? I've never had any information of vital importance and I've always been a bit of an outsider amongst you lot."

"Perhaps to throw you off the track," Boris ventured.

"That too: there's never been a real 'track,' unless I really did get too close to something and became important to the case without being aware of it."

"But when it happened at the motel you'd only just got here. And that rules out the hypothesis of throwing you off the track," said Goran.

"Then there's only one explanation left…whoever followed me wanted to *intimidate me*."

"What for?" said Sarah Rosa.

Mila ignored her. "In both cases, my pursuer didn't give himself away involuntarily. In fact I think he revealed himself deliberately."

"Fine, we've understood. But why should he have done that?" Rosa insisted. "It makes no sense!"

Mila turned abruptly towards her, using their difference in height to her advantage.

"Because from the outset I was the only one among you who was capable of finding the sixth girl." She looked at them all again. "Don't take this the wrong way, but the results I've got so far prove me right. You're great at finding serial killers. But I find missing people: I've always done it and I know how to do it."

No one contradicted her. From that perspective, Mila represented the most concrete threat to Albert because she was the only one capable of blowing his plans sky high.

"Let's recapitulate: he kidnapped the sixth child first. If I'd found out straightaway who number six was, his whole plan would have collapsed."

"But you didn't find out," said Rosa. "Perhaps you're not as good as you think."

Mila didn't rise to the provocation. "By coming so close to me outside the motel, Albert may have made a mistake. We've got to get back to that moment."

"How do we do that? You're not trying to tell me he's got a time machine!"

Mila smiled: without being aware of it, Rosa had come very close to the truth. Because there was a way of going back. Ignoring his nicotine breath once again, she turned towards Boris. "How good are you at questioning people under hypnosis?"

"Now relax..."

Boris's voice was barely a whisper. Mila was lying on his camp bed, her hands along her sides and her eyes closed. He was sitting beside her.

"Now I want you to count to one hundred..."

Stern had put a towel over the lamp, plunging the room into a pleasant gloom. Rosa had taken up position on her bed. Goran was sitting in a corner, carefully observing what was happening.

Mila slowly articulated the numbers. Her breath began to assume a regular rhythm. By the time she finished counting she was perfectly relaxed.

"Now I want you to see things in your mind. Are you ready?"

She nodded.

"You're in a big meadow. It's morning and the sun is shining. The rays warm the skin of your face, and there's a smell of grass and flowers. You're walking and you're barefoot: you can feel the cool of the earth under your feet. And there's the sound of a stream calling to you. You walk over to it and lean down to the bank. You plunge your hands into the water, and then bring it to your mouth to drink it. It's very good."

The image was not chosen at random: Boris had evoked those sensations to take control of all of Mila's senses. That way it would be easier to bring her back in her memory to the exact moment when she was crossing the area outside the motel.

"Now that you've quenched your thirst, there's something I'd like you to do for me. Go back to a few evenings ago..."

"All right," she replied.

"It's night, and a car has just brought you back to the motel..."

"It's cold," she said suddenly. Goran thought he saw her shiver.

"And what else?"

"The officer who drove me back nods good-bye, then reverses. And I'm left alone in that space outside the motel."

"What's it like? Describe it to me."

"There isn't much light. Only the neon sign, creaking in the wind. In front of me are the various bungalows, but the windows are in darkness. I'm the only guest tonight. Behind the bungalows there's a strip of very tall, swaying trees. There's gravel on the ground."

"Go on walking..."

"I can only hear my own footsteps."

She almost thought she could hear the sound of the gravel.

"Where are you now?"

"I'm heading towards my room, walking past the porter's office. There's no one there, but the TV is switched on. I'm carrying a paper bag containing two cheese toasted sandwiches: it's my dinner. My breath is condensing in the chilly air, so I quicken my pace. My footsteps on the gravel are the only sound I can hear. My bungalow is the last one in the row."

"You're doing very well."

"Only another few yards and I'm concentrating on my thoughts. There's a little hole in the ground, I don't see it and I trip...*And I hear him*."

Goran wasn't aware that he was doing it, but he instinctively lunged towards Mila's bed as if he could join her in that gravel square, protecting her from the threat that she faced.

"What did you hear?"

"A footstep on the gravel, behind me. Someone is copying my steps. He wants to approach me without me noticing. But he lost the rhythm of my footsteps."

"And what are you doing now?"

"I'm trying to stay calm, but I'm scared. I continue towards the bungalow at the same pace, even though I'd like to start running. And at the same time I'm thinking."

"What are you thinking?"

"That there's no point taking out my gun, because if he's armed he will have plenty of time to shoot first. I'm also thinking about the television that's switched on in the porter's office, and telling myself that he's already killed him. Now it's my turn...the panic is mounting."

"Yes, but you manage to stay in control."

"I'm rummaging in my pocket for my key, because my only chance is to get to my room...as long as he lets me."

"You're concentrating on that door: you're just a few yards away now, yes?"

"Yes. That's all there is in my field of vision, everything else around me has disappeared."

"But now you've got to make it come back..."

"I'm trying…"

"The blood is thundering through your veins, the adrenaline is pumping, your senses are on the alert. I want you to describe the *taste*…"

"My mouth is dry, but I can smell the acid smell of saliva."

"Touch…"

"The cold of the key to my room in my sweaty hand."

"Smell…"

"The wind carries a nasty smell of rotting rubbish. The bins are on my right. And pine needles, and resin."

"Sight…"

"I see my shadow stretching across the square."

"And then?"

"I see the door to the bungalow, it's yellow and the paint's flaking. I see the three steps leading to the porch."

Boris had deliberately left the most important sense to last, because Mila's only perception of her pursuer had involved sound.

"Hearing…"

"I can't hear anything except my footsteps."

"Listen more carefully."

Goran saw a frown appearing on Mila's face, right between her ears, as she struggled to remember.

"I can hear him! Now I can make out his footsteps as well!"

"Excellent. But I want you to concentrate even harder…"

Mila obeyed. Then she said, "What was that?"

"I don't know," Boris replied. "You're alone there, I didn't hear anything."

"But there was something!"

"What?"

"That sound…"

"What sound?"

"Something…metal. Yes! Something metal falling! Falling on the ground, on the gravel!"

"Try to be more precise."

"I don't know…"

"Come on..."

"It's... *a coin!*"

"A coin, are you sure?"

"Yes! A small coin! He's dropped it and he hasn't noticed!"

It was an unexpected trail. If they found the coin in the middle of the gravel square, and took prints from it, that might take them to Mila's pursuer. The hope was that this was Albert.

Mila kept her eyes closed, but she couldn't stop repeating: "A coin! A coin!"

Boris took control again. "That's fine, Mila. Now I'll have to wake you up. I'll count to five, then I'll clap my hands and you will reopen your eyes." He slowly began to articulate: "One, two, three, four... and five!"

Mila opened her eyes wide. She looked confused, bewildered. She tried to stand up, but Boris gently sat her back down by resting a hand on her shoulder.

"Not yet," he said. "Your head might spin."

"Did it work?" she asked him, blinking at him.

Boris smiled: "It seems we may have a clue."

You absolutely have to find it, she said to herself as she swept the gravel in the square with her hand. *My credibility depends on it... my credibility and my life.*

That was why she was being so careful. But she had to get a move on. There wasn't much time.

She only had a few yards to search. The distance separating her from her bungalow, as it had done that night. She was on her hands and knees, unworried about getting her jeans dirty. She plunged her hands into the little white stones, and on her knuckles she already had the bleeding marks of little cuts peeping through the dust that covered them. But the pain didn't bother her; in fact, it helped her concentration.

"The coin," she went on repeating to herself. "How could I not have noticed?"

It would have been very easy for someone to find her. A guest, or even the porter.

She had come to the motel before the others, because there was no longer anyone she could trust. And she had the feeling that her colleagues didn't trust her anymore either.

"I've got to hurry!"

She moved the stones by throwing them over her shoulder, biting her lip. She was nervous. She was angry with herself, and with the world at large. She breathed in and out a number of times, trying to overcome her agitation.

For some reason she found herself remembering something that had happened when she was a raw recruit at police academy. Even then it had been apparent that she had a very reserved character and found it difficult to make contact with other people. They had put her on patrol with an older colleague who couldn't stand her. They were chasing a suspect down the alleyways of Chinatown. He was too fast and they hadn't managed to catch him, but her colleague had thought that as they passed the rear of a restaurant the suspect had thrown something into a vat of oysters. So he forced her to climb up to her knees in that stagnant water, and rummage around the rotting mollusks. Obviously there was nothing there. And he had probably only wanted to teach her something a recruit has to learn. She had never eaten another oyster since. But she had learned an important lesson.

And the rough stones that she was throwing aside with such intensity were a test as well.

Something to demonstrate to herself that she was still capable of getting the best out of things. It had been a gift of hers for a long time. But just as she was beginning to feel pleased with herself, a thought ran through her head. Like her older colleague that other time, someone was making fun of her now.

There wasn't really a coin. It had just been a trick.

Just as Sarah Rosa reached this realization, she raised her head and saw Mila approaching. Unmasked and powerless, her rage fled at the sight of her younger colleague and her eyes filled with tears.

"He has your daughter, hasn't he? *She's number six.*"

34.

Her mother is in the dream.

She is speaking with her "magical" smile—that's what she calls it, because it's lovely when she isn't angry, and becomes the loveliest person in the world, but it now happens less and less.

In the dream her mother is telling her about herself, and also about her father. Now her parents are getting on better, and have stopped arguing. Her mother is telling her what they are doing, about work and life and home in her absence, and she even lists the films that they've been watching on the video recorder. Not her favorites, though. They'll wait for those. She likes to hear it said. She'd like to ask her when she can come back. But in the dream her mother can't hear her. It's as if she's talking to her through a screen. However much she tries, nothing changes. And the smile on her mother's face now seems almost ruthless.

A caress slides gently through her hair, and she wakes up.

The little hand goes up and down from her head to the pillow, and a tender voice murmurs a song.

"It's you!"

Such is her joy that she forgets where she is. What matters now is that she didn't imagine the little girl.

"I've been waiting for you for so long," she says to her.

"I know, but I couldn't come before."

"Weren't you allowed?"

The little girl looks at her with big, serious eyes: "No, I was busy."

She doesn't know what tasks could have kept her so busy that she couldn't come and see her. But for now it doesn't matter. She has a thousand questions for her. And she starts with the one closest to her heart.

"What are we doing here?"

She takes it for granted that the little girl is a prisoner too. Even if she's the only one tied to the bed, while the other one is apparently free to wander at will around the belly of the monster.

"This is my house."

The answer takes her aback. "What about me? Why am I here?"

The little girl says nothing and concentrates on her hair again. She understands that the girl is avoiding the question and doesn't insist—the moment will come for that as well.

"What's your name?"

The little girl smiles at her: "Gloria."

She takes a closer look at her. "No..."

" 'No' what?"

"I know you... your name isn't Gloria..."

"Yes it is."

She struggles to remember. She's seen her before, she's seen her before, she's sure of it.

"You were on the milk carton!"

The little girl still doesn't understand. "I only came here recently. Four weeks at the most."

"No! It's at least three years."

She doesn't believe her. "It's not true."

"Yes it is, and your parents made an appeal on television!"

"My parents are dead."

"No, they're alive! And your name is... Linda! Your name is Linda Brown!"

The girl stiffens: "My name is Gloria! And the Linda you're talking about is someone else. You're getting mixed up."

Hearing her voice crack like that, she decides not to press the point: she doesn't want the girl to go away and leave her on her own again. "All right, Gloria. Whatever you like. I must have made a mistake. Sorry."

The girl nods contentedly. Then, as if nothing had happened, she goes on combing her hair with her fingers again, and singing to herself.

Then she tries something else. "I feel terrible, Gloria. I can't move my arm. I have a fever all the time. And often I faint..."

"You'll be better soon."

"I need a doctor."

"Doctors just mess things up."

The phrase sounds false on her lips. It's as if she has heard someone else saying it, so often that over time it has entered her own vocabulary. And now she's repeating it for her benefit.

"I'm dying, I can feel it."

Two huge tears fall from her eyes. Gloria stops and collects them from her cheeks. Then she starts staring at her fingers, ignoring her.

"Did you understand what I said to you, Gloria? I'll die if you don't help me."

"Steve said you'd get better."

"Who's Steve?"

The little girl is distracted, but she answers anyway. "Steve, the one who brought you here."

"Who kidnapped us, you mean!"

The little girl stares at her again. "Steve didn't kidnap you."

Even though she's afraid of making her angry again, she can't compromise on this point: her survival depends on it. "Yes he did, and he did the same to you. I'm sure of it."

"You're wrong. He rescued us."

She doesn't want to lose her temper, but the question is too much for her. "What the hell are you saying? Rescued us from what?"

Gloria hesitates. She can see her eyes draining, making way for a strange fear. Gloria takes a step back, but she manages to grab her wrist. She tries to escape, tries to break away, but she isn't going to let her go without an answer.

"From who?"

"From Frankie."

Gloria bites her lips. She didn't want to say it. But she did.

"Who is Frankie?"

Gloria manages to wrench herself free, she's too weak to stop her.

"We'll see each other again, won't we?"

Gloria walks away.

"No, wait. Don't go!"

"You need to rest now."

"No, please! You won't come back!"

"I will: I'll be back."

The girl leaves. She bursts into tears. A bitter lump of desperation rises into her throat. And it spreads to her chest. She is racked with sobs, her voice breaks as she cries into the darkness.

"Please! Who is Frankie?"

But there is no reply.

35.

Her name is Sandra."

Terence Mosca wrote it at the top of his notepad. Then he looked back up at Sarah Rosa.

"When was she kidnapped?"

The woman rearranged herself on the chair before replying, trying to get her ideas in order. "Forty-seven days have passed by now."

Mila was right: Sandra had been taken *before* the other five. And then Albert had used her to attract Debby Gordon, her blood sister.

The two girls had met one afternoon in the park, watching the horses at the riding stables. They had exchanged a few words and a rapport had immediately been established. Debby felt low because she was so far from home. Sandra because she was separated from her parents. United by their respective sadnesses, they had immediately become friends.

They had both been given free horse rides. It was no coincidence. It was Albert who had brought them together.

"How was Sandra kidnapped?"

"It was while she was on the way to school," Rosa replied.

Mila and Goran saw Mosca nodding. They were all there—

including Stern and Boris—in the big archive room on the first floor of the Federal Police building. The captain had chosen this unusual place to avoid the news getting out, and to keep the conversation from seeming like an interrogation.

The room was deserted at that time of day. Long corridors of shelves full of files spread out from the place where they were assembled. The only light came from the consulting table that they were all sitting around. Sounds and voices were lost in the echoing darkness.

"What can you tell us about Albert?"

"I've never seen or heard him. I don't know who he is."

"Obviously..." observed Terence Mosca, as if this must be an aggravating circumstance for her.

Sarah Rosa still hadn't been put in any kind of custody. But soon she would be charged with complicity in abduction and the murder of children.

It was Mila who had identified her when investigating the kidnapping of Sabine at the merry-go-round. She had thought that Albert might have used a woman so that the abduction passed unobserved in front of everyone. Not just any accomplice, though, but one who could be blackmailed. The mother of child number six, for example.

Mila had received confirmation of this incredible hypothesis when going through the photographs from that evening at the fair on her laptop. In the background of a snapshot taken by a father, she had noticed a mass of hair and a foreshortened profile that had provoked an intense tickle at the base of her neck, followed by an unmistakable name: Sarah Rosa!

"Why Sabine?" Mosca asked.

"I don't know," said Rosa. "He let me have a photograph of her and let me know where I would find her, that's all."

"And no one noticed a thing."

In the Thinking Room, Rosa had said, *Everyone was looking only at their own child. People don't give a damn, that's the truth of it*. And Mila had remembered. Mosca went on: "Then he knew the families' movements."

"I suppose so. His instructions to me always seemed very accurate."

"How did he get his orders to you?"

"All by e-mail."

"And you never tried to trace them?"

There was an answer to the captain's question: Sarah Rosa was a computer expert. If she couldn't do it, it meant it was impossible.

"But I did keep all the e-mails." Then she looked at her colleagues: "He's very cunning, you know. And he's smart." She said it as if trying to justify herself. "And he's got my daughter," she added.

Mila wasn't moved by her plea.

She had been hostile to her since the first day, putting her life in jeopardy, because she was really the only one capable of discovering the identity of the sixth child.

"Was he the one who ordered you to get rid of Officer Vasquez as soon as possible?"

"No, that was my initiative. She could have given him problems."

She had wanted to display her contempt once more. But Mila forgave her. Her thoughts went to Sandra, the girl who suffered from an eating disorder—as Goran had told her—and who was now in the hands of a psychopath, with one arm amputated, and prey to unspeakable suffering. For days she had been obsessed by her identity. Now she finally had a name.

"So you followed Officer Vasquez twice, to frighten her and force her to abandon the investigation."

"Yes."

Mila remembered that after being followed in the car she had gone to the Studio, and there had been no one there. Boris had told her in a text that they were all at Yvonne Gress's villa. And she had joined them. Sarah Rosa was there, getting ready by the mobile unit's camper. Mila hadn't wondered why she hadn't been in the house with the others. Her lateness hadn't aroused her suspicions. But just in case, Sarah Rosa had attacked her verbally so as not to give her time to think, sowing doubts about Goran.

And by the way, he fooled you... because I voted against you.

Except she hadn't, because she would have risked drawing suspicion to herself.

Terence Mosca wasn't in a hurry: he wrote down Rosa's answers in his notebook and thought about them before continuing with his next question.

"And what else have you done for him?"

"I sneaked into Debby Gordon's room at the boarding school. I stole her diary from the tin box, tampering with the padlock in such a way that no one would notice. Then I took the photograph with my daughter in it off the wall. And I left the GPS transmitter that led you to the second discovery at the orphanage..."

"Didn't you ever think that someone might discover you sooner or later?" asked Mosca.

"Did I have a choice?"

"It was you who put the fifth girl's corpse in the Studio..."

"Yes."

"You got in with your key, and faked the damage to the armored door."

"So that no one would get suspicious."

"Yeah..." Then Mosca stared at her for a long while. "Why did you take that body to the Studio?"

It was the answer they had all been waiting for.

"I don't know."

Mosca breathed deeply through his nose. That gesture meant that their conversation was over. Then the captain turned to Goran. "I think that might be enough. Unless you have any questions..."

"None," said the criminologist.

Mosca turned back to the policewoman: "Special Agent Sarah Rosa, in ten minutes I am going to phone the Prosecutor, who will officially formulate the charges against you. As agreed, this conversation will stay between us, but I advise you not to open your mouth except in the presence of a good lawyer. One last question: is anyone apart from you involved in this business?"

"If you're referring to my husband, he doesn't know a thing. We're in the middle of a divorce. As soon as Sandra disappeared, I threw him out of the house using some excuse to keep him in the dark about everything. We'd also been arguing a lot lately because he wanted to see our daughter and thought I was stopping him."

Mila had seen them talking animatedly outside the Studio.

"Fine," said Mosca, rising to his feet. Then he turned to Boris and Stern, pointing at Rosa: "I will mandate someone immediately to formalize the arrest."

The two officers nodded. The captain bent down to pick up his leather bag. Mila saw him putting his notebook next to a yellow folder: on the cover she could see some typed letters: "W…on" and "P."

Wilson Pickett, she thought.

Terence Mosca walked slowly towards the exit, followed by Goran. Mila stayed with Boris and Stern along with Rosa. The two men were silent, waiting to guard the colleague who hadn't trusted them.

"I'm sorry," she said with tears in her eyes. "I had no choice," she repeated.

Boris didn't reply, barely able to contain his rage. Stern said only, "Fine, but stay calm now." But he didn't sound very convincing.

Then Sarah Rosa looked at them imploringly: "Find my little girl, please…"

Mila found Stern outside, sitting on one of the steel steps of the fire escape. He had lit a cigarette and brought it to his lips, balancing it between his fingers.

"Don't tell my wife," Stern said to her as soon as he saw her coming out of the fire door.

"Don't worry, it'll be our secret," Mila reassured him as she went to sit beside him.

"So what can I do for you?"

"How do you know I've come to ask you for something?"

Stern replied by raising an eyebrow.

"Albert will never let himself be caught, you know that yourself," Mila said. "I think he's already planned his death: it too is part of his plan."

"I don't care if he kicks the bucket. I know it isn't Christian to say certain things, but that's how it is."

Mila stared at him and grew serious. "He knows the team, Stern. He knows lots of things about you, otherwise he would never have put the fifth corpse in the Studio. He must have followed your cases in the past. He knows how you move, which is why he's always able to get ahead of you. And I think he knows Gavila in particular…"

"What makes you think that?"

"I've read one of his statements in the Tribunal about an old case, and Albert behaves as if he wants to prove his theories false. He's a serial killer sui generis. He doesn't seem to suffer from a narcissistic personality disorder because he prefers to draw attention to other criminals rather than himself. He doesn't seem to be governed by an unstoppable instinct, he's very good at controlling himself. He doesn't get pleasure from what he does, he seems more attracted by the challenge that he has presented. How can you explain that?"

"It's simple: I can't. And I'm not interested."

"How can you not care?" snapped Mila.

"I didn't say I didn't care, I said I wasn't *interested*. It's different. As far as I'm concerned, we never took up his 'challenge.' He can only keep us on our toes because there's still a child to save. And it isn't true to say that he hasn't got a narcissistic personality, because what he wants is our attention, not someone else's: just ours, you understand? The press would be over the moon if he gave them a sign, but Albert doesn't feel like it. Not for now, at least."

"Because we don't know what finale he has in mind."

"Exactly."

"But I'm convinced that Albert is trying to draw attention to you at the moment. And I'm talking about the case of Benjamin Gorka."

"Wilson Pickett."

"I'd like you to talk to me about that…"

"Read the file."

"Boris told me there was some kind of hitch…"

Stern tossed aside what was left of his cigarette. "Boris sometimes doesn't know what he's saying."

"Come on, Stern, tell me what happened! I'm not the only one interested in this whole affair…" She told him about the card she had seen in Terence Mosca's bag.

Stern grew thoughtful.

"All right. But you're not going to like it, believe me."

"I'm ready for anything."

"When we caught Gorka we started going through his life. He practically lived in his truck, but we found a receipt for the purchase of a certain quantity of food. We thought he'd realized that the circle was closing in on him, and that he was getting ready to hide away in a safe place, waiting for the waters to calm."

"But that wasn't the case…"

"About a month after he was captured we had a report of a missing prostitute."

"Rebecca Springher."

"Exactly. But the disappearance dated back to sometime around Christmas…"

"When Gorka was arrested."

"You've got it. And the streets she walked fell within the area covered by the truck."

Mila drew a conclusion: "Gorka was keeping her prisoner, the supplies were for her."

"We didn't know where she was, and how long she could survive. So we asked him."

"And obviously he denied it."

Stern shook his head. "In fact he didn't. He admitted everything, and he agreed to reveal the place where she was imprisoned, but on one small condition: he would only do it in the presence of Dr. Gavila."

Mila didn't understand. "So what was the problem?"

"The problem was that Dr. Gavila couldn't be found."

"And how did Gorka know that?"

"He didn't, the sadistic bastard! We were looking for Gavila, and meanwhile time was passing for that poor girl. Boris subjected Gorka to all kinds of questioning."

"And did he get him to talk?"

"No, but listening to the recordings of the previous interrogations he noticed that Gorka had casually mentioned an old warehouse where there was a well. It was Boris who found Rebecca Springher, on his own."

"But she'd already died of starvation."

"No. She cut her veins with one of the box cutters that Gorka had left her along with the food supplies. But the most infuriating thing is something else...according to the medical examiner, she killed herself just a few hours before Boris found her."

Mila felt a chill run through her. Then she asked anyway: "And what was Gavila doing all that time?"

Stern smiled, to hide his true feelings.

"He was found a week later in a gas-station toilet. Some motorists had called an ambulance: he was in a drunken stupor. He had left his son with the nanny, and gone home to work through his wife's desertion. When we went to see him in hospital he was unrecognizable."

That story perhaps included the reason for the unusual bond between the officers on the team and a civilian like Goran. Because it's more often human tragedies than successes that unite people, Mila thought. And she recalled a phrase she had heard from Goran, when they had been at his place, after she had discovered that Roche had tricked her about Joseph B. Rockford.

We think we know everything about people, when in fact we know nothing at all...

It was absolutely true, she thought. Try as she might, she would never be able to imagine Goran in the state they had found him in. Drunk and delirious. And that thought at that moment troubled her. She changed the subject.

"Why did you call the case Wilson Pickett?"

"Good nickname, don't you think?"

"From what I've learned, Gavila usually prefers to give a real name to the criminal he's after, to make him more three-dimensional."

"Usually, but this time he made an exception."

"Why was that?"

The special agent stared at her: "There was a survivor."

You don't survive a serial killer.

Weeping, despairing, pleading, they're all pointless. On the contrary, they feed the murderer's sadistic pleasure. The prey's only hope is flight. But fear, panic, the inability to understand what's happening all play to the predator's advantage.

Still, in a few rare cases, the serial killer doesn't manage to complete his killing. It happens because just as he is about to finish off the act, something—a brake suddenly activated by a phrase or gesture from the victim—stops him.

That was why Cynthia Pearl was a survivor.

"She said something to him...it came to her spontaneously, perhaps it was panic, I don't know. She said, 'Please, when I'm dead take care of my son. His name is Rick and he's five years old'...She couldn't believe she'd done it afterwards, but it saved her."

"It halted his rage."

"He dropped her off at a parking lot. As they walked, 'In the Midnight Hour' came on the radio...then she fainted and woke again in hospital: she didn't remember a thing. We asked her how she'd got those injuries and she had no idea. Even when we showed her Gorka's photograph, his face meant nothing...Until one Tuesday afternoon, she was at home alone and turned on the radio. They were playing the same Wilson Pickett song. It was only then that the memory came rushing back." Stern threw down his cigarette and returned to the building.

Mila understood that the team had given Gorka the nickname only after he had been caught. And they had chosen it as a warning and a reminder of all their mistakes.

Goran Gavila's team had fallen to pieces. And the investigation had collapsed with it. And the other thing that was shattered was the hope of saving little Sandra, who was now, somewhere, using up the last of the energy that still kept her alive. In the end she would have been killed not by a serial killer with a made-up name, but by the selfishness and shortcomings of other men and other women.

This was the best finale that Albert could have imagined.

As she was formulating those thoughts, Mila saw Goran's face appearing in the glass door in front of her. He was behind her. But he wasn't looking into the building. He was looking for her eyes in the reflection.

Mila turned round. They looked at one another for a long time, in silence. They were united by the same discomfort, the same distress. It was natural to lean towards him, close her eyes and try to find his lips. To plunge her own into his mouth, and for him to respond.

Dirty water poured down on the city. It flooded the streets, poured down the manhole covers, the gutters tirelessly swallowed it up and spat it back out again. The taxi had brought them to a small hotel near the station. The facade was blackened by smog and the shutters were always closed, because the people who stayed there had no time to open them.

There was a constant bustle of people. And the beds were constantly being remade. In the corridors, sleepless chambermaids pushed squeaking trolleys of linen and pieces of soap. Breakfast trays arrived at all hours. Some people stopped there only to freshen up and change their clothes. And some came to make love.

The porter gave them the key to room 23.

They went up in the elevator, without saying a word, holding one another by the hand. But not like lovers. Like two people afraid of losing one another.

In the room, mismatched furniture, spray deodorant and stale nicotine. They kissed again. More intensely this time. As if to shed their thoughts before they shed their clothes.

He rested a hand on one of her little breasts. She closed her eyes.

The light from a Chinese restaurant sign filtered through, gleaming with rain, and carved out their shadows in the darkness.

Goran began undressing her.

Mila let him do it, waiting for his reaction.

First he revealed her flat belly, then rose, kissing her, towards her chest.

The first scar appeared, level with her hip.

He slipped off her sweater with infinite grace.

And saw the others.

But his eyes didn't linger on them. That task was reserved for his lips.

To Mila's great surprise, he began to kiss those old wounds, very slowly. As if he could somehow heal them.

When he slipped off her jeans, he repeated the operation on her legs. Where the blood was still flesh, or had just congealed. Where the blade had recently paused, before plunging into the living flesh.

Mila felt again all the anguish she had felt when inflicting that punishment on her soul through her body. But along with that old pain, there was now something sweet.

Like the tickle of a healing wound, at once stinging and pleasant.

Then it was her turn to undress him. She did it as you take the petals from a flower. He too wore the signs of suffering. A thin ribcage, slowly dug from despair. And protruding bones where the flesh had been consumed by sadness.

They made love with strange violence. Full of anger, of rage, but also of urgency. As if each of them, with that act, were trying to pour all of themselves into the body of the other. And for a moment they even managed to forget.

When it was all over, they were left there side by side—separate but still united—listening to the rhythm of their own breathing. Then the question came, disguised as silence. But Mila could see it floating above them like a black bird.

It concerned the origins of the pain, her pain and his.

Which was first imprinted on her flesh and which she then tried to hide with her clothes.

And inevitably, the interrogation was interwoven with the fate of a child, *Sandra*. As they exchanged that feeling, she—somewhere, near or far—was dying.

Anticipating the words, Mila explained. "My work consists in finding missing people. Especially children. Some of them have been away for whole years, and then they don't remember anything. I don't know if that's good or bad. But perhaps it's the aspect of my job that causes me the most problems..."

"Why?" asked Goran, interested.

"Because when I lower myself into the darkness to pull someone out, I always have to find a motive, a strong reason to bring myself back into the light. It's a kind of safety rope to bring me back. Because, if there's one thing I've learned it's that the darkness calls to you, it seduces you with its pull. And it's hard to resist the temptation... When I come out with the person I've rescued, I'm aware that we're not alone. There's always something else that comes with us out of that black hole, stuck to our shoes. And it's hard to get rid of."

Goran turned to look into her eyes. "Why are you telling me?"

"Because it's from darkness that I come. And to darkness that I must, from time to time, return."

36.

She is leaning against the wall, with her hands behind her back, in the shadows. How long has she been there, staring at her?

Then she decides to call her. "Gloria…"

And she comes over.

She has the usual curiosity in her face, but this time there's something different. A doubt.

"I've remembered one thing…I used to have a cat," says Gloria.

"I've got one too: he's called Houdini."

"Is he nice?"

"He's mean." But she immediately knows that that's not the answer the little girl wants from her, and corrects herself: "Yes. He has white and brown fur, he's always sleeping and he's always hungry."

Gloria thinks about that for a moment, then asks again: "Why do you think I'd forgotten mine?"

"I don't know."

"I thought…if I forgot him, I'll forget lots of other things as well. Maybe even my real name."

"I like 'Gloria,'" she says encouragingly, thinking of her reaction when she told her that her real name was Linda Brown.

"Gloria…"

"Yes?"

"Will you tell me about Steve?"

"Steve loves us. And soon you'll come to love him too."

"Why do you say he saved us?"

"Because it's true. He did."

"I didn't need to be saved by him."

"You didn't know, but you were in danger."

"Is Frankie the danger?"

Gloria is afraid of the name. She's undecided. She doesn't know whether to speak or not. She weighs up the situation, then comes closer to the bed and speaks in a very low voice.

"Frankie wants to hurt us. He's looking for us. That's why we have to stay hidden here."

"I don't know who Frankie is, or why he's angry with me."

"He isn't angry with us, he's angry with our parents."

"With mine? Why?"

She can't believe it, it sounds like a ridiculous story. But Gloria is very convinced.

"Our parents swindled him, something to do with money."

Once again she sounds like she's saying something borrowed from someone else, and passively learned by heart.

"My parents don't owe money to anybody."

"My mother and father are dead. Frankie killed them. Now he's after me to finish the job. But Steve is sure that he won't find me if I stay here."

"Gloria, listen to me…"

Every now and again Gloria wanders off, and she has to go and get her from wherever she has ended up in her thoughts.

"Gloria, I'm talking to you…"

"Yes, what is it?"

"Your parents are alive. I remembered seeing you on TV a while ago: they were on a talk show and they were talking about you. They were wishing you a happy birthday."

She doesn't look surprised by the revelation. But now she starts considering the possibility that it's all true.

"I can't see the TV. Only the tapes Steve gives me."

"Steve. Steve is the bad man, Gloria. Frankie doesn't exist. He's only an invention of Steve's to keep you prisoner here."

"He exists."

"Think about it: have you ever seen him?"

She thinks about it. "No."

"So why do you believe in him?"

Even if Gloria is the same age as her, she seems much younger than her twelve years. It's as if her brain had stopped growing when she was nine. When, that is, Steve had kidnapped Linda Brown. That's why she always needs to think about things a bit.

"Steve loves me," she repeats, more to convince herself than anything else.

"No, Gloria. He doesn't love you."

"So you're saying that if I try and leave here, Frankie won't kill me?"

"It'll never happen. And we're going to leave together, you won't be alone."

"Will you be with me?"

"Yes. But we have to find a way to escape Steve."

"But you're ill."

"I know. And I can't move my arm."

"It's broken."

"How did that happen? I don't remember…"

"You fell down the stairs together when Steve brought you here. He's very angry about it: he doesn't want you to die. And then he won't be able to teach you how to love him. That's very important, do you know that?"

"I'll never love him."

Gloria takes a couple of seconds. "I like the name Linda."

"I'm glad you like it, because it's your real name."

"So you can call me that…"

"All right, Linda." She articulates it clearly, and she smiles at her. "So now we're friends."

"Really?"

"When you swap names you become friends, didn't anyone tell you that?"

"I already knew your name… you're Maria Eléna."

"Yes, but all my friends call me Mila."

37.

The bastard's name was Steve, *Steve Smitty*."

Mila uttered the name with contempt, as Goran held her hand on the three-quarter-sized hotel bed.

"He was just an idiot who'd never done anything with his life. He moved from one stupid job to another, and couldn't hold one down for as much as a month. Most of the time he was unemployed. When his parents died he had inherited a house—the one in which he kept us prisoner—and the money from a life insurance policy. Not much, but enough to let us bring his 'grand plan' to life at last!"

She said it with exaggerated emphasis. Then she shook her head on the pillow, thinking of the absurdity of the story.

"Steve liked girls, but he didn't dare to approach them because his penis was the size of a little finger and he was afraid they'd laugh at him." A mocking, vindictive smile brightened her features for a moment. "So he started taking an interest in children, sure that he'd have more success with them."

"I remember the Linda Brown case," said Goran. "I'd just been given my first chair at university. I thought the police had made a few mistakes."

"Mistakes? They made a complete mess of it! Steve was an unskilled slob, he'd left a trail of clues and witnesses behind! They couldn't find him straightaway, so they said he was clever. When in fact he was a complete fool! A very lucky fool…"

"But he had managed to convince Linda…"

"He had tortured her, exploiting her fear. He had invented this evil character—Frankie—and given him the role of the bad guy, so that he could set himself up as the good one, the 'savior.' That imbecile hadn't even had much imagination: he'd called him Frankie because it was the name of a turtle he had when he was a child!"

"It worked."

Mila calmed down. "With a child who was terrified and distressed. It's easy to lose your sense of reality in those conditions. All along I thought I was in some damned basement, and called it the 'belly of the monster.' But there was a house above me, and the house was in a suburban area with a lot of other houses around it, all the same, all normal. People walked by and didn't know I was down there. The worst thing about it was that Linda—or Gloria, as he had rechristened her, giving her the name of the first girl who had rejected him—could move freely. But she didn't even think of going outside, even though the front door was practically always open. He didn't lock it even when he went out for a walk, he was so sure that the story of Frankie would work!"

"You were lucky to get out alive."

"My arm was almost in a state of necrosis. For a long time the doctors despaired of saving it. And I was starving, too. The bastard gave me baby food and treated me with out-of-date medicine that he stole from a pharmacy dump. He didn't need to drug me: my blood was so poisoned by that filth that it was a real miracle that I was conscious!"

The rain outside was pelting down, washing the streets of leftover snow. Sudden gusts of wind shook the blinds.

"Once I woke from that kind of coma because I'd heard someone say my name. I'd also tried to attract attention, but Linda had appeared and persuaded me to stop. So I'd bartered my safety for the small happiness of not being alone. But I hadn't been mistaken: up above me there really had been two police officers scouring the area. They were still looking for me! If I had called out more loudly, perhaps they would have heard me. Basically we were separated only by a thin wooden floor. There was a woman with them, and she had been the one who called my name. But she hadn't done it with her voice, just her mind."

"It was Nicla Papakidis, wasn't it? That's how you met her..."

"Yes, it was. But even though I didn't reply, she had still heard something. So she had come back over the next few days, she'd walked around outside the house in the hope of hearing me again..."

"So it wasn't Linda who saved you..."

Mila snorted. "Her? She always went and told Steve everything. She was his small and involuntary accomplice by now. For three years he had been her whole world. As far as she knew, Steve was the last adult left on earth. And children always trust adults. But Steve had already thought of getting rid of me. He was sure that I would die soon, so he had prepared a hole in the shed behind the house."

The photographs in the newspapers of that hole had struck her more than anything else.

"When I left that house I was more dead than alive. I didn't notice the paramedics carrying me away on the stretcher, up the same stairs that that klutz Steve had dropped me down when he'd been carrying me to the basement. I couldn't see the dozens of policemen gathering around the house. I didn't hear the applause of the crowd that had collected there to celebrate my freedom. But I was accompanied by Nicla's voice, which was still describing everything to me and telling me not to go towards the light..."

"What light?" Goran asked curiously.

Mila smiled. "She was convinced that there was one. Perhaps because of her faith, she believed that when we die we become detached from our bodies, and after we have gone quickly down a tunnel, a beautiful light appears to us...I've never told her that I didn't see anything. Just darkness. I didn't want to disappoint her."

Goran leaned over her and kissed her on the shoulder. "It must have been terrible."

"I was lucky," she said. And her thoughts ran suddenly to Sandra, girl number six. "I should have saved her. But I didn't. What chance did she have of surviving?"

"That's not your fault."

"Yes, it is."

Mila drew herself up, still sitting on the edge of the bed. Goran stretched an arm out towards her again. But he could no longer touch her. His caress touched her skin but couldn't reach her, because she was far away again.

He noticed, and let her go. "I'm going to have a shower," he said. "I have to go home, Tommy needs me."

She stayed there motionless, still naked, until she heard the water running in the bathroom. She wanted to empty her mind of those horrible memories, to have a white void to fill with the weightless thoughts that children have, a privilege that had been torn from her.

The hole in the tool shed behind Steve's house had not been left empty. Her ability to feel empathy had ended up in there.

She stretched out a hand to the bedside table and picked up the television remote. She turned it on in the hope that, like the water of Goran's shower, meaningless chatter and images would wash away the remains of all the pain in her head.

On the screen a woman was clutching a microphone as wind and rain tried to carry her away. To her right was the logo of a television news program. Below her, the scrolling text of breaking news. In the background, a long way away, a house surrounded by dozens of police cars, their flashing lights splitting the night.

"...and in an hour Chief Inspector Roche will issue an official statement. Meanwhile I can confirm that the news is real: the maniac who has been terrorizing the country by kidnapping and killing innocent little girls has been identified..."

Mila couldn't move, her eyes were fixed on the screen.

"...he is the offender, released on probation, who this morning opened fire on two correction officers who had visited his house for a routine check..."

Mila couldn't believe it.

"...following the death in hospital of the wounded correction officer, the special units sent to the site decided to break in. It was only after killing the offender and entering the house, they made the unexpected and surprising discovery..."

"The little girl, tell me about the little girl!"

"...for the benefit of viewers who have just joined us: the name of the offender was Vincent Clarisso..."

"Albert," Mila corrected her in her head.

"...Department inform us that the sixth child is still in the house behind me: we believe she is receiving first aid from a medical support team. We have no confirmation, but it would seem that little Sandra is still alive."

Electronic surveillance report n° 7
23 December
3.25 a.m.
Duration: 1 min. 35 sec.

Prisoner RK-357/9:

...know, be ready, be prepared [followed by words incomprehensible to the transcriber]*... deserving of our rage... do something... trust above all...* [incomprehensible phrase] *too good, condescending... must not be tricked... know, be ready, be prepared* [incomprehensible word] *there's always someone who will take advantage of us... the necessary punishment... serve our sentence... it isn't enough to understand things, sometimes you have to act consistently... know, be ready, be prepared* [incomprehensible word]*... kill, kill, kill, kill, kill, kill, kill, kill, kill, kill, kill, kill, kill, kill.*

38.

Department of Behavioral Sciences,
25 February

Vincent Clarisso was Albert. Or was he?

He had been out of jail for less than two months, after serving the remainder of a sentence for armed robbery.

Once he was free, he had started his plan.

No record of violent crime. No symptom of mental illness. Nothing to mark him out as a potential serial killer.

The armed robbery had been a "setback," according to the lawyers who had defended Vincent in that trial. The stupidity of a young man with a serious codeine dependency. Clarisso came from a good bourgeois family, his father was a lawyer and his mother a teacher. He had studied, graduating as a nurse. He had worked for a while in a hospital, as a theater nurse. It was probably there that he had acquired the knowledge necessary to keep Sandra alive after amputating her arm.

Gavila's team's hypothesis that Albert might be a doctor was not far from the truth.

Vincent Clarisso had allowed all those experiences to settle in an embryonic layer of his personality, before going on to become a monster.

But Mila didn't believe it.

"It's not him," she went on repeating to herself as her taxi reached the Federal Police building.

After learning the news from the TV, Goran had spent about twenty minutes on the phone to Stern, who had told him of the latest developments. The criminologist had paced up and down the hotel room, beneath Mila's anxious gaze. Then they had parted. He had called Mrs. Runa to ask her to stay with Tommy that night, and had immediately hurried to the place where Sandra had been found. Mila would have liked to go with him, but her presence would no longer have been justifiable. So they had arranged to meet later, at the Department of Behavioral Sciences.

It was after midnight, but the city was one big snarl-up. People were pouring into the streets, heedless of the rain, to celebrate the end of a nightmare. It was like the middle of a New Year's party, with car horns sounding and everyone hugging everyone else. To complicate the traffic situation there were roadblocks to intercept any possible fleeing accomplices of Clarisso, but also to keep onlookers away from the area where the story's epilogue had taken place.

As the taxi proceeded at a walking pace, Mila was able to hear a new report on the radio. Terence Mosca was the man of the hour. Solving the case had been a stroke of luck. But, as often happened, the only one to benefit directly had been the man in charge of operations.

Tired of waiting for the line of cars to move, she decided to confront the pelting rain and got out of the taxi. The Federal Police building was a few blocks away, so she had pulled up the hood of her parka and continued on foot, immersed in her reflections.

The figure of Vincent Clarisso didn't coincide with the profile of Albert drawn up by Gavila.

According to the criminologist, their man had used the corpses of the six little girls as a kind of pointer. He had put them in specific places to reveal horrors that had never come to light, but of which he himself was aware. They had hypothesized that he was a secret associate of those criminals, and that they had all met him in the course of their lives.

They're wolves. And wolves often hunt in packs. Every pack has a chief. And Albert is telling us this: he's their leader, Goran had asserted.

Mila had become even more convinced that Vincent wasn't Albert when she had heard the serial killer's age: thirty. Too young to have known Ronald Dermis as a boy in the orphanage, or indeed Joseph B. Rockford—in fact she and the team had deduced that he must be between the ages of fifty and sixty. And nor did he resemble the description given by Nicla after she saw him in the mind of the billionaire.

And, as she walked through the rain, Mila found something else that justified her skepticism: Clarisso was in jail when Feldher was slaughtering Yvonne Gress and her children in the villa in Capo Alto, so he couldn't have witnessed the massacre, leaving his outline in blood on the wall!

It's not him, they're making a mistake. But Goran will have noticed, and he's bound to be explaining it to them now.

She reached Federal Police headquarters and became aware of a certain euphoria in the corridors. The officers were slapping one another on the back, many of them were returning from the crime scene still wearing their swat team uniforms and passing on the latest news. Then the report passed from mouth to mouth, increasingly enriched by new details.

Mila was intercepted by an officer who told her that Chief Inspector Roche urgently wanted to see her.

"Me?" she asked, startled.

"Yes, he's waiting for you in his office."

As she climbed the stairs, she thought that Roche had summoned her because they had noticed that something didn't square with the reconstruction of events. Perhaps all that excitement that she could see around the place would soon settle or subside.

There were only a few plainclothes officers in the Department of Behavioral Sciences, and none of them were celebrating. The atmosphere was the same as any working day, except that it was nighttime and they were all still at work.

She had had to wait for a long time before Roche's secretary called her into his office. Outside the door, Mila had been able to catch some of the words of the chief inspector, who was probably having a telephone conversation. But when she stepped inside, she discovered that he wasn't alone. Goran Gavila was with him.

"Come in, Officer Vasquez." Roche waved her over. He and Goran were standing on opposite sides of the desk.

Mila stepped forward, approaching Gavila. He turned slightly towards her, with a vague nod. The intimacy they had shared only an hour earlier had completely disappeared.

"I was just telling Goran that I'd like you both to attend the press conference that will be held tomorrow morning. Captain Mosca agrees with me. We would never have caught him without your help. We need to thank you."

Mila couldn't contain her surprise. And she saw that Roche was just as confused by her reaction.

"Sir, with the greatest respect…I think we're making a mistake."

Roche turned back to Goran: "What the hell's she saying?"

"Mila, it's all OK," the criminologist said calmly.

"No, it isn't. This guy isn't Albert, there are too many incongruities, I…"

"You're not going to say that at the press conference?" the chief inspector protested. "If that's how things are, you can't take part."

"Stern will agree."

Roche waved around a piece of paper from his desk. "Special Agent Stern has resigned with immediate effect."

"What? What on earth's going on?" Mila couldn't believe it. "This guy Vincent doesn't match the profile."

Goran tried to explain, and for a moment she saw in his eyes the same gentleness with which he had kissed her scars. "There are dozens of corroborations that tell us he's our man. Exercise books full of notes about kidnapping children and where to put their corpses, diagrams of the security system at Capo Alto, a plan of Debby Gordon's boarding school and electronics and computer manuals that Clarisso had started studying when he was still in jail…"

"And have you also found all the links with Alexander Bermann, Ronald Dermis, Feldher, and Rockford?" Mila asked, exasperated.

"There's a whole team of investigators at work in that house, and they're still finding clues. Something will come out about those links, you'll see."

"It's not enough, I think that—"

"Sandra has identified him," Goran interrupted her. "She has told us that he was the one who kidnapped her."

Mila focused on this for a moment. "How is she?"

"The doctors are optimistic."

"Happy now?" Roche broke in. "If you want to cause some kind of trouble for me, you should go home right now."

At that moment, the secretary's voice from the intercom told the chief inspector that the mayor urgently wanted to see him, and that he should get a move on. Roche took his jacket off the back of a chair and set off, after saying to Goran: "You tell them that the official version is this: either you agree, or you fuck off!" Then he left, slamming the door.

Mila hoped that Goran would tell her something different when they were on their own. But instead he said: "Unfortunately all the mistakes were ours."

"How can you say that?"

"It was a total failure. We created a false trail and followed it blindly. And I was the one chiefly responsible: all those conjectures were mine."

"Aren't you wondering how Vincent Clarisso knew about all those other criminals? He was the one who let us catch them!"

"That's not the point... The point is how it took us so long to find out about them."

"I don't think you're being objective at the moment, and I think I can guess why. In the days of the Wilson Pickett case, Roche saved your reputation and helped you keep the team going when his bosses wanted it to disband. Now you're returning the favor: if you accept this version of events, you'll take some of the glory away from Terence Mosca, and save his job as chief inspector!"

"That's enough!" Goran exploded.

For a few seconds, neither of them said a word. Then the criminologist headed for the door.

She was left alone in the room, fists clenched at her sides. Cursing herself and that moment. Her eye fell on Stern's letter of resignation. She picked it up. In those few formal lines there wasn't a trace of the real reasons for his decision. But it was obvious to her that the special agent must have felt somehow betrayed, first by Sarah Rosa and now by Goran as well. This was all wrong. She had to get into the monster's lair.

39.

The taxi wheels splashed up the water that had accumulated on the tarmac, but luckily it had stopped raining. The streets glittered like the stage of a musical; it seemed that at any moment brilliantined dancers in dinner jackets might appear.

"This is as far as you're going to get," the taxi driver said, turning towards her.

"That's OK, I'm there."

She paid and got out of the car. Ahead of her was a cordon of policemen and dozens of cars with flashing lights. The vans of various TV channels were lined up along the street. The cameramen had set up their equipment so that they always had a good view of the house.

Mila had reached the place where it had all started. The crime scene that went under the distinctive name of *site zero*.

Vincent Clarisso's house.

She still didn't know how she would get past the police checks and into the house. She just took out her pass and hung it around her neck, in the hope that no one would notice that she wasn't under their jurisdiction.

As she came forward, she recognized the faces of the colleagues she had seen in the Department corridors. Some of them were holding improvised gatherings around the boot of a car. Others were taking a break to eat snacks and drink coffee. She also spotted the medical examiner's van: Chang was writing a report, sitting on the running board, and didn't look up when she passed in front of him.

"Hey, where are you going?"

She turned and saw an overweight policeman panting towards her. She didn't have a ready excuse; she should have thought of one before she came, and now she'd probably flunked it.

"She's with me."

Krepp walked towards them. The scientific expert had a plaster on his neck, from which the head and claws of a winged dragon appeared, almost certainly his latest tattoo. He turned to the police officer: "Let her in, she's authorized."

The officer accepted his assurance and turned on his heels to go back where he had come from.

Mila looked at Krepp, unsure what to say. The man winked at her, then continued on his way. In a way it wasn't that strange that he had helped her, Mila thought. Both—albeit in different ways—wore part of their personal history imprinted on their skin.

The path leading up to the front door of the house was on a slope. On the gravel there were still cartridge cases from the shoot-out that had cost Vincent Clarisso his life. The front door had been slipped off its hinges for easier access.

As soon as she stepped inside, Mila was struck by a very strong smell of disinfectant.

The sitting room was furnished with seventies-style Formica furniture. A swirly-patterned sofa, still in its plastic covering. A fireplace with a mock fire. A mobile bar that harmonized with the yellow carpet. The wallpaper had a pattern of huge brown stylized flowers that looked like snapdragons.

Instead of halogen lamps, the room was lit by table lamps. That too was a sign of the new course taken by Terence Mosca. No "scene" for the captain. Everything had to be kept sober. Old-school policing from a long time ago, Mila thought. And in the kitchen she glimpsed

Mosca, holding a little summit with his closest collaborators. She avoided going in that direction: she had to remain as unobserved as possible.

They all wore shoe covers and latex gloves. Mila put them on and then started to look around, mingling with the others.

One detective was taking out the books from a library. One at a time. He picked them up, quickly flicked through them and set them down on the floor. Another was rummaging in a chest of drawers. A third was classifying the ornaments. Where the objects had not yet been moved and examined, everything seemed to be obsessively tidy.

There wasn't a speck of dust, and everything could be cataloged just by looking round, as if everything had been assigned a precise place. She felt as if she was in a completed jigsaw puzzle.

Mila didn't know what to look for. She was only there because it was the natural place to start. She had to see if this really was Albert. She had to know why the fifth corpse was found at the Studio.

Mila worked out the source of the smell of disinfectant when she saw the room at the end of the short corridor.

It was an ascetic room, with a hospital bed wrapped in an oxygen tent. There were large quantities of drugs, sterile overalls and medical equipment. It was the operating theater where Vincent had performed the amputations on his little patients, then turned into the room where Sandra had been kept alive.

As she walked by another room, she noticed a police officer watching a plasma screen with a digital video camera plugged into it. In front of the screen was an armchair with audio-surround speakers around it. On either side of the television was a whole wall of mini-DV cassettes, classified only by data. The detective slipped them into the video camera one by one to view their content.

Right now they were running through the images of a playground. Children's laughter on a sunny winter's day. Mila recognized Caroline, the last little girl to have been kidnapped and killed by Albert.

Vincent Clarisso had studied his victims meticulously.

"Hey, could someone come and give me a hand with this thing? I don't know a thing about electronics!" the policeman said as he tried to pause the film. When he noticed her in the doorway, for a moment he had the happy sensation of having had his wish granted, even though he then realized that he had never seen her before. Before he could say anything, Mila continued on her way.

The third room was the most important.

Inside there was a steel table and the walls were covered with noticeboards full of notes, Post-its of various colors and other things. That material set out in detail Vincent's plans. Street maps and timetables. The blueprints of Debby Gordon's boarding school, and of the orphanage. There was Alexander Bermann's number plate, and the stages of his business trips. The photographs of Yvonne Gress and her children, and a picture of Feldher's dump. There were cuttings from society magazines dealing with the fortunes of Joseph B. Rockford. And, obviously, snapshots of the kidnapped girls.

On the steel table there were other diagrams, with confused annotations. As if his work had suddenly been interrupted. Hidden among those pieces of paper—perhaps forever—was the finale that the serial killer had imagined for his plan.

Mila turned and froze. The wall that had been behind her until that moment was completely papered with photographs showing the members of the violent crimes investigative unit while they were at work. She was there too.

Now I'm really in the belly of the monster…

Vincent had always kept a close eye on their movements.

"Shit! Could someone give me a hand here?" came the voice of the officer in the next room.

"You all right, Fred?"

At last someone came to his aid.

"How can I tell what I'm looking at? And how can I classify something if I don't know what it is?"

"Let me see…"

Mila drew away from the wall of photographs, preparing to leave the house. As she passed by the television room, she noticed something on the screen. A place that the officer called Fred and his colleague couldn't identify.

"It's an apartment, what else am I supposed to say?"

"Yes, but what do I write in the report?"

"Write 'unknown apartment.'"

"Are you sure?"

"Yes. Someone else can work out where it is."

But Mila knew where it was.

It was only then that they noticed her and turned to look at her, while she couldn't take her eyes off the film on the TV.

"Can we help you?"

She didn't reply, and walked away. As she hurried through the sitting room, she looked in her pocket for her mobile phone. She called Goran's number.

By the time he replied she was on the path outside.

"What's happening?"

"Where are you now?" Her voice was alarmed.

He didn't notice. "I'm still at the Department, I'm trying to organize a visit by Sarah Rosa to her daughter in hospital."

"Who's at your place at the moment?"

Goran started to get worried. "Mrs. Runa is with Tommy. Why?"

"You've got to get there right now!"

"Why?" he repeated, full of concern.

Mila passed by the group of policemen. "Vincent had film of your apartment!"

"What does that mean?"

"That he'd searched your place…what if he had an accomplice?"

Goran fell silent for a moment. "Are you still at the crime scene?"

"Yes."

"Then you're closer than me. Ask Terence Mosca to give you a few officers and go to my place. In the meantime I'll call Mrs. Runa and tell her to shut herself in."

"Fine."

Mila hung up, then turned back towards the house to talk to Mosca.

And let's hope they don't ask me too many questions.

40.

"Mila, Mrs. Runa isn't answering the phone!"

It was dawn.

"Don't worry, we're nearly there, it won't be long."

"I'm on my way, I'll be there in a few minutes."

The police car stopped with a screech of rubber in the quiet street of the affluent district. The tenants of the surrounding buildings were still asleep. Only the birds had started greeting the new day, perched among the trees and on the rooftops.

Mila ran towards the front door. She rang the entry phone several times. There was no reply. She tried a different bell.

"Yes, who is it?"

"It's the police, sir: open up, please."

The lock clicked open electronically. Mila pushed the door open and dashed towards the third floor, followed by the two officers who had come with her. They didn't use the goods lift that served as an elevator, but took the stairs to get there as quickly as possible.

Please let nothing have happened... let the boy be all right...

Mila was invoking a divine being that she had stopped believing in a long time ago. Even though it was the same God that had freed her from her tormentor through Nicla Papakidis's gift. Because she had encountered children less lucky than herself too often to keep her faith.

Please don't let it happen again, let it not happen this time…

Reaching the third floor, Mila started knocking insistently on the closed door.

Maybe Mrs. Runa sleeps deeply, she thought. *Now she'll come and open the door and everything will be all right.*

But nothing happened.

One of the officers stepped towards her. "Do you want us to knock it down?"

She didn't have enough breath to reply, she just nodded. She saw them taking a brief run up and then delivering a kick. The door burst open.

Silence. But not a normal silence. An empty, oppressive silence. A lifeless silence.

Mila drew her pistol and walked in ahead of the police officers.

"Mrs. Runa!"

Her voice rang out through the rooms, but no one answered. She nodded to the two officers to split up. She walked towards the bedrooms.

As she walked slowly down the corridor, she felt a tremor in her right hand, gripping the handle of her pistol. She felt her legs growing heavy and the muscles in her face contracting as her eyes still stung.

She reached Tommy's room. The door was ajar. She pushed it with her open hand until she revealed the room. The shutters were closed, but the clown-shaped lamp on the bedside table rotated, casting the figures of circus animals on the wall. In the bed resting against the wall, a little body could be seen.

It was curled up in a fetal position. Mila walked gently over.

"Tommy…" she said in a low voice. "Tommy, wake up…"

But the little body didn't move.

As she reached the bed, she set her pistol down beside the lamp. She felt bad. She didn't want to move the blankets aside, she didn't want to uncover what she knew already. In fact she wanted to give the whole thing up and leave the room straightaway. Not to have to face this along with everything else, damn it! She'd seen it happen too many times, and now she was afraid that it would end like this every time.

But she forced herself to move her hand towards the edge of the blanket. She gripped it and pulled it away in a single tug.

She stood there for a few seconds holding the corner of the blanket raised, looking into the eyes of an old teddy bear smiling up at her with a beatific and immutable expression.

"I'm sorry…"

Mila gave a start. The two officers were watching her from the door.

"There's a locked door back here."

Mila was about to order them to knock it down, when she heard Goran coming into the apartment and calling his son: "Tommy! Tommy!"

She walked towards him. "He isn't in his room."

Goran was desperate. "What do you mean he's not there? Where is he?"

"There's a locked room over there, did you know that?"

Confused and anxious, Goran didn't understand. "What?"

"The room is locked…"

The criminologist froze… "Did you hear that?"

"What?"

"It's him…"

Mila didn't understand. Goran pushed her aside and headed quickly towards the study.

When he saw his son hiding under the mahogany desk, he couldn't hold back his tears. He bent down under the table and hugged him tight.

"Dad, I was scared…"

"Yes, I know, my love. But it's all over now."

"Mrs. Runa went away. I woke up and she wasn't there…"

"But I'm here now, isn't that right?"

***

Mila was still standing in the doorway, and had put her pistol back in her holster, reassured by what Goran was saying as he crouched under the desk.

"I'll bring you your breakfast now. What would you like to eat? Are doughnuts all right?"

Mila smiled. The terror was past.

Goran said again, "Come here, let me pick you up..."

Then she saw him coming out from under the desk, struggling to his feet.

But he wasn't holding a little boy in his arms.

"I'd like you to meet a friend of mine. Her name is Mila..."

Goran hoped his son would like her. He was often a bit shy with people he didn't know. Tommy didn't say anything, he just pointed at her face. Then Goran looked at her more closely: she was crying.

The tears came unexpectedly, from who knows where. But this time the pain that had provoked them was not mechanical in origin. The wound that had opened up was not in her flesh.

"What's up? What's going on?" Goran asked her, acting as if he was really holding a human weight in his arms.

She didn't know what to say. He didn't seem to be pretending. *Goran really thought he was holding his son in his arms.*

The two officers who had joined her in the meantime watched them, stunned and ready to intervene. Mila nodded to them to stop where they were.

"Wait for me downstairs."

"But we aren't..."

"Go down and call the Department, tell them to send Agent Stern. If you hear a gunshot, don't worry: it'll have been me."

The two policemen reluctantly obeyed.

"What's happening, Mila?" Goran's voice sounded helpless now.

He seemed so scared of the truth that he couldn't react in any way. "Why do you want Stern to come?"

Mila brought a finger to her lips, to keep him quiet.

Then she turned round and went back to the corridor. She headed towards the room with the closed door. She fired at the lock, shattering it into pieces, then pushed the door.

The room was dark, but they could still smell decomposition gases. There were two bodies in the big matrimonial bed.

One big, the other smaller.

The blackened skeletons, still wrapped in scraps of skin that fell like fabric, were melted in a single embrace.

Goran walked into the room. He smelled the smell. He saw the bodies.

"Oh, my God…" he said, unable to understand who those two corpses in his bedroom belonged to. He turned towards the corridor to keep Tommy from coming in…*but he couldn't see him*.

He looked back at the bed. That little body. The truth descended on him with ruthless force. And then he remembered everything.

Mila found him by the window. He was looking outside. After days of snow and rain, the sun had started shining again.

"This was what Albert was trying to tell us with the fifth little girl."

Goran said nothing.

Her breath was glass that shattered each time she tried to draw air into her lungs. "Why?" asked Mila, in a faint voice that broke in her throat.

"Because, after *she* left, she came back to this house. She hadn't come back to stay. She wanted to take from me the only thing I had left to love. And *he* wanted to go with her…"

"Why?" Mila repeated, unable to hold back the tears that now flowed freely.

"One morning I woke up and heard Tommy's voice calling to me from the kitchen. I went and saw him sitting in his usual place. He asked me for breakfast. And I was so happy that I *forgot* he wasn't there…"

"Why?" she begged.

And this time he thought hard before answering: "Because I loved them."

And before she could stop him, he opened the window and threw himself into the void.

41.

She had always wanted a pony.

She remembered tormenting her mother and father to let her have one. Without thinking that where they lived there wasn't even a proper place to keep one. The courtyard at the back of the house was too small, and beside the garage there was barely a strip of land where her grandfather had his vegetable garden.

And yet she insisted. Her parents thought that sooner or later she would tire of that ridiculous whim, but every birthday and in every note to Father Christmas there was always that same request.

When Mila emerged from the belly of the monster to come home, at the end of her twenty-one days of prison and three months in hospital, she found a beautiful brown and white pony waiting for her in the courtyard.

Her wish had been granted. But she couldn't enjoy it.

Her father had asked for favors, had persuaded his few acquaintances to get a good price together. Her family certainly wasn't rolling in money, and they'd always had to scrimp and save at home. It was chiefly for economic reasons that she had stayed an only child.

Her parents couldn't afford to give her a brother or sister, so they had bought a pony. And she wasn't happy with it.

So many times she had imagined finally getting that present. She talked about it all the time. She imagined cuddling it, putting colored bows in its mane, brushing it properly. Sometimes she forced her cat to undergo similar treatment. Perhaps that was why Houdini hated her and stayed away from her.

There's a reason why children like ponies so much. Because they never grow, they're immortalized by the enchantment of childhood. An enviable condition.

In fact, after she was freed, all Mila wanted to do was grow up all at once, to put a distance between her and what had happened to her. And, with a bit of luck, she might even be able to forget.

But the pony, having absolutely no chance of growing, represented an unsustainable pact with time as far as she was concerned.

When she had been pulled, more dead than alive, from Steve's stinking basement, a new life had begun for her. After three months in hospital to recover the use of her left arm, she had had to regain trust in the things of the world, not only with everyday life in her house, but also with the routine of her emotions.

Graciela, her very best friend, with whom she had celebrated the blood-sisters rite before disappearing into the void, now treated her strangely. She was no longer the one with whom she always rigorously shared the last chewing gum in the pack, the one she wasn't embarrassed to pee in front of, the one she had "French-kissed" to practice for when the boys came. No, Graciela was different. She talked to her with a fixed smile on her face, and she was worried that if it went on like that her cheeks would soon start to hurt. She tried to be pretty and nice, and had even stopped teasing her, when until recently they'd called each other things like "stinky old cow" and "freckly slut."

They had pricked their index fingers with a rusty nail so that they would always be friends, because no boyfriend would ever come between them. And instead it had taken only a few months to dig a trench that no one could fill.

If you thought about it, that prick in her finger had been Mila's first wound. But it had caused her more pain when it had healed completely.

"Stop treating me as if I'd just come back from the moon!" she had wanted to shout at everyone. And that expression on people's faces! She couldn't bear it. They turned their heads to one side and pursed their lips. Even at school, where she had never excelled, her mistakes were now indulgently tolerated.

She was tired of other people's condescension. She felt as if she was in a black-and-white film, like the ones they showed on TV in the small hours, in which the earth's inhabitants have been replaced by Martian clones, while she had been saved by staying in that strange lair.

Then there were two possibilities. Either the world really had changed, or after twenty-one days of gestation the monster had given birth to a new Mila.

No one around her mentioned what had happened. They let her live as if suspended in a bubble, as if she was made of glass and could explode into pieces at any moment. They didn't understand that all she wanted was a bit of authenticity after all the illusions she had been subjected to.

Eleven months later Steve's trial had begun.

She had waited for that moment for a long time. It was in all the newspapers, on all the television news programs which her parents wouldn't let her see—to protect her, they said. But which she watched in secret as often as she could.

Both she and Linda had been supposed to testify. The public prosecutor counted much more on her, because her terrified fellow prisoner still defended her tormentor. She had started demanding that they call her Gloria again. The doctors said that Linda suffered from serious mental problems. So it was up to Mila to get Steve put away.

In the months after his arrest, Steve had done everything he could to appear mentally ill. He had made up ridiculous stories about hypothetical accomplices that he said he had only obeyed. He was trying to convince the world of the story that he had used with Linda. The one about Frankie, his evil associate. But that had been disproved as soon as a policeman had discovered it was only the name of the turtle he had had as a child.

But people had swallowed the story anyway. Steve was too "normal" to be a monster. Too much like themselves. The idea that there was someone else behind it all, someone who was still mysterious, a real monster, paradoxically reassured them.

Mila had arrived at the trial determined to put all the blame on Steve, paying him back for the harm he had done her. She would make him rot in jail, and for that reason she was also willing to play the part of the poor victim, which she had obstinately refused to perform until then.

She sat in the witness box, facing the cage in which Steve was held in handcuffs, planning to tell everything without ever taking her eyes off him.

But when she saw him—in that green shirt buttoned up to the neck, too big for him now that he was little more than skin and bone, with his hands trembling as he tried to take notes on a pad, with his hair that he had cut himself, which was now much longer on one side—she felt something she had never expected to feel: pity, but also rage for that wretch, precisely because she felt sorry for him.

That was the last time that Mila Vasquez felt *empathy* for anyone.

When she had discovered Goran's secret, she had wept.

Why?

A memory lost somewhere inside her told her that those tears had been tears of empathy.

Suddenly a dam had burst somewhere, releasing a surprising range of emotions. Now she even thought she was aware of what other people felt.

Like the time Roche had come onto the scene and she had been aware of his intense feeling that his days were numbered, because his best man, the pinnacle of his task force, had given him the worst kind of poisoned bait.

Terence Mosca, on the other hand, had seemed caught between joy about his certain promotion, and unease about his motivation.

She was clearly aware of Stern's perplexity as soon as she crossed the threshold of that house. And she immediately knew that he would roll up his sleeves to bring some order to this horrible case.

Empathy.

The only person for whom she could feel nothing was Goran.

She hadn't fallen into Steve's snare as Linda had: Mila had never believed in Frankie's existence. Instead she had fallen for the illusion that a little boy, Tommy, lived in that house. She had heard about him. But she had also heard his father phoning his nanny to check that he was all right and to say good night to him. She had even believed she had seen him as Goran was putting him to bed. All things that she couldn't forgive herself for, because they made her feel a fool.

Goran Gavila had survived a forty-foot fall, but now he was caught between life and death in an intensive care bed.

His house was guarded, but only on the outside. Only two people walked around inside. Special Agent Stern, who had put his resignation on ice for the time being, and Mila.

They weren't looking for anything, just trying to put events in chronological order, to find answers to the only possible questions. At what point had a calm and balanced human being like Goran Gavila brought his murderous project to fruition? When had the impulse of revenge been unleashed? When had he begun to turn his rage into a plan?

Mila was in the study, and she heard Stern inspecting the adjacent room. He had carried out many searches in his career. It was unbelievable how revealing the details of someone's life can be.

As she was exploring the refuge in which Gavila had formed his theories, she tried to remain detached, taking note of the details, the little habits that might accidentally reveal something important.

Goran kept his paper clips in a glass ashtray. He sharpened his pencils straight into the wastepaper basket. And he kept a picture frame on his desk, with no photograph in it.

That empty frame was a window on the abyss of the man Mila had thought she could love.

Mila looked away, for fear of being swallowed up by it. Then she opened a drawer in the side of the table. In it was a file. She picked it up, and put it on the ones she had already looked through. This one was different, because it seemed to deal with the last case that Gavila had dealt with before the story of the missing little girls had come to light.

Apart from the documents, it contained a series of audio cassettes.

She started reading the contents of the papers; she would listen to the tapes if it seemed worth it.

It contained the correspondence between the director of a prison—one Alphonse Bérenger—and the public prosecutor's office. And it concerned the peculiar behavior of an inmate who was identified only by his prison number.

RK-357/9.

The subject had been found, months before, by two policemen, wandering at night, alone and naked, in the countryside. He had immediately refused to supply his personal information to the public officials. An examination of his fingerprints had revealed only that he had no criminal record. But a judge had sentenced him for obstructing the course of justice.

He was still serving his sentence.

Mila picked up one of the audio cassettes and looked at it, trying to imagine what it might contain. The label showed only a time and a date. Then she called Stern and quickly summed up what she had read.

"But listen to what the prison director writes…'Since the moment he set foot in the penitentiary, inmate RK-357/9 has never shown any sign of indiscipline, and has always respected prison rules. The subject is of a solitary disposition and reluctant to socialize…Perhaps for that reason no one has been aware of one particular trait of his, which has only recently been noticed by one of our warders. Prisoner RK-357/9 wipes and rubs with a piece of felt each object with which he comes into contact, he collects all the hairs that he loses each day, he polishes to perfection the sink, the taps and the toilet each time he uses them.' What do you think?"

"Hm, I don't know. My wife is obsessed with cleanliness."

"But listen to how it goes on: 'We are plainly dealing with someone with a mania for hygiene, or, more likely, an individual who wants at all costs to avoid leaving behind "organic material." We therefore seriously suspect that prisoner RK-357/9 has committed a particularly serious crime and wants to prevent us from taking his DNA to identify him.'...See?"

Stern took the piece of paper from her hands and read it. "This was November...Didn't they eventually learn something from his DNA?"

"It would seem that they couldn't oblige him to take the test, or take it against his will, because that would have violated his constitutional freedoms..."

"So what did they do?"

"They tried to collect some skin or hair with surprise inspections in his cell."

"Did they keep him in solitary?"

Mila ran through the papers for the passage where she had read something on the subject. She found it. "Here it is, the director writes: 'So far the subject has been sharing his cell with another recluse, which has certainly helped him in his task of mixing up his own biological traces. Thus our first measure since discovering his habit has been to remove him from this social setting and put him in isolation.'"

"So, did they manage to take his DNA or not?"

"Apparently the prisoner was cleverer than they were, and always left his cell perfectly clean. But then they noticed that he was talking to himself, and put a bug in the cell to understand what he was saying..."

"And what did Dr. Gavila have to do with it?"

"They asked him his expert opinion, I don't know..."

Stern thought for a moment. "Maybe we should listen to the cassettes."

On a little table in the study there was an old tape recorder that Goran probably used to record his verbal notes. Mila passed one of the cassettes to Stern, who walked over to the machine, put it in and was about to press play.

"Wait."

Surprised, Stern turned to look at her: she had turned pale.

"Fuck!"

"What's wrong?"

"The name."

"What name?"

"The name of the prisoner he shared his cell with before he was put in solitary."

"Yes?"

"His name was Vincent... *Vincent Clarisso*."

42.

Alphonse Bérenger was a baby-faced sixty-year-old.

His ruddy face looked as if it was held together by a dense network of capillaries. Every time he smiled, his eyes narrowed to two slits. He had run the prison for twenty-five years, and he was a few months away from retirement. He was a passionate fisherman; in a corner of his office he kept a rod and a drawer of bait and hooks. Soon that would be the main occupation of his days.

Bérenger was seen as a good man. During his governorship of the prison, no serious episodes of violence had been recorded. He had a human touch with the inmates, and his guards rarely resorted to the use of force.

Alphonse Bérenger was an atheist but read the Bible. He believed in second chances, and always said that every individual, if he so wishes, has the right to forgiveness. Whatever crime he has committed.

He had the reputation of being an upright man, and considered himself to be at peace with the world. But for some time he hadn't been able to sleep at night. His wife told him it was because he was about to retire, but that wasn't the case. What troubled his dreams was the thought that he would have to release prisoner RK-357/9 without knowing who he was and whether he had committed some terrible crime.

"This guy is…ridiculous," he said to Mila as they passed through one of the security gates, heading for the wing that held the solitary confinement cells.

"In what sense?"

"He's completely imperturbable. We've stopped his running water, hoping that he would stop washing. He went on cleaning himself all over with rags. We confiscated those as well. He started using his uniform. We forced him to use prison cutlery. He stopped eating."

"Then what?"

"We certainly couldn't starve him! He responded to all our attempts with disarming perseverance…or mild determination—you decide."

"And the scientists?"

"They spent three days in that cell, but they never found enough organic material to extract DNA. And I wonder: how is it possible? We all lose millions of cells every day, in the form of tiny eyelashes or scales of skin…"

Bérenger had used all his patience as an experienced fisherman in the hope that it would be enough. But it hadn't been enough. His last resort was the policewoman who had turned up by surprise that morning, telling a story so crazy that it sounded true.

As they walked down the long corridor, they reached an iron door, painted white. It was solitary confinement cell 15.

The director looked at Mila. "Are you sure?"

"In three days this man will get out of here, and I have a sense that we won't see him again. So yes, I'm absolutely sure."

The heavy door was opened and closed right behind them. Mila took the first step into the little universe of prisoner RK-357/9.

He wasn't as she had imagined him from the identikit that Nicla Papakidis had drawn after looking into the memories of Joseph B. Rockford. Except for one detail. The gray eyes.

He wasn't a tall man. He had narrow shoulders, and protruding collarbones. His orange prison overalls were too big for him, so much so that he had had to roll back both the sleeves and the hem of the trousers. He had very little hair, and it was concentrated on the sides of his head.

He was sitting on his folding bed, with a steel bowl on his knees. He was wiping it with a yellow duster. Laid out in an orderly fashion on the bed beside him were some cutlery, a toothbrush and a plastic comb. He had probably just finished polishing them. He lifted his head slightly to look at Mila, rubbing away as he did so.

Mila was sure the man knew why she was there.

"Hello," she said. "Do you mind if I sit down for a moment?"

He nodded politely, pointing to a stool against the wall. Mila took it and sat down.

The regular, insistent rubbing of cloth against metal was the only sound in that narrow space. The typical sounds of jail had been banished from the solitary section, rendering the mind's solitude even more oppressive. But prisoner RK-357/9 didn't seem to mind.

"Everyone here is wondering who you are," Mila began. "It's become a kind of obsession, I think. It certainly is for the director of this prison. And for the public prosecutor's office. The other prisoners tell the story of your legend."

He went on imperturbably looking at her.

"I know you're the person we called Albert. The person we've been hunting."

The man didn't react.

"You were in Alexander Bermann's armchair in his pedophile lair. And you met Ronald Dermis at the religious institution, when he was still a little boy. You were at Yvonne Gress's villa while Feldher was slaughtering the woman and her children: that's your outline in the blood on the wall. You were with Joseph B. Rockford when he killed for the first time in that abandoned house... They were your *disciples*. You instigated their disgrace, inspired their evil, always crouching in the shadows..."

The man went on rubbing, without losing his rhythm even for a moment.

"Then, just over four months ago, you decide to get yourself arrested. Because you did it on purpose, I have no doubts about that. In jail you meet Vincent Clarisso, your cell mate. You have almost a month to teach him, before Clarisso serves his sentence. Then Clarisso, just out, starts pursuing your plan…kidnapping six children, amputating their left arms, placing the corpses in such a way as to reveal all those horrors that no one had ever been able to discover…While Vincent took his task to its conclusion, you were here. So no one can incriminate you. These four walls are the perfect alibi…but your masterpiece is still Goran Gavila."

Mila took from her pocket one of the audio cassettes that she had found in the criminologist's study, and threw it onto the bed. The man watched it travel before landing a few inches from his left leg. He didn't move, he didn't even try and avoid it.

"Dr. Gavila never saw you, he didn't know you. *But you knew him.*"

Mila felt her heartbeats getting faster. It was rage, resentment, and something else.

"You found a way of contacting him when you were still inside. It's brilliant: when they put you in solitary confinement, you started talking to yourself like some poor lunatic, knowing that they would plant a microphone so that they could have the recordings listened to by an expert. Not any old expert, but the best in his field…"

Mila pointed to the cassette.

"I've listened to them all, you know? Hours and hours of electronic surveillance…those messages weren't just ramblings. They were for Goran…'*Kill, kill, kill*'…He took notice of you and killed his wife and son. It was patient work on his psyche. Tell me one thing: how do you do it? How do you manage it? You're brilliant at it."

Either the man didn't catch the sarcasm, or he didn't care. In fact he seemed curious to know the rest of the story, because he didn't take his eyes off her.

"But you're not the only one who can get into people's minds…Lately I've learned a lot about serial killers. I've learned that they're divided into four categories: visionaries, missionaries, hedonists and power seekers…But there's a fifth kind: they're called subliminal killers."

She rummaged in her pockets, took out a folded piece of paper and opened it up.

"The most famous is Charles Manson, who inspired the members of his famous 'Family' to carry out the massacre of Cielo Drive. But I think there are two even more emblematic cases..." She read: "'In 2005, a Japanese man called Fujimatsu managed to persuade eighteen people he had met on chat lines, all over the world, to take their lives on St. Valentine's Day. Different in age, sex, financial status and social origin, they were very normal men and women, without any apparent problems.'" She looked up at the prisoner: "How he managed to subjugate them all remains a mystery...but listen, this one's my favorite: 'In 1999, Roger Blest of Akron in Ohio kills six women. When he's arrested, he tells the investigators that the idea was "suggested" by a certain Rudolf Migby. The judge and jury think he's trying to pass as mentally ill, and sentence him to death by lethal injection. In 2002, in New Zealand, an illiterate workman called Jerry Hoover kills four women and then tells the police that it was "suggested" by a certain Rudolf Migby. The prosecution psychiatrist remembers the case in 1999 and—since it's unlikely that Hoover could know the case—discovers that the man has a work colleague by the name of Rudolf Migby, who lived in Akron, Ohio, in 1999.'" She looks at the man again: "So, what do you say? Do you see any similarities?"

The man said nothing. His bowl was gleaming, but he still wasn't entirely satisfied with the result.

"A 'subliminal killer' doesn't commit the crimes in a material sense. He's not chargeable, he's not punishable. To put Charles Manson on trial they resorted to a judicial trick, whereby the death sentence was commuted to several life sentences...Some psychiatrists call you *whisperers,* because of your ability to impress weaker personalities. I prefer to call you wolves...wolves act in packs. Every pack has a leader, and often the other wolves hunt for him."

Prisoner RK-357/9 stopped rubbing the bowl and set it down next to him. Then he rested his hands on his knees, waiting for the rest.

"But you defeat them all..." Mila shook her head. "There's nothing to demonstrate your involvement in crimes committed by your disciples. Without proof to convict you, soon you will be a free man again…and no one will be able to do anything."

Mila sighed deeply. They stared at one another.

"Shame: if only we knew your true identity, you'd become famous and go down in history, I can assure you."

She leaned towards him, her tone of voice suddenly subtle and menacing: "Anyway, I'll find out who you are."

Standing up, she cleaned her hands of imaginary dust and hurried from the cell. First, though, she allowed herself a few more seconds with the man.

"Your last pupil failed: Vincent Clarisso couldn't complete your plan, because child number six is still alive…which means that *you too have failed*."

She studied his reaction, and for a moment she almost thought that something had stirred in his face, which had until then remained inscrutable.

"We'll see each other outside."

She held out her hand. He looked surprised, as if he hadn't expected that. He studied her for a long time. Then he raised a slack arm and shook it. At the touch of those soft fingers, Mila felt a sense of repulsion.

She let her hand slip from his.

She turned her back on him and walked towards the iron door. She knocked three times and waited, knowing that his eyes were still on her, burning into a spot between her shoulder blades. Someone outside started to turn the key in the lock. Before the door opened, prisoner RK-357/9 spoke for the first time.

"It's a girl," he said.

Mila turned towards him, not understanding. The prisoner had returned to his rag, meticulously rubbing another bowl.

She left, the iron door closed behind her and Bérenger came towards her. With him was Krepp.

"So…did it work?"

Mila nodded. She held out the hand with which she had shaken the prisoner's hand. The scientific expert picked up a pair of tweezers and delicately detached from her palm a thin transparent film in which cells from the man's skin were trapped. To preserve it, he immediately put it into a flask of alkaline solution.

"Now we'll see who this bastard is."

43.

5 September

The sky was crisscrossed with isolated white clouds that enhanced its pure blue. Had they been put all together, they would have covered the sun for good. And yet there they were, carried on the wind.

It had been a very long season. Winter had made way for summer, without a break. It was still warm.

Mila drove with both windows open, enjoying the breeze in her hair. She had let it grow, and that was only one of the little changes that had happened recently. Another was the clothes she wore. She had abandoned her jeans, and now wore a floral-patterned skirt.

On the seat beside her was a box with a big red bow. She had chosen the gift without thinking too hard about it, because now she trusted to instinct in everything she did.

She had discovered the fertile unpredictability of life.

She liked this new course of things. But the problem now was the whim of her emotions. Sometimes she found herself stopping in the middle of a conversation, in the middle of a task, and bursting into tears. For no reason, a strange and pleasant longing took possession of her.

For a long time she had wondered where those emotions came from, the ones that regularly filled her in waves or spasms.

Now she knew. But she hadn't wanted to know the sex of the child.

"It's a girl."

Now Mila was avoiding thinking about it, trying to forget the whole affair. She had different priorities now. There was the hunger that assailed her too often and unexpectedly, and which had restored some femininity to her figure. Then there was the sudden, urgent need to pee. Finally there were those little kicks in her belly, which she had started feeling some time ago.

Thanks to them, she was learning to look only to the future.

But inevitably, from time to time, her mind drifted back towards the memory of those events.

Prisoner RK-357/9 had come out of prison one Tuesday in March. Without a name.

But Mila's trick had been successful.

Krepp had extracted the DNA from his epithelial cells, and it had been fed into all available data banks. Comparisons had also been made with unidentified organic material from unsolved cases.

Nothing.

Perhaps we still haven't discovered the whole plan, Mila said to herself. And that hunch worried her.

When the nameless man had regained his freedom, the police had at first kept him under constant surveillance. He was living in a house put at his disposal by the social services and—ironically—had taken a job as a cleaner in a big department store. He revealed nothing about himself that they didn't already know. So, over time, the policemen's checks had drawn a blank. The senior officers were no longer willing to pay overtime, and the voluntary surveillance had lasted only a few weeks. In the end they had given up.

Mila had kept her eye on him, but he had become increasingly exhausting for her as well. After the discovery of her pregnancy, her checks had become less frequent.

Then, one day in mid-May, he had disappeared.

He had left no traces of himself, and no one could imagine where he might have gone. At first Mila had been angry, but then she had discovered that she felt a curious sense of relief.

The policewoman who found people who had disappeared basically wanted that man to disappear.

The road sign to her right indicated the road towards the residential district. She turned into it.

It was a lovely place: the streets were lined with trees which cast the same repeated shadow, as if they didn't want to offend anyone. The little villas stood side by side, with an area of land in front of them, all identical.

The directions on the piece of paper that Stern had given her ended at the junction in front of her. She slowed down and looked around.

"Stern, damn it, where are you?" she said into her phone.

Before he answered she spotted him in the distance with his mobile to his ear, waving to her with one arm held aloft.

She parked the car where he indicated and got out.

"How are you feeling?"

"Apart from the nausea, the swollen feet and always running to the bathroom... pretty good."

He put an arm around her shoulders: "Come on, they're all round the back."

It was strange to see him without his jacket and tie, with his blue trousers and a floral shirt open at the chest. If it hadn't been for his inevitable mints, he would have been almost unrecognizable.

Mila let him guide her towards the back garden, where the former special agent's wife was laying the table. She ran to hug her.

"Hi, Marie, you're looking great."

"Obviously—she has me at home all day!" said Stern with a laugh.

Marie slapped her husband on the back. "Shut up and cook!"

As Stern walked away towards the barbecue, ready to cook sausages and corncobs, Boris came over holding a half-empty bottle of beer. He hugged Mila with his strong arms and lifted her in the air. "How fat you've got!"

"You're one to talk!"

"How long did it take you to get here?"

"Were you worried about me?"

"No, I was just hungry."

They laughed. Recently Boris had put on weight because of his sedentary life and the promotion he had been given by Terence Mosca. Roche had presented his resignation immediately after the official closure of the case, but had first drawn up an exit procedure that involved a ceremony featuring the award of a service medal and a solemn commendation. It was said that he was considering the possibility of going into politics.

"I'm such an idiot: I left the box in the car!" Mila suddenly remembered. "Could you go and get it for me, please?"

"Of course, straightaway."

As soon as Boris shifted his bulk, she was able to see all the other people.

Sandra was sitting in a wheelchair under a cherry tree. She couldn't walk. It had happened a month after she was let out of hospital. The doctors said her neurological block was the result of shock. Now she was on a strict rehabilitation program.

She had a prosthesis where her missing left arm had been.

Standing beside the girl was her father, Mike. Mila had met Mike when visiting Sandra, and had liked him. In spite of his separation from his wife, he had gone on looking after his daughter, with affection and dedication. Sarah Rosa was with them. She had changed a lot. She had lost a few pounds in jail, and her hair had turned white very quickly. She had received a stiff sentence: seven years and a dishonorable discharge, which had also cost her her pension. She was there on special leave. Not far away was Doris, the surveillance officer who had come with her, and who nodded a greeting to Mila.

Sarah Rosa got up and walked over to her. She tried to smile at her.

"How are you? All OK with the pregnancy?"

"The worst thing is the clothes: my size is constantly changing, and I don't earn enough to change my wardrobe so quickly. One of these days I'm going to go out in my bathrobe!"

"Listen to me: enjoy these moments, because the worst is yet to come. For the first three years, Sandra didn't let us get a wink of sleep. Isn't that right, Mike?" And Mike nodded.

They had all met up several times. But no one had ever asked Mila who her child's father was. God knows how they would have reacted if they'd known she was carrying Goran's child.

The criminologist was still in a coma.

Mila had gone to see him only once. She had seen him from behind a pane of glass, but she had managed only a few seconds before having to leave.

The last thing he had said to her before throwing himself into the void was that he had killed his wife and child *because he loved them*. It was the incontrovertible logic of someone justifying evil with love. And Mila couldn't accept it.

Another time Goran had claimed: *We think we know everything about people, when in fact we know nothing at all…*

She thought he was referring to his wife, and she remembered the words as a banal truth, no real match for his intelligence. Until she had found herself involved in what he was saying. And she of all people should have understood. She who had said to him, *Because it's from darkness that I come. And to darkness that I must, from time to time, return.*

Goran too had often visited that same darkness. But one day, when he had reemerged, something must have followed him. Something that had never let him go.

Boris came back with the present.

"What took you so long?"

"I couldn't close the door on that old banger of yours. You should get a new car."

Mila took the box from his hands and gave it to Sandra.

"Hey, happy birthday!"

She bent down to kiss her. The little girl was always pleased to see her.

"Mum and Dad gave me an iPod."

She showed it to her. And Mila said, "It's fantastic. Now we've got to fill it up with some good honest rock."

Mike disagreed: "I'd rather have Mozart."

"I'd like Coldplay best," said Sandra.

They unwrapped Mila's present together. It was a velvet jacket, with various kinds of frills and studs.

"Wow!" exclaimed the birthday girl when she recognized the label of a famous designer.

"Does that 'wow' mean you like it?"

Sandra nodded with a smile, without taking her eyes off the jacket.

"Let's eat!" said Stern.

They sat down at the table in the shade of a gazebo. Mila noticed that Stern and his wife were constantly coming back to one another and touching each other like young lovers. She felt a little bit envious of them. Sarah Rosa and Mike were acting out the role of good parents for the benefit of their daughter. But he was also very solicitous of Sarah. Boris told a lot of jokes, and they laughed so much that officer Doris choked on a mouthful of food. It was a pleasant, carefree day. And Sandra probably forgot her condition for a little while. She received lots of gifts and blew out thirteen candles on a chocolate and coconut cake.

They finished lunch just after three. A gentle breeze had blown up, making them want to lie down on the lawn and sleep. The women cleared the table, but Stern's wife let Mila off because of her belly. She took advantage of the fact to join Sandra under the cherry tree. With a little effort she even managed to sit down on the ground, next to her wheelchair.

"It's lovely here," the girl said. Then she watched her mother carrying in the dirty dishes and smiled. "I'd like this day to go on forever. I kept missing my mother a lot…"

The use of the imperfect tense was revealing: Sandra was talking about a different kind of longing from the one she felt when her mother went back into jail. She was talking about what had happened to her.

Mila knew very well that those little hints were part of the effort that the girl was making to put the past in order. She had to arrange her emotions and come to terms with a fear that, even though it was all in the past, would lie in wait for her for many years to come.

One day the two of them would broach the topic of what had happened. Mila thought of telling the girl her own story first. Perhaps it would help. They had so much in common.

First find all the words we need, my little one, we have all the time in the world.

Mila felt great tenderness for Sandra. In an hour, Sarah Rosa would have to go back to jail. And each time that separation was a source of great distress to both mother and daughter.

"I've decided to let you in on a secret," she said to distract her from that thought. "But I'm going to tell only you…I want to tell you who my baby's father is."

Sandra gave a cheeky smile. "Everyone knows."

Mila was paralyzed with amazement for a moment, and then they both burst out laughing.

In the distance Boris saw them, without knowing what was going on. "Women," he called out to Stern.

When they finally recovered, Mila felt much better. Once again she had underestimated someone who loved her, creating pointless problems. But in fact things were often incredibly simple.

"*He* was waiting for someone…" Sandra said seriously. And Mila understood that she was talking about Vincent Clarisso.

"I know," she said simply.

"He was to come and join us."

"That man was in jail. But we didn't know. We'd also chosen a name for him, did you know that? We called him Albert."

"No, that's not what Vincent called him…"

A gust of warm wind stirred the leaves in the cherry tree, but that didn't stop Mila from feeling a sudden chill running down her spine. She turned slowly towards Sandra, and met her big eyes, which stared at her completely unaware of what she had just said.

"No…" the girl repeated calmly. "He called him *Frankie*."

The sun was shining on that perfect afternoon. The birds sang their song in the trees, and the air was full of pollen and perfumes. The grass of the lawn was inviting. Mila would never forget the precise moment when she had discovered she had much more in common with Sandra than she imagined. And yet those similarities had always been there, in front of her eyes.

He always took girls, never boys.

Steve preferred girls too.

He chose families.

And like herself, Sandra was an only child.

He cut off a left arm from each of them.

She had broken her left arm when she fell down the stairs with Steve.

The first two were blood sisters.

Sandra and Debby. Like her and Graciela many years before.

"Serial killers, with the things they do, are trying to tell us a story," Goran had once said.

But that story was her *story.*

Every detail sent her back into the past, forcing her to look the terrible truth in the face.

Your last pupil failed: Vincent Clarisso couldn't complete your plan, because child number six is still alive… which means that you too have failed.

And yet it hadn't happened by chance. And that was Frankie's true finale.

It was all meant for her.

A movement behind her brought her back. Then Mila lowered her eyes to her ripe belly. She struggled not to wonder if it too was part of Frankie's plan.

God is silent, she thought. *The devil whispers.*

And in fact the sun was still shining on that perfect afternoon. The birds hadn't tired of singing their song in the trees, and the air was still full of pollen and perfumes. The grass of the lawn was still inviting.

Around her, and everywhere, the world contained the same message.

That everything was the same as before.

Everything.

Even Frankie.

Who had come back, to vanish once more into the vast expanses of shadow.

Author's Note

Criminology literature began to address the issue of "whisperers" during the rise of cults and sects, but had great difficulty finding a definition of "whisperer" for use in a legal trial, because mere suggestion is so hard to prove.

Where there is no causal connection between the guilty party and the whisperer, it is not possible to envisage any type of crime for which the latter might be liable. "Incitement to criminal activity" is usually too weak to lead to a sentence. The activity of these psychological controllers involves a subliminal level of communication which does not *add* criminal intent to the psyche of the agent, but *brings out* a dark side—present in a more or less latent form in each of us—which then leads to the subject committing one or several crimes.

Often cited is the Offelbeck case of 1986: a housewife who received a series of anonymous phone calls and who then, out of the blue, exterminated her family by putting rat poison in their soup.

Anyone who sullies himself with heinous crimes often tends to share moral responsibility with a voice, a vision or imaginary characters. For this reason it is particularly difficult to tell when such manifestations spring from genuine psychosis and when they may be traced back to the hidden work of a whisperer.

Among the sources I used in the novel, apart from manuals of criminology, forensic psychiatry and texts of legal medicine, are quoted studies by the FBI, an organization with the merit of having assembled the most valuable database concerning serial killers and violent crimes.

Many of the cases quoted in these pages really happened. For some, names and places have been changed because the investigations relating to them are not closed or the trials have not yet taken place.

The investigative and forensic techniques described in the novel are real, even though in some circumstances I have taken the liberty of adapting them to the needs of the narrative.

Acknowledgments

Many people think that writing is a solitary adventure. In fact, many people contribute, however unconsciously, to the creation of a story. They are the ones who have nourished, supported and encouraged me throughout all the months of gestation of the novel and who, in one way or another, are part of my life.

In the hope that they will stay beside me for a long time to come, I should like to thank them.

To Luigi and Daniela Bernabò, for the time and the dedication that they have given to this story and its author. For their valuable advice that allowed me to mature as a writer, helping me to mold the style and effectiveness of these pages. And for putting their hearts into it. If these words have reached your eyes, I owe it mostly to them. Thank you. Thank you. Thank you.

To Stefano and Cristina Mauri, who invested their name in mine, believing in it until the end.

To Fabrizio, my "whisperer," for his ruthless advice, for his kind firmness, for having loved every page, every word.

To Ottavio, the friend anyone would wish to have beside them their whole life long. To Valentina, who is truly special. To little Clara and Gaia, for the affection they fill me with.

To Gianmauro and Michela, in the hope of finding myself close to them when it truly matters. And to Claudia, my light.

To Massimo and Roberta, for their support and their sincere friendship.

To Michele. My first and best friend. It's good to know that he will always be there when I need him. And it's good that he knows I'm there too.

To Luisa, for her infectious smiles and the songs sung loudly at night, in the car driving along the streets of Rome.

To Daria, and the destiny she gave me. For the way she sees the world and the way she makes me see it through her eyes.

To Maria De Bellis, who guarded my childish dreams. If I am a writer, I also owe it to her.

To Uski, my peerless "companion."

To Alfredo, volcanic companion in a thousand adventures.

To Achille, who isn't there…but is always there.

To Pietro Valsecchi and Camilla Nesbit, and the whole Taodue.

Thanks to everyone at the Bernabò Agency, who followed the first stages of this novel. And all the friends who read this story from its beginnings and helped me to improve it with valuable suggestions.

To my whole big family. The ones who are, the ones who were…and the ones who will be.

To my brother Vito. The first eyes to meet this story, and many others, always. Even if you can't hear it, the music in these pages belongs to him. And to Barbara, who makes him happy.

To my parents. For what they have taught me, and what they have let me learn on my own. For what I am, and what I will be.

To my sister Chiara. Who believes in her dreams, and in mine. Without her my life would be terribly empty.

To all those who have reached the end of these pages. In the hope that I have given them a gift of emotion.

Part of the proceeds from this book will go to an association for long-distance adoption.

About the Author

Donato Carrisi studied law and criminology before he began working as a writer for television. *The Whisperer,* Carrisi's first novel, won five international literary prizes, has been sold in nearly twenty countries, and has been translated into languages as varied as French, Danish, Hebrew, and Vietnamese. Carrisi lives in Rome.